WAIL NOT

By:

J.D. Oliver

First Edition

ISBN: 978-1-60388-128-9
ISBN: 1-60388-128-X

J.D. Oliver

Wail not for the past, for it is dead.
Weep and cry out and rub ashes in your wounds.
Mourn, yes mourn for the yet to be.
Listen! Listen! Can you not hear?
The blood of the lost are calling out to me,
From the ground on which you weep.
Fields of blood, hock deep they run.
Wail Not! Wail Not!
For the future you cannot change.
Listen! Listen! Can you not hear?

Chapter One

I awoke with those words ringing in my ears. What the hell they meant, I hadn't the slightest idea. One thing I did know was that we're burying Ma this day. I lay in my bunk listening to the horses chomping on their hay. My bunk was in the barn. I usually went in the house and had breakfast with the rest of the family. I would not be doing that this morning.

I reached into my saddle bags, that were hanging from a nail beside my bunk, and got some pemmican and jerky, that would do me. I propped myself up against the wall and pulled my blanket around me, the spring air had a chill in it.

I heard Pa come in the barn, "Come on, Buck, help me saddle the team and hook up the wagon."

"Be right there," I said. I looked around my room at the books lining the walls. I had read all of them. From Blackstone's Law to Plutarch. The books, them, I would miss the most. I pulled on my buckskins and boots. Grabbing my old felt hat, I went to give Pa a hand. Pa said, "How come you didn't come in for breakfast?"

"Didn't figure the boys wanted me there."

"I am still boss on this ranch, you're welcome here, this is your home too."

"I know that Pa, but I just didn't want to make a fuss on the day we buried Ma."

"I know that those four boys have made your life miserable. I was always so busy that a lot of the time I didn't pay much attention and if it wouldn't have been for Ma taking your side, they probably would of killed you."

"Well, they might of tried, and I guess they did a few times. But this child is a hard one to put under. And I guess this is a good as time as any to tell you Pa, I have all my plunder packed on Jill and Lil, all I have to do is saddle Jim and I'm pulling my freight. As you know, those horses belong to me, I won't be taking anything from the ranch."

Pa turned around and hugged me, "But Buck, you're only twelve years old, Oh I know you're smarter than the Devil and stand man grown, but still, I guess what I am trying to say is, I love you son, and will miss you like the dickens. I always considered you my son, right from the time we found you beside the trail back in Nebraska. And you know how Ma felt about you, she considered you heaven sent. Especially since we just buried the still born baby, then there you were, wrapped in white deer skin, just laying there looking at us."

"I know that You and Ma, and Caleb always treated me right. I am not scared of Carl, Robert , Charles or Wilbur, its just that they're your sons and I don't want to kill them, that's what I would have to do if I stuck around. Did Caleb, Harriet and Penny spend the night?"

"Yes, Harriet and Penny dressed Ma in her Sunday go-to-the-meeting dress, Caleb brought the casket with him yesterday. I guess we're already, the Preacher got here just before dawn. The neighbors are trickling in. You are coming to the grave side services aren't you?"

Ma was loaded into the wagon, the procession was long. I dropped into the back of the line. The four boys had dug a grave at the foot of Castle Rock yesterday. The ranch was called Castle Rock Ranch, some twenty thousand acres under deed, more they laid claim to. I guess they could hold it, if they shot straight. Caleb and Harriet had their own place on the North Fork of the Shoshone. Caleb was the oldest son, Harriet his wife, and Penny their ten year old daughter.

Caleb had married Harriet when I was a year old, Penelope had come along a year later. Her family had a spread on the North Fork, Caleb moved in and took over, her parent's were old and glad to have him. Castle Rock was on the South Fork.

Now Penny was a caution, every chance she got, she dogged my steps. She was a ten year old going on thirty. I taught her a lot of stuff, how to hunt, shoot, fish, fight. She was good at all of them. She didn't know I was leaving.

I seen Carl turn around in his saddle. Looking at me he said, "What's that Indian doing here?"

Pa cuffed him upside the head, he turned back around and shut up. Penny looked at me and winked. I smiled back, her eyes lit up. Lets see, Caleb would be 28 years old now, Carl 26, Robert 24, Charles 22 and Wilbur 20. It sure was a wonder somebody hadn't killed them yet.

The four of them wanted to bash my head in when they found me beside the trail back in 1860. Ma and Pa Butler and their five boys were driving a herd of Long Horns from Texas to the Wyoming Territory. Pa's brother had come across the twin valleys of the Shoshone back in the twenties. He died of old age before they started north. The Civil war was on the horizon, they had just made it in time.

I stood in the back of the crowd, with my old hat in my hand, with the cold wind from the snowy vaults of Colter's Hell blowing through my shoulder length black hair. The neighbors glanced at me, shrinking smaller as they tried to put space between us. They considered me an Indian. I was I guess, a half breed anyway. Depends on how I dressed as to what breed I was. My eyes were green, I could make people back peddle by just staring at them. I stood almost six feet tall, wide of shoulder and lean of hip. They knew I was only twelve years old. They thought I was a freak.

The preacher finally got done with sending Ma to heaven. Now me, I don't know if there is a heaven, or even a hell. But if he wanted to believe there was, I guess I couldn't fault him. Some of the neighbors had volunteered to fill in the grave. I gave them a sign to back off, told them I would do it.

I stood there with the shovel in my hand, I tried to erase all of the pain in my heart by thinking of all the loving things Ma used to do. I thought about the finality of death. I looked at the hills around about, they seemed to be drawing closer, saying don't worry we will watch over her. Then I knew there is life that death cannot strike out, that the hills know, they would remember, even though man may forget, the creator would not.

I went back to the barn, rolled up my bedroll, took a couple of books to read, remembering what Ma said, "if nothing else, read." I had a new Henry repeating rifle, and a new Colt .45. All what I had I worked for. The Shoshone on the Wind River had showed me where to dig for gold. Every time I went out to ride herd, I took a short handled shovel with me. I had gold stashed most every where. I found out one thing, if you didn't care about wealth, its not hard to find.

Pa and Penny had seen me ride in, they came out to say goodbye. Penny was crying, I took her hands in mine and stared into her eyes. Reaching into her soul, she quieted down. She said,

"You Promise, you really will come back for me?"

"Yes, before your eighteenth year, I will come back." I looked at both of them and said, "if you need me, the Shoshone on the Wind River will know how to get a hold of me."

I rode southwest toward the Needles, with Jill and Lil in tow. Jim was dancing, anxious for the trail ahead. More so than me, I am afraid, somewhere inside of me the twelve year old boy was screaming. I told him to shut up. I told him he was coming of age, it was time for his vision quest.

The Needles were made up of lava, in a volcanic field. I would have to leave my horses at there edge. The sharp edges would cut their feet up. They were quite spectacular and a little spooky. I was half Lakota Sioux, and with my green eyes, I bet the other half was Irish. Anyway most Sioux youth went on their vision quest with no weapons or food or water. But like I said I was half white, I took it all with me. I figured if my totem wanted to find me, he could find me just as well, if I had a full stomach or not. And I am sure my weapons would not scare him off.

I left my horses on the banks of the South Fork and climbed toward the base of the main formation. It was just coming on to dark by the time I rolled into my covers. I was exhausted, emotionally mostly. I fell asleep quickly.

The dreams started, not just one, all kinds. They came like a kaleidoscope, all creation passed before my eyes. So which one was my totem? I was still dreaming, the kaleidoscope slowed down and stopped. Old Man Coyote came padding up and sat down. He said,

"Wake up Buck, I am not going to talk to you while you're sleeping."

"Huh? What the hell you're real, you can you talk?"

"Really Buck, you're too young to cuss. But to answer your question, yes I can talk. It's just to special people, of which you are one."

"What makes me so special?"

"Really Buck, do you know of any other twelve year olds who are man grown and smarter than a college graduate?"

"No, I don't, so are you saying you had something to do with making me a freak?"

"You might say that. Your unfortunate birth turned into an opportunity, we needed a tool, you are it."

"That's all I am? A tool?"

"Isn't that enough? To be one of the Great Spirit's tools, is an honor. I know I am honored to be one."

"So if you know so much about me, Who were my Father and Mother?"

"Your Mother was Lakota Sioux, as you have already figured out, her name was: She Who See's the Light. Your Father's name was Sir Phillip Gentry, he was half Irish and half English. Your Mother died at your birth. Your Father thought that you did too. Your Mother's family did not like your Father, they only put up with him on account of your Mother. When she died, they told him you also did. He left for the east a day after they buried your Mother. Your Grandfather took you and waited beside the trail, it was foreordained. He waited out of sight tell Pa picked you up."

"So my name is Gentry? I suppose I am a Junior. Phillip, that sounds like a prissy name. I think I prefer Buck."

"As you wish, you have the ability to become anything that you want. When in the white man's world, you can be white, in the real world, you can be Indian. Did you fail to notice that your father's name was preceded by a Sir?"

"No I didn't, I preferred to ignore it."

"Yes, well, you will come to find out, that, that designation will open many a door for you. Use it wisely. You are a complex person. Phillip is only twelve years old, he is naive. He has a lot to learn, you two will grow into one."

"What are you trying to say, that I am two people?"

"No, not really. It's just that your body and ability's have outgrown your actual years. Phillip will be shocked by the things you will encounter. Buck will not. It is your responsibility to see that Phillip is not scared and lose the innocence of the pure at heart."

"It sounds like two people to me."

"No, everyone is the same. One is who they want to be, and one is who they are. It is only when they put the two together that they become whole. You are just a little bit more pronounced, you realize it, they don't."

"So what am I supposed to do now?"

"I would suggest you get some sleep. Life is about to catch up with you. Just follow your nose. You will know what to do, when it needs done. I am going to tell the Shoshone where you are and where you are going. And don't worry about Penny and Pa, they will be fine."

He turned and became one with the shadows of the night. I laid back down and thought about what Old Man Coyote said. Well Phillip old boy, it sounds like we have some exciting times ahead, are you game? Of course he didn't answer me, I may talk to myself, but I don't answer myself, as of yet anyway.

I awoke with the sun to find a Rattlesnake coiled on my chest for warmth. I looked at him and said, "It's time to get up." He shook himself, and went on his way. A man's first inclination is to kill the snake, but this was probably my first lesson, at times its better to negotiate than fight.

I went down to the horses, built a fire and made breakfast, filled my canteen and re-packed Jill and Lil. I asked

J.D. Oliver

Jim, "Where are we going this fine morning?" He looked at me, then set off cross country, heading southeast.

Chapter Two

It took us five days to get to Cheyenne. We had taken our time. The wild flowers were in bloom, I think spring is my favorite season. But then again I like all four seasons. Cheyenne was in its infancy. A brawling baby was she.

I had tied my hair back in a pony tail. My hat hung from its stampede string on my back. My .45 was tied down. I was one bad looking Indian. I caught stares right away. Most with a frown. I rode to the town's only stable. There was a dirty looking fellow with a tobacco plug in his cheek, sitting there whittling. As I dismounted he spat a stream of tobacco juice at my feet.

I grabbed him by the hair, with my Texas Bowie knife to his throat, I asked him, "Did you see the sun rise this morning?" He nodded. "Do you want to see another one?" He nodded again, swallowing his plug, "Then, you will apologize, you will take the best of care of my horses, graining them twice a day, currying them three times a day, do you understand?"

I let him go, he threw up all over himself. I grabbed him again and dunked him in the horse trough. He came up a changed person. He said, "I am sorry Sir, I will do as you say."

"My name is Phillip Gentry, my friends call me Buck, what is your name?"

"It's Carl Hatfield, Sir."

"Alright Carl, you will take my saddle and packs and lock them in your storeroom. They will not be stolen, do you understand? Good, can you point me to a decent boarding house?"

He did, I took my saddle bags and rifle and walked to the boarding house. In front of the Cheyenne Supper Club, one so-called town tough stepped in front of me, so as to make me walk around him. I simply used the butt of my rifle to his groin, when he bent over I kneed him in the nose. Then went on my way. "You see Phillip, it would do no good to negotiate with him, he was not as smart as that Rattlesnake. Oh, I know, I know, I will have to kill him before we leave here, but maybe not."

I knocked on the door of the boarding house. A youngish looking woman came to the door. At first glance she started to sniff, then I held her with my eyes. She said, "Won't you come in, Sir, I presume you're looking for a room? Do you want it by the day or week?"

I slowly looked her up and down, she blushed. "My name is Phillip Gentry, may I ask yours?"

"It's Felicity Wells, the rooms are ten dollars a week, with board."

"I will take it by the week, and you may call me Buck, Felicity, are you married?"

"I was Sir, but my husband was killed by a stray shot, he was in the wrong place at the right time. I am afraid we do not have much law around here."

"But you do have a lawman, don't you?"

"I guess you could call him that, he is the biggest crook of all of them. He is always trying to get me to marry him, I loathe him."

"Do you have bathing facilities? And I need a haircut, can you do that?"

"Yes, I will have the boy bring up hot water to your room, I will come up and cut your hair. The room is this way."

I followed her up the stairs, she had a sway to her hips that I had never seen before. Strangely appealing. "Phillip, look away, you shouldn't be watching that." He didn't look away.

A young boy brought the water up. Staring at me all the time, he poured the water in the tub. He left and Felicity came in with scissors and a razor. She said, "I will cut your hair first, do you want to take your skins off?"

I stood up and pulled my buckskin shirt off and sat down on a stool. She started to cut my hair, her breasts brushing up against me. She sure smelled good. She was breathing hard. She finished with my hair and then shaved my neck. "When you get in the tub I will pour water over your head." She didn't leave. Oh, well I didn't mind. I took my boots off and then my pants. She stood there looking at me, she was holding her breath. I got in the water and started washing.

I glanced up at her, she was staring, all of a sudden she ripped her clothes off and stepped into the tub with me. Now I didn't know for sure what was going on, but I found out that I liked it.

She got out of the tub, wrapping a towel around herself, she grabbed her clothes and ran from the room. I sat there, so that's what it's all about, Yep a person could sure get used to that. But thinking about it, I was sure that wasn't all there was to it, that was sex, not love. "Hey Mr. Coyote, was that part of my education?" I heard him laughing in the background.

I was drying off, when I heard a light knock on the door. It was Felicity, she said, "I brought you some of my late husbands underwear, I saw that you didn't have any, a gentlemen should always wear underwear. I feel so ashamed, its just that its been so long, I am sorry, can you forgive me?"

I smiled at her, as I put on the underwear, strange, but it did feel good. "Sure I guess so, that was sure some experience though, I think I could get used to that."

"Do you mean to say that was your first time?"

"Yep, sure was, I am only twelve years old."

"What, no, you can't be, you look at least twenty?"

"Fraid not, back home they think I'm a freak. But don't worry you didn't hurt me none."

She got all white and sat down on the bed, "You Ok, Miss? Felicity are you Ok?" She started to fan herself. Then started to fall over sideways, I grabbed her and held her up. She came around and said, "Buck, please don't tell anyone about this. And don't tell anyone you're only twelve years old. They wouldn't understand. Oh, Lord, what am I going to do?"

"I don't see what the Lord has to do with this, but if you want to call on him, I can't see that it hurts anything. In fact I stayed overnight at Caleb's house one time and heard Harriet calling Lord, Lord, during the night too. I guess that's something you women do."

She looked at me and broke out laughing. Go figure, here she was almost bawling, now she was laughing like mad. One thing I was learning about women, was that I didn't know anything about them. She said, "When you get dressed come on down to supper."

I did just that, but something told me to buckle on my .45 and my Bowie in a scabbard at my back. I walked into the dinning room, everyone turned and stared at me. I said, "Hi There, my name's Phillip Gentry, what's yours?"

That took them by surprise, one thing I had always found to be true, when in doubt. Go on the offensive. Felicity introduced me around. They were right friendly now. I would tell you their names, but it wouldn't make much difference, you would forget them anyway. The food was good, reminded me of Ma's. I almost shed a tear. One brash fellow looked at me and said, "So Phillip, where are you from? England?"

"Well my Dad was, lately though, from the South Fork of the Shoshone." Coyote was right, I could pass for white, or Indian, just depended on the eye of the beholder. I smiled at him and transfixed him with my eyes. He lowered his and went back to eating. Felicity was looking at me with a confused look in her eyes.

After supper everyone went their own way, I volunteered to help with the dish's. Even though Felicity did have a couple of young girls to do the kitchen work. Felicity said, as I brought an armload of plates in, "Buck, you sure are a conundrum, at times you act like a cold hearted gunslinger, other times, like a true twelve year old. I just can't figure you out."

"I suppose you could say that I am what I have to be to fit the situation. I hope someday to combine the two. Phillip is coming along, but he is a little stubborn. You see he enjoys being a kid. Says he is being robbed of his childhood."

"I swear Buck, are you pulling my leg?"

"No, I haven't even touched your leg, have I?"

"Oh, grab a tea towel and dry these dish's."

It must of been about seven P.M. but the noise of gunfire already was making itself heard. Every time a shot went off, the women cringed. I said, "You mentioned that Cheyenne had a lawman, but he doesn't seem to be very effective."

"No he isn't, he is one of them. He's been trying to force himself on me. I can't even go out after dark, really no woman can. I wish someone would just shoot him."

"Your wish is my command, where can I find him?"

"You're joking, you are aren't you?"

"Sure, I was just joking. I won't shoot him, unless he shoots at me first. I think I will go and see what the night life is like." I handed one of the girls the tea towel and left. I kept to the shadows. I went in the side door of the Cheyenne Club Bar. I pulled my hat low over my newly cut hair. The place was crowded. No one noticed me, except the bar tender. He came over and asked what I wanted. I told him a warm bad tasting beer. He gave me a dirty look and slapped one down on the bar. I gave him a silver dollar, he didn't give me any change, even though the sign said that beer was fifteen cents.

I put my back to the bar and sipped my beer. It was lousy. The saloon girls were working the crowd. One of them came by and started giving me the eye. I locked eyes with her, she lowered hers and scuttled away. The town marshal was the loudest one in the bar. A great big dirty fellow. Slapping everyone on the back and pinching the girls. I took an instant dislike to him.

There was a poker game going on, over in the corner. I walked over and stood there watching. Ma and Pa had taught me how to play poker one winter night. There was one empty chair, a slick hair gambler looked up and said, "If your going to stand there, take a seat, otherwise get the hell out of here."

I pulled out the chair. As I sat down I untied my tie down on my leg, so I could tilt my holster. They didn't notice. The slick hair gambler was sitting across from me. The other four players were run of the mill cowboys. The gambler had a large pile of chips in front of him. I played very conservative. Losing some, winning some. Ma had taught me to watch the other players, she said they all had their ticks. The cowboys were easy to figure out. The gambler was the easiest, he was cheating. So I would do him one better. Pa had taught me a few things when Ma wasn't looking.

I made sure that the cowboys didn't lose to me. They started winning some. The gambler was losing. It wasn't long before I had his pile of chips in front of me. He was mad, every time he gave himself a good hand, we all folded. I seen him give the Marshal the high sign. They were about ready to make their move. The Marshal came over and stood behind the gambler.

The gambler said loudly, "You are cheating, I am going to blow your head off." He palmed his pistol, so did the Marshal, they were not going to give me a chance. The gambler got one shot off, he missed. I shot him in the balls, then put another round in his heart, then I put a shot right in the Marshal's badge, then one through his head. All without taking my .45 out of its holster. I was using a soft lead bullet. When they went through the wood of the table to get the Marshal, they flattened some. Sure made a mess of him.

"I am sure everyone seen they drew first, they even shot first. Is there anyone who thinks otherwise?" I said, as I stood up and punched new shells in my revolver. There wasn't. The piano player started pounding on his keys, the bouncers came over and gathered up the carrion. Another evening in Hades. But things were a little different now, they all knew who I was.

I walked up to the bar, they parted and made room for me. The four cowboys came with me. They wanted to buy me a drink. I said, "How about a cup of coffee?"

The bartender said, "Sure thing, I just put on a new pot of Arbuckle's."

I said, "So boys, in town for a night of fun, Huh?"

"Three of us are, John here, we just met. He just got here from Dodge City, he used to be a Deputy there."

I looked at him, he nodded and said, "That was some shooting, best I've seen, where did you learn that?"

"I just do what comes naturally. They needed killing so my .45 obliged. I didn't catch your full name."

"Its, John Wesley Harden, I don't believe I heard yours either?"

"It's Phillip Gentry, my friends call me Buck. Where are you staying John?"

"I don't have a place yet, do you know of a good place?"

"Sure do, I believe Felicity has another spare room, come on, I will introduce you. And Boys," I looked at the other three, "I believe you had better be heading back to your ranch, tomorrow is a work day, isn't it?"

"Sure, we're doing just that, say Buck, you forgot your money, here it is."

"I tell you what boys, why don't the three of you split that, and sock it away for a rainy day, don't drink it up."

"But Buck, there must be three hundred dollars there."

"That's Ok, Boys, use it wisely."

John and I walked out, he looked at me and said, "What are you rich?"

"No, John, I'm not, it just don't take much to keep me alive, I live on love."

"Bullshit, if I ever heard it."

"Yeah, you got that right, that was plain bullshit. But really them boys needed it more than me. I got money socked away, they don't."

I introduced John to Felicity, I could feel the attraction between them. Well maybe I could move on quicker than I thought. I think I just killed two birds with one stone, got her a man, and the town a new Marshal. Was my job done here?

I went back to my room, the bed sure felt good, I was almost asleep when Felicity stuck her head in, she said, "I heard what you did tonight, thank you."

"That's Ok, I want to sleep, don't be calling on the Lord tonight, Huh?" She slammed the door. I hadn't heard from Phillip, I think he was in shock. I was almost asleep, when I got up and put a chair under the door knob, then slid the mattress off of the bed, to the floor. Now I could sleep.

Tap, tap, tap-tap, tap woke me from my sleep. With my.45 in hand I went to the door, "Who's there," I asked.

"It's me, Felicity, may I come in?" I opened the door, she was standing there in her nightgown. She brushed by me, her perfume smelled good. She looked at the mattress on the floor. "Why in the world is the mattress on the floor?"

"Because its out of the direct line from the window. What's wrong? Why are you here? I thought that you and John might like each other?"

"No, I think he was interested in me, but his eyes, their so cold, like their already dead."

"Well he is a gunfighter, but then again, I just killed two people last night, what do my eyes look like?"

She stepped close in the dim light from the coal oil lamp, the female smell of her was strong. She stared into my eyes. "I see life, hope and kindness, but I do not see love for me in there. But I don't care, I just need you to hold me tonight," she said, as she dropped her nightgown to the floor.

The morning light was peeking over the window sill, I rolled over on one elbow and looked at her naked body sleeping like a little girl. She opened her eyes and looked at me. I said, "You know there is no future in this?" She nodded, I went on, "Isn't there someone in town that you are interested in?"

"Well yes, but every time I try to talk to him, he stutters, lowers his eyes and runs away."

"Who is this shy fellow?"

"He's only shy with me, when he talks to other people, he's Ok. His name is Walter Oglethorpe. He's runs the newspaper, The Cheyenne Bugle."

"It's time you got back to your room, I will go see this Walter, have a little talk with him. You know he wouldn't stutter and run away if he didn't like you."

She got up and walked to the door, dragging her nightgown, Old Walter didn't know just how lucky he was. But he was going to find out, if I had anything to do with it. I put the mattress back on the bedstead and made it nice and neat. Poured water in the wash bowl and cleaned up.

Felicity and the two hired girls were already in the kitchen. I think I forget to mention that the girls were Chinese. Anyway their eyes were red, like they had been crying. I walked over to the stove and poured myself a cup of coffee. Leaning against the wall, I watched them as they made breakfast. The girls took arm loads of food to the dinning room table. I asked Felicity, "Ok, what's with the red eyes on the those girls?"

"As you can see they are Chinese, being so, a lot of the Cowboys around here think they are fair game. Especially Jelly Belly Farr, the son of the owner of the J-Bar-J. He is the only son and Jake Farr thinks his son can do no wrong."

"Jelly Belly? Really? What is he fat or what?"

"Well, some. But he's strong too, he's a bully. He not only picks on people, he's mean to animals also. But his name comes from his sweet tooth."

"How did these girls get here to Cheyenne?"

"A lot of them worked on the railroad in the Sierras, when it was done, they and the girls' parents drifted in here, the parents run a laundry. The girls help me for extra money."

I went in and had breakfast with the rest of the borders. John Wesley Harden sat beside me. We talked, we decided to go uptown and talk to the city fathers about John being Marshal.

We went to the General Store, it was all the further we had to go, they hired John on the spot. When their eyes turned to me, I seen a glint of fear. Oh, well I wasn't going to stick around that long anyway. One bad thing about being Marshal, his jurisdiction ended at the city limits. Mine didn't.

John went to the Marshal's office, I headed toward the Bugle. I went in, Walter was setting type, he had sleeve garters, green eye shade hat, and glasses. He was about thirty-five or so, sandy hair that was slightly balding. You know it was strange, there is no rhyme or reason to a woman's taste in men.

I leaned both elbows on the front counter, watching him. He looked up and seen me. Coming over, he offered his ink stained hand, I shook it, he said, "May I help you?"

"Yeah, I want to place a notice in your paper, a full page, can I do that?"

"Yes, yes I can do that, it'll cost thirty dollars, do you have that much?"

"I reckon I can scrape my penny's together, I am going to leave the exact layout to you, but I want to warn any miscreants to either change their ways, or move on. Or face the consequences. You can expand on that word miscreants to include any unsocial behavior that comes to mind. You fill in the blanks. Just sign it, Sir Phillip Gentry, the second."

I reached into my pocket and gave him thirty U.S. Greenbacks. I studied his face, he had level gray eyes, a strong chin, Yep, maybe Felicity might have a winner here. I said,

"Oh, one other thing, you know Felicity Wells, don't

you?"

"Yes, of course, a fine looking woman."

"Yes a fine looking woman, any man would be fortunate to have her. You get your butt down to her boarding house, and you ask her to marry you. No buts. Don't worry she will say yes. Come on, lock the door, go right now."

He did, Yep, he had his hustle on. You ought to of seen him scurrying along. Maybe I could get some sleep tonight. "What do you think Phillip, did we do the right thing?" He allowed that we did. He wanted to get some sleep too.

That ad came out the next day, along with their wedding announcement. John was a little upset about the ad. It didn't take long for his jail to fill up. But Jelly Belly hadn't came to town yet. It was him I wanted.

You are probably wondering why I was bothering about such grown up things, you probably think I should be out under that old cottonwood, playing marbles with the rest of the boys. My time for playing was long gone from the time I was laid in that white tanned deer skin beside the trail.

The days passed, three of them to be exact. I became friends with Yin-Li and Yang-Su, turned out the girls were twins, they were fourteen years old. And like the Yin and the Yang they complimented each other. There parents came from Yentai, a seaport on the Shantung Peninsula in China.

On the fourth day, Jelly Belly came to town. I was rocking on the porch of the General Store. Of course he came with his entourage. Phillip said, to me of course, "My, he is an ugly one, isn't he?" I replied, "Why tell me? Tell him how ugly he is."

Wrong thing to say. I had noticed that Phillip was coming out of his shell. He picked a fine time to get brave. So I had to back his play. Phillip got out of the rocking chair, leaned against the porch support post and said, as they were tying their nags to the hitching post,

"What did you need horses for? A Neanderthal like you could of run here on all fours."

Jelly Belly looked confused, "Huh, what's that you say, were you speaking English?"

"I said that you are fat and ugly, what do you have to say to that?"

One of his hired hands said, "Be careful boss, that's the gunslinger that killed the Marshal, they call him Buck. Let it go, come on lets get a drink." They, all six of them, lowered their eyes and headed for the saloon.

I looked around, John was standing in the doorway of the store. No wonder they didn't take the bait. Six to two odds wasn't good enough for them, they would wait and try and dry-gulch me. John said, "You had better watch your back from now on, Buck. You made a fool out of him, he won't forget it."

"I hope not, because that was the purpose, to get him to come after me and leave other people alone." Phillip said. Yep, that old Phillip he was coming right along.

John said, "Well I hope your mouth didn't overload your ass."

I squared around and looked into John's eyes. He said, "Nope, I reckon it didn't."

He turned and followed them into the saloon. Me, I drifted down toward Yin-Li and Yang-Su's Father's laundry. He did more than just run the laundry. He was also the town's undertaker. How them two fit together I don't know. But anyway the dead always wore clean clothes to the hereafter.

I went in the back door, Yin-Li brought me a cup of coffee. Her Father had a work bench in one corner of the kitchen. On it was powder and shot. And all the tools to reload with. Makes sense, after all the Chinese invented gun powder. He was hunched over the bench reloading some cartridges.

I walked over, drinking my coffee, looking over his shoulder. He looked up and invited me to sit down. I did. Now most of the cartridges of the day had a little piece of wadding between the powder and the bullet. He was taking that out, dumping the powder into a coffee can, then taking some different powder out of a crock, pouring the shell full, without the wadding, then replacing the bullet. The powder of the day, when shot, caused a lot of smoke. He told me his powder burned clean.

I said, "I see that your leaving the wadding out, and adding more powder."

"Yes, the extra powder, how you say, causes a magnificent difference. Then I drill a little hole in the end of the bullet, the result is magnificent."

"That's twice you used the word magnificent, Chen-Lee, have you named your new cartridge yet?"

"No, do you have a suggestion?"

"Well you could call it a Magnum, just shorten the word magnificent. I see those bullets are .44 caliber. Do you have a revolver to fit them?"

"Yes, I have many, rifles too. Being the undertaker, the belongings of the dead are left with me, those that are not claimed by relatives that is. A great many of them are not. In fact that gambler you killed, in this trunk, there is a matched set of Navy Colts, .44 caliber."

"Let me help you with the reloading, then perhaps you will show me those guns?" We spent the rest of the day working on the reloading. Then after supper (his wife was a good cook) we went down to his basement. He opened the trunk. They were beautiful, they had pearl handles. Under the guns was clothes. I looked through them. The labels were from London. Hand made, beautiful. Who was this gambler? I bought the whole trunk full of goodies.

I asked Chen-Lee, "I see that you have an extra room out back that is not being used, do you think I could rent it? The town seems to be filling up, I guess since some of the bad crowd has been eliminated, people feel safe now. The boarding house is getting too crowded for me."

He was glad to have me around, I went to my old room. Told Felicity that I was leaving, for Chen-Lee's house. She wasn't too upset, her and Walter were due to get married next week. But she did pinch my butt as I left. When I got back to my new room, Chen-Lee had the trunk in my room. I went through it.

His name was Charles Nottingham, from, where else, Nottingham, England. Going thru his papers, I found out his Father was a Duke. How far the great have fallen. I tried on some of his suits, they fit me. He even had some high quality underwear. Did I feel funny wearing a dead man's clothes. No, I didn't. To the victor goes the spoils.

I was awoke by the sounds of wild shouts and gunfire. I strapped on my new .44's over my new underwear. Jelly Belly and his crew were hoorawing Chen-Lee and his family. One man had a torch he was about to throw into the front window. My first shot hit the torch thrower in the hand taking the hand clean off. The hollow point mushroomed on impact. The so called torch thrower was none other than Jelly Belly.

His stump was squirting blood all over. Chen-Lee came out of the house with some bandages. He stopped the flow of blood and wrapped it tight. I told his crew to get him to the Doctor. And reminded them that if it wasn't for the charity of Chen-Lee, their Boss would have been dead by now from blood loss.

Yin-Li and Yang-Su were standing there with their hands over their mouths, looking at me and giggling. I looked down, Yeah I was quite a sight. Gun belts over underwear. But at least my fly was closed.

The next morning there was a citizen's committee at my door. Seems I was determined to be a hazard to the community. I was being given five days to get out of town. I fixed my gaze upon their souls, staring them down to their beginnings. They lowered their gaze and allowed as how they made a mistake. I was free to stay as long as I wanted. I told them to go home and make love to their wives and from now on to check with the Marshal before trying to eject someone.

I finished getting dressed, black suit, ribbon tie, black boots. My old felt hat didn't quite fit the getup though. I went into breakfast. Chen-Lee asked me what the good citizen's of Cheyenne wanted. I told him. I also told him I was getting a little tired of Cheyenne anyway and thought I might just drift.

He allowed as to maybe I would do him a favor. The twins wanted to go spend the summer with his youngest sister, their Aunt in Denver. Maybe I would see them there, safely? I told him I would. We decided to leave three days from now. I went to town to make arrangements.

The first thing I did was buy a new hat. Then I went to the stable's. I bought a spring wagon, suitable for the trip. Bought harness for Jill and Lil, they could pull the wagon, Jim could tag along behind. Carl had kept my belongings safe. Good thing, I had a couple of hundred pounds of gold in them packs. I took fifty pounds out and went to the bank.

I laid the fifty pound sack on the counter. The clerk looked at it and said, "I don't know if we can accept raw gold or not, let me get the owner." The president of the bank came over. Looked at it, I could see the greed in his eyes.

He said, "Where did you get that gold, Boy?"

"I got it up in Bannack, Montana. Yes Sir, I dug it out of the ground myself. Can you weigh it out for me?"

"Sure we can, do you want to deposit it?"

"Yes Sir, I do." He brought the scales over to the counter. I kept my eye on his thumb, he only tried to cheat once. I cleared my throat, he took his thumb off of the scale. Gold was going for fifty dollars an ounce, fifty pounds, that's sixteen ounces per pound, eight hundred ounces, that comes to forty thousand dollars. I had that all figured out in my head. He could see that I wasn't going to put up with any nonsense.

"Yes Sir, forty thousand dollars. We'll put that in your account, what's the name?"

"It's Phillip Gentry, and I will need a receipt for that, plus," I looked around, there were a couple of women customers in the bank, "I want those women, as well as all of your employees to sign and witness that you received that amount and that it was deposited to my name."

"I assure you, sir, this is an honest Bank." He blustered.

"Oh, I know that, and I aim to keep it that way."

They all signed, I put the receipt in my pocket. I withdrew four thousand dollars, traveling money. Now four thousand dollars was a lot of money, to anybody. It wouldn't take long for this transaction to be known all over town. Perhaps my reputation would keep the miscreants from shooting me in the back for the money, most likely not, though.

I went over to the Cheyenne Supper Club for supper. Chinese food was good, but I wanted steak and beans, with taters. I went to the table in the back, I sat with my back to the wall. The waitress knew who I was. As she set a glass of water on the table, she bent over so I could see her wares. Told her all

I wanted was a steak, well done, and to pile on the beans and taters. And to drink, a pint of beer. Beer didn't bother me, as long as I had it with food. But why a person would drink it just to get drunk was beyond me.

Before she was done taking my order, John Wesley Harden walked in, seeing me, he came over and sat down. I told him I was buying, to order what he wanted. He told the waitress, "Make mine the same as his." He smiled at her and patted her ass as she left. Then he said, "You've been pretty busy, you've made the big wigs nervous, they sent me to ask if you would please leave town for awhile. Now if you don't want to that's Ok. They just wanted me to ask."

"You know what, I have just made plans to go to Denver for awhile. Chen-Lee wants me to take the twins down there to see their Aunt. I told him I would."

"I heard that you made quite a deposit at the Bank today. Where did you get the gold?"

"I dug it out of the ground. Just like everybody else, if it's anybody's business." I shifted in my chair, so I could look directly into his eyes. We locked stares, he broke first.

"I was just asking, no offense." A drop of sweat ran down the side of his cheek.

"And none taken," I said, with a smile.

Phillip said to me, "You know, you are really quite mean, he was just curious, he didn't mean any harm."

I said, "yeah, just like a Rattlesnake doesn't mean it, when he bites me."

John was looking at me, "Is anything wrong, you Ok?"

"Sure I was just thinking, that's all. Here comes the food, dig in partner." Then I continued, "John, tell me, when did the good city fathers decide I was an undesirable person? Was it after I moved into Chen-Lee's house or before?"

He laid his fork and knife down and looked at me. "It was after you moved into Chen-Lee's place. I never made the connection, but yes, they're a bunch of prejudice pricks. What are you going to do about it?"

"Nothing at this particular time. But while I am gone, I want you to keep watch over the rest of Chen-Lee's family. If they come to any harm, I will wipe Cheyenne off the face of this land."

John stared into my eyes. Then said, "And I do believe that you could do it too."

"If I couldn't, I know people who can."

"I just bet you do Buck. But I will keep a lid on things. This town has such a good start it would be a shame to see it wiped out."

"That's what this land is all about, if all the people cannot be free, then no one is."

"Don't worry Buck, no harm will come to your friends. Or anyone else in Cheyenne if I have anything to do with it. If you're done, do you want to go in and watch the floor show?"

Most of the town fathers' were in there watching. I stood in the back of the room. The girls were kicking up their heels. I enjoyed it for awhile. Till their costumes started to slip, showing things that they shouldn't. But the good citizen's of Cheyenne kept egging them on. Till some of them were nude. The girls not the citizens. I turned around and left. They didn't like the Chinese or Indians, but they put up with lewdness. Go figure.

I spent the next three days getting things ready for our trip, which took about thirty minutes. The rest of the time I spent playing poker, till no one would play with me anymore. I took their money and gave it to Chen-Lee, told him to invest it. I was not very popular. In fact the night before we left, a couple of ne'er-do-wells tried to knife me in the back. I didn't kill them, I carved some designs on them with my Bowie Knife. They were marked for life, everyone would know what happened to them. That was worse than death, right?

We left the next morning. I had bought the girls riding habits' with linen dusters to cover them. Their hats were gray wool felt, they did look cute. I loaded my belongings out of the hostler's store room into the traveling trunk of the late gambler. I tied it secure under the spring seat. I guess you could call this wagon a surrey. The top even had fringes on it, to wick the rain away.

My Henry was a .44, the same as my new revolver's. So I had plenty of ammunition, the new stuff Chen-Lee made. I had bought two .36 Caliber 12-shot revolvers for the girls, told them they could practice on the trail. They were naturals. In return they said they would teach me how to defend myself. I didn't know what they were talking about. But the first night out, around the fire, they showed me.

In fact they kicked my ass. They said it was called Tai Chi. Started with some weird posturing, then wham. I was seeing stars. We spent a couple of hours practicing. I was a fast learner, it only took me maybe twelve times of landing on my back. The girls went to bed in their tent. I crawled over to my bedroll beside the fire.

I awoke the next morning with a wolf washing my face. When I opened my eyes he sat down on his haunches with his tongue lolling out. When I got a better look I could see that he wasn't all wolf. He was part Husky or some such.

There was some corn fritters left over from supper last night, I tossed him some, he caught them in mid-air. Where he came from I had no idea. But when we got ready to go, he hopped up in the rear seat beside Yang-Su. Yin-Li sat beside me. I guess we adopted him, or to be more precise, he adopted us. I didn't have too good an imagination when it came to names, so I just called him, Wolf.

We were in the month of May, there were more and more travelers' on the road. Some stopped to yarn, some just stared at us as they went by. Mid-afternoon the next day there was some dust coming down the road. Wolf was growling. Now Ma didn't raise me up to be stupid, when a Dog doesn't like someone, you had better take it to heart.

There were four of them red-necked louts, dirty and nasty. They stopped in the middle of the road, blocking our path. Saying, "Well, what do we have here, two Chinie girls, with only some dumb Indian to guard them. You two just hop on down here and take those fancy duds off, and we'll have some fun."

I said, "I don't think so, I'll give you four thirty seconds to make your peace with your maker, then I am going to kill you." I lied. I really didn't mean to, but it was Yin-Li and Yang-Su's fault. You see, when those four idiot's went for their guns, Yin and Yang pulled their guns and shot them out of the saddle. I didn't even clear leather.

I looked at the girls, "Now you shot them, what are you going to do with their bodies'?"

They got out of the buggy, went over and took the saddles off of their horses and turned them loose. Then they took the saddles and lined them up beside the trail, then pulled the bodies' over and laid their heads on the saddles. And then covered them with their saddle blankets', like they were sleeping. Then they pinned a note on each of them, "This is what happens to Highway Men in this country, Be Warned."

Wolf and me, we didn't even get out of the surrey. The girls got back in and started singing some kind of a Chinese dirge. I clucked at Jill and Lil, we went on our way, with Jim following like usual. It wasn't long before their tune changed to some kind of a happy song.

That night we came to a little town called Greeley, twernt much, but it did have a nice hotel and stable. I let Phillip do the talking, when he got done explaining how we were escorting two Chinese Princesses, they gave us the royal treatment. We even had hot water for bathes. You see it depended on who was doing the talking, me or Phillip, as to whether we was white or Indian.

I did the talking at the stable though. The hostler was a fellow of about forty years old, receding salt and pepper hair and moustache. His brown eyes showed a twinkle that belied his job. He looked at me and said, "What can I do for you son?"

"I reckon we need to put three horses up for the night. And I would like to pull our buggy in the barn. It has all of our belongings in it, I sure would hate for them to get stole."

He looked me up and down, "How old are you son? Now I know how big you are, so don't lie to me."

I gave him the same appraisal that he did me. So I figured I would tell him the truth, "I am going on thirteen Sir, although I look to be in my twenties."

"I thought so, I ran across the same thing once, back east. The boy didn't handle it too good. But I think you have a handle on it. What's your name son?"

"It's Phillip Gentry, sir, my friends call me Buck."

"Phillip Gentry? I knew a Phillip Gentry, just about thirteen years ago. I was in Denver then, he was some kind of an English Duke. He was a nice man, in fact he gave me the money to start this livery. Said it was a gift. He was sad though. Said his wife died in child birth, along with the baby. But looking at you I reckon he was mistaken. He was traveling the west trying to assuage his grief."

"Do you know where he ended up?"

"I sure do, he is in Pennsylvania. I received a letter from him just last winter. How do you know your name is Phillip Gentry?"

"The spirits' told me. Old Man Coyote, to be exact."

"Well that's good enough for me, I will dig out that letter for you in the morning. You get a good night's sleep, I will take care of your horses and buggy."

"I reckon I must be tired, did you tell me your name? Or did I just forget?"

"I thought I did son, but maybe I didn't, it's Festus McGovern, from Tennessee."

"Well Festus from Tennessee, I will see you in the morning and please call me Buck"

Chapter Three

Yin-Li and Yang-Su were both in the tub when I returned. For a small town, this hotel was ahead of its time. Our room was on the top floor. I say room, but it was really three rooms, two bedrooms and a setting room. The bedrooms had a tub in each of them. The girls had left their bedroom door open. I stood in the doorway and said, "Girls from now on please close your door when you are naked, I know you consider me your brother, but there might be other people around, you know you didn't even lock the outside door?"

"We know that Buck, but you didn't have a key, did you?"

"No, but I could of knocked. Denver is a big city, when we get there you're going to have to change your ways."

"Don't worry, our Aunt Mee-Ling, we hear, is very strict, even though her name means Beautiful Dawn."

"So, how old is your Aunt?"

"She is only twenty-six, she was just a baby when our family came over."

"Well, you girls get out of that tub and let's get some chow, I heard they have good food."

The next morning at breakfast, Festus came in and ate with us. Said, he would accompany us to Denver, he had some business there. We were glad to have the company. He had already hooked up Jill and Lil to our wagon. Jim was getting fat and lazy, just tagging along. Of course, I wasn't working too hard either.

Festus was riding a Tennessee Walker, looked pretty smooth. As we were leaving, he handed me a letter. It was from my dad to Festus. Details weren't important, much, but he was living in Williamsport, Pennsylvania. He was married and had three children. The rest of the letter I didn't pay much attention to, it was just words. Yin-Li and Yang-Su took turns handling the team. I sat and pondered.

We stopped for lunch beside a small stream. I unhooked the team to let them graze. I didn't bother to hobble them, they wouldn't go anyplace. Turned out Festus had another stable in Denver. That was good, I trusted him. I was hatching a plan in the back of my mind. I thought I would like to go see my Dad. And since Festus had a stable in Denver, I could trust him to take care of my horses and gear.

There was a moderate amount of people on the road. They waved as we passed. It was a fine spring day. A day to lift the spirits. That is if you had any. I didn't. I was down in the dumps. The girls were looking at me and so was Festus. We got into Denver as the sun was going down. We pulled up to a big house on the outskirts of Denver.

The front door opened, out came Mee-ling. A vision in the latest Paris fashion. She hugged the girls. Looking at Festus and me, she said, "Hello Festus, who is this?"

Yin-Li said, "This is Phillip Gentry, our friend. He kept our house from being torched."

She held out a well manicured hand and said, "Glad to meet you, Phillip, I am Mee-Ling."

I said, "Glad to meet you, Miss Beautiful Dawn. It is

Miss isn't it?"

"Yes, of course. I see by your demeanor, that, you are single too. Although you are spoken for. The little girl on the Shoshone loves you very much."

"How in the hell did you know about Penny?"

"You are not the only one that has spirit helpers."

"She may love me, but she is only ten years old."

"And you are not quite thirteen. Not that much older than little Penny."

"That's right Phillip is that young. But I am not." I looked around. "I am older than these hills you see in the light of the moon."

She stepped closer, "As well as I, but trapped we are, isn't that so?"

"Trapped? I suppose you could look at it that way, but I think it's much more like being hemmed in by circumstances."

"Hey you two," Festus said, "do you want me to take the horses and buggy to my stables or what?"

"Yes," Mee-Ling said, "take them, but we had better unload the buggy first. Buck will be staying with us. Won't you Buck?"

She had called me Buck, instead of Phillip. "Sure, can I bring Phillip?"

"I really don't know how you cannot bring him, it will be a good experience for him."

We unloaded the buggy, all except the gold. I asked Festus, "Would you put that buggy under lock and key. I will be by in the morning for what's under the seat?"

"Sure," he looked at me, "we have a good bank here, see you in the morning."

The girls were already in the house. I followed Mee-Ling back into the house. She turned around just inside the door, stepping close, her essence was overpowering, she kissed me. She pulled back and said, "I have been waiting for you Buck, I had the servants' draw a hot bath for you, it's in my room. After you're done, dinner will be ready."

My trunk was already there. Well anyway, it was my trunk now, that gambler sure didn't need it. The water was fine. I soaked away, then fell asleep.

"Hey sleepy head, wake up, the food is on the table. Here is a towel, stand up, I will dry you off."

I opened my eyes. Mee-Ling was standing there, like a beautiful dawn. I stood up, she smiled, then dried my back. Patience was its own reward. I got dressed and we went down to dinner. Later that night patience lost out to expediency. And that expediency was a good night's sleep. I bet you thought it was sex. The tub was in her room, I had my own room.

The next morning Yin-Li and Yang-Su woke me. Mee-Ling had already left for her dress shop. They made me breakfast. Flap Jacks and Churned Butter, with Maple syrup. Not very Chinese, but we were Americans, not Chinese.

The girls accompanied me to Festus's Stable. The gold weighed one hundred and fifty pounds. How were we to get it to the bank? We could hook up the horses to the wagon, but it was only two blocks to the bank. So we used a wheel barrow. We got all kinds of looks. Two beautiful girls following a dandy, wheeling a barrow of sacks through the streets.

You noticed I called myself a dandy? Well that's what I looked like, all duded' up in that Duke of Nottingham's clothes, you know the gambler. It was all Phillip's idea, I wanted to wear my buckskins. But he said Nooo, you had to play the part.

Yin-Li held the bank's door open for me. The clerk behind the counter said, "Here, you can't bring that thing in here."

"Hold your horses, little man, appearances tend to deceive, don't let your eyeballs overload your ass." That was me, Buck, talking. "Trot out the owner of this here bank, I have a deposit to make."

"Please Buck, let me do the talking, you're so crude." said Phillip. "This dray is but a curricle of the gods. Holding the lustrous opulence of the heretofore said gods."

The clerk said, "Huh?"

"You see there, Phillip, he didn't understand one word you said. You have to get down to their level."

I walked up to the window, with the twins beside me, "My good man, this wheel barrow holds one hundred and fifty pounds of gold nuggets. I wish to deposit said gold. Do you understand?"

He said, "Yes Sir, I will get the president of the bank." He hurried off. Thirty seconds later, he scurried back with a rather portly individual in tow. Why would I modify the word portly by putting the word rather in front of it? I thought that sounded better than saying that he was fat.

"May I help you?" he wheezed.

"I see by your size, that you run to excesses, perhaps even to greed. Does that perhaps translate as to how you run this bank also?" Phillip said.

"Really Phillip, that was a little cruel, wasn't it?" I said.

The fat man said, "Uh, no, I assure you Sir, this is an honest bank." His face was beet red. I was a little worried that he might have a heart attack.

"I didn't catch your name," I said.

"It's Herman Ratcliff, Sir. I am the President of this bank. What can I do for you?"

"Well Mr. Ratcliff, I have one hundred and fifty pounds of gold nuggets, I would like to deposit them in your bank. Now to save time, don't tell me you don't have the facilities to handle gold, I know you do."

"Yes Sir, we can handle that. The price of gold just went up to fifty dollars an ounce, as of yesterday. If you will wheel that behind the counter, Mr. Jefferies will start weighing it."

I wheeled it as directed. I said, "Yin-Li, Yang-Su, will you monitor Mr. Jefferies?" I turned to Mr. Ratcliff, "Herman old pal, my name is Sir Phillip Gentry, the Second. The name on this account will be just Phillip Gentry. If I kick the bucket, Yin-Li and Yang-Su will be my beneficiary's. We will need the deposit slip witnessed by everyone present."

"And Mr. Ratcliff, I will need ten thousand dollars in cash, if that's Ok? You can give it to my girls. I am going over to Mee-Ling's dress shop, they can bring it over there when they're done."

"Yes Sir, Mr. Gentry, it will be done."

I moseyed over to the dress shop. Have you ever moseyed? Anyway, I did. To me this was a big city. Full of hustle and bustle, there was even some in the dress shop window's. Bustles that is. Anyway that's what Mee-Ling told me they were.

"Have you ever sold any of them?" I asked her.

"A few, they aren't too big here in Denver, yet. I personally think that they are stupid, the bustles, not my customers. After all, how can they be stupid, they are smart enough to buy from me."

I looked her up and down, she was dressed in a gown with a tight waistline, she did not need a bustle. Mee-Ling was taller than most oriental woman and belied the image of a so-called China Doll. Under those graceful curves she had muscles of steel. And a will to match. I am afraid I was staring. So was she. I said, "I dislike to lose and I can see that you do too. I know you would consider it a loss, if you broke the stare first. So what I am going to do, is, step forward and kiss you. When our lips meet we can both close our eyes. That way nobody loses, it will be a draw."

"Yes, but who is it, that I will be kissing? Buck or Phillip?"

"Who do you want to kiss?"

"Well I certainly don't want to kiss a little boy, so it had better be you, Buck."

We both stepped forward and met in the middle. We both opened our eyes at the same time. She was breathing hard, so was I. She said, "That was certainly not the kiss of a little boy. I know some about you, Buck. But not enough. Just who or what are you?"

"I? Who am I? I am just starting to find out. It seems there are two parts to me. One a naive boy and the other? I am afraid I do not know. It seems I have been around for centuries. I know what people are going to say before they say it, most times. Sometimes not, as with you. Every breath you take, every blink of your eyes. The way you move, is a beautiful surprise to me."

"That is the most romantic thing anyone has ever said to me. I do think you are old, centuries old. Oh, not in years, but in experience. I think in years your body match's mine. In all ways. As to Phillip, I do not know. I think he was given to you to raise and when that is accomplished, you two will become one. Phillip is the auspicious one to have you."

"Mee-Ling, you said you know about Penny? What about her and me? Is she waiting for me?"

"She thinks she is, she is in love with the idea of you, not you. After all you trained her to be able to take care of herself. Before her eighteenth year she will meet her love. Old

Man Coyote told me. But you also gave a promise, that you would be back before her eighteenth year. For some reason that is important, Old Man Coyote said."

"Boy, you and him really had quite a talk. Anything else?"

"No, not right away. But when the girls get here, you can take us to lunch. There is a nice restaurant in the Denver House, that's the big hotel you walked by."

"I didn't walk, I moseyed, you do know the difference, don't you?"

Mee-Ling was walking away, she half turned, looked back over her shoulder and gave me that look. You know the one that says, we both know that you don't have a sense of humor, but I love you anyway. Yep, that's the look, I melted inside.

"Uh, Mee-Ling, I need a hair cut. I seen a barber shop two doors down. I am going to go over there, I'll be back just before lunch, Ok?"

Denver was a town, becoming a city, as such it had the same growing pains as all the west had. Everyone was still wearing weapons. So was I. I walked, I didn't mosey. I had Mee-Ling on my mind. Being occupied, I didn't notice the man coming out of the hardware store. I bumped into him, he fell down, scattering his packages. He was a man in his forties, a rancher by dress.

I said, "I'm sorry Sir, I didn't see you, I apologize. Here let me help you."

I reached down and helped him up. Then started to pick his packages up. As I was doing so, another man came out of the store, "Here, what's this? Did that man hurt you, Mr. Peters?" Then he turned towards me, saying, "You clumsy oaf, do you know who you knocked down? Mr. Peters is the owner of the P Bar P, the biggest ranch in these parts, I am his foreman. I think a beating would put some manners in you."

Mr. Peters said, "No Claude, it was my fault too, I wasn't watching where I was going either."

Claude didn't pay any attention to his Boss. He took a swing at me. I side stepped him. He had put all of his body in that swing, when he missed he fell on his face. I laughed. Really I couldn't help it, I didn't mean to make fun of him, it was just funny. A big man like him laying on his face in the mud of the street.

Claude sat up, wiped the mud from his eyes, they were mighty mean looking eyes. He said, "You did that on purpose."

"Well of course I did, do you think I wanted to get hit with that ham you call a fist?"

He sat there staring at me, all of sudden he started to laugh, the mean left his eyes. He went to get up, I stepped forward to help him. He let me give him a hand up. Mr. Peters said, "Claude, the next time you don't listen to me, you're fired, do you understand?'

"Yes sir, I'm sorry Boss."

"It's not me you owe an apology to, it's to Mr.? I don't believe we know your name."

"My name is Phillip Gentry, my friends call me Buck, however."

"Well Buck, I would like to be considered a friend of yours, so may I call you Buck?"

"Yes Sir, Mr. Peters, you may, I don't believe I know your first name either."

"It's Simon. Don't laugh, I know, Simon Peters, is redundant. But it is what it is. May I ask your purpose in our fine City?"

"Purely pleasure Simon. I am staying with Mee-Ling, I brought her two nieces from Cheyenne. But I hail from the Shoshone country. I was just heading to get a haircut."

"I might just join you, we have three barbers now, no waiting. Claude, gather these packages up and get the rest of the supplies and take them to the ranch. I'll be along later."

We went into the Barber Shop, one barber was busy. We sat down. I told them I wanted the works, this being the first time I was ever in a Barber Shop. I didn't know what the works consisted of, but figured I could afford it. Simon was a talker. I said, Yep, Sure, You Bet. While the barber cut my hair, put a hot wet towel on my face, then shaved me. Now I really didn't need a shave, but what the heck. Then when all that was done, he leaned my chair back and washed my hair. Now, no one ever done that since Ma did it, when I was a little fellow.

When he was all done he put some kind of oil in my hair, and some kind of flower smelling water on my face. I bet I could be smelled for at least a mile. The Shoshones' would of laughed their heads off at me....

Simon and I walked out, on the sidewalk he invited me out to his ranch, I told him perhaps I could get out that way, maybe in a few days. He shook my hand and we parted. I walked back to the dress shop. The twins were there. Mee-Ling looked at me and quietly smiled. The twins couldn't stop giggling. Yang-Su said, "Didn't take long to turn you into a dude, did it?"

"Appearances can be deceiving, can't they Mee-Ling?"

"Yes Buck, in your case, that is definitely true. You are certainly not what you appear to be. Sometimes a chameleon lives longer. Come, lets go to dinner."

She took my arm, the twins followed along behind. Every head turned to watch the procession. The Maitre d` showed us to our table. Big difference from Cheyenne. There was no prejudice here, against Mee-Ling anyway. Could be a reason for that. Just could be. This was a pretty fancy place. I think they were a little ahead of the times though. Me thinks they were putting on airs. That's alright, life can be pretty basic here in the west, sometimes even short. Why shouldn't they live it up, while they could?

"Would you like a glass of wine, Buck?" Mee-Ling asked me.

"Wine? I have heard of it, but all I have ever tasted is beer and whisky. I guess I could try a glass."

The waiter brought a bottle out with a fancy cork in it, he made a show of taking the cork out, it went pop and flew across the room. I think he did that on purpose. I could of taken that cork out without even making a sound. He said it came from France. Big deal. I tasted it, it wasn't bad, but not much bite. Probably just a ladies drink. Oh, heck I might just as well play along. I drank my glass down in one gulp.

Mee-Ling said, "Buck that was gauche, now pay attention as I drink, see just small sips, savor the flavor."

"Why, I see some of the other men taking big gulps?"

"Because, when we go back east to see your Dad, manners will be important."

"Go back east? Are we going back east?"

"Yes, of course, why else did you think you brought the twins to Denver? They will stay here and run the dress shop."

"How can they stay here by themselves, they are too young."

"How do you think I could stay here, without anyone bothering me? Our family belongs to the Tong. They will take care of them, like they have taken care of me."

"How come they didn't take care of Chen-Lee's family

in Cheyenne?"

"He didn't want them to, he knew you would be along. Then things would improve and they did. That John Wesley Harden is taking care of things."

"How come everybody knows more about me than I do?"

"Oh, you are so full of questions, aren't you? Are not you enjoying yourself?"

I took a few seconds to ponder that question. Looking at the three beautiful Chinese women. I said, "Of course I am. I seemed to have moved out of the past into a new life. At times I think things are moving a little fast for me. But then again, looking at you, Mee-Ling, I think everything is right on track."

"Of course it is, silly boy. Eat up that wonderful food, use that fork for your salad, not the big one. When we get back east, people will judge you on your manners. Seems rather shallow, doesn't it? But not really, manners show that you respect the people around you and also at the same time, that you respect yourself."

"Please, I beg you, do not under estimate the naive boy you see before you. It is but a facade, a passing shadow. As you well know, deep inside you, under those beautiful breasts that are straining at your bodice."

Mee-Ling blushed, beautifully, and dropped her eyes to the food on her plate. The twins just sat there grinning. "Come finish your food, would you like to go for a ride, the three of you? Have you ever rode straddle, not side saddle?"

"No we have not, but we can learn. I have some clothes at home that should be suitable for the occasion."

And did she ever. "I had these made special, a wool blend on the outside of the trousers, with leather on the inside of the leg. The jacket is of the same wool, silk blend, woven tightly to keep wind and water out. The color being in earth tones, so as to blend in with the country side."

"I applaud your creativity and foresightedness my love, may I call you that, 'My love'?"

"What else would you call me? Not to be factitious, but we were created for each other." I looked at her, it taking all of my self control to keep my hands off of her, "Good, you three get dressed, I will go see to the horses." I did so after going to my room and changing into my buckskins.

Festus was at his stables. Jim, Jill and Lil would be suitable for the women. Festus put my saddle on a big black stallion. He asked, "Where are you going to ride?"

"I thought I would go see Mr. Peters at his ranch, the P Bar P. He invited me out."

Festus said, "Mr. Peters is a good man, I think he is in a little bit of financial trouble, though. His last roundup was several hundred head of stock short. If you ask me, I think some of his crew has something do with it."

"Do you think it's his foreman?"

"No, he has been with him for years. Just about a year ago, a tough bunch of riders showed up, Peters hired them on. Now he can't get rid of them. Both he and his foreman are not gunfighters, but those toughs are."

"Well, well. I guess I had better dig my .44's out of my trunk. I wouldn't want to ride in there naked."

I threw the reins on Jim, Jill and Lil, around their necks, they followed us to Mee-Lings house. "You women practice getting on and off. I have to get something out of my trunk."

"Is that something your guns? If it is, we have them, they are hanging on the gate post."

"Ah, the inscrutable oriental, what would I do without you?"

"Let's hope you never have the chance to find out."

Mee-Ling took the reins of Jim in one hand, then sprang into the saddle, she didn't even use the stirrup. Yin-Li and Yang-Su did the same. Damn, they made me look like an old man. Well I couldn't let them show me up. So I did the same as they, but I hit the saddle horn a little bit. I thought I hid the pain, but Mee-Ling said, "Are you alright? You be more careful, you know they belong to me, also."

"Oh, they do, do they? Well perhaps we had better make it legal then?"

"Are you asking me?"

"Are you accepting?"

"If you are asking, I am."

"This could go on all day, when do you want to tie the knot?"

Mee-Ling leaned over toward me and we kissed. She said, "There is no hurry, or is there?"

"No, I can control myself, can you?"

"I am the model of self-control, haven't I waited all these years for you?"

Yin-Li and Yang-Su looked back and said, "You know you two are not alone, we can hear everything you say."

"Good," I said, "then you must know this is a private conversation. Although not that private. Because we have no secrets from the two of you. And yes I am going to tell her about Felicity."

"Oh, you don't have too, we already have."

I looked at Mee-Ling. "Yes, I know, I knew before they told me. I know it was not your fault, don't worry, I love you." She said.

I didn't know what to say. So I just leaned over and kissed her again. Then I pulled my Henry out of the saddle scabbard and checked its load. Love is fine, but life goes on, that is if you are prepared.

It was a beautiful afternoon. Isn't it strange how often we use the word beautiful. There is a saying that beauty is in the eye of the beholder. Now some Anglo-Saxons' would not think anyone but their race was beautiful. I don't know how anyone could think Mee-Ling was not beautiful. She was about five foot, eight inches in height, weighed about a hundred and twenty pounds. Black hair, brown eyes. She was not one hundred percent Chinese though, I could tell. But what ever the rest was, she was the most breath taking woman I had ever seen, or even dreamt about. Her background held secrets.

I awoke out of my reverie when a Magpie lit between my horses ears. It just sat there looking at me. The black didn't even spook, his ears just twitched a couple of times. "Ok," I said, "What's your story?"

It didn't say anything, but flew over and lit on my shoulder. I guess I had acquired a pet. I think pet was not the right word, because pet to me is just another word for slave. I think the proper word to use would be friend. Friend left me and flew up to Yang-Su's shoulder, well couldn't blame him, she probably smelled better.

We were about six or seven miles from town. In rolling hills and wild flowers. The grass was already hock deep. If the spring rains kept up, the grass would be good this year. "Just how far is the P Bar P," I asked Mee-Ling.

"About three more miles, we are already on their range. Strange, the last time I was out here, there were a lot more cattle."

"Perhaps they moved them to different grass, although I wouldn't think so, the grass looks pretty good here. Festus did tell me that Simon had been losing some stock. He also told me that he has some hard cases on his payroll. They won't leave, even though he has tried to fire them."

"Yes, I have seen some of them in town. A few of them are just boys that fell in with bad company. But most of them are rotten to the core. I believe there are ten of them."

We topped a little hill and below in a nice little valley with its own stream was the headquarters of the P Bar P. Around the main house, large old Cottonwoods grew, with many out buildings arraigned around a large ranch yard. The biggest building of course was the barn. Yep, it was a nice layout.

We rode down the hill and through the large gate. It had a big sign over it, with the brand P Bar P on it. As we rode in, there were a couple of hands leaning against the corral gate, watching a bronco being rode. They turned and stared at us, well not us so much, but at the girls. They had smirks on their faces. Oh, this was going to be fun!

We stopped at the hitch rack and dismounted. The two loafers were walking toward us. The ranch house door opened and Simon came out. "I see you took me up on my invitation, glad to see you." Simon looked at the two hands and said, "You two get back to work."

They just stood there, "We don't think so, we want to meet your guests." One of them said with his legs planted and his thumb hooked in his gun belt.

I patted the dust from my buckskins. Unhooking the hammer loops from my guns, I stepped out from behind my horse. The sun was hanging about to the three o'clock position in the naked blue sky.

I said, " I suppose its none of my business, but I could of sworn I heard Mr. Peters give you two an order, or was I mistaken?"

They both squared around to face me. The tall one said, "Yeah you're right, it's none of your business and you are making a big mistake, which will be your last."

The small one said, "Pete, slow up, I know who that is..."

"Shut up Shorty, I don't care who he is, I'm going to kill him."

His right hand dropped toward his gun, I let him clear leather and start to bring his gun level, then I drew and put one .44 Magnum bullet straight up his arm, starting with his trigger finger and traveling up his hand into his forearm to the elbow. Shorty was standing there with his hands in the air. I said, "Drop your gun belt, Shorty, then take that pigging string and tie it off around his upper arm just above the elbow. Then you had better get him to town to the Doc. After you're done there, you had both better light a shuck for a climate more conducive to your health."

Yin-Li said, "That was mean Buck, it would of been more kind to have killed him. You ruined his right arm, he'll never be able to work as a Cowboy again."

I said, "Nor will he be able to shoot anyone, either. It might have been mean, but that was the point, there are some things worse than death to some people. He is one of those."

Simon said, "I am sorry about that, the rest of his ilk are out checking the cows, they will be back before supper time, then there will be hell to pay. I am ashamed that I have been so weak, but they said they would kill my family, then when they put the run on the rest of my crew, I just didn't have any choice. I had to knuckle under."

"Don't be ashamed Simon, you did the right thing. Your family comes first," said Mee-Ling. "Where is your foreman, Claude?"

"He is in the south pasture, we have some late calves we have to take care of."

"Could he hear the gunshot from here?"

"Yes, in fact I think I hear him coming now."

Claude came at a dead run, his horse lathered. Shorty was just helping Pete on his horse. "Everything alright here?" He said, as his horse slid to a stop.

Simon said, "Sure, thanks to Buck. Glad you're here, we will need your gun, when those others get back." The door on the ranch house opened again and Simon's wife came out with a little girl about eight years old. Simon said, "This is my wife, Hazel and my little girl, Brenda. Hazel, Brenda this is Mee-Ling, Yin-Li and Yang-Su, and this is Buck, he sent Pete and Shorty packing."

Hazel said, "Glad to meet all of you, you are more than welcome, we were giving up hope that anyone would help us."

Mee-Ling and the girls assured her that we were there to help. Yang-Su looked at me and said, "Have you forgotten about that boy that was breaking that bronc in the corral, he is standing there watching us."

"No, I haven't forgotten. Why don't all of you go into the house, I'll go talk to him." They did so. I sauntered over and leaned on the corral post. He pulled out the makins' and offered me some, I declined. Smokin' was a Mex habit, that showed me this hombre was from Texas.

"Well son, it's your move," I said.

"How so? I seen what you did to Pete. My Mother didn't raise any idiots, besides I don't hold with that bunch anyway."

"How come, you rode in here with them, didn't you?"

"Yeah, that's right, they came across me on the trail, offered me a job. I didn't know he didn't own this outfit."

"Who's he?"

"Jack Gamber, he's the 'he-wolf' of these boys."

"Gamber, huh. I think I heard his name mentioned up in Cheyenne. So what's your handle?"

"Troy Ford, from El Paso. I know who you are, your reputation has preceded you, you're Buck Gentry."

"You're half right, I answer to Buck, but it's Phillip Gentry also. There's two of us rattling around in here."

"That's funny, you have a sense of humor anyway. But I have met a lot of people with nick names. And they only make one target."

"Yeah, that's right, Buck is my nick name. I was just joshin' you. You said my reputation has preceded me, how so?"

"You killed that stupid Marshall in Cheyenne. And that gambler, he was a Duke, name of Nottingham. That Nottingham had him quite a rep also. The word was he had ten notch's on his gun's."

"I don't know how many men he killed, but I do know he didn't have any notch's on his guns. Cause I am wearing them." Troy glanced down at my guns, his tan faded a little bit. "So Troy, lets get down to brass tacks. Where do you stand?"

"Well I don't stand with Jack Gamber and that bunch. I am my own man, as such I reckon I would like to stay on here, if that is Ok, with Mr. Peters and his foreman. And I guess with the way things stand, with you also."

"You're a wise boy Troy, as such I predict a long life for you. I think their going to whip up some chow. After you get your chores done, come on up to the house. Would you mind taking care of our horses also? Put them somewhere they won't catch any stray bullets."

"Yeah, sure thing, I'll bring along my hogleg, you might need another hand."

I walked over to the Black and pulled my Henry out of the scabbard, then dug more shells out of my saddle bags. Then went into the house. I was right, the women were preparing supper. Mr. Peters and Claude were in the Den, they went quiet when I walked in. I said, "Don't stop on my account, that is of course unless you have some secret you don't want me to know about?"

"No. No. We don't have any secrets from you Buck. We were just talking about what to do when Gamber and his bunch comes back." Mr. Peter's stammered.

"Well the way I see it, you don't have any choice, fight or die. That's the only choice you have. And I am sure you don't want to die, or at least you don't want your family killed or raped." I looked from one to the other. They were scared, but the question was, were they too scared to fight?

"Cheer up boys, Troy is going to join us. The way I see it, with us three, Troy and my women, that makes seven of us that can shoot. That gives us the edge, there are only seven of them left. The way I see it, we out number them two to one."

"How do you figure that?" Claude said, "The way I see it, that makes us even."

"Well you just have to have faith boys, don't you know right always triumphs over wrong? Besides Mee-Ling and the twins, they are worth their weight in wildcats, shoot they could do for that bunch by their selves. Shoot fire boys, buck up we're on the winning side here."

"But you don't know the whole story. Even after we get rid of those cut throats. They still have robbed us blind. The bank payment is coming up, we just don't have the cattle or the cash. I am afraid we may win the battle and lose the war." Mr. Peters said.

"How much do you owe the bank?"

"Fifty thousand dollars, the whole note was only for one hundred thousand dollars. I had the place half paid for, now I'm afraid it's all gone."

"So, say, I have an idea, would you like a partner? I'll pay off your note for half of this ranch. What do you say?"

"You would do that, even knowing that all of the young stock has been stolen?"

"Sure, I need an investment, what the hell, life is full of risks."

"Ok, then, let's shake, you have half of the P Bar P." Said Mr. Peters, as he held out his hand. I shook it and the deal was done.

Mee-Ling came into the Den, "Supper is ready, Troy is here also. He says we have about an hour before Jack Gamber and his bunch gets back. So we had better eat now."

We followed her into the dinning room, she sure had sway in her get-along. Those riding breeches she had on emphasized her attributes. We sat down to a roast beef dinner with all the fixins'. Even had apple pie for dessert. We were just drinking our coffee, when we heard them ride in.

"Tell you what," I said, "I will help you do the dishes after we finish this task. Mee-Ling you and the twins stay in the house. Don't break the window glass please, raise the windows to shoot through. The four of us will go out. If we call our targets ahead of time, we won't waste any bullets." The four of us filed out of the house. They were just tying the horses to the corral, they turned and seen us.

A big guy with fancy clothes said, "What's going on here, who the hell are you?"

I said, "I take it that you are Jack Gamber. The Jig is up. And we can do this two ways, well, maybe not, we can do this my way, that's the only way."

He went for his gun, so did two others. The other four held their hands high. Jack's gun came level, I shot him through the tag on his tobacco sack. It made a nice target. Troy got one and Mee-Ling got the other one. Mr. Peters and Claude never even cleared leather.

"Mr. Peters if you and Claude would please take their guns then tie them up. Then after I do the dishes, maybe Troy could help us get them to the Sheriff in town. I guess you had better tie the dead ones to their saddles. The undertaker in Denver can take care of them.

Mee-Ling said, "Did you check their saddle bags for money? And their bedrolls in the bunkhouse?"

"No, not yet, that's a good idea, their ill got gains have to be somewhere. I'll go do that." I did, I found twenty thousand dollars, all told. Troy came over and said that he would help us get the rustlers to town, then he was going to drift for California. I asked him if he had any money. He had one hundred dollars. I gave him a thousand that I took from Jack's saddle bag. I took the rest of the money over to Mr. Peters.

I said, "Here is some of the money that they stole. It will help to buy cattle for our ranch. We are going to take them to town, that is after I help with the dishes."

Mrs. Peters was standing there, she said, "Oh no you're not, I will do the dishes, for heaven's sake I thought you were joking. No man does the dishes in my house. You just take those bad people to jail. I just thank God that you were here."

I said, "Ok, if you insist. Mr. Peters, I will see you at the Bank in the morning, say around ten, if that's alright? We can pay off that note and write up a partnership agreement."

"Yes, yes, thank you so much Mr. Gentry, you've given me back my life, thank you so much." I could hardly get away from him, he was still pumping my hand when I tried to swing into the saddle.

We strung out on the trail, Mee-Ling and I were riding drag. She was quiet, so I asked, "What's the matter? What are you thinking about?

"Oh, I don't know, it's Mr. Peters, he's a fine man, but I am afraid he's not much of a manager. He knows cattle, but I am afraid that's not enough."

"Yes, I got the same impression, we'll have to do something about that. Let's not rush things though, something will turn up. Besides I have more important things on my mind."

"What's that?"

"You, I have a hard time concentrating on business with you in that outfit. When do you want to get married?"

"Oh Buck, we've been waiting for each other for eons, I think we can take our time and wait for the opportune time, don't you?"

"What do you mean the opportune time?"

"When the time is right we will know, perhaps after we go see your father. Who knows?"

"Well not me, that's for sure. But yeah, you're right, we can wait. Believe me, you're worth waiting for." She leaned over and gave me a kiss, I almost fell out of the saddle. As I said before, Mee-Ling had some other race in her. It made her all the more beautiful, maybe she thought the same about me. Not beautiful, but handsome maybe?

I rode along thinking about that, "Mee-Ling, you know I am half Indian and half white. I also have eyes, you are not all Chinese, even though your brother is. Would you like to tell me about that?"

She looked at me and said, "No, not now, perhaps

sometime after we're married. It's no big deal, I just don't like to talk about it."

"Ok, I will say no more. Till you get ready, the subject is closed."

We rode the rest of the way billing and cooing at each other. Isn't that what lovers do? We delivered the live and the dead to the Sheriff's Office. They had all kinds of questions. I answered as best I could. Finally, Mee-Ling told them that was enough. If they had anymore questions, that Mr. Peters would be in town in the morning. Then Troy said his goodbyes. Said he was going to get a room in the hotel for the night, then ride west tomorrow. We told him if he ever needed anything to just ask.

We went home. Home? I called Mee-Ling's house home, it felt sort of good. Even with Ma and Pa, I never considered it home, it was just Ma and Pa's place. It was probably on account of the boys. They never let me forget where I came from. Which was good in a way, otherwise I would of probably stayed right there. Then I would of never met Mee-Ling. One thing I have learned, is never look back. What if's, should of's and could of's, don't cut it. All they do is make a person bitter.

Mee-Ling made the four of us a pot of tea. I had never drank tea before, I had tasted it, but never drank it. It was pleasant the four of setting there, discussing the days happening's. Just like a family should. Mee-Ling said the tea would help us sleep, I didn't know the name of it, but she was right. My head no more than hit the pillow and I was out.

I awoke the next morning to find Mee-Ling sleeping with me. I turned on my side and watched her sleeping. It wasn't long before she opened her eyes. She smiled. I said, "Uh, we didn't? I didn't? Did we?"

"No, silly. And we aren't going to, till we're married. I was just lonely. Besides anticipation is part of the joy. Come on, I see by the sun coming in the window that it's past eight o'clock." She jumped up and yanked the cover's off of me. I slept in the nude, but then again, so did she, I noticed, did I ever! She grabbed her nightgown and ran from the room.

It took me a few minutes to dress. I met her in the hall, she was dressed also. But that didn't make any difference. In my mind, I still seen her as she was when she pulled those covers off of me.

Yin-Li and Yang-Su had breakfast ready for us, those girls were efficient in everything they did. We lingered over breakfast, not taking our eyes off of each other. Yin-Li said, "I hope you two don't take too long to get married, you are making us sick!"

Chapter Four

We were almost late in meeting Mr. Peters at the Bank. Hazel and Brenda came with him. There was no problem in paying off the note. All I had to was transfer some money from one account to another one. Herman Ratcliff, as it turned out, was also a lawyer. He helped us work up a partnership agreement. I don't know if that is a good combination, a banker and a lawyer, all in one. But one thing I did know, if he turned out to be a crook, a .44 bullet between the eyes would always remedy the situation.

We bought everyone lunch at the hotel restaurant. This was the first time that Brenda had eaten out. After lunch, Hazel and her daughter, Brenda, went shopping. Mr. Peters, myself and Mee-Ling went to the Hotel Lobby to discuss the running of the ranch.

"Mr. Peters would you be hurt if I hired a business manager to help run the business part of the ranch?"

"No, I wouldn't be hurt. I know cattle, but I'm afraid at times business is not my strong suit."

"Good, Mee-Ling and I are going back east. Till we can find someone, I would like Yin-Li and Yang-Su to handle that part of the ranch. I know most people think they are only little girls, but that couldn't be further from the truth. So from now on any business decision's and financial transactions will have to be run through them. We can inform Mr. Ratcliff of our arrangement."

Mee-Ling said, "Don't worry Mr. Peters, you will be in complete charge of the day to day running of the ranch. There will be nothing underhanded taking place."

"I know that, I trust you both, completely."

"Good, have you found any replacement cattle yet?"

"I got a line on some, about fifty miles west of here. But I don't have time to go check on them. We are still trying to count what we have left. I haven't been able to hire any hands yet, so it is going slow. And one more thing, Claude has given his notice, he wants to go back home, to Tennessee. So hiring some hands is probably our first priority."

"Right, so it looks like we will have to hold off on our trip back east, at least for a little while. What do you say Mee-Ling, would you like to go get some cattle?"

"Yes, that might be fun. We could also look for some hired hands while we're at it."

"Ok, Mr. Peters do you have the money we took off of those crooks?"

"Yes, I have been carrying it with me, here in my money belt."

"Good, give me half of it, keep the rest for operating money. We will get the cattle we need. Perhaps even some help."

Mr. Peters took off his money belt, counted out ten thousand dollars and gave it to Mee-Ling. Ten thousand dollars?

"How much money did they have?" I asked.

"We found more stashed in the bunkhouse. It came to twenty thousand altogether. Some of it must of been from previous jobs." Mr. Peters said.

"Isn't it funny how sometimes you can fall into a pile of manure and come out smelling like a rose?" Mee-Ling said.

"Quite so, do you know how many cattle ten thousand dollars will buy? More than your ranch can comfortably graze." I said.

Mr. Peters looked at me and said, "How do you know how many acres I have? And how do you know so much about cattle?"

"Before I even came out to your ranch the other day, I went by the land office. I know how many deeded acres you have and how many you are grazing free. Since we do not know what the future holds, we should only have the cattle that our deeded grass will maintain without over grazing."

"Your knowledge astounds me for a man as young as you are. Why?"

"Why what? Why I have such knowledge or why you are astounded?"

"Your knowledge?"

"I was raised on a cattle ranch. Also I read a lot, everything I can get my hands on. And I am cursed with common sense, which at times can be quite boring."

Mee-Ling looked at me with those eyes that made me melt and said, "You boring? No, I think not. Of course it just could be me, others might find you boring."

"I don't find you boring, but I guess not for the same reason Mee-Ling does." Mr. Peters said. "But enough said, I had better be gathering up my wife and daughter or they will bankrupt us."

"Uh, before you go, where is the cattle that you had a line on, located?"

"You go west from here, it's a little northeast of

Loveland Pass. It's close to a little town that's just getting settled, called Central City. It's a new outfit, they just brought in a bunch of cattle from Texas and they don't have enough graze to get them through the winter. Should be able to make a good buy. The guys name is Mark Roberts."

Peters left, Mee-Ling and I spent the rest of the afternoon gathering supplies for our trip. If we did get the cattle, it would take a few days to drive them to the ranch. Therefore we would need enough food. Not only for us, but if we hired any hands. We dropped everything off at the stables. Festus said he would have Jim and the Black saddled, as well as Jill and Lil packed with our supplies.

Yin-Li and Yang-Su made us supper. They wanted to go also. But we told them they were needed here. Not only for the Dress Shop but also to keep a check on the ranch. So no one would try to move in on Mr. Peters, since he would be alone there after Claude left. There was some law in Denver, but it only reached as far as the city limits.

Mee-Ling was eating slowly, I could tell she was thinking about something. She said, "I think we should have the girls go and stay at the ranch. I can have Mrs. Tuttle look after the dress shop. I just have a feeling, something is nagging at me."

"One thing that I never doubt, is a women's intuition. Ma's never failed her. Where does Mrs. Tuttle live?"

"Right next door, I will go over after supper and talk to her."

"Good, I will help the girls with the dishes. My hands need washed anyway."

"Buck, you will wash your hands before you do the dishes, didn't you wash before supper?"

"Yes I did. But doing dishes gets that ground in dirt out

better than anything else I know."

"I see the logic of your reasoning, but it's just the idea, don't tell anyone else that you wash your hands in the dish water."

The morning dawned clear and bright with a wisp of clouds over the mountains. Mee-Ling brought me a cup of coffee in bed. She was dressed for riding, same outfit, different color.

"How many of those outfit's you have anyway?"

"Oh, this old thing, I have four of them altogether. I have some new buckskins for you. Come on get up and try them on."

"Have you forgotten that I sleep in the nude?"

"No I haven't. Why do you think I want you to try them on now?"

I threw the covers back and stood up. She stepped back and smiled. Her dark eyes twinkling. I stood there feeling stupid. She said, "There, that's what I was waiting for, you can get dressed now."

"What makes you think that I can get those breeches on over that?

"I'll leave, it'll go down." She did so and it did.

I think she was delaying getting married to just torment me. I don't think there is a man in the world who has ever figured women out. The buckskins fit. How she knew they would I don't know.

The girls walked to the stables with us. Since we would be taking Jill and Lil with us, Festus saddled two other horses for the girls.

I said, "Festus do me a favor, will you?" Keep an eye on things. Yin-Li and Yang-Su are going out to the P Bar P. They can pretty well take care of themselves. But it always helps to have a leg up."

"Sure Buck. I don't know what good I can do if they are out there and I am in here?"

"I tell you what Festus, if a Magpie comes by and starts yakking at you, get yourself a posse and hurry out there."

"Magpie huh?"

"Yeah, this particular one has taken a shine to the girls. Fact is, there he sits, over yonder in that Cottonwood tree. Ever since we went out there the other day, he's been hanging around. You know, I can't think of a better totem for a woman. I've heard some women that sound just like a Magpie."

Mee-Ling kicked me in the shins. I hopped around making a big deal out of it, really it didn't hurt. And she knew it didn't. She came over and grabbed me by the ears and kissed me. Now that really didn't hurt!

We said our goodbye's. We went west, the girls went east. Festus didn't go anywhere, but back to work. The morning was a little crisp. Mee-Ling had a canvas slicker on. Under it I could see she had strapped a gun on. And in her scabbard was a rifle, it had some kind of a fancy sight on it. I said, "What kind of a sight is on your rifle?"

"Chin-Lee made it for me, it adjusts for yardage and wind."

"Can you hit anything with it?"

She looked at me with a steady level gaze, "What do you think?" She said.

What did I think? "I think at times, I speak without thinking, that's what I think. Because I know you can hit anything that you aim at, I'm sorry I said that."

I returned her gaze. The smile started in her eyes and ended with her beautiful mouth. She said, "That was the proper answer and aimed just right, you are a good shot yourself." She wasn't talking about with a gun either.

The morning warmed up, she took her slicker off. Mine was tied on the back of my saddle. She turned sideways and tied hers on the back of her saddle. In doing so, her breasts strained against their restraints. Like two wild fillies wanting to get out and kick up their heels. All I knew was that we had better get married pretty soon, she was driving me crazy.

We were about twelve or thirteen miles out when we stopped for lunch. There was a little stream running under some birch trees. I loosed the cinches on the horses, let them loose to graze. They wouldn't wander off. Mee-Ling dug some sandwiches out that she had made. I filled our canteens at the creek. We sat on a fallen log beside the stream. Not saying anything, enjoying the warm breeze and the singing of the birds. A monarch butterfly lit on the toe of Mee-Ling's boot, then flew up and sat on her outstretched finger.

Have you ever had a perfect moment? I think this was one. Everything seemed to slow down. The Butterfly's wings were in slow motion. A bumble bee flew slowly by my nose. Its buzz a song in my head. The black bottle fly's buzz was even in tune. The slight breeze was ruffling Mee-Ling's bangs over the light freckles on her forehead. Her hat was tilted back on her head. Her delighted laugh tinkled through the air to join the brook's babbling.

The moment was broken by the raucous scolding of a big black crow. I looked up and said, "What the hell do you want?" He stopped his noise and looked into my eyes, we sat that way for a moment. "Oh, I see." I said. "Come Mee-Ling, he wants to show us something."

We tightened the cinch's on the Black and Jim, then on Jill and Lil our pack horses. We followed the crow. He was heading west, at least he wasn't leading us out of our way. In the distance we could see a covered wagon, what was called a Prairie Schooner. As we got closer we could see some children standing by the wagon, they were black. I had never seen any black people before, I had heard about them. As we rode up a man came out of the wagon. He was about six foot two. A woman followed him out, they were both black. The man had a Army issue Springfield Rifle in his hand.

I put on my Indian face, I held up my hand and said, "Howdy, you folks lost?" I winked at the children, a boy in his teens and a girl a year or so behind him.

The man said, "Could be, could not be. Just depends."

I said, "My name is Buck Gentry, this here is my woman, Mee-Ling. I do suppose that you all have a name, right?"

He was eyeing our outfit, specially our guns. I detected a note of caution in his eyes. He said, "My name is Clifford, Hank Clifford. This is my wife, Jezerel, my boy, Henry and my daughter, Cheche, my small one."

"To get back to my first question, what are you folks doing out here in the middle of nowhere?"

"Just trying to escape."

"Escape what?"

"The past. Were looking to start new. To forget. Do you think that's possible?"

"I reckon to some extent. It's partly up to you to make it happen. I suppose there are some people will try to give you a hard time. Not us though."

He sat his rifle butt on the ground. He was dressed in remnant's of a Union Army Uniform. He said, "That's good to know. We do seem to be in a tangle. One of the horses died, we only have three left to pull this wagon, don't know where I can get another one, do you?"

"Not right off the top of my head. But I am sure we can find one. Would you be open to a job offer?"

"What kind of a job?"

"Well do you know anything about cattle?"

"Yeah, sure, we're from Texas, before the war I worked on a cattle ranch. During the war I went north and fought with the Union. When I got home, I wasn't welcome, we have been drifting since then."

"I tell you what Hank, we are going after a herd of cattle, you stay put here and watch over your family. We will bring back a horse for your wagon. Perhaps a few more besides. Then you can come back to the P Bar P with us, we need someone with a little cattle savvy. How are your supplies holding out?"

"We's getting down there, that's part of our tangle."

I looked around at Mee-Ling, she said, "I have an idea, does Henry have the same savvy as you? He does? Good. Our pack horses are loaded with food. We could put that food in your wagon. And Henry could go with us, we need hands to help with the herd. He could ride Jill, you could use Lil to help pull the wagon. We could use your wagon as the chuck wagon. If everything goes as planned we should be back this way in four days. We will take some food with us in our saddle bags. How does that sound?"

He said, "That sounds mighty nice. We would be beholden to you."

So far his wife and children hadn't said one word. Jezerel said, "Why would you help us? White people usually won't even talk to us, but I see that you both aren't all white. You Buck, look part white, Mee-Ling, I don't know what you are?"

"I am Chinese, mostly. Don't worry Jezerel, we're not

66

prejudice. We have no ulterior motive."

"Huh? I don't understand what you just said."

Mee-Ling smiled and said, "I meant that we will not hurt you, we are friends."

Hank said, "Are you sure, you don't want me to ride with you?"

I said, "No, Hank, your place is here with your wife and daughter, you never know who will come by. There are a lot of scalawags around. Henry will be fine, we'll watch over him." Henry was staring at me, he looked a little spooked. Henry was shorter than his father. A little gangly, like any teenager. He took the initiative and went over and started taking the food and pack saddles off of Jill and Lil. Jill turned her head to look at him and then snatched his handkerchief out of his pocket.

Henry laughed and rubbed her ears. Then said, "What do you say old girl, are we going to be friends?" Jill whinnied. Henry glanced at me and I seen confusion in his eyes. We would have to see what that was all about.

They had a couple of saddles in the wagon. Henry threw an old Kak on Jill and cinched it up. Then tied an oil slicker on over his bedroll. He affixed a worn scabbard under the right stirrup then stuck an aged single shot Sharps in it. He rummaged around in the wagon and came out with a braided rawhide lariat about fifty feet long. I had heard of those. Mexican vaqueros used them, usually they were about eighty to a hundred feet long. Had to be quite an artist to drop a loop on a steer with a lariat that long. Henry grabbed his hat, an old Union Calvary hat, with a gold rope hat band and screwed it down on his head. Then swung up in the saddle.

I shook hands with Hank and said, "I know you must be a pretty good hand to get your family this far, but I also know that a lot confederates have been moving into this country.

Some have changed their outlook and some haven't. Anyway I suppose I don't have to tell you that, but, hell, keep an eye out will you?"

"I always have, Buck. But thanks for your concern, I appreciate it. Just take care of my boy."

"We will, don't worry, see you in four days." Mee-Ling said.

We sat out at a mile eating trot. All the time checking the grass along the way. Also for water for the cattle. That is if we we're able to buy some. It didn't take long for the sun to get about one thumb above the horizon. One thumb meant we had about twenty minutes before it sat. One finger would of been about fifteen minutes. So we stopped at the next likely place to camp.

Henry immediately started to gather wood for the fire. There was a little spring bubbling up beside the roots of a Red-Osier Dogwood tree. Its flowers were white, growing in clusters. I picked some and gave them to Mee-Ling. She thanked me with a kiss. Then put them in a little pocket of water beside the spring. I sort of got the impression that I shouldn't have picked them. Anyway, I got a kiss out of them. Mee-Ling produced a frying pan from her saddle bags. Put Pemmican and water in it and sat it on some rocks in the fire. Wasn't long before we had Pemmican stew. She had some kind of powdered salt she put in, it was good.

After we ate, we sat around the fire, jawing. Henry produced a harmonica and played a few tunes. Mee-Ling had a nice clear voice. It was sort of funny watching her sing Jimmy Crack Corn. But she did a good job on Dixie. Me? I couldn't sing. They almost tarred and feathered me one time when at a Sunday meeting I tried singing. We rolled out our bedrolls near the fire, we slept like logs, but was up at dawn and on our way.

I got to thinking about the three of us as we rode, a black, a yellow and a red, with tinges of white around the edges. Why the white? Because we were in a white man's world. You remember I told you I had heard about Black people before. Well where I heard about them was from the Shoshone Indians, they called them Black, White people. Because they may have been a different color, but they acted just like white people. Of course my white around the edges was because I was half white. Mee-Ling was half something too. I remember a saying Pa had; when one of the boys didn't do a good job on something, "You did that half-assed." Well a sack half full is better than a sack half empty. The musings of the mind at times do not make sense.

We stopped only long enough at noon to water the horses and eat a little dried pemmican. We were making good time. We rode into Central City with four fingers of daylight left. They had a boarding house, two saloons, general store and other various establishments. All set along one main street with private houses along side streets. We secured two rooms at the boarding house. One for Henry and one for us. Why did Mee-Ling room with me? Because she just liked to tease me. Anyway it was teaching me self-control. Or maybe it was for her benefit.

The woman that ran the boarding house was on the plump side as was most of the women that lived in towns. Most of the homestead women were wore down from work, no fat there. She was a little uncomfortable about Henry. But after looking into my eyes, she got right peaceable. We stabled our horses in the towns only barn. The hostler was a friendly fellow, about sixty years old, with a hitch in his get-along. He looked like he was waiting for a Chinook that never came. He had a long white beard and moustache. He was wearing greasy buckskins. And would you believe it? A coonskin cap. Now what do you reckon his past held?

He looked at me and said, "Sioux?"

"I reckon your eyes haven't failed you yet, old timer. Do you have any objections?"

"No Son, I don't, my wife was a Sioux. She died in the winter of sixty nine. Seeing you brings back nothing but good memories. How long will you be staying?"

"Well, Mr.? I didn't catch your name?"

"It's Pike, just Pike."

"My name is Buck, that is the Sioux side of me. The white side is Phillip Gentry. But Phillip has been pretty quiet lately, he must be off in la-la land."

"So they're two of you in that new set of buckskins?"

"Yep, but we work well together."

"What was your mother's name, Son?"

"She who see's the light."

"Well I'll be dad-gummed, she was my wife's cousin. That sort of make's you a relative."

"In my book too, Pike. Say how about after we get settled in, you'll have supper with us, and a drink maybe?"

He said he would. That was when we went to get our rooms. Then we went back to the stables. Pike was waiting for us. He said that the Silver Slipper Saloon had good food. So we adjourned to there.

When we walked in, all conversation stopped and all heads turned. The hair on the back of my neck stood up. Shit, I knew right then that we wouldn't get out of here without trouble. Hostile stares were directed at Henry and me. But they leered at Mee-Ling. We went over to a corner table and sat down.

A big tough looking puncher at the bar started toward

us, with his spurs ringing he sauntered over. He stood there with his thumbs hooked in his gun belt and said, "They don't serve Nigger's and Indians in-," He never got to finish his sentence. I reached up and grabbed him by his shirt front and slammed his head into the table. The table split right in two.

I said, "Looks like we will need another table."

Henry reached down and plucked the unconscious puncher's guns from his holsters. There was another empty table right beside us, we moved over. The bartender came over and asked what would we have.

Pike ordered steak, beans and potatoes for all of us, with beer all around. We were almost finished eating before the puncher woke up. He sat up and looked around, stood up and staggered off. Henry kept his guns.

Pike sat back in his chair and ordered us another beer, around. Then said, "Well Buck, what are the bunch of you doing here?"

"We're here to buy cattle. Is there a fellow around called Mark Roberts? He is supposed to have some Texas Longhorns for sale."

"Yeah, his outfit is southwest of here. He has a pretty tough crew. He probably does have some stock for sale, he's overstocked. I could go with you, that is if you're looking for help. This town is no place for an old mountain man."

"Sure we would be more than happy to have you. In fact we can offer you a steady job at the P Bar P. You won't have any trouble with your old boss, will you?"

"No, not any, I was pretty much doing it for nothing anyway. Just killing time till I died."

"Ain't we all?" I said.

Mee-Ling looked at me and said, "Well not me, I am going to live till I die."

"Now Mee-Ling, you know what I meant. I am not going to role over and die, either. That is unless you leave me."

She looked at me with lowered eyes and pressed up against me, kissing me, she said, "That is the same with me. Without you, there would be no use in living."

I went over to the bar and asked, "What do I owe you?"

"Ten bucks should cover it, unless of course you want to pay for the table?"

I started twirling an empty shot glass, then looked up at him, "Do you think I should pay for that table?"

He was turning red and sweat was dripping from his face, "No, no of course not, that was not your fault, Sir."

I reached into my pocket and pulled a double eagle out and tossed it to him. "We will be in for breakfast in the morning, that should cover this meal and breakfast."

He nodded and said, "Yes Sir, we open at six."

We went outside. Pike took his leave, saying he would see us for breakfast. We ambled over to the boarding house. Henry went to his room. Mee-Ling and I undressed and took a spit bath. The water in the wash basin was dirty when we got through, all of the trail dust we had on us. We crawled into bed and was instantly asleep.

We woke to the song of birds on the window sill. The sun was peeking at us through the fly specked window glass. Mee-Ling sat up, her hair falling down over her shoulders, tickling her nipples, they stood bravely out. I couldn't stop staring. I got out of bed and pulled the curtains closed. I didn't want anyone but me seeing her. Turning, I said, "Mee-Ling, just when are we going to get married?"

She said, "When that stops standing straight out."

"Well I guess that will be never, cause as long as I live, it will be like that when you're naked."

"And that's just like it had better be, when I'm naked you had better be hard. But, yes, it won't be long now, we will get married before we go back east. What does Phillip have to say."

"You know, I don't hear from him very much."

"Good, that's what I have been waiting for. So when we get back, we will get married."

We met Henry downstairs, then met Pike for breakfast. Everybody that was there, was extra nice to us. We walked over to the stables, Pike had our horses saddled. All the four of us had to do was tighten our cinches. The day was pleasant with a slight southwest wind blowing. The mountains were looming closer. Pike said the ranch we were going to was close. It was.

We had started to run into Long Horns. The grass was short. And it shouldn't have been this early in the year. The ranch house was half sod and half log. The barn was big, with holding corrals ranged about it. The corrals held about forty head of horses. They heard us riding up.

It was mid-morning. A man came out of the house, he had twin guns tied low. He said, "Howdy, what can I do for you?"

"Are you Mark Roberts?" I asked.

"Yep, I sure am."

"We heard you might have some cattle for sale?"

"Yeah, I reckon I do. How many head are you looking for?"

"How many are you willing to part with?" I asked.

He spit a stream of tobacco at a grasshopper. He missed. Shuffled his feet and said, "Oh, maybe thousand to fifteen hundred head."

"Mind if we have a look at them?"

"Let me catch up a horse and I'll show you around." He

was giving us a once over. "You sure are a colorful bunch, red, black, yellow and white."

I looked at him and said, "Is that a problem?"

He missed a step at my tone, turning he said, "No, heck no. My Mom didn't raise any fools, and if she did, they would be dead by now."

"It's a wise man who listen's to his parent's Mark. It's also a wise man who listens to his inner self. Perhaps, if we do buy some of your stock, you would be able to let us hire some of your hands to help drive them?"

"Chance and circumstances have been kind to you, four of my hands, vaqueros, wish to return to Mexico. I suppose they would be able to help you for a small numeration of money."

"I can tell by your vocabulary that you are an educated man, Mr. Roberts. Did you go to the University of Alforja?"

"Very clever Buck. Yes, I did go to Alforja, since Alforja in Spanish means saddlebags. I was self taught from the books in my saddlebags. As I bet you were too? I noticed that you pronounced it right also, changing the 'J' to 'H'."

"Yes, but I had a good tutor, Ma used to make me study every night. I still read every chance I get. In fact, there are some books in my Alforja's right now. But daylight is a wastin', let's see those cows."

We ended up buying a thousand head with calves at side. It would take us longer driving a herd with calves'. But time is only relative to the need. Since there would be eight of us pushing this herd. I couldn't see much of a problem, that is if we stopped often and let them mother-up. We also bought a small remuda, eight head of small Texas horses. I was used to the horses of the north country, who were mostly sixteen hands tall. These Texas broncs stood between thirteen to fourteen.

We spent the night and got an early start. Mark Roberts

now stood a chance of getting the cattle he had left through the winter, since his range wouldn't be over grazed. The four vaqueros; Arturo, Berto, Chico and Diego were more than willing to help us. I decided to pay them double their usual wage.

We only made eight miles that day. It's always that way the first day of a drive, till you get all the kinks shook out. I rode drag. Most people hate riding drag, cause of the dust. But I preferred it. That way when the tail end of the herd got heavy with calves, I could call a halt and let them mother-up.

The next day while riding drag, Phillip decided to surface. "Buck, are you sure you know what you're doing?"

"What's to know about riding drag?"

"I mean about our life? Are we ready to get married?"

I glanced over at Mee-Ling riding flank to my right, she was cutting back a herd quitter. That little Texas bronc she was riding knew what it was doing. I envied the horse. "Phillip, you just put your fears at rest, we know exactly what we are doing. I will tell you something else, Phillip, Mee-Ling is a little worried about you. Isn't it about time you stopped being so childish and joined me?"

"I guess so, Buck, but I enjoyed my time with Ma so much, it's just hard to realize she's gone and so is that part of our life. I know, I know most people have a hard time growing up. But we've had to do it so fast, look at us we are only thirteen years in actual age, but at the same time we're as old as these trees we're passing through."

I looked around at the Ponderosa Pines and thought about the marvels of creation. "Yeah, those trees are a lot older than us, Phillip." He didn't answer. "Phillip are you there?" He still didn't answer. Phillip had decided to join me in the common purpose. What purpose? Life and any variable there of.

We stopped for lunch and let the herd mother-up. Mee-Ling came up and dismounted. She came over and gave my dusty lips a kiss, looking into my eyes, she said, "Well I see Phillip has decided to join us, I am glad. As soon as we get back we'll get married."

Diego had rode ahead and already had lunch prepared, enchiladas and frijoles. How he did it, I don't know. After lunch we pushed on. Had an hour of daylight left, when we found water and grass enough for the night. We set up a schedule for two of us to be with the herd all night. I pulled the hoot owl shift; mid-night till four. Didn't need much sleep anyway. Arturo was with me. The herd was quiet and bedded down.

The moon was full. If there would of been snow on the ground, it would be like daylight. I was sitting with one leg around the horn. I was on one of the Texas horses. I heard a rustle in the grass, a big black wolf came up and sat on his haunch's beside us. The mustang I was on didn't even flinch. The wolf looked at me, then looked at the herd. I asked him, "What you doing here Pardner, you hungry?"

He shook his head no. We sat there a little while longer, then he got up and walked a few steps toward the timber, he stopped and looked over his shoulder at me and made come-on motion with his head. "Ok, feller, you lead I'll follow." He moved at a walk, his attitude let me know that I was to be quiet also. We went about a mile southwest of the herd. I seen the glow of a campfire through the trees. Wolf stopped, I dismounted and ground tied my horse. I left my rifle in the scabbard. I had my guns and my bowie knife.

It was about two A.M. by the stars. Wolf crouched on his belly and crawled closer, I did the same. There were four men in the camp, three in their bedrolls and one man just sitting a coffee pot on the fire. Then he got out a frying pan and put some sow belly and potatoes in it. Then he went over and kicked each man awake, saying, "Come on, get up, we want to catch them just before the shift change." They got up. I was sure I had seen them before, then it came to me. They were part of that outlaw crowd that rustled the P Bar P stock. They were supposed to be in Jail in Denver. How in hell did they get out!

They gathered around the fire, pouring themselves some coffee. One big fellow said, "I get that Yellow Girl. I been dreaming about her ever since I seen her when we got took. I'm going to use her till she's no good anymore, then I'm going to kill her."

"Now Swede, you ain't the only one that wants a crack at her, you're going to share."

"Ah, Jake, alright but I get her first."

I backed away about twenty yards, then crawled over to where their horses were tied on a picket line. They just looked at me, meeting my gaze, they just stood still. I cut them loose. I tied their reins to the saddle horns. Told them to follow my trail back to the herd. I'll be damned but I think they understood. They had stood there saddled all night. I don't think they liked them fellers any.

I stayed there by the cut picket line, waiting. It wasn't too long before I could hear one of them coming. He was right in front of me before he noticed the horses were gone. I clamped one hand over his mouth and slipped my blade between his ribs to his heart. I pulled him back in the brush. I waited for the next one. Because when he didn't return with the horses, another would come to see what the hold up was. This one, I was true to my Sioux nature and cut his throat. I just left him lying there. The Wolf was just watching me, he didn't make a yip. I knew it wouldn't work again, next time both of them would come. So I slipped back to the camp. They were just packing up.

I picked up a rock as big as my fist, I set myself and let fly. It caught one of them right on the forehead, he dropped like a rock, no pun intended. I stepped into the fire light, the only one left was that big fellow who wanted my wife. When he seen me, he went for his gun. I shot first, I blew his gun right out of his holster. He never even got his hand on it.

I put my gun back in it's holster. I pulled out my knife. I motioned for him to palm his knife. He smiled like, now I was dead. He made a rush for me, I side stepped and flicked a cut along his side. He whirled and made another lunge, I put a cut along his other side. He was really mad now. Over confidence and rage was his downfall. He came at me once more, his last. As he passed me I made a swipe at his groin, he stood there holding it. I could either let him bleed to death or put him out of his misery. I slit his throat. Never let it be said I wasn't merciful.

When I got back to the herd, everyone was up. They had heard the shot, besides the four horses had trailed in. Mee-Ling came up, noticing the spots of blood on me she said, "Go wash up and get a little sleep, you can fill us in later."

Diego had made tortillas and frijoles for breakfast. We were sitting around eating, all except Chico. I didn't miss him till he rode in. "Where has he been?" I asked.

Mee-Ling said, "I sent him to bury them, we just couldn't leave them for the birds."

"How did you know where they were?"

"I heard the shot, didn't I? I have a great sense of location, I told Chico where they would be. We are about a day away from meeting up with Henry's parents. I thought we would push the herd hard till about three this afternoon. Then bed them down. Henry can go get them and they can spend the night with us. That is if that is alright with you?"

"Sure, I guess so. Aren't you interested in why I killed them?

"I thought you would get around to telling me sooner or later."

Pike was lounging on one elbow, sipping a cup of coffee. He looked up and said, "Well Old Son, I reckon they weren't the first, were they?"

"No Pike, they weren't. But I hope they are the last."

"You know Son, what I have found out, is, when lemmings want to jump off a cliff, it don't matter if someone push's them or not, they're still dead."

I don't know if that made any sense or not, but I am sure there was some wisdom in it somewhere. What I was surprised about was that he knew what lemmings were. But why should I be surprised, Pike was a reader, he should know what Lemmings are.

We got the herd started, they were starting to get trail wise. Mee-Ling dropped in beside me on drag. I told her all about the Wolf coming to get me and about what they were going to do. She wasn't surprised when I told her who they were. She said, "I never liked that Judge Pugh, I thought he was on the take. I take it personal now. Since they were going to kill me. I will have to do something about him." Then she rode off to ride flank. I would not want to be that Judge.

We bypassed Central City, stopping at noon to let them mother up. We ate some cold frijoles. Then we pushed on, stopping a little later than we planned. It was close to four. Diego fixed us some supper, I am not going to tell you what it was, I am sure you can guess. After we ate, Henry saddled a fresh horse and left to find his parents.

We were camped at a stream fed pond, with belly deep grass around it. I was dirty and so was Mee-Ling. We grabbed some soap and towels and walked upstream to find a secluded spot to take a bath. We came across another pond. There was no mud around the edges, grass grew right up to the water.

Mee-Ling started disrobing. I just stood and watched her. She had everything off but her drawers, she looked at me and said. "Come on now Buck, get those skins off, there's not that much daylight left and I want to see what I'm going to get."

"Huh, what do you mean? We're going to."

"No silly, I like to look at what I am going to get on our wedding day. Come on, take it off." Then she dropped her drawers and jumped in. She floated around on her back, and she could float real good. I followed in short order. Even shorter when the cold water hit it. But she seemed to like looking anyway.

We got back before dark. Of course we slept in the same bedroll. Neither one of us had to ride herd this night. It felt good to be clean and also to be able to sleep all night. We draped ourselves around each other. When we woke the next morning, Wolf was sleeping beside us.

I looked at him and said, "Are you going with us or did you just stop by for breakfast?" He told me that he just stopped to say goodbye, he was moving north. There were too many people in this country anymore, but he would eat with us. I told him I knew how he felt, but it was only going to get worse. He said he knew that. Said he was going to the Yellowstone, the land of steam. Told him he was wise, I had been there, he would like it.

It was mid-morning before we hooked up with the Clifford wagon. Jezerel was driving. Mee-Ling and I rode over to the wagon, leading one of the rustler's horses that was already saddled, for Hank. Henry rode off to the herd. I said, "Well Hank, did you have any problems while we were gone?'

"Nope, nary a one. Is that horse for me?"

"Yep, you'll have to adjust the stirrup's tho. You'll notice there is already a rifle in the scabbard. Courtesy of the last owner."

"I notice there is no blood on the saddle"

"Nope they never had a chance to get in the saddle. There are three more just like it. Do you think Cheche would like to ride?"

Cheche said, "Can I Dad?"

"I reckon you're capable, so the question is, may I. And the answer is yes, you may."

"She can hop up behind you, the other three are in the remuda, over there."

After Jezerel swung the wagon on the upside of the herd to stay out of the dust and Cheche got mounted. Hank and I rode to the point. Mee-Ling had Cheche ride with her. I said, "Hank, I have a proposition for you. I own half of the P Bar P, and as such, I am in need of an agent to look after my interest's. He would live and work on the ranch. Mr. Peters is the other owner. He is a good cattleman, but I don't think he is a good manager. Would you like the job? Your pay would include a percentage of the business."

Hank looked at me and I could see the surprise in his eyes. "You don't know me that well, why would you want me?"

"Well, I know your son and you raised him. Besides with your Calvary background, I think you can handle it."

"Ok, then, I accept."

"Good. The future of the cattle business is good right now. It will last this way for the next twenty years. But things will change. Free range will be a thing of the past. Too many people moving west. Right now, not many of the ranch's are putting up hay. That will be one of your tasks. Have you ever heard of irrigation? Good. That will be another task. Dam streams and run ditches."

"Sounds like you have some progressive ideas, how did you come by them?"

"I seen it. In my vision quest. You see, the only thing that remains constant, is change."

"I understand, if you want to stay ahead, you have to think ahead."

"I see that you do understand, Hank. We will need hands. I am going to try to talk the four vaqueros, Arturo, Berto, Chico and Diego to stay on. They did say they wanted to return to their families. But perhaps they can get their families to move up here. Oh yes, you will have to oversee the building of yourself a new house and if their families do move, they will need proper housing."

"One thing more, this Mr. Peters, is he prejudice?"

"I certainly don't think so, Hank. He wasn't, of myself and Mee-Ling. And when he sees what an asset you are to the ranch, he won't be."

"What about that old mountain man, with the white beard, will he be staying on?"

"His name is Pike, he was married to my Mother's cousin. No, he will be going with us. Even tho he doesn't know it yet. I consider him my Grandfather, although he doesn't know that either."

"Alright then, I will scout ahead for a nooning spot."

The rest of the drive went without event. We skirted around Denver and drove straight to the ranch. Yin-Li and Yang-Su saw us coming. The cloud of dust would of been hard to miss.

They asked, "How did it go?"

Mee-Ling answered, "Good, we did what we set out to do. How are things here?"

"We finally got the books straightened out. They were a mess, but they will probably go back to being a mess after we leave."

"No, I've hired a ranch manager, Hank Clifford, that's him over there, with his family. In fact, I want you both to show him the books and familiarize him with the operation. The vaqueros settled the cattle along the creek, below the ranch. It turns out I didn't have to talk to them about staying, Hank did. They were going to send for their families.

Mr. Peters and his family was standing in the ranch yard. There was no problem. Hazel Peters invited the Clifford family to stay with them till the new house was built. Brenda and Cheche were already yakking as only girls can. Hazel and Jezerel were already planning supper. Hank and Mr. Peters were talking to the vaqueros and showing them to the bunkhouse. We had the girls gather their belongings. And we headed for town. I don't think they even knew we left. I had talked with Pike, he said, sure, he'd like to go back east. All five of us rode back to Denver. Pike and I stopped at the Barber Shop. They had bathing facilities. After we took a bath. We got haircuts, I got a shave, Pike got his beard trimmed. By the time we got back to the house Mee-Ling and the girls had done their ablution's. I did change clothes. Pike didn't have any new one's. We would have to take care of that on the morrow. Anyway, we headed for the Denver House to eat.

On the way we dropped our horse's off at Festus's stables. It was Saturday Night. The restaurant was fairly full, but when they saw us, we had no trouble getting a table. I let

Mee-Ling do the ordering. She ordered, we sat back sipping our wine, looking around. Two tables over sat Judge Pugh. I didn't know who he was till Mee-Ling leaned over and told me. There was two ladies of the night sitting with him, sounded like they were deep in their cups, all three of them.

"Do you want me to kill him now?" I asked.

"Goodness No. He has a wife and family. Don't you think it is better to turn a sinner around instead of killing him?"

"Well, Yeah! But."

"No buts. You see how much pleasure he is getting out of his way of life? Wouldn't it be better to take that pleasure away from him? You see if you want to play, you have to have money. We will simply take his money, most of it anyway. Leave him enough to support his family, but not to play in the pig pen."

"How are you going to do that?"

"Oh, did I forget to tell you? I own controlling interest in the bank, maybe I will transfer his bank account into his wife's name. But first I will talk to her. I am sure she will leave him enough money to buy a cigar. Maybe not. We will see what kind of man he really is. Might be he will turn around, maybe he will just kill himself. That is up to him."

Pike downed his drink and said, "Whew, and people say the female is the weaker sex."

"Oh but Grandfather, we really are. That is till some man tries to kill us." Mee-Ling said.

I said, "What else have you forgotten to tell me?" It was the first time I had seen Mee-Ling flustered.

"Oh My, I am sorry Buck, but it truly was an oversight. I own fifty one percent, but I roll all of my profits over, I have never drawn any of my Dividends. Therefore it just slipped my mind."

84

"How long have you owned those shares?"

"About five or six years, I really don't know how much is in my account."

"Don't worry, I am not mad that you didn't tell me, how could I be, really it's none of my business, we're not married yet."

"Why don't we correct that situation, say next Wednesday, are you willing?"

"Of course, how many times have I asked you?"

"I have said yes, every time and I meant it."

Pike said, "Ok, I think we have that Bronc rode, it's time to stop spurring. You are both going to get married Wednesday, can I give the bride away?"

"Of course you can Pike, but I think we will just have a civil ceremony, but the three of you are invited. But who can marry us? Certainly not that Judge Pugh."

Yin-Li said, "I have an idea, why don't we go back to Cheyenne?"

Chapter Five

"You know that's not a bad idea, the Union Pacific Railroad goes right through there. And your brother would like to be present when we get married. We would have to postpone the wedding for a few days, but that's Ok, isn't it?"

"You mean you would be able to wait?" Mee-Ling said, while holding my hand.

"Yes, we have some loose ends to tie up here anyway, one of them is setting two tables over."

"Ah, yes. He will be taken care of, if nothing else the Tong can do it. But I also have financial affairs to take care of, you can go with me to the bank, Phillip." Mee-Ling said.

"Why did you call me Phillip?"

"Because that is your name Phillip, Buck is only your nickname. A grown man goes by his real name, not a nickname. Except maybe in the heat of passion."

Pike was just taking a drink of water when she said the last, he started to choke and sputter. Yin-Li and Yang-Su giggled and their eyes twinkled.

"What? What did I say wrong?" Mee-Ling asked looking at the three of them.

Yang-Su said, "It was not wrong, just surprising, Aunt Mee-Ling."

"You are surprised that I am a human female and have feelings?"

Yin-Li said, "Well yes, you have always been so perfect and straight laced and to think of you in the heat of passion, boggles our minds."

I said, "As it does mine, but for a different reason."

Pike stood up and said, "If you libertines will excuse me, I am going to the bar and get a shot of whisky."

"Really, all of you had better grow up or I will really start saying what I think."

I said, "That's all right sweetheart, we love you and you can tell me what you think any old time." She took my hands in hers and smiled her special smile. Then the food came. I said, "I hand better go get Pike, so we can all eat before the food gets cold." I got up and went to the bar. Pike was drinking his shot. Now that he was trimmed and brushed he looked distinguished. "Come on Pike, our food just came, we don't want it to get cold." He sat his glass on the bar. We turned to leave, in doing so his sleeve spilled the drink of the man standing next to him.

The man said, "Watch out what you're doing, you doddering old fool."

Pike turned back around and said, "That was my fault, I am sorry, let me buy you another drink."

"Why? So you can spill that one too? You old sack of shit."

I didn't even see Pike's arm move, but the man was laying on the floor, out cold. Pike straightened his tie and said, "Come Phillip, I am hungry." We walked back to our table, the subject of all eyes.

As I was eating, I was thinking. Yeah, I could do two things at once. Anyway, It was strange, the behavior of that man. A spilled drink was nothing new in a bar, happens all the time. Why was he so antagonistic? It was like he did it on purpose. Like maybe he was paid to pick a fight? I glanced over at Judge Pugh, he was glaring at us.

I said to Mee-Ling, "There is something afoot, I do believe it has something to do with you, my love. Or perhaps the both of us?"

"And what leads to most skullduggery? It's money." Mee-Ling answered. "Monday morning we will go the bank and check on our accounts." She added.

"But first I am going to make a call on the Sheriff and see how those rustlers got out of jail. I bet Judge Pugh had a hand in it, but why?" I said between bites.

"Money of course, my love." Mee-Ling said, as she skillfully cut her steak into small pieces. Cold chills went down my back as I looked into her eyes. Fire and Ice stared back at me. I was sure glad she wasn't mad at me. Women, the most complex creature's in the universe.

It was going on ten by the time we arrived back at Mee-Ling's house. Pike was to sleep in one of the downstairs rooms. I went to my room and changed into my buckskins and moccasins. Then I silently slipped downstairs and out the back door. The clouds were flirting with the moon. An owl hooted at me from the Cottonwood tree in the backyard.

I went back to the Denver House and stood in the shadows of the alley. Sure enough, I did not have to wait long. Judge Pugh came out of the backdoor, with his girls of the night. I fell in behind them, they lurched on, unaware of my presence. I came up behind them, I slit the stays on the back of their dresses, their over abundant breasts fell out. They felt not the slight tug of the knife point on the silk of their dress.

They stopped. Judge Pugh thought they had exposed themselves on purpose, he started to fondle them. They pushed

him away. I slid from one shadow to the next, till I was behind
the Judge. The women saw me, appearing and disappearing,
they spooked and ran. The Judge stood there in his drunken
stupor, weaving back and forth. With a few deft flicks of my
knife point I carved the figure of the Thunderbird on his right
cheek, my touch was so light, he felt it not. It bled but little. He
staggered his way home.

I awoke to the sound of a Robin singing on my window
sill. I called to him, he came and sat upon my finger. Telling me
the wonders of his world, I felt the envy of his perfection. A
knock upon my door, the robin flew on his way. "Come in." I
said.

My love stood there, dressed in a black silk dress, it
clung to her every curve. She glanced at my buckskins and
moccasin's laying upon the bedside chair. "I see you were busy
last night, you didn't kill him, did you?"

"No, you told me not to, you said you had plans for him,
I thought I would just help them along?"

"It's Sunday, would you like to go for a picnic, down by
the river? Or, would you like to go to Church. You mentioned
about attending meetings before your Mother died."

"No, no Church, I never had much use for those self-
righteous pulpit pounders. I only went to please Ma. Although,
if you read the Bible carefully, it does make a lot of sense.
There is a lot of practical wisdom in there."

"Perhaps, I will have to read it someday and see."

"Maybe we can read it with our children."

"Yes, we will see what the future holds. Come to my
room, I have some new clothes for you."

I got out of bed, she handed me a clean pair of shorts.
Watching while I put them on, she motioned for me to follow
her. On her bed was a suit, made out of the silk and wool blend,

like her riding habit. The color was hard to describe, I do believe the color depended on the shade of the light that shone upon it. Right now in the darkened bedroom it was black. She said, "The weave is one I invented, a knife will not pass through it, a light caliber bullet will bounce off. Try it on, I want you to wear it tomorrow."

"Do you have one of similar weave?"

"Yes, those riding habits I have are of that weave. Also the dress I will wear on the morrow is of the same material." I pulled the pants on, she stepped forward and started to button the pants. Patience, patience, her touch sent shivers down my spine.

She was on the last button, when I reached to her bosom and unbuttoned her top button, then the second one, then quickly the third. She raised her eyes to mine, her hand still on the last button. I pulled the dress top to the side, enough to expose the rise and fall of her breasts, she shivered herself. Then, Knock, Knock, "Aunt Mee-Ling are you busy? The Sheriff is down stairs."

"We'll be right there, your Uncle Buck is here with me."

"Yes, we know."

She looked at me and said, "That was close, one more button and I wouldn't of been able to stop." She buttoned my top one. I did the same with her dress. Then I finished getting dressed in the new suit she gave me. Then I went back to my room and slipped on my black boots. Then I strapped on my guns. Mee-Ling was just opening the door for the Sheriff as I was coming down the stairs.

Mee-Ling was saying, "Come in Harold, I am glad you are here, we were coming to see you Monday. What can Phillip and I do for you?"

He looked at me, I saw fear in his eyes. He said. "It has

to do with Judge Pugh, he seems to have some kind of an idea that you were responsible for an attack on him last night. He has a Thunderbird symbol cut into his right cheek. I asked him if he seen you do it, he said No, he didn't even know it was there till he woke up this morning. But he insists you must be responsible."

"That is really quite preposterous, don't you think, Sheriff? Why would he accuse me?

The Sheriff just shrugged his shoulders, looking miserable. Yin-Li came into the foyer, saying, "There is hot coffee in the kitchen, would the three of you like some?"

I said, "Sure we would, come on Harold, I believe they might also have some bear sign, you know, doughnuts. You know, there is a question I would like you to answer Sheriff." We sat down at the table. Yang-Su poured the coffee. I went on, "What I was wondering is, how did those rustlers get out of your jail?"

He sat his cup on the table, clearing his throat, he said, "Judge Pugh came in and said he was going to have an inquest, a pre-trial hearing. He had me bring them over to the court house, it was the biggest farce I had ever seen. He more or less just slapped their hands, then turned them loose. Strange thing about it, they all seemed to know the Judge."

"And you didn't object?" Mee-Ling said, in a purring tone that sent shivers down his spine.

"I did, yes I did. He said if I didn't shut up, he would hold me in contempt, whatever that means. Another thing that you should know, the banker and the Judge are thick. I seen them meeting together several times late at night. None of this is my fault, Miss Mee-Ling."

I said, "Well you don't have to worry about those rustlers, they were sent to kill Mee-Ling and rustle our herd. In other words the Judge wanted Mee-Ling dead. Now why do suppose that was?"

He said, "I don't know for sure, but I bet it has something to do with the Banker."

Mee-Ling said, "I tell you what Sheriff, I heard the fish are biting over at the lake. I think that you should go fishing for a few days. By the time you get back, all of this will be settled."

"Have another Bear Sign Harold, they're good aren't they?" I said. We sat and jawed about various things, then the Sheriff left. It wasn't even a half hour later that we seen him riding out of town with his fishing pole.

We did the same. Except we went on a picnic, the five of us. That evening we sat around and listened to Mee-Ling play the Piano, she sang also. The girls chimed in, I didn't. Pike did though, he actually was pretty good. We retired around nine.

I just got settled in bed, when there came a light knock, Mee-Ling came in, she didn't say anything, dropping her robe, she climbed into bed, snuggling close, she said, "Go to sleep." Another exercise in self control? My dreams were full of wild fantasies, at least I think they were fantasies. I wonder what her dreams were like?

The next morning we woke up looking into each other's eyes. She leaned forward, she kissed me, a long time. When we came up for air, she got out of bed. Standing in front of the mirror she brushed her hair, her robe was still on the floor. When she finished with her hair, she went over to the closet and pulled the night pot out, squatting, she went and wiped herself, then put on her robe, blowing me a kiss she left the room. It was a few minutes before I could move.

While I was dressing, I was pondering about Mee-Ling. She had as many facets as a diamond. She could ride, shoot, rope. Playing piano and singing, she was a sweet young girl. Just now she was temptress, a vixen. But to sum it all up, she was a woman. A beautiful, all encompassing woman.

We all had breakfast altogether, the five of us. Afterwards, Mee-Ling went into the Den and got some papers. "What are those," I asked.

"The deed to the bank, I own the building outright. These others are what passes for stock certificates."

"Can I see them?" I asked.

"Sure," Mee-Ling said, as she slid them across the table.

I looked at them, then said, "These are made out to an Elizabeth Drake, is that you?"

"Yes, Drake was my fathers name. Yes, it's a long story. Chen-Lee and I had different fathers. His father died. My mother remarried, an Englishman. They both are still alive, I think.

"If I'm not being too nosy, where did you get the money to invest in the bank?"

"It's what is called a dowry. I talked my Father into giving it to me, told him I wasn't going to get married, I guess I lied."

"Things change Mee-Ling, the only thing that remains constant is change. I don't think you are capable of lying. Tell me, does Herman Ratcliff know that you are Elizabeth Drake?"

"I don't think so, you see I had a lawyer handle all of the paper work on this transaction. But he died two years ago. I didn't need the money, so I sort of just forgot about it. Why?"

"I was just trying to figure out why the Judge wanted you dead. Of course we know it must be about money. But if no one knew you were Elizabeth Drake, why would they want you dead?"

"Uh," Yin-Li said, "I, we didn't know that was a secret.

When Yang-Su and I, were in the bank, watching them count Phillip's gold. We were poking into things and Mr. Ratcliff told us not to handle bank property. We told him our Aunt owned the bank, so there. We thought it was strange, when he turned pale and left the counting to his clerk, Jefferies."

"Did he leave the bank right then?"

"Yes, he ran out of the back door, We looked out the front window, he went into the court house."

"Everything is starting to make a little more sense now. Does this Jefferies own any stock in the bank?" I asked.

"No, not that I know of. That is unless Ratcliff sold some of his."

"What about the rest of the bank employee's?"

"No, not even the widow Hetland, she has been there the longest."

"Which one was she?"

"She was the one with salt and pepper hair, about forty five to fifty years old."

"Oh, I remember her now. For her age she didn't look too bad."

"Is that right." Mee-Ling scowled.

"I said for her age, sweetheart. Now say, if I were Pike, I might be interested."

"I have seen her, Yes, I might be interested." Pike said, turning a little red.

I said, "But we're getting too far afield, back to the point. The only reason, I think, that they would want you dead, is that they have been fast and loose with Elizabeth Drake's money. And when they found out that you were her, whom they thought did not exist, that you would demand an accounting."

"Well I wouldn't have, but now they have overplayed their hands. I am going to demand more than an accounting. I want justice."

"And justice you will have, because I do believe that they are probably hatching another plot to do all five of us in."

Pike cleared his throat and said, "I have been in a lot of tight spots and have found out that a good offensive is the best defense."

Mee-Ling said, "My thoughts exactly, when the bank opens this morning, we will be there. All five of us. Phillip and I will confront Ratcliff in his office. Pike you interview the Widow Hetland, see what she knows. Girls, you be sure and take your weapons and see what Jefferies knows or doesn't know. If he is in on it, don't be gentle. I am sure when we are done with Ratcliff, he will spill his guts, one way or another."

Mee-Ling (I didn't know if she would want me to call her Lizzy or maybe Beth.) And I went into the bank first. Pike and the girls were to wait till we got into Ratcliff's office, before they came in. Jefferies didn't give us any trouble, in fact he seemed friendly. He showed us in.

Ratcliff was taken by surprise, he jumped to his feet, stammering "What are you doing here, who said you could come in here!" He started to reach into his desk drawer, I beat him to it, I slammed the door on his hand. He howled and held his hand, I was sure I broke a finger or two. I reached into the drawer and put a .41 caliber derringer in my pocket.

Mee-Ling said, "Herman, Herman, Herman, you have been a bad boy, haven't you? No need to answer, it would be redundant. You did not know I was Elizabeth Drake?" He shook his head. "Herman, have you been stealing my money? Now don't lie, the girls and Mr. Pike are checking the accounts right now."

He said, "After Lawyer Daggert died, I didn't hear anymore about you. I thought you were just an alias of his. I asked the judge what I should do with the past and future money. He said, that we could just split it. He said no one would ever find out. Then when your nieces said you owned the bank building, I ran over to tell the Judge, I wanted to give the money back, but he didn't want to, he said he would take care of you. It wasn't my idea."

Boy when you got him started, he couldn't wait to spill his guts. I asked, "So Herman, how much money have you stolen?"

He was wilting, growing smaller right before our eyes, "I think about two hundred thousand, I don't know for sure."

"Do you have any of it left, between the two of you?" Elizabeth Drake asked.

"I have about fifty thousand, I don't know about the Judge."

"How much do you have of your own money in my bank?"

"I have one hundred thousand that I have saved over the years."

"Didn't you move here from somewhere back east?"

"Yes, St. Louis. My family still lives there."

"I tell you what I am going to do, me being the soft hearted fool, that I am. I am going to let you take fifty thousand of your own money and take your wife and children back home to St. Louis. That is plenty of money, if you watch your spending, to live your life out."

I looked at her, "What about the Judge, Lizzy?"

"Lizzy?" She looked thoughtful, "Yeah, I like it. But I don't like the Judge. Will you take care of him?"

"What do you want done with him?"

"Please Phillip, just let Buck do what comes natural."

"Well I guess I could let his actions be my guide, for

every action there is a reaction." I turned and left the building. I walked over to the Court House. The judge had a young receptionist, she looked somewhat like one of those harlots from the alley the other night. She started to rise, I stopped and laid the point of my knife against her left breast, she sat back down, I motioned with my knife toward the door, she hurried out.

I opened his office door, he was sitting with his feet up on his desk. I walked in and sat across the desk from him. He sat his feet down and said, "What can I do for you? Mr..? I didn't catch your name."

"I didn't give it. Just call me Buck. That's quite a tattoo you have on your cheek, where did you get it?" Now, I couldn't see his hands and he couldn't see mine.

"That's none of your business, what do you want?"

"Why Judge, all I want is justice, isn't that what you want too?"

"Of course, I am a Judge. What is this justice that you want?"

"Someone has just tried to kill my fiancée. I just want them brought to account. They stole vast amounts of money from her. Do you have any idea who that felon might be?"

A shot exploded from under his desk, it hit me in the left shoulder. I was wearing that new suit Mee-Ling had made me. It hurt like hell, but did not penetrate. My return shot did, right between his eyes. I sure wouldn't want to be the person who had to clean that mess up.

The Records clerk from down the hall rushed in, I said, "He shot first, I was just being polite and returned it."

He said, "Couldn't have happened to a nicer man. Thank you."

I walked back to the Bank, they were just finishing up.

Elizabeth had appointed Pike as the new President of the Bank. He was leaning over the Widow Hetland's desk, studying some forms. Hers included.

I said, "Hey Lizzy, the Judge is no longer a problem. But my left arm is. I let him have the first shot. Your suit works fine. But the impact almost broke my shoulder. She came over and unbuttoned my jacket and shirt. The whole shoulder was starting to turn black and blue. And it still hurt like hell.

"I have some special salts, come on I'll draw a hot bath and you can soak that shoulder. And Buck, no more letting the bad guy shoot first. I don't want to be a widow, before I am even a wife."

The four of us went back home, Mee-Ling was as good as her word. The kitchen range had double boilers, so there was plenty of hot water for a bath. She filled the tub in her room. Poured in some kind of concoction. I got in and slid down so the water was over my shoulder.

It did feel good. Mee-Ling took the empty buckets back to the kitchen, I drifted off. Woke up to her getting in the tub with me. I forgot all about my shoulder.

After supper that night, we had a family meeting. It was agreed that on the morrow we would start preparations for our trip to Cheyenne.

Mrs. Tuttle would continue to run the dress shop. Pike would run the bank. Mee-ling's local Chinese friends would look after the house. We had already made arrangements for our share of the ranch to be looked after, Hank and family would do that. So I guess we were free to travel. Or anyway as free as possible. You see, minority's were considered fair game.

Chinese were in the minority, Negroes were in the minority, and us Indians were fast becoming a minority in the west. So the word freedom was relative, say like, as to who your relatives were. There was one breed that was in the majority, bigots. There was a never ending supply of them.

It took us all day to gather stuff and tie up any loose ends. We made sure that all the financial things were in order first. We bought a carriage that was big enough for the four of us and all our baggage. It took four horses to pull it, with two trailing behind. Things were happening so fast in the west, you had to stay at lope or get left behind.

Chapter Six

Festus decided to ride along with us back to Greeley, he thought it would be safer for all of us. A lone man on the trail was taking his life in his hands. There were several bands of outlaws reported to be working the trail between Denver and Cheyenne. Of course we knew four of them that would not be giving anyone any trouble. You remember, the ones the girls did for on our way to Denver.

Festus met us with the Carriage. I asked him. "Why does it take four horses to pull this? It doesn't look that heavy."

"I know it doesn't, but if you look inside, you will see it is lined with one eighth inch thick steel plate. I modified it myself. It's almost like a War Wagon."

We were just loading up, when the Sheriff came back from his fishing trip. He rode up, "Is there anything I should know about?"

Mee-Ling said, "Well there are a few changes, Mr. Ratcliff is moving to St. Louis. And you will need to have them send a new Federal Judge, Judge Pugh committed suicide, he missed, Buck didn't. Our friend Francis Pike is now president of the Bank. He might need a best man in the near future. Maybe you could do that?"

"Sure and I would be glad and I want to thank you for

getting rid of that corrupt Judge."

I said, "Believe me, that was no problem, it was pure pleasure."

Yin-Li and Yang-Su were going to take turns driving. We sat in back, I said to Mee-Ling, "I thought Pike didn't have a first name?"

"You didn't know his name was Francis? He told me that the first time we met."

She punched me in the arm, like a school girl. I punched her back, one thing led to the other, we started kissing. The girls looked back and said, "Hey, you're not alone, you'll corrupt our morals." Then they broke up laughing.

Does it seem at times we revert to the silly? Like maybe we missed our childhood? I know I felt that way, a lot. Like when I seen kids playing marbles. I would like to get down on my knees and lag for first shooter. I would like to go swimming on a hot summer day, lay in the shade with a cane pole, catch fish and throw them back. Because cleaning them would be too much work.

We wrapped our arms around each other and just sat there and watched the miles go by. We stopped for lunch and watered and fed the Horses their oats. We swapped the two trailing horses for two of the four horse team. Letting two of them rest. We stopped once more before we got to Greeley and swapped the other two out. We pulled into town an hour before dark. It was a nice trip with no problems.

We left the Carriage and horses with Festus at his stables. We walked to the hotel. We got the same suite of rooms that we had the last time we were here. They brought hot water up for us, so we could bathe. After we got back from eating we turned in early. This time I didn't have to sleep alone. Our dreams seemed to mesh with each other, comforting, holding the terror's of the night to the shadows where they belonged.

We awoke together, nose to nose and toes to toes. I have already told you the color of my eyes, green. But hers were special, brown. What's special about brown? Hers had specks of gold, that sparkled down deep, into her soul. She leaned forward and kissed the tip of my nose. I kissed the bottom of her throat. She moaned, then, "Will you two stop that, we're hungry." Yang-Su was standing at the foot of our bed.

Mee-Ling looked at her and said, "Well then, maybe you had better get dressed, do you realize that you don't have any bottoms on?"

Yang-Su looked down, a mortified expression came across her face and she ran out of the room. Mee-Ling looked at me, "Did that bother you?"

"No, why should it? They are just like sisters to me. I mean I saw that she didn't have any bottoms on, but it didn't make any difference. Sometimes I think there is too much emphasis put on the wearing of clothes."

"Good, that was what I wanted to hear. Wouldn't it be nice if nobody wore any clothes?"

"No, good lord, no. Can you imagine, say, if Mrs. Tuttle wore no clothes, how awful. Or say if that Herman Ratcliff wore no clothes?"

Mee-Ling started laughing and didn't stop till she rolled out of bed and her naked butt hit the cold floor. She sat there, straddle legged, still giggling. I got up and held my hand out, she took it and stood up into my arms.

"Come on, we're hungry." This time it was Yin-Li, and she was dressed. "You know," she added, "You two do make a nice couple." Then she winked, turned and walked out.

The dining room was almost full, but there was a corner table open. We were watched by every eye in the room. Some with appreciation, some with contempt. Those with contempt I marked in my memory.

The waitress came over with a pot of coffee, we all held our cups out. She said, "Do you want the standard breakfast, or something special?"

Mee-Ling said, "And just what is your standard?"

"Eggs, potatoes, beef and beans."

I said, "Sounds good to me, what about you women?"

"Ugh, but that's fine, when in Rome." Lizzy said. Am I confusing you with the many names I am calling my wife? I hope not. You see, women are not just one person. There are many inhabiting their beautiful bodies. And they will bring them out to suit their fancy. That was Lizzy that said that, the outspoken one. Mee-Ling was too polite to say anything like that.

I was conscious of everyone in the room. On the far side sat four men, dressed in the style of the range. But somehow their clothes did not fit their demeanor. Their attire did not ring true. The hair on the back of my neck was tingling. They kept glancing our way, but when they saw me looking back, they would look away. Trouble, trouble, boil and brew.

Who were they and what did they want? They were not simple highway men. They did not belong in the west. But then again, there were a lot of people out here who did not belong, according to my people. Excuse me, I was just being facetious.

We finished eating, it was good. I enjoy the simple things of life. Like life itself and I intended that all of us keep on living. We went back to our room and gathered our things. As we left the hotel, one of them was trying to follow us, surreptitiously. Oh, shoot, I am sorry, I'm afraid big words like that are Ma's fault. She drilled the dictionary into my head and sometimes they just spill out, unasked.

At the first alley, I sent the women ahead. Ducking down the alley, I circled around behind him. I laid the point of my Bowie against his neck below his right ear. He stiffened.

"Who are you and what do you want?" I said. He pissed his pants. He really didn't belong out here.

"Don't kill me, I'm from the Pinkerton Agency, we're looking for Elizabeth Drake, we think that woman you're with is her."

"What do you want with her?"

"Elizabeth Drake's family is looking for her, not her family exactly, their solicitors. She is heir to their fortune. Quite sizable, I'm led to believe."

"She don't need anymore money. She has enough to last her the rest of her life."

"It's not just the money, it's the matter of a title, some kind of English thing."

"What if I said you can't talk to her?"

"I'm afraid that would not be acceptable, it just wouldn't."

"Ok, come on, walk in front of me, toward the stables." I put my knife back in it's sheath. He seemed docile, so I walked beside him. My family was waiting for us.

"Mr. Pinkerton Man, this is Mee-Ling, my wife. Mee-Ling he is looking for Elizabeth Drake, has he found her?"

"That depends on what he wants her for?"

He told her everything, she admitted she was Elizabeth Drake. Shit, so long to the simple life. "Ok, Pinkerton," I said, "Why does it take four of you to find one woman?"

"Oh, it doesn't, the other three are on different cases. We were only eating together."

"Well I tell you what, we are going to Cheyenne, you can come with us, go get your plunder. You can rent a horse from Festus, if you don't have one."

"I have one, he is stabled here. I rented him in Cheyenne."

"Oh, one other thing, don't try to be something you're not, lose those duds, change back into your suit. Oh yes, do you have a name?"

"It's William Custer."

"Fine, shake your hocks, like Pa used to say, we're burning daylight. That was hokey, wasn't it?"

"Yes Dear, it was. But I love you anyway. Are we going to ride in back again?"

"Sure, the girls did a good job yesterday. Besides if one of us are driving, we can't cuddle in the back." I said. Then I checked the carriage and harness over. I found several cuts in all four sets of reins.

"Festus, come over here will you." He came, I showed. "Was there anyone strange in here last night?"

"No...Wait, yes, that man you was just talking to. He came in last night, said he left something in his saddle bags. I didn't think anything of it."

"Ok, thanks Festus, fix these will you, better yet, let's put new ones on. Don't say anything about this, will you?"

I went over the carriage again, this time I found a loose bolt on the axle spindle. I was getting madder by the second. After fixing it, and we were getting in the carriage, I said,

"Mee-Ling, I've changed my mind, I am driving. You three will set in the back seat, all three of you. And would you please look to your weapons? Something's afoot, trust no one."

"Not even you?" Lizzy said.

"You know what I meant, Smarty Pants."

"I know, what's wrong sweetheart?"

"Someone has tried to sabotage both the harness and the

carriage. And I think I know who it was. That so called Pinkerton Man. But what I don't know is why. Another thing, why didn't he just approach you in the restaurant, why skulk around?"

"You know one thing I have found out about deceitful people? Always keep them where you can watch them. When he gets back here Buck, invite him to ride up front with you, he can put his horse in back with the other two," said Elizabeth Drake.

He came walking up with his suit case and rifle. I said, "Hey, Mr. Custer, how would you like to ride up front with me?"

"Uh, that's Ok, I can ride my horse."

"No, no, I insist. Throw your suitcase in the boot. I will tie your horse in back. Here let me hold your rifle while you crawl up there." When he turned his back to get in, I reversed his rifle and drove the muzzle in the dirt, reversing it again, I wiped the loose dirt away with my hand. He was a shade paler. He didn't see what I did with his rifle, he was thinking of the sabotage.

We were just leaving town, when I seen a cloud of dust on the trail ahead of us. Oh yes, I think the last leg of our trip would prove to be very interesting. Mr. Custer was hanging on for dear life. I had a hunch they would make their play just before the noon break. I think I knew the exact spot also. There was a cut in the trail where they could ambush us from the high banks on either side.

As the morning wore on, he was getting more and more nervous. I said, "What's wrong, Bill, this carriage ride making you nervous?"

"No, I just seem to be a little nauseous, is that wheel loose?"

"I don't know Bill, you think we should check it?"

"Yes, it looks loose to me."

I hauled back on the reins, we came to an abrupt stop. Setting the brake, I climbed down over the wheel. Making a show of checking it, I said, "Nope Bill, that spindle bolt is as tight as a banker's wallet." He turned even more pale and fingered his rifle. I got back up and we went on.

Another hour went by, I let the rein of the off wheel horse slip out of my hand. He held on tighter. I said, "What's wrong with that rein?" I stopped and got down again. Bill's eyes followed me. I walked around checking all the reins. I got back up. "Nope they're all fine. How about that?" He started to retch and threw up over the side. We were just short of the spot where they could ambush us. I looked in the back seat, Mee-Ling reached forward and clipped him behind the ear with her pistol. He crumpled to the floor boards.

"Thank you, Sweetheart." I said. "Girls, why don't you tie him up. I am going to injun up on them."

"Not without us, you're not." Mee-Ling said. "But I have an idea; Jim, Jill and Lil are in the team. Why don't we have them take the carriage thru the cut. We will go with you. You take Yin-Li and I will take Yang-Su. When they start shooting at us, we will kill them."

I thought a little on it, she was right, hell they were a match for any ten dudes. The girls had old Bill all tied up, we threw him in the back. I told Jim to wait till we got up the trail. Then I would whistle, Bob White probably. He nodded as if he understood. Maybe he did. At least I hoped he did.

Mee-Ling and Yang-Su went left, Yin-Li and I went right. It was so easy, it was almost criminal. There were two of them hunkered down behind some boulders on our side. So that meant there must be one of them on the other side. We got within ten feet of them. I even gave the Bob White whistle, they didn't even look around.

I could hear the carriage coming. When it rounded a curve, they stood up and started shooting. So did the one on the other side. Shit, Ma always taught me to be kind to dumb animals. So I just shot them in the legs. Found out later that Mee-Ling did the same. After we stopped the bleeding, we hauled them down to the road.

We set up camp on the far side of the cut. Bill had woke up, he was scared shitless. We had all four of them tied to trees. We decided to stay there till morning. Yin-Li went off to find their horses and bring them to water.

I built a nice hot fire. I had noticed a loose piece of strap iron in the boot. I went and got it, putting it in the fire, I started a nice slow dance around the fire, singing a low rhythmical chant. I was even starting to scare myself. Mee-Ling and the girls were watching me, fighting to control their laughter.

I didn't get within ten feet of them, before they started to spill their guts. Turns out they were really Pinkerton agents. But they sold out to the highest bidder. She was really an heir, but her Dad's family did want to find her, but to kill her.

"I suppose Bill, that you have some kind of proof to back up your claims?" I said.

"Yes, sure, in my suitcase. There are our orders from Pinkerton, telling us to find her and tell her she is an heir to a fortune. Her Father died last year in San Francisco. But there is also a letter from an Ardel Drake, with his signature. Giving us one hundred thousand dollars, to kill her instead. He gave us half in advance. Not too bright was he? Not only in giving us that much money in advance, but signing his name to that letter."

"You will find most criminals are stupid, including you

four. Look at you now, we have you for attempted murder. We would have been in the right, if we would of killed you."

Mee-Ling came back with his suitcase. We popped the lock. We found the papers. The Pinkerton papers told us not only about the inheritance, but it gave the New York Lawyers names that were handling the case. And the prize, the letter hiring them to kill one Elizabeth Drake.

"Well Elizabeth, it was you they were trying to kill, what do you want to do with them?"

"I don't know, some people are their own worst enemies. Let me sleep on it. Then we all will decide what to do with them."

"We are only a few hours out of Cheyenne, should we load them up in the carriage and sleep in a bed this night?"

"No I don't think so. Let's stay here and go in tomorrow. They won't die will they?"

"No, I guess not, they seem stable. I'll gather all of their guns and lock them in the boot." I did just that, almost. I left William Custer's rifle on the floor boards of the carriage on purpose. I knew if they got loose that would be the first place they would look. Cause he was watching me as I gathered the guns, he noticed I did not get his rifle.

There was an old saying that Ma used to like: "If you give a person enough rope to hang himself, he usually will." We made supper and fed the prisoners. Gave them a blanket to keep warm. We went to bed as soon as dark fell. I had the girls sleep under the carriage. Mee-Ling and I rolled our bed roll under a tree across from the four would-be killers. I had my .44's close at hand.

The moon peeked at me through the trees, playing hide and seek. Mee-Ling's breathing had become regular. She didn't know, but I did. I saw them untie their bonds and sneak to the carriage. Custer got his rifle and coming toward us, he stopped about six feet away.

"Wake up, you dumb Indian, give us the key to that boot. Or I will kill her right now."

"Now why in the world would I give you that key? You would kill her anyway. Why don't you just go ahead and shoot us both, then you could rape and kill the girls over there, is that what you want to do?"

The other three had dragged themselves over beside Custer. They all said, "shoot him, damn it. That wasn't a bad idea, we could use them girls."

You could see that he was arguing with himself, he said, "No dammit, I won't, I've changed my mind, I don't want nothing to do with this." One of his late friends, hit him over the head with a tree limb. He took his rifle and aiming it at me, he pulled the trigger. That was his last act in this world. The other two were standing right next to him, when the rifle blew. It killed all three of them. I didn't even have to fire a shot.

Mee-Ling gasped, "How did you know that rifle would blow up?"

"Easy, I had jammed the muzzle in the dirt back at Greeley, when I first suspected him."

I got up and went over to where Custer was laying, "Hey, he's still alive, that blow didn't kill him, but he is sure going to have a headache."

He moaned and rolled over, looking at me he said, "What happened?" He sat up and seen his friends laying there dead. "Did you kill them?"

"No, you did, well your rifle did anyway. You see I had jammed the barrel full of dirt. If you would of pulled that trigger, you would be laying over there with your friends. Now what are you going to do with your friends? There is a shovel over there, I think you should bury them."

It took him awhile, but he did it. It was an hour before dawn, when he rolled up in his blanket and went to sleep. We woke him up for breakfast. I asked him, "Well Bill what are you going to do?"

"What do you mean, what I am going to do? Aren't you going to turn me over to the law?"

"Naw, I figure you can either run, or you can make things right, do what the Pinkerton's hired you to do. If you do, they don't have to know about you almost going bad. In fact, I think you can help us to put the real murderer away, that Ardel Drake. What do you say there, Billy Boy?"

"What about the money he already paid us?"

"Well now, that is quite the question. Mee-Ling what do you think he should do with the blood money Ardel Drake paid these men?"

"I am sure there are many charities that would love that money. But we have plenty of time to figure out which one. Besides I think there will be expenses that will have to come out of that money."

"Well there you have it, William. Right from the boss." I said. "Let's load up, I'm anxious to see the bright lights of Cheyenne."

The girls drove, William had the whole back seat to himself. Mee-Ling and I rode and ponied the extra horses. We made it to Chen-Lee's for lunch.

We ate lunch, then I said, "Well here we are in Cheyenne, you said we could get married when we got here."

"Ok, come on, who wants to go with us? We are going to the court house to get married. We will need some witnesses." Mee-Ling said.

Chin-Lee sat there, drumming his fingers on the table,

then he said. "I tell you what, I'll go get the Judge, we'll have the wedding here in our living room. A lot must of went on down there, you have only known each other for three weeks."

Mee-Ling said, "Oh, we've known each other forever, he's the one I told you I was waiting for. Isn't that why you sent the girls to Denver with him?"

Chen-Lee looked surprised, "Why come to think of it, it was, somehow I knew he was the one." He looked at our guest, Bill. "Do you want me to take him to the hotel?"

"No, he will stay in your extra room. But you can reserve the best room the hotel has, for Buck and me. In the meantime, we'll take the carriage and horses to the stable's."

Carl Hatfield was glad to see us, especially since we had his rental horses. "Carl, you see this carriage, its special. I want you to put it in the corner of the barn and cover it. Also I will pay you extra to take care of all six of my horses. We might be going back east for awhile. As to how long we will be gone or when we will leave I don't know. It doesn't matter, I want them here when I get back. Even if it's years from now. Do you understand?" I handed him a thousand dollars. He understood.

"Mee-Ling how would you like to get a drink at the Cheyenne Supper Club?"

"Cheyenne Supper Club? What's that, a fancy name for a saloon?"

"Yeah, I guess it is, proper ladies usually don't go in there, but we're not proper, are we?"

"Oh I think we are proper, but unusual, but yes, I would like a glass of wine."

We moseyed, with me pointing out places of interest to my wife. We came to the Bugle, I told her about Walter Oglethorpe and Felicity Wells. We went in. Felicity was standing behind the counter. The bell on the door sounded, she

J.D. Oliver

looked up and started to say, "May I help- Oh my, Buck." Then she fussed with her hair, "It's good to see you, who is this?"

"Felicity, this is my Wife, Mee-Ling, or will be this evening. Mee-Ling this Felicity Wells, it's still Wells isn't it?"

"No, no, now it's Oglethorpe, see my ring." She held her hand out. Damn, that is what I forgot, I didn't have a ring for Mee-Ling. I looked and so did Mee-Ling.

"Felicity where did Walter buy your ring?" I asked.

"At the General Store, they have a selection of rings there."

"Ok, say do you want a news story? You can write one up on us. You can say that a renowned rancher from Denver, a Phillip Gentry, and the heiress Elizabeth Drake were married, blah, blah, and plan to honeymoon in New York city and the East Coast area. Just put a lot of uppity things in, use your imagination. Of which, I am sure, you have an abundance."

"Yes, I will. And let me congratulate the both of you, Buck and Mee-Ling. Mee-Ling you are getting quite a man there. I am sure you will be more than satisfied with him."

We said our goodbyes and left. Mee-Ling looked at me and said, "So that's her."

"Huh, what do you mean, that's her?"

"Oh, you know exactly what I meant, she still has the hots for you."

"No she doesn't, Ok, well maybe. She sort of seduced me, I didn't even really know what the sex act was, but she sure showed me. Are you jealous?"

"For heaven's sake, no. I think I will be grateful to her. Anyway we'll see this night, won't we?"

"Alright then, let's go get you a ring."

We put a little step in our get-along. As we stepped into the General Store, John Wesley Harden was talking to the store

113

keeper. He turned as we came in, "Buck, it's good to see you, now maybe things won't be so dull around here. Trouble always seems to follow you. Just don't make it too interesting." Then he laughed, somehow I didn't think he was funny.

"John, this is my wife, or will be this evening, Mee-Ling this is our Marshall, John." He stepped forward and took her hand, looking into her eyes. He didn't hold his gaze for more than a few seconds. He dropped her hand and stepped back. His demeanor had slipped a little bit.

"What's wrong John, you look shaken?"

"It's just as if I looked into the eyes of both heaven and hell, all at the same time. Uh, if you will excuse me, I have business at the office."

He ran out the door. Mee-Ling said, "The damned often react that way, don't worry, Honey, I won't hurt him. Are these the rings?" She said to the storekeeper, pointing to a display of jewelry.

We picked out a wedding set, the cost was not important, cause she liked it, that's all that was important. I slipped the engagement ring on her finger, the other one went in my pocket. Then we walked over to the Supper Club and found a table in the corner.

The girl came over, I ordered two glasses of wine, the girl said, "Uh, I see you are a lady, ladies usually don't come in here, there are some real jerks in here, there might be trouble. Some of them don't know who you are, Buck, I do. You see that boy at the end of the bar? Please don't kill him, I love him." Then she left to get our drinks.

"My, you must be one bad ass. Do you go around killing people willy-nilly?"

"No, I don't, you know how people blow things out of proportion. I just killed a couple of really bad people, they deserved it."

The girl brought our wine, we sat there sipping it, making eyes at each other. Why can't people just leave us alone? Mee-Ling nudged me under the table. I looked up, there stood three jerks, one of them was the boy, whom our server didn't want killed.

We looked up at them, the big one in the middle said, "Hey little lady, do you want to dance with me?"

Mee-Ling said, "You know you ought to stop banging your head against the bar, you may hear music in your head, but there is no music playing."

"The only music I need is your body against mine." He said, leaning over he made a grab for her. She grabbed him by the hair and slammed his face into the table. I made a grab for the wine glasses, waste not, want not. The one to his left made his play, she pinned his hand to the table with her knife. I never even seen her produce it. The boy that the waitress didn't want killed just stood there, not moving. The girl ran over and grabbed him, pulling him away, all the while scolding the hell out of him.

I said, "Come on Hon, this table is dirty, there is a clean one over here," I still had the drinks in my hand.

Mee-Ling said, as she pulled her knife and wiped it on his shirt. "Sweetheart if you get any slower, I swear you'll grow roots."

"What do you mean, I saved the drinks, didn't I?"

The bouncer came over, "Sorry about them, I'll toss them out." He picked the unconscious one up and tucked him under one arm, the other one was holding his bleeding hand. He took him by the shoulder, then he took them both out the back way.

We sat down at the clean table. I said, "I'm sorry too, I

shouldn't have brought you in here. I don't know what I was thinking. Here it is our wedding day, it should be all flowers and soft summer breeze's. Instead it's all blood and sawdust."

Mee-Ling took my hand, "Of course it should, but life isn't like that. And you have to live the hand you're dealt. Look at us, we have it good, compared to most of the population here on the frontier. And being who we are, a lot of the population would like to see us dead."

"Yeah, I know. Ever since I was born, I have been fighting to survive. As you have had to do also. Face it, we're not only both members of a minority race here, but also breeds. Do you think things will ever change?"

"Some, but not in our lifetime. That is just the hand we have been dealt. No use crying about it. I think our diverse background has made us strong. Now that we two are becoming one, that makes us even stronger."

She had mentioned living the hand you're dealt, twice. In other words accept things you cannot change. Well, we had both accepted who we are, but that was no sign we were going to lay down and let the bigots of the world walk all over us. At the same time we were not going to go looking for trouble. Discretion was the better part of valor.

So therefore, when we left the saloon, we left by a little used side door. No use tempting fate. We went to the hotel. They had our room ready for us. Chen-Lee even had our bags there. He had left a note, he wanted us there by six that evening, the ceremony was to be at seven. That meant we had time to take a bath and get something to eat.

I went down to the front desk and made arrangements for hot water to be brought up. As well as some food from the kitchen. They weren't in the habit of bringing food to the rooms, but money spoke the loudest. Plus they were still scared of me. I swear you kill a few hard cases and they think you're Attila the Hun.

The hot water came, they said the food would be up in a half hour. The tub was big enough for two. Mee-Ling started to undress, I sat on the bed and watched her. She was perfect, there are no words to describe her, so I won't even try. She lowered herself into the water, her breasts floated, peeking in and out of the bubbles.

I started to undress, hurriedly, she said, "No, slowly, I like to look also. Anticipation is part of the pleasure, this bath is part of that anticipation, do you understand?"

Sadly I did. We dried each other off. Mee-Ling had robes for the both of us. The food came, I tipped the girl, she looked at Mee-Ling and giggled. She probably had a vivid imagination.

After we ate and brushed our teeth. Mee-Ling tossed her robe on the bed and went to the suitcases. She started to lay out our clothes. New underwear for the both of us. Her dress looked like Black Velvet, but it was of that same new weave, silk and wool. She had black kid leather boots, almost knee high. She stood in front of the mirror and fixed her hair, before even putting on underwear. She was going to drive me completely out of my mind. She said, "Your clothes are there. Put them on while I finish my hair." I rushed to do so. My suit was black, same material, different sheen. The jacket was short cut, ending just below the waist. The shirt was white, Spanish looking. The tie was Spanish also. She even had a new pair of black boots, same leather as hers. I put them all on, she was standing there watching me, she was breathing hard, her breasts rising and falling. At least I wasn't the only one hot and bothered.

She hurried to get dressed. I asked, "How in the world did you know my size, you had to of had these clothes made up a long time ago?"

"I seen you in my dreams, for at least two years, I know every inch of your body."

As she was pulling up her panties, I said, "As I do yours."

The only thing old that we put on, was our weapons. Hers were hidden of course. My twin .44's looked at home on my hips. To finish our ensemble, she went to a hat box and brought out two new hats. Hers cut smaller, but still a replica of mine, black and Spanish. We put them on. As we got ready to leave, she said, "Oh, I almost forgot," She handed me a silver pocket watch. "If you look at your shirt, you will see two watch pockets on either side, there. That does look nice." The silver chain was just the right length, with a double eagle for a fob. I made sure that her wedding band was in my pocket.

As we walked through the lobby, everyone turned to watch us. I felt self-conscious. I bet I looked quite the dandy in these clothes. But I bet they weren't looking at me, why would they, with the most beautiful girl in Wyoming Territory walking beside me?

As we stepped out on the boardwalk, there sat Jelly Belly Farr on his horse. I stopped, my hands went to rest on my pistols. He said, "Whoa, I'm peaceable, I just wanted to thank you for not killing me, when you had every right too. Since you shot my hand off, my life has changed. I'm even engaged to be married, I want to thank you again. If I can ever do anything for you, just ask." Then he spurred away.

"Well, how about that, I thought not killing him that night would come back to haunt me. Well, I guess it has, but not in a bad way."

Mee-Ling said, "Could be that was a good omen, on our wedding day."

J.D. Oliver

"I'll take any good news that I can get, on this the first day of the rest of our lives."

Chapter Seven

We awoke the next morning to the cooing of Doves outside of our open window. I opened my eyes to see two beautiful feet. I assumed Mee-Ling had the same view. How did we get in this position? Oh yes, all of our anticipation was not in vain. "Phillip, get up here, I don't want to talk to your feet."

"Yes, my Dear, your wish will always be my command." I reversed my position, she laid a sloppy wet kiss on me. After we broke for air, I noticed the wedding band that I had placed closest to her heart, with the diamond engagement ring backing it up. Yes, we were married, forever.

"From now on, I think we should use our legal names, mine, Elizabeth Drake-Gentry and of course yours, Phillip Gentry II."

"Why do you get to use a hyphen and I don't?"

"Oh, alright then, I will drop the hyphen, It will just be Elizabeth Gentry, but you will have to drop the Second."

"Ok, deal." We started to laugh and of course it turned into sex. It was just the start of any little excuse we used to initialize love making. That habit was to go on the rest of our lives.

She sighed and rolled off of me, "We had better get up, we are supposed to have lunch at my brother's. And we have the future to plan, if such a thing is possible."

"To a certain degree it is, we can plan, no sign it will turn out that way."

Lizzy got up and went over to the commode, pouring water in the basin, she took a washrag off of the rack and started washing herself, glancing over at me she said, "Come on, there's another washrag, or do you want me to wash you?"

"No, that might just start something again, and you said we didn't have time."

"Right, in that other case over there, are our everyday clothes, get them out will you?"

As we came through the lobby this time, there was a lot of tittering. Understandably. People loved to speculate. There was a lot of envious looks tossed my way. The walk was refreshing, Lizzy glowed like the proverbial Golden Apple. I basked in her glow.

When we got there, they were all waiting for us. Even the Pinkerton man, Custer was all smiles. Yes, now, there was a piece of unfinished business. I think I knew what our immediate future would hold.

Do you want the details of our wedding feast? I thought not. It was a nice family get together. Yin-Li and Yang-Su were happy for us, but were a little sad. We sat down with them and talked about that. Turns out they didn't want to stay here. They had become used to the action of the last few weeks. They wanted to go back to Denver. Lizzy and I thought that could be arranged. They could oversee all of our investments in the Denver area.

We talked about that in bed that night. We both agreed that they would have to have some backup. In the Chinese community in Cheyenne, there were some young men that would jump at the chance to escort the girls. Lizzy said that the boys could handle themselves, they had a lot of experience in defending themselves. I said, "They wouldn't try putting any moves on the girls would they?"

"Of course not, if they tried they would lose face, that would bring shame on them and their families. Really the girls don't need any help, they could whip their weight in wild cats. And they can shoot better than most men, around here. But there is security in numbers."

"How would they get down there?" I asked.

"Didn't you notice the new stage office? I hear they even have two shotgun riders."

"Well I guess that would be Ok, I wouldn't want anything to happen to our girls."

I turned on my back, "That only leaves us, when do we leave for New York?"

She ran her fingers through the few hairs that were on my chest, "how about the day after tomorrow? We will need a day to get our tickets on the Union Pacific to Chicago. Then east. Do you think we can get private accommodations?"

"Sure money talks, we'll see what we can do."

"Good, since that is settled, stop talking and get to work." Lizzy moaned.

When it comes to my wife, I always do what I'm told.......

****

The morning dawned as all mornings should, with a warm southwest breeze blowing sweetly through the trees. We didn't lay abed too long. As, what I was to learn, was her habit. Liz stood in front of the mirror brushing her hair with no clothes on. She turned, "Do you think, after we get our trip arranged, that we could go on a picnic in the afternoon? I know the girls would like to."

"Sure, I see no reason why not. I suppose Chen-Lee doesn't mind keeping an eye on our Pinkerton Man, Mr. Custer, does he?"

"No, they have been talking quite a bit. Seems Custer really isn't too bad of a man."

"Yeah, I got that impression too. Some people do learn from their mistakes. Uh, do you think you could put some clothes on now?"

"Oh, I don't know, this feels pretty good, I might stay this way all day."

"Well, you wouldn't want me to stay this way all day, would you?" I said looking down.

"No, I certainly would not, I'll get dressed." I guess what's good for the Goose, isn't necessarily good for the Gander. That was a cliché, but you know, I've found out that clichés wouldn't be clichés, unless they were worth repeating. I guess you could say wisdom was ageless.

After we ate, we walked over to Chen-Lee's. We had William Custer go with us to the Union Pacific Depot. The ticket agent was an irritable old fellow with a nasty attitude. But that soon changed, as soon as he picked himself up from the floor. I didn't hit him, Lizzy did. Wisdom is supposed to come with age, he just got some knocked into him.

As he rubbed the knot on his cheek, he said, "How can I help you, Ma'am?"

I spoke up, as much to assuage his feelings, as to let Liz cool down. "Well, my good man, we would like passage for three to New Your City. But as my wife and I are newly weds, we would like private accommodations. Mr. Custer here would like a sleeping birth also."

"There is no problem on the single for your Mr. Custer, but private accommodations for the two of you, let me think. Yes I know what. It just so happens that we have a private car for sale. It belonged to a Lord Dunraven. It has been setting on a side track here for over a year. We just got word that we can sell it for storage costs."

"How did that all come about?" I asked.

"Lord Dunraven and his party came to hunt Buffalo. They were told it wasn't safe to go into Indian territory. But you know how arrogant some of these English Lords are, they would not listen. They have not been seen since."

"How much are the storage costs?" Lizzy asked.

The ticket agent glanced sideways at her and spoke to me. "I was told eight thousand dollars, but they might take less." He said, as Liz cleared her throat. He was scared of her.

"How much less?" My mean wife asked.

"Would five thousand be too much?"

"No, that would be fine," I said. "Then how much to pull it to New York?"

"A thousand dollars, as long as you took care of your own food and water needs. Two thousand if you want Porter service."

"Ok then, seven thousand dollars, how much for Mr. Custer's ticket?"

"Oh, I will throw that in."

"Done," My wife said, as she reached into her purse and handed him seven thousand dollars. "Now where is this car located so we can inspect it?"

"We have it pulled up next to the Depot, right out the back door."

He handed us the keys. "One thing more," Liz said, "I want a bill of sale and paper work showing we have passage to

J.D. Oliver

New York, so no station agent can give us a hard time."

"I will do that while you are inspecting your property."

It was just as luxurious as one would expect of an English Lord. Someone had recently dusted it. Everything was complete, right down to toilet facilities. There were even clothes in the closets. Women's clothes, hence there must of been a woman in his party. A fool and his wealth are soon parted. In this case it was also their health.

The master bedroom was in the rear. I sat down on it, not hard, not too soft. I pulled the covers back, silk sheets. Wow! All of their personal belongings adorned the dressers. I felt a little uncomfortable, like I was invading their privacy. But I was sure where they were, they wouldn't mind.

In the living area, there were comfortable leather chairs, ash trays and spittoons. Chess tables and card tables. Everything to help the rich pass the time. There was even a bookcase, full of books. Now there was a treasure! One I hoped to take advantage of. Over in the corner there was something else, a safe. With a combination lock. I looked at our Pinkerton Man,

"Do you know anything about how to open that?" I asked.

"Some, that was part of our training. I could play with it, it might take awhile."

"Well we will have a lot of time before we get to New York." Lizzy said, while she surreptitiously slipped her hand down the back of my pants and pinched my butt. What a little vixen she was.

There was even a built in gun case, most of the guns were gone. The Sioux probably had them. There were a few small caliber pistols still there tho. I'll have to check them out later. On one wall was a Coat-of-Arms. Two lions doing something behind a shield and spears. It was quite a heraldic device. I wonder if either Elizabeth or my family had one of those.

We went back in the ticket office, he had the paper work ready. He said they would have the car ready to be hooked up to the east bound train, when it came through at noon tomorrow.

We all went back to Chen-Lee's. The girls were anxious to go on a picnic. They said they knew exactly where to go. William Custer was going to spend the afternoon with Chen-Lee. So we made up a picnic lunch, got a light surrey from the stables and headed out.

A few miles northeast, was a hot spring that fed into a deep pool and the pool drained into Lodgepole creek. It had everything, grass, trees, flowers. And above all privacy. We were a little hungry, so we laid out our food on a blanket and ate. The girls didn't eat much, they said, "Are you ready to go swimming?"

I said, "How, we didn't bring any swimming suits?"

"Don't need any here, there's no one around, come on." Then they started to disrobe. To my astonishment Mee-Ling was yanking her clothes off also. All tho I don't know why I was surprised. Given her penchant for nakedness. They all three made a dash for the water, they looked at me and said, "Come on, you big chicken, haven't you ever went skinny dipping before?"

"As a matter of fact, I have. With the Shoshone kids. We went that way all the time. With both boys and girls. But I don't know, I'm older now, are you all sure you want me too?"

"Why not, we're all family?"

So I did. The water near the spring inlet was about ninety-eight degrees. I stuck one toe in. Then I inched my way, till Yin-Li grabbed my foot and gave a yank, dousing me all at once. I found an under water rock and sat on it, enjoying the mineral rich water. They were swimming around in the cooler end, splashing and throwing mud at each other, family or no, I knew enough to stay out of it. I said, "There are some things we need to talk about, why don't all three of you come over and sit?"

They swam over and floated on their backs. "What do you want to talk about?" Yang-Su said, as she splashed water in my face.

"About business, you two are going to be in charge of all of our interest's in Denver. The ranch, not too much to do there, but just keep an overall eye on everything. The bank, you will have to keep a close eye on that. And of course the dress shop and your Aunt's house. We will give you both Power of Attorney, in both of our names. You never know, something might happen to us. One thing I want to caution you about, you will have a lot of power over people and their destiny. And one thing I know for sure, power corrupts, and total power totally corrupts."

They got serious. Treading water, they all came over and sat down beside me.

"We know that, Uncle Buck, you don't have to worry, we have been on the receiving end of that power before, we won't misuse our power."

"Oh, and one other thing," I said, "Boys. You two are very beautiful young women. As such you are going to have to beat them off with a switch. And remember they will tell you anything to get in your pants or steal your money."

"Is that what you did with Aunt Mee-Ling?" They laughed.

Mee-Ling said, "No, that's what I did with him." Then they all three went back to playing around. This time I joined them, carefully.

That night in bed Mee-Ling said, "You don't think we're putting too much responsibility on them, do you?"

"No, I don't think so. I have seen them in action. They are two real cool characters. I know they would never do anything to hurt us. And if chance and circumstance should befall our business adventures, don't worry. I know where there is plenty more where that came from."

"What do you mean?"

"Gold, I have enough stashed away, more than we will ever need. But even if we didn't, I don't care. I have you. You're heavenly, and just like the scriptures say, 'Store up your treasures in heaven, where the moth and rust do not consume.'"

"I am sure that's not what that means, I'm sure that's referring to spiritual matters. But I appreciate the thought." Then we got down to more carnal endeavors.

We packed what little clothes we had at the hotel, then went down to eat. Afterward we went to the stables and Carl Hatfield harnessed a team to a buckboard, to haul our luggage from Chen-Lee's to the railroad. Everyone went with us. It was nice to have family and friends that care about you.

By the time we got there, the train from the west was already there and our car was hooked on. The conductor was standing beside our car. Our friends, including John Wesley Harden loaded our stuff in our car.

The conductor took Mr. Custer's ticket, then looked at us, "Tickets please."

I looked at him, "What the hell you talking about?"

"You need Ticket's to ride on my train."

"Your train?"

"Yes, it's my train."

"Did the ticket agent show you that we are paying two thousand dollars for our passage?"

"No, he said that you paid seven thousand dollars for the private car."

"No, we paid five thousand for the car and two thousand for passage to New York. In fact, here are the papers." I handed the Bill of Sale and the passage agreement to him.

He looked at it and threw it back at me. "I don't care, you still need ticket's. You pay or I will have your car disconnected."

Now this was a case of a person's mouth overloading his ass. I said, "You look like you're about thirty five years old. And I see you're wearing a gun on your hip. And I expect by your attitude that you've taken advantage of pilgrims right along. Now you take a close look at me, what do you see?"

"I see a pile of shit that will be staying in Cheyenne, with his trashy wife." Now that was a wrong thing to say, calling my wife trash. He seen the rage in my eyes and went for his gun. I let him clear leather, then I put a .44 Magnum between his eyes.

John was standing there, "I've seen some fools before, but he sure enough committed suicide. Do you think the City of Cheyenne should pay to clean that mess up or should the Union Pacific clean up its own trash?" We all voted, the Union Pacific should handle it's own fools. The ticket agent, got a couple of gandy dancers that were lazing around to haul him away.

The Engineer came back from the Engine. "You killed the Conductor, now who the hell is going to take his place?"

I said, "That should be no problem, how about him?" I pointed to a Steward standing by the train. "Hey come over here," I said to him and then picked the Conductor's hat from the platform, where it had fallen. I looked at it, it didn't have any blood on it. I tossed it to the Steward, "Here, you're the new Conductor."

The Engineer said, "But. But, he's black."

"Is that a problem." I said.

He said, "No, I guess not, there's a first time for everything".

"What's your name?" I asked the new Conductor.

"It's George Washington, Sir."

"Well George, there lies his ticket pouch, with his ticket puncher, you can do this job, can't you, George?"

"Yes Sir, I can. Being a Steward, I know his job, as well as I know my own."

"Good, then Mr. Conductor, do we owe you any money?"

"No Sir, you don't. He was just pocketing the money, at times he cheated the railroad, also."

"Well George, if you have any problems, just refer them to me, that includes any railroad people also. Isn't it time to say 'all aboard'?"

Chapter Eight

They had filled the water tanks, thank goodness. Because there was a small kitchen area, complete with a small cook stove. We could cook, anyway. When we had examined the car before, I hadn't paid much attention, but there was even bunks in the far end for the servants.

This was the first time I had ever been on a train. It started with a lurch, I almost fell down. I sat down, before I fell down. Turning to the bookcase, I scanned the titles. Two stood out, Great Expectations by Dickens and Moby Dick by Melville. I had heard of them, but this was the first time I had seen them. I plucked Moby Dick from the shelf and started to read.

Between the clackity-clack of the rails and my lack of sleep, the next thing I knew, Lizzy was waking me up.

"Come on, sleepy head, I have supper ready. That book must really be boring or was it our calisthenics the last few nights that made you so sleepy?"

"Well this book isn't boring. But it's just not our lovemaking, I have been on the go for weeks. Ever since Ma died, I guess it just caught up with me."

I helped with the dishes, I washed, Lizzy dried. A lot of people would call washing the dishes a chore. But when two people who love each other share the 'chore', it becomes a pleasure. Afterwards, we lit the coal oil lights. And just sat and talked.

It's just not in times of difficult situations that you get to know people. But on how they handle silence. I have heard some people say that they're bored. But how can you be bored, if you have a brain? Especially one as beautiful as my wife has.

I was just sitting there watching her eyes as she talked. I almost knew what she was going to say before she said it, by the expression in her eyes. They were absolutely glowing. I contributed to the conversation at the proper time, just enough to keep her talking. She had such enthusiasm that you couldn't help but to be sucked in. Her enthusiasm became yours.

I was completely enthralled with my wife. She seen the expression on my face,

"What? What's wrong.?"

I got up from my chair and leaning over I gave her a kiss, then picked her up and carried her to bed. I wasn't tired anymore......

We awoke the next morning to silence, the train had stopped. We were in sand hills of the state of Nebraska. Nebraska had only been a state for five years. Turns out, the train was waiting for a small herd of Bison to move out of the way. I opened the window and looked out. I heard a shot and saw a Bull fall. I had dressed when I got out of bed. Grabbing my guns I jumped to the ground, running up along the train, I reached the window with a rifle poking out.

Instead of just yanking the gun out, I grabbed it and shoved it back toward whoever it was that held it. I heard a crunch and a yell. Then I jerked the gun out of his hands. Going to the car door, I yanked it open and barged in.

There were three of them. One holding a bloody nose. They were what was called drummers. Salesmen. I said. "Were you planning on eating that Bull?"

"No," said the one with blood running down his hand, that was holding his nose.

"Well you are, the three of you get out there right now and start butchering."

One of the other two said, "Who says so? And he started reaching for a gun, I laid the barrel of my left hand gun upside of his head. I said, "Now there are only two of you and that is a pretty big job, that Bull must weigh almost a ton."

They had just started when Conductor Washington came up. "How long is that going to take? We have a schedule to keep."

"Well George, it will take as long as it takes. My Ma taught me not to kill anything if I wasn't going to eat it. So I guess if you are in a big hurry, grab a knife and pitch in. I am sure you can use the fresh meat, huh?"

Several of the other passenger's must of been in hurry, cause some of them helped. I took a haunch back to our car myself. Lizzy cut off a roast for supper and started smoking the rest. Sort of makeshift, she pulled the stove pipe apart, hooked the meat on wires and then put the stove pipe back together. Well anyway, it would sure enough be smoked. I don't think there was anything she couldn't do.

After the Clackity-Clack resumed, I sat down to read. An hour or so later William Custer came back to visit. Then our Conductor, George Washington drifted in. So we started a friendly game of poker, no money, just chips. Lizzy sat in with us.

Didn't matter who won or lost, but we did find out a lot about our guests. Turns out Bill had a wife and two small children. Made me glad I didn't plug him back on the trail. They were waiting for him in New York City.

George had a wife and three children. Also his kid Sister lived with them. They were in Chicago. The home office of the Union Pacific. George was a little worried about his job. I told him not to worry, I would talk to his boss when we got to Chicago.

He looked around and said, "I notice that you do not have a maid, Mrs. Gentry. My sister needs a job, she's eighteen years old. I hated to ask you, but I am afraid for my sister. You see she has a different Father than me. She is half white. You see before the war we were slaves. Sometimes the master forced himself on the women. She doesn't feel at home in our world. I am afraid she would not be accepted in the white world, either. Don't take this wrong, but you both have mixed blood. That is why I am being so bold."

Lizzy looked at me, I nodded. She said, "Of course, George. Are you sure she wouldn't mind leaving home and going on the road? You know we plan on moving around quite a bit."

"I am sure. She has tried to run away before, but we caught her."

"Alright then George, ante-up."

That's how the whole trip went. Frequent stops for fuel and water for the engine and passengers getting on and off. It took us three days to get to Chicago. They parked our car beside the main terminal. Turns out it would be a couple of days before we could get clearance for our car to be hooked up on the Pennsylvania Railroad. Which would take us through to New York.

George asked me to go with him to the main office of the Union Pacific. Of course I went. Pretty fancy layout. In the front office sat an overstuffed secretary. She sniffed when she seen George. I was dressed like an English Lord, I was behind George. I stepped out and said, "Sir Phillip Gentry the II, to see your, what do you call it, your Boss. Come my good woman, close your mouth and tell your superior I am here."

She got up, all flustered and bustled toward the door. She went in and came right out.

"Mr. Billings will see you now."

I went in with George right behind me. Mr. Billings stood up and came around his desk, holding his hand out, I shook it. He said, "What can I do for you Sir Gentry?"

"As you probably know, your conductor committed suicide in Cheyenne. No big loss, since he was robbing you blind. I took the liberty of appointing Mr. George Washington the conductor. He was a steward on your train. He has done a superb job. Is there any reason that the appointment should not be permanent?"

"Uh, he is a Negro, we usually don't have black conductors."

"Do you usually hire people that rob you?"

"No, of course not."

"You do want to hire the best man for the job, don't you?"

"Yes, I do."

"Then I see no problem, the color of a man's skin has no bearing on his ability. I assure you Mr. Billings, he is the best man for the job. And if you are worried about what people may think, don't be. Thousands of our citizens have just died in the Civil War to overcome that kind of thinking. Don't make their sacrifice worthless."

"You're right, Sir Gentry, George you have the job, at equal pay also. You'll have the western run. Is there anything else you need, Sir Gentry?"

"I would like to have my private car restocked. Perhaps you can see to that, then let me know the cost, so I can pay you."

"Yes, of course, George can you see to that. They can be stocked out of the same stores that our trains are supplied from."

"Good, and I do wish to thank you, Mr. Billings. And if any of your stockholders have a problem with a 'black conductor', let me know, I am sure I can set them straight."

And on that note, we left. The secretary had been listening, she was respectful as we left. She had got up and opened the street door for us. I guess she knew what side of the bread the butter went on.

George said, "May I bring my Sister by this evening?"

"Sure George, bring her possibles along with her. Might as well make the cut nice and clean. Maybe in the mean time you could get our car restocked."

That afternoon, William Custer showed us around Chicago. He knew it as well as he knew New York City. We had supper at a Café on Michigan Street. Chicago had one of the biggest stockyards in the country. The steak was about two inches thick and as big as the plate. They had some kind of steak sauce in a bottle setting on each table, I tried some, it was good.

Remember I told you before how good my wife was with a knife, anyway she made a production out of cutting her meat. I would hate to have her mad at me. William couldn't take his eyes off of her sideshow. "What? Why are you two watching me?"

"Uh," William said, "I haven't seen anybody cut their meat quite like that, no offense, I'm sorry for staring."

"I'm not, I love to stare at you, would you cut my meat too?" I said.

"I'll cut your meat alright, you won't like it."

I stuck my tongue out at her, she flipped a piece of meat at me, it missed and hit a guy at the next table. It stuck to his cheek. Oh shit, I thought, here comes trouble. He stood up to his full height, at least six foot six. He took the meat off of his cheek and came over.

"I believe this belongs to you Ma'am." Then he handed it to her and went back to his table.

I sat there stunned for a second. He wasn't mad? I got up and went over, "I want to apologize for that. My wife and I are newlyweds and sometimes we to get acting like kids, I am sorry. My name is Buck Gentry," I held my hand out.

"That's Ok, I knew it was just an accident." He stood up and took my hand, his grip was like a vise. "My name is Victor Wade. Lately of Texas. We just brought a herd in by rail."

"My wife and I are from Wyoming Territory, we're going to New York, have you ever been there?"

"No, don't ever want to, either. I heard about it tho. I hear they have all kinds of gang violence. All those buildings so close together, I hear you can't even see the sky."

"Yeah, its not my favorite place either. But we have some business to take care of, are you going back to Texas?"

"Yeah, I reckon, if I can round up the fare. After I pay for this meal, I'll be stone cold broke. You see my Boss done ran off with the money from the herd."

"Are you dead set on going back to Texas, a wife maybe, children?"

"No, no wife or children. I'm open to suggestions."

"What would you say about Colorado? You see I have

half interest in a ranch, east of Denver. We need hands, if you want, I would pay your way back there, what do you say?"

"I'd say you just hired yourself a hand."

He stuck his hand out and I shook it. Then I reached into my pocket and peeled off a thousand dollars. Lizzy had a pencil and paper in her purse. I wrote out a note to Pike, telling him to take Vic out to the P Bar P and introduce him to Mr. Peters and Hank Clifford. I handed the note to Victor and said, "Take this note to Mr. Pike at the Bank in Denver, he will take you out to the ranch. You can take the train to Cheyenne, go to the stables and tell Carl Hatfield that I told him to give you a horse. When you go to get your ticket here in Chicago, tell the conductor, George Washington, that you work for me, he'll fix you up. Oh, yeah, when you get to Denver, my wife's nieces sort of are our agent's, they speak for us, on all of our investments. Watch out for them, they are hell on wheels. They look like angel's, but fight like hell unleashed."

After we parted company, Lizzy said, "What did you tell him that for, about the girls, they're not that bad."

"I had my reasons, I don't want him getting sweet on them. I did it for his own safety. I didn't want him to get hurt."

We went to a saloon and had two drinks and we didn't have any problems, no fights or anything. We went back to the depot and waiting at the car was George and his half sister.

They were standing under a gas street light, she was about the same height as my wife, she was wearing a gingham dress and carrying a carpet bag. She looked scared to death. I could see why she didn't fit in, in a black community. Her color was just a shade different than mine.

"This is Louisa, my Sister. Louisa, this is Phillip Gentry and his wife, Elizabeth."

Lizzy stepped forward and hugged her, I took her carpet

bag. Her brother hugged her, a tear ran down his cheek. He turned and ran. We walked to the car. We lit the coal oil lamps.

In the warm light from the coal oil lamps, her beauty came through. She was shaking, scared to death. This was probably the first time she had been away from her brother's family.

I said, "You don't have to be scared of us Louisa. We are just like you, Lizzy is half white and half Chinese. I am half white and half Sioux Indian. You are half Negro and half white. You see you fit right in."

Lizzy said, "Another thing, you are not our maid. You are our friend and as such part of our family. We all chip in with any work to be done, as family's should. Why don't we get your bed made up, things will look better in the daylight."

They made the bunk up, Louisa started to crawl in. Lizzy stopped her, "Don't you want to use the toilet and brush your teeth?" Louisa nodded. Lizzy showed her where it was. When she came out, she went straight to bed, she didn't take her dress off.

We went to bed, to sleep, for the first time since we got married. That didn't mean the honeymoon was over, just delayed for a day.

We awoke the next morning to the smell of coffee, it smelled like heaven. Lizzy threw on a robe, I slipped into a pair of pants and the rumpled shirt from last night. We went out of our room. Louisa was up, her face scrubbed clean, she poured us some coffee, "Do you want anything in it, cream or sugar?" She asked. Her voice was low and melodic. She had a cute, shy smile. We fell in love with her right away. Not that kind of love, you know what I meant.

"I don't believe we have any cream." Lizzy said.

"Yes we do, right there in the Ice Box, George had

everything stocked yesterday, there is even ice in there. He said, we're supposed to leave for New York today."

We drank our coffee and then went back to our room and got cleaned up and dressed. By the time we got done, Louisa had breakfast ready.

"Hey, you're not supposed to be our maid or cook."

"That's Ok, Mrs. Gentry, I am used to fixing food for my family, it's Ok, isn't it?" Louisa said, with a tremor in her voice.

"Of course it's Ok, I wasn't scolding you, I just didn't want you to think that you had to do this."

Louisa smiled her shy smile and put the food on the table. We all three sat down to eat. After we ate, I said, "Since Louisa cooked breakfast, I will wash the dishes, do I have a volunteer to dry?"

"No, I am going to help Louisa find some decent clothes in the closets, you can wash and dry, that's Ok, isn't it?"

I made a face then said, "Of course, your wish is my command."

So I cleaned the table off and started washing. They went to the closet and got an armload of dresses out and put them on one of the chairs in the living area. They didn't pull the privacy curtain to the servants sleeping area. Louisa pulled her dress off over her head. She wasn't wearing any underwear, I turned my back and put my full attention to washing the dishes. I could hear them giggling and laughing as they tried dresses on Louisa.

I finished with the dishes, I said, "Hey I'm done with the dishes, may I turn around?"

"Sure, why not?" Lizzy said, "You've seen naked women before."

I turned around, crap, they were both naked, trying on

dresses. I put my hand over my eyes and stumbled my way to the door. I sat on the stoop, pouting.

The Depot was busy. And only due to get more business as the west was becoming more open to settlement. There were whole families boarding the trains, with all of their belongings. One family was walking by, they stopped and stared at our car. I followed their gaze. For heaven's sake, the shades weren't pulled!

I jumped up and ran back inside. Yelling, "pull the shades, pull the shades!"

"What?" Lizzy said.

"The shades, people can see in, in fact look, see that family? They can sure see the two of you." I hurriedly pulled the shades, turning, they both stood there, with dresses half on. Were they embarrassed or upset? No, they giggled some more. Then finished pulling the dresses up and over their abundance. I sat down in my chair and looked at them.

"Well since you're here, what do you think of these, do they fit Ok, or do they make us look fat? Is my butt too big?" Lizzy said.

Now I didn't know too much about women, but I knew enough to never give fashion advice, especially on the size of their derrieres. Now if I would of said, "No, it doesn't make you look too fat." They would say, "Oh, you think we're fat, but just not too fat?"

Instead, I said, "Is there any coffee left, I need something to wake me up. I think I will go get me some coffee, do you want me to bring some back?"

"How are you going to bring coffee back? They won't let you take their cups, why don't you take the coffee pot, maybe they will fill it up for you." Then they started to pull those dresses off. I grabbed the coffee pot and ran.

People were staring at me, walking along with a coffee pot in my hand. One woman was staring, I stuck my tongue out at her. She said, "Well, I never..."

I said, "That's right lady, you never, but I have." She stuck her nose in the air and grabbed her little kids hand and hurried off. That was pretty infantile of me, wasn't it? Oh, well at times I acted my actual age.

That got me thinking, just who the hell was I? Or better yet, what was I? Thirteen years old, man grown, married and what some would call a gunman. Two different personalities pulling me this way and that.

Buck's memories and experience's went back centuries. I hadn't heard from Phillip for awhile. He was the one with all the book learning. Some of it must be wearing off on Buck tho. Because he seemed to know a lot of stuff too. What the hell was I thinking about, I was Buck, I was Phillip, they were me.

I went into the first café I came to. Went to the counter and handed the girl the pot. She said, "What am I supposed to do with this?"

"Fill it up, please."

"With what?"

"Uh, coffee?"

"You have got to be kidding, no one has ever came in with a coffee pot and told us to fill it up."

I reached into my pocket and handed her a twenty dollar gold piece. She said,

"Coming right up." Then shook her fanny into the kitchen.

When I got back, they were just starting to hook our car on the train, the great Pennsylvania Railroad. "Where were you? You almost missed the train, goodness sake, Buck, do I have to put a leash on you?" Lizzy said. At least they were both dressed. I didn't say a word, just went and sat down and grabbed Moby Dick. I wished I had a harpoon.

William Custer came back to visit. I put my book up and we set up the chess board. I had read a book on chess years ago, never had a chance to play it tho. I wasn't really too interested in it, but Phillip was. Pretty soon his enthusiasm wore off on me. We played three games, and I won two of them. It wasn't really fair, cause it was two against one, you know, Phillip and I.

Lizzy invited Custer to stay for supper. He was full of questions about Louisa, just curious, I was sure he didn't have any ulterior motive, after all, he wanted to live.

Lizzy sat the table, they had fancy silver and china. She said it was time to start teaching Louisa proper etiquette. Custer knew all about it, he helped teach us hayseed's. Louisa was a fast learner. Me, I was a little slower. Couldn't see why you had to dirty so many forks, when one would do. Anyway this proper manners thing went on for the entire to trip to New York. I for one was getting a little sick of it, but Louisa ate it up.

But I am getting a little ahead of myself, I am sure you wanted to hear a little about our trip. Because on the road of life, it's the trip, not the destination. Although at times its sure nice to rest when you get there.

The first night out everything got back to normal, you know, our honeymoon. The clackity clack was even starting to get soothing. We took turns on the chores. We got into a pretty good routine. But what I liked best about the trip was the scenery. The well laid out farms, the neat little towns. There were some open spaces. But I was sure it wouldn't take long and people would be wall-to-wall. I made it a point to get out at every water and wood stop. Plus the Depots. I made the effort to talk to anybody who would talk to me. The trick was finding a common point of interest. I made friends all along our route. Never could tell when friends would come in handy. I did the same thing on the train. But I wasn't the only one, Lizzy and Louisa did the same thing, but they didn't have to make an effort, it came natural to them.

Louisa caught the eye of every young man on the train. It wasn't long before I had to set down some rules. She was like a kid in a candy store. So I substituted a few sour lemons. They got the point. Louisa pouted for a while, but she got over it.

Lizzy was teaching her about life. That was probably why she got over it so quick. She had common sense, which a lot of young women of the day lacked. Did I say just young women? I should of said people in general and every generation. Perhaps even me, at times.

As I said, Lizzy and Louisa were circulating through the train, making friends. One of them was a young widow with two small children, a boy of ten and a girl of eight. They were a casualty of the movement west. Her husband fell victim to the cattle and homesteader wars. She was going back home to Philadelphia. Only thing was, she was out of money.

Lizzy and Louisa came back to our coach at midday the next morning after we left Chicago. "Phillip," said Lizzy, "we found someone that needs help."

"Then help her, what do you need my permission for?"

"Well, cause the help she needs involves all of us. You see, she and her children are to be put off the train at the next stop. She only had money enough to take her that far. We could just pay her fare, but she is a pretty woman with two small children. And there is no end to the cads that would like to take advantage of her. We, Louisa and myself, thought that sense we have three bunks that are empty, why, she could just live with us. What do you think?"

J.D. Oliver

"What's her name? Helen of Troy, I presume?"

"No smart alec, it's not, its Charlene Russell. Her children are Toby and Edith. And they are well behaved."

"Well they had better be, I don't need any competition in bad behavior, I have a lock on that."

"You most certainly do, don't worry there is no one that can take your crown away." Said my lovely bride. She went on, "You haven't said yes or no, what's it to be?"

"Of course she can stay with us, you really didn't have to ask, but asking did assuage my male ego."

"Of which you have an abundance, my love." She plastered herself against me. Louisa went to tell her. We went to our room, we had time enough, if we hurried.

She was right, Toby and Edith were well behaved. I was a little concerned about their reticent behavior. But it didn't take me long to bring them out of their shells. Edith had a set of Jacks. I got on her good side, by letting her beat me, ten times. Oh well, maybe I didn't let her, she was just good at Jacks. Toby and I started out with checkers, then advanced to chess. He was good at checkers, I was still the champ when it came to chess, tho. I tried to keep everything light and airy with the children. They had not recovered from the loss of their Father. I didn't know the details on his death. I hesitated to approach Charlene on the subject. But if I was going to help her kids to get over it, I would have to know.

So the next night after the kids were put to bed, I broached the subject. She immediately broke into tears. When Lizzy and Louisa finally got the tears turned off, I asked, "So, Charlene, I know it hurts to talk about it, but in order to get over it, you need to greave. I know how there is a lack of proper law enforcement on the frontier. So if we are going to get justice for you, we need the details."

145

"What can you do about it, you are only one man, they are many?"

"Ok, that's one detail, he was killed by more than one man. Go on. Where did this happen?"

"On our homestead, west of Laramie. They waited till he came out to feed in the morning, then shot him. Dragged us out and burned our house."

"Did you see who shot your husband?"

"Of course I did, four of them, I see them every night in my dreams. Artus McNally and his three sons. Plus of course his whole crew. They laughed about it. They threw a hundred dollars in the dirt, told me to take my trash and go. If it wasn't for the General Store owner in Laramie we wouldn't even have had a change of clothes."

"Alright I will need a few more details later, but rest assured they will be punished, what kind of numeration will you want for your husbands death?"

"Huh, what do you mean?"

"I mean do you just want your land back? Or perhaps you would like their ranch in place of yours? I am just talking about tangible things here, because as far as you're concerned they are already dead."

"How can you be so sure, you are on a train to New York? And you are only one man."

Lizzy said, "Oh, he is a lot more than that. Besides he has me and all of my relatives."

"Are you going to kill them?"

"Oh no, they will commit suicide. Cowards like them always do."

"Good, I'm afraid I don't believe in killing. I would prefer it if the law would handle it."

"Oh, the law will. The law of survival of the fittest." I

said. "Because out there, that is the only law that applies."

Lizzy added, "Yes, you just take care of your children. Do you have any relatives in Philadelphia?"

"Yes, my late husband's older brother, Charles Russell. He owns a bunch of stores. I know he will help us."

"Good," I said, "You stay with him, while we go on to New York to take care of some business. On our way back we will stop to either see you, or take you back with us. Your choice."

"Just who are you people?"

"Who do you want us to be?"

"Are you angels?"

"No, we're flesh and blood, cut us, we will bleed, but not as much as those who cut us."

"I know your friend Mr. Custer, is a Pinkerton man, are you Pinkertons?"

Lizzy and I looked at each other, just who were we? Hell, we didn't even know. I said, "Don't worry Charlene, my Ma used to say, 'Don't look a gift horse in the mouth'."

"Then I won't, thank you, all of you."

On that note everyone retired for the night, except Lizzy and myself. We made us some herbal tea, to help us sleep. We sat there sipping it, idling talking.

"Mr. Custer hasn't had any success in opening the safe, I see." Lizzy said.

That drew my attention to it, as I mentioned before, Dunraven's Coat of Arms, were prominently displayed, even on the front of the safe. But on the safe it was more elaborate.

"Lizzy if you were going to hide something, where would be the best place to hide it?"

"Well I suppose in some secret out of the way place, I think. But no, wait, I know, the best place to hide something is right out in the open, right?"

"Yes, look at the front of the safe, you see the coat of arms? You see all of that fancy scroll work around it? That's not just scroll work, I think in between all of the squiggly lines, those letters are Latin. I can't read Latin, can you?"

"You mean the combination to the safe could be written right on the front of it?"

"That answer's my question, you can't, but I bet I know who can. Did you notice that Priest in the front coach?"

"Yes, of course, they are supposed to know Latin, they say Mass in Latin. Do you think he would read it to us?"

"I bet for a healthy donation, he would read it to the Devil. Whom he probably thinks we are. Why don't you ask him in the morning?"

"Me? What not you?"

"Even with all of his robes and foo-fa-raw, he is still a man. And as such he will find it hard to resist the wiles of a pretty woman. And my love you are the prettiest of them all."

"Flattery will get you everywhere, but you don't need it, let's go to bed."

In my dreams of the night, the past was yapping at future's heels, threatening to devour the present. Or maybe it was just the clickity-clack of the rails? No, for I opened my eyes and Old Man Coyote was sitting on the foot of the bed, staring at us.

"I see you have been busy, Buck. You have a very pretty wife. I would like to meet her, wake her up will you?"

I reached over and poked Mee-Ling in the ribs, "Huh, what's the matter, why did you wake me up?" She said, as she sat up. She seen him setting on the foot of the bed, she took it in stride. "And who do we have here?"

"This is Old Man Coyote, he wants to meet you."

Old Man Coyote looked at her tousled hair and proud breasts, "Yes you have a pretty wife, and she has great presence of mind. A rare find indeed, I would say Buck."

"I always thought so. What can we do for you?"

"I just stopped by to remind you of your purpose, the both of you. And to make sure the luxuries of the world didn't suck you in."

"Our purpose? Luxuries of the world? What is our purpose?"

"My, my, so full of questions. Maybe it would be better if I gave you the answer and let the question, be your goal." Then he went on, after making himself comfortable.

"The answers to all of your questions lie with the Creator. And the question and answers are the same. They can not be separated. If you ask, where am I going? The answer is mute, because you are already there."

I looked at Mee-Ling, "Do you understand anything he is saying?"

"Strangely, I think I do. I think he is saying the answer is in the questioning itself. It is enough that you care enough to ask the question, the answer doesn't matter."

"Oh, I think it does matter, if I ask what direction is North, the answer damn well does matter, or you will be going the wrong way."

Old Man Coyote said, "If I tell you what direction North is, the next thing you will be asking what direction South is. Without bothering to find out for yourself. You see, the question causes you to seek and the main thing is to keep seeking. Because you will never find out all the answers."

"Oh Crap, you are giving me a headache. Are you going to tell us what our purpose is?"

"I just did, seeking, that is your purpose. Sometimes

Buck, you can be rather dense, on some things you would be well advised to ask Phillip, till you completely become one, as you and Mee-Ling are."

"Are you saying that we are three people, instead of two?"

"Oh Buck, don't be obtuse. Sometimes I think you just like to argue. You are many people. Not only of the past, but in you lies many people of the future. We are part of the chain of creation. We are but a link in that chain."

With that, he stood up, said goodbye and disappeared. I looked at Mee-Ling, she looked back. She shrugged her shoulders, pulled me down and we went back to sleep.

Chapter Nine

I sat there watching the guy in the black robes deciphering the squiggles on the safe. He hummed and wrote, hummed and wrote. Then handed me the paper. I handed him a thousand dollars, he smiled and left.

Inside was a multitude of personal papers, stacks of money, and what looked like the Crown Jewels, to me. Of course I was no judge of jewels. But Lizzy and Louisa were having a ball trying it all on.

Dunraven's will was in the safe also. He had no kin. Looked like he was some kind of a rake. He wanted to leave his money to a brothel in New York. Man it takes all kinds. But who was I to judge. Who was I? I was the one that held his will in my hand. Maybe they would get it, or maybe they wouldn't. I would have to see. And by that, I mean I would do just that, go and see if they were worthy. We put everything back and locked it.

Philadelphia by day was a busy city. I don't know what night was like. We spent about two hours there. Long enough for us to find this Charles Russell. Turned out he was more than happy to help his brother's widow. He was some kind of a Bible Student, anyway that was what he called himself. I think it was more like a Bible scholar, he sure knew his Bible. He thanked us profusely, even offered to reimburse us for their fare. Of course I said no. I think his wife was glad we said no. You know women, until you get on their good side, you were on their bad side.

We took Charlene aside to say goodbye. I asked her if she still wanted us to bring justice on her Husband's killers, she said most definitely. She didn't hold with her Brother-in-Law's turning the other cheek philosophy. She wanted us to stop on our way back.

It was just a short hop to New York City. What a conglomerate of dismal. I had to hire a special guard to watch over our coach, they were recommended by our Mr. Custer. So I guess I could trust them. William Custer's family lived on the upper west side. We went to a hotel. It was nice, comparatively.

One thing the women liked was the shopping. I found the hotel bar quite comfortable. I sat in the corner with my back to the wall watching humanity flowing in and out. Some of it quite liquid.

A spoiled dove drifted by my table. She was just a kid. An Irish kid. Complete with red hair. "Would you like some company?" She shyly asked.

I looked at her, she was shaking. I said, "Sit down, no I don't want any sex, I am married. How old are you girl?"

"I'm fourteen, I'm old enough."

"Like Hell you are." I said. "No one is that old. Where are your parent's?"

"They died on the way over, they're buried at sea."

"How long have you been here?"

"The boat got in the day before yesterday."

"How did you get here?"

"There was a woman at immigration, she said I could live with her, I didn't know what she was. I know now. This was to be my first time."

"Where is she at?"

"Over at the bar, with that man from the house where we live. That big man at the end, the one watching us. The woman beside him is the woman."

I looked at them, yes, they were watching us. The waitress came over, I ordered a Sarsaparilla for the lady and for me. I asked her to tell the manager to come over to the table. She said, "Is there a problem, did I say something wrong?"

"No, Ma'am, you didn't, I just want to talk to him, I have a proposition for him." The girl started to get up. "You sit, don't move." She sat back down. I asked her, "What is the name of the house where they took you?"

"They called it the Palace of Delight, I didn't see where either word applied." The girl was not dumb, she had some schooling, I could tell by her elucidation. That was the same name that Lord Dunraven had left his money to. Well, well, I just made my decision, they would not get the money.

The two leeches at the bar were getting nervous. The manager came over, "What can I do for you, Sir?"

I said, "Do you see those two at the end of the bar? He looked.

"Are they regular customers? I asked.

"Yes, they come in here often."

"Do you know what they are?" He started to turn red. He cleared his throat. "I see by your reaction, that you do." I said.

"Yes Sir. But it is not my fault, the owner of the Hotel said it was alright if they plied their wares here, I think he gets a kick-back, not me."

"Where is the owner of the Hotel?"

"He is setting at the other end of the bar. That fat man

with the silk top hat on."

"Would you please ask him to come over here? If he doesn't want to, tell him it's a matter of life and death, his."

"Yes Sir, I will." He turned and hurried over to the fat man. He whispered in his ear, the fat pig gave me a stare out of his narrow set eyes. Then slid off of the bar stool and waddled over to my table.

"What can I do for you?" He said, with a wheeze.

"Are you a pimp?" I asked. His breathing got worse.

"No, I am not."

"How can you say that you are not, when you take a kick-back from those brothel owners setting at the end of the bar?" He got redder and redder, I thought he was going to have a heart attack. Guess what, he did. He fell down, grabbing his chest. The bar manager ran over, along with the bar maid. We gathered around him, of course there was nothing we could do, or wanted to.

The pimps came over and took the girl by the arm, I whirled and laid my blade up against the big man's throat. "Are you an apple tree? You are about ready to lose your apple, Adam." He dropped her arm. "I suggest you take Eve, here, and go back to your garden while you still live there. Because I think you're about to be kicked out of your paradise."

Of course like all big men, they only learn from the school of hard knocks. He started to turn away, then swung back and tried to kick me in the groin. My Sioux blood came through, I left his Adam's Apple alone, his lower appendage was my target, he would not be fathering any more little pimps. His woman had her hand on it, trying to staunch the flow of blood. Good thing there was a Hospital close. When everything calmed down. I asked the manager if the previous owner had any kin. Turns out he didn't. I told him to keep me informed when the Hotel came up for sale, I might be interested. Then I looked at the girl that was the cause of all of this mess, "What's your name?" I asked.

"Carleen O'Reilly, it is Sir."

"Well Carleen, it looks like we are stuck with you. My wife's name is Lizzy. We have another girl that is in our charge, her name is Louisa Washington, you will like her, she can be your sister." About that time, in they walk. It took me a while to explain, like half the night.

We were just leaving the bar, when the Police finally showed up and started asking questions. I didn't feel like talking, so I just pressed a hundred dollar bill in the Sergeant's palm. He smiled and asked if there was anything else he could do for me. I told him probably. That we had some business here that we might need some help with, he said to just ask for Sean. I said I would.

We had two adjoining rooms. So it was no problem with Carleen, she could bunk with Louisa. You could tell Carleen probably came from a poor close nit family, cause she had no compunction about taking her clothes off in front of people. That more or less came from all the family living in a one room house in Ireland. When Lizzy said it was time to get ready for bed, she, Carleen just pulled her dress off over her head. Only problem was, she wasn't wearing any under clothes.

Now she was a mite smaller than either Lizzy or Louisa, so the night shirt that Lizzy gave her was sort of an over kill. She looked like what she was, an orphan waif. But I bet she wouldn't look that way for long, that is after they went shopping on the morrow.

Growing up back on the ranch, it was all boys, that is except Ma. This all female house-hold would take me a little time to get used to all the female fuss. Now I'm not saying I didn't like it, cause I did. But just the same, they were sure full of surprises. I don't know what they considered me to be, but they took no note of me being a male. Thinking about it, that didn't bother me much either. The view sure was fine.

The next morning after breakfast we all went shopping. Now when I say all, I mean they went shopping. Now me, I spied a park across the street. I told them to just go ahead and shop, when they got done, I would be sitting over in the park, contemplating my bad ways. Of course of which I had none, being so perfect.

I picked my way across the shit laded street. Now I don't mind the smell of a good clean barnyard. Or even the smell of a stockyard, like in Chicago. But this New York had a stink all of its own. I don't think all of that manure in the street came from all the horse traffic. I suspect some of it was human in nature. Now the good Lord never intended for humans to gather up in such a big pile of crap that this New York City was. It sent shivers down my spine.

I wasn't the only one seeking respite in the green of the park. There were many men, reading their morning paper and smoking their cigars or pipes. One such gentleman was sitting on a bench by himself. He was sucking on a cigar, with his legs stuck out in front of him, like maybe he was trying to trip somebody. Which perhaps he was. He had a devil may care twinkle in his eyes. I liked him right off. I said, "Well Sir, I see by your demeanor, that you don't want any company. So I says to myself, since I don't want any company either, then there might as well be two of us setting there, not wanting any company."

He looked up at me, "Yes Sir, you are a man after my own heart, I like people that tell it like it is. My name is Sam. And since we are of a like mind, sit down stranger."

J.D. Oliver

As I sat down, I stuck out my paw, "My name is Buck, Buck Gentry, from Wyoming Territory, to be more precise, the South Fork of the Shoshone."

He shook my hand, then said, "My full name is Samuel Clemens, I hail from Hannibal, Missouri, on the Mississippi River. What are you doing in New York, Buck?"

"My wife has some business to take care of here. I am here to make sure she is not taken advantage of, although I am quite sure she can whip her weight in wild cats. But while she is doing that, there is always the danger of a Rattlesnake sneaking up behind her."

"Well there are a lot of sneaky snakes in New York, you are wise to take precautions. Now me, I am here on account of my wife, Livy, she is from Elmira, New York. We've only been wed two years. We are in the City doing a little shopping. We have a boy, a year old, Langdon is his name, he is the apple of my eye."

"I am glad for you Sam, what do you do for a living? If you don't mind me asking."

"I was a river boat pilot on the Mississippi. Till I became a writer."

"Well we do have something in common, you're a writer and I'm a reader, where would one be without the other?" I said. When he got done laughing, I added, "What are some of the books that you have written?"

"Well in Sixty-Seven I wrote the Celebrated Jumping Frog of Calaveras County, then in Sixty-nine, I wrote Innocents Abroad. Along with a lot of other twaddle. But let me ask you Buck, what do you do for a living?"

"I kill people," He looked shocked, so I added, "But only those that need it, if they aren't really bad people, I just make them wish they were dead." I gave him my really innocent look. He stared for a few seconds then broke out in loud guffaws. He laughed so hard that he dropped his cigar. I stomped it out before it caught the grass a fire.

"No seriously, what do you do to make money?" He finally asked.

"Not much, I dug a lot of gold out of the earth, now I just follow my wife around, like a little puppy dog." He started laughing again. That man sure could laugh. I said, "Where can a man get copies of your books?"

"See there, across the street, that bookstore? But I use a pen name, It's Mark Twain."

He went on about a few other things he had written, all the while I was looking into his soul. Right now his life was going pretty good. But I could see there was a sadness coming. I could also see that he didn't know I was half Sioux. I went back further into his mind, he didn't like Indians. He felt sorry for how the blacks were treated. Oh well, no body's perfect, I still liked him. I would read his books. I shook my head, what was I doing looking into his mind, why had I done that? I really didn't even know I could. I also knew I wasn't going to do that again, unless I really had to. It takes all the mystery out of people. And hell that's half the fun.

I seen my family coming across the stinky street and William Custer was with them. Custer said, "I see you have met Samuel Clemens." Then he said, "Good Morning Mr. Clemens, this is Elizabeth Drake-Gentry, I think you know her half brother, Ardel Drake? These other two ladies are Louisa Washington and Carleen O'Reilly, Mr. And Mrs. Gentry are their guardians."

Sam stood up and bowed over Elizabeth's hand, kissing it, he said. "It is an honor to meet such a lovely lady and so rich a one, also." Then he did the same with our charges, that is kiss their hands.

He turned back to Elizabeth and said, "I have been visiting with your husband, a most unusual fellow and funny too. He said he kills people for a living, isn't that funny?"

"Oh, he told you that, did he? Well don't you believe him, he only kills half of them, I get to kill half, after all marriage is fifty-fifty." That broke Sam up in laughter too. When he had recovered, Elizabeth added, "Mr. Clemens you mentioned I was rich, how so?"

"Why, its common knowledge, you and your half brother are heirs to one of England's biggest fortunes. Didn't you know?"

"I knew I was an heiress to something, but I didn't know how big it was. I really didn't even know I was an heiress, until Mr. Custer here was hired to kill me."

Sam started to laugh again, "You people are so funny, I am going to have to write a story about you folks. Mr. Custer was hired to kill, hilarious. One of Pinkerton's best, hired to kill you." I thought he was going to choke he was laughing so hard.

They say laughter is good for you, so maybe we added a few years to his life. Anyway we left him laughing. We would probably see him again before we left. We went over to the hotel's restaurant with Mr. Custer. After we ordered, we got down to brass tacks.

"Mr. Custer have you been in touch with Ardel, or the lawyers?" I asked.

"Yes, with both. I have a meeting set up for eleven in the morning, in the lawyer's office. And then one set up to meet Ardel Drake at two in the afternoon at the country club."

"Does he know that Elizabeth is alive, that you didn't kill her?"

"I told him she was here, that I would bring her to the

meeting with me. He knows nothing of you. I don't trust him, he may try and kill her, not in front me of course."

"Why not? Didn't he hire you to kill her? He may just try it, right in front of you. I think I will go as her agent. She can wait outside the door till I invite her in. What do you think?"

"Yeah, but I am sure I can protect her."

"Hell you couldn't even kill her, much less protect her."

"Buck, cut him some slack, he was up against the best. And you are the best, Dear."

"Thank you, Sweetheart, but I plan on keeping you alive, so we will do it my way. Bill please do it, like I said. And I will let you keep what's left of the fifty thousand. If you don't you won't need the money anyway, do you get my drift?"

"Yes, Mr. Gentry, I do. I know I made a mistake and it was wrong. But I am not a bad man, if you will remember, it wasn't me that pulled the trigger on that rifle."

"I know that Bill, I trust you, but I don't trust this Ardel Drake. I think he will try something. He knows she is still alive, I think he will have his ace in a hole and I want to make sure it's an ace of spades with his name on it."

"The food is coming, the food is coming." Carleen said. Squirming in her seat. She knew what was important in life. 'Food.'

Louisa was helping her with the proper fork selection. I just picked up the biggest one and dug in. Everyone was staring at me. I didn't care, I was hungry. When I was paying for the food, I would eat it anyway I wanted to. That is till my wife said, "Put that fork down and use the salad fork, it's the smaller one." I did what I was told.

After lunch we went back to our room, Bill went home. I asked them where all the clothes were, they went shopping didn't they? The packages were to be delivered this afternoon. I went and laid down, till I heard the knock on the door. I jumped up, Lizzy was just about to open the door, I said, "Stop, don't open that door, let me. It might not be whom you think it is."

She stepped back. I jerked the door open and grabbed the man standing there by the neck. Yeah, that's right, it was only the delivery man. I gave him a big tip. He went away rubbing his throat, but he was smiling.

The rest of the afternoon was spent with giggling females trying on clothes. That evening we went to the opera, yeah that's right, the opera. I couldn't understand a word they said, but the women acted like they had died and gone to heaven. I spent more time watching the audience than the play. My eye was drawn to a box a couple of box's over. There was an obnoxious fellow with two underdressed women. They were drinking what looked like some kind of wine. The usher had to ask them to be quiet a couple of times. He would slip his hand under their dresses. They would giggle and wiggle. Oh, yeah, they were having fun. But there was something about him that seemed familiar. I glanced at Lizzy and then back to him. Yeah, it could be, I bet it was. But how could siblings be so different, even half siblings?

Lizzy and the girls were paying rapt attention to the Opera. I wasn't. Lizzy had some light freckles on her shoulders. I was busy counting them. I was up to fifty, when she kicked me.

"Will you pay attention," she whispered, "I swear your attention span is like a two year old." I stuck my tongue out at her. She kicked me again. That's alright my shins were starting to get calluses. I made a concerted effort to pay attention. Despite my concocted indifference, it was starting to make a little sense. Anyway they sure could yell.

When it was all over and everyone was milling in the lobby, I got a chance to get close to Lizzy's half brother. He was still groping his women companions. But two men came up to them and one said, "Come on Sir, it's time to get you home, you have a big day tomorrow." Then they escorted the trio out. The men were more than just footmen, they were body guards. Good to know.

Lizzy had her arm through mine, the two girls on either side, their eyes were glowing. It made me happy to see them happy. Yeah the big city was exciting. A nice place to visit, but I wouldn't want to live here. I missed the wide open spaces.

I was watching the crowd, good thing, cause I spotted one well dressed fellow that was doing the same thing. His eyes were darting all around. He was looking to score. A pickpocket if I ever seen one. And I never had seen one, being a hick from the sticks. But I wasn't stupid. But he didn't have a companion with him. A man by himself at the Opera? That was an oxymoron.

I wasn't mistaken, he made his snatch from an older gentleman, the man didn't even notice. As the pickpocket came by me, I grabbed him by the nape of the neck and lifted him off of the floor. Holding him up, I walked over to the older gentleman, "Give it back to him." I said. He handed the man back his wallet. I shook him like a dog. "Ok, now empty your pockets." He did.

A Policeman rushed over, and took my burden from me. Another Policeman gathered up the crooks plunder from the floor. The gentleman said to me. "I want to thank you young man, my name is Judge Fellows. If there is ever anything that I can do for you, just ask. And your name is?"

"It's Phillip Gentry the Second, Sir. And let me

introduce my wife, Elizabeth Drake-Gentry. And these are our adopted daughters, Louisa Washington. And the rambunctious young woman is, Carleen O'Reilly.

"Drake? Are you any relation to Ardel Drake, the man who just left?"

"I am afraid she is, he is her half brother. We have a meeting with him on the morrow, over an inheritance, I believe."

"Yes, yes, quite, I believe it is coming up before me to adjudicate, I was under the impression that Elizabeth Drake was deceased? I believe it's to appear on my docket the day after tomorrow."

"Well as you can see Judge, she is alive and well and she has in her possession her birth certificate. We have a meeting set up with Ardel tomorrow. Perhaps there won't be a need to go to court, then again, it might be best to get an official ruling, so this can be put to rest."

"Yes, quite. I will be looking forward to helping you both with this case.

We got back to our room without anymore exciting distractions. Unless of course, you don't take into account walking behind your wife as she ascended the stairs to our room. A prelude to ecstasy.

As the sun rose the next morning so did the smell from the street below. I got up and shut the window. We lay there, entwined, listening to the girls in the next room. They were telling each other about their childhood. Twernt much difference between the Irish in Ireland and the Negro in North America. Both of them were persecuted and poor. But isn't that the way with most minorities?

We got up and put on our robes, opening our door, we went into the common room. The girls were comfortable with each other now, since they were sitting there with no clothes on. I put my hand over my eyes and said, "Come on girls, put some clothes on, I know we're family but really have a little mercy on an old man."

"Aye, and ye be not that old, Uncle. We hear the both of you in the night, we like to not of got nary a bit of sleep." Said Carleen. Then they both bounced off to get dressed.

Lizzy looked at me and winked, "And just so you know, Smarty, you won't be getting any sleep this night either." She said to their butts as they disappeared into their room.

I said, "Was that a promise?"

"You wish." She said. How come women always make out it's the man that wants sex. When really it's them, or they wouldn't go along with it?"

The girls went with us to the eleven o'clock meeting with the lawyers. We thought they might as well know what was going on. Mr. Custer had come by our Hotel around ten. We were shown in promptly. We were all dressed to the nines. To the nines was a saying I heard at the opera, I heard a couple of men talking. Anyway to go on. The Lawyers were real polite to us. There must be a lot of money involved.

There were three of them. The oldest said, "Miss Drake, maybe we could see your birth certificate?"

I said, "Sure you may, but first be advised Elizabeth is my wife, her full name is: Elizabeth Drake-Gentry, My name is: Phillip Gentry the Second. You may proceed now."

Elizabeth handed him her birth certificate. He looked it over and said, "Yes, it seems to be in order, but there is a little smudge here beside one signature, I don't know?"

I took the certificate and looked at it, then I looked at him. "That smudge is nothing, I can read the signature alright, are you having trouble with your eyes?" Then I sat on the corner of his desk and hitched my .44 around. He looked at me, then said, "On second thought, I see no problem with the certificate. Your wife is entitled to the entire inheritance. As the older sibling. I am afraid Ardel will be very disappointed, he will be penniless."

"Ok, just what does this inheritance consist of?"

"All the property in both the United States and England. Including the monies deposited in the Bank of England, as well as here in New York. A very considerable sum, I am afraid."

I looked at Lizzy, she cleared her throat and said, "I would like an accounting of the total holdings. Here in the United States and in England, split up by country. Can you do that?"

"Yes, yes, I am sure we can, it might take a few days, but it can be done. Give us tell Wednesday next week." The gray headed lawyer said.

"Oh, I afraid that won't do, you see I know that Judge Fellows has a hearing on this tomorrow. And since this was already set up, when you thought I was dead. I am sure you will be there with the needed facts," said my wife. Then she stood up, smiling sweetly she wished them a good day. We three followed her out. Bill came trailing after.

I said, "Well that went well, how about lunch, Bill do you know of a good and expensive place?" He said he did. It was called DeMarcos. We got a chance to use our new found manners. They were a pretty snooty bunch. I enjoyed every minute of it, turns out I was a good actor, I even used an English accent. It was all the girls could do to keep from losing their composure. Bill was enjoying the show as well as the food.

We made the lunch last till it was time to go to our two o'clock meeting. But first we took our girls back to the hotel.

When we got to the country club, Ardel was already there. He was seated at a table by himself. The waitress showed us to his table.

He looked up and his face went pale, or anyway paler than it had been. He knew who Elizabeth was, there was no doubt. He said, "I thought she was dead, you were paid...." Then his mouth snapped shut.

"No Brother, I am not dead. But I see you are about ready to have heart failure. Don't worry, I am not going to kill you. But I might kill those two goons over there, if you don't call them off."

I walked over to the same two guys I seen at the opera. They were sitting at another table. "Do you two want to live to take another breath?" They nodded their heads. "Good, shuck your weapons on the table, then walk out of here, go home and count your blessings."

They did as they were told. Saying on the way out, "We always thought he was a weak Johnny, but the pay was good."

I picked up their pistols, knives and brass knuckles. Took a napkin and made a nap sack out of them. Get it, napkin, nap sack. Oh well, I thought it was good.

Setting back down, I said, "Well brother-in-law, it's good to finally meet you. Be nice and you will live to see another day. Say one disrespectful word to my wife and I will slit your throat." He started to turn purple, way past pale.

Lizzy took his hand in hers, "Don't worry Ardel, he will not kill you. But you have been a bad boy. You need to be punished. What shall I do with you? I know, you are your own worst enemy. You should be left to make yourself miserable. I know, I am going to split the inheritance. Everything in England will be yours, everything here in the United States will be mine. The only requirement is, that you must go back to

J.D. Oliver

England and never come back to my country again. What do you think, can you do that?" All he could do was nod his head, his mouth working. "Ok then, Ardel, we will see you in court tomorrow." Lizzy said as she patted him on the head.

In court the next day, the lawyers were there, with the needed information. It turned out the lion share of the estate was here in New York. He was planning on moving here, so he had transferred most of the money here. But he had large real estate holdings in England. Maybe he would be land poor, lets hope so anyway. He also had bought a large house and acreage here in New York state. At Elmira, in fact. Close by the Langdon house.

Ardel sailed for England on the next ship out. We bought a carriage with a matched set of Morgans. And loaded up all of our stuff and headed for Elmira. We were very glad to get out of the stinking city.

We spent the rest of the summer at Drake's Rest, that was what we named our property at Elmira. We got to know Sam and Livy well. He was a hoot. But Livy kept him in control.

Before the leaves started blushing, I was getting restless. It was time to go home. But it wasn't as easy at that, the girls wanted to stay. Lizzy and I spent many long nights getting our minds around that. But really, they would be out of place back on the frontier. They knew how to be good hostesses. They knew nothing of survival, I mean of killing or being killed. Yes, we decided they should stay. We had hired a good staff, they came well recommended.

Our housekeeper, or I guess you could call her our home manager, was a freed slave. Her husband was one also, he handled everything else. As you can well imagine, Lizzy and me, we didn't do one damn thing around the place. Why? Well

167

as far as I could figure, we sort of felt like fish out of water. Temporary residents you might say. The housekeeper's name was Anana and her husband was Abu Obote. They were sort of the Grandparents the girls never had.

We waited till after breakfast, then called them all together. We had discussed this ahead of time with the girls. But it would be a big surprise to Anana and Abu. I asked them.

"Are you both happy here?"

Anana answered, After looking quickly at her husband, "Yes, of course we are, are you happy with us?" More glances at her husband.

"You know we are, but you're probably wondering why I was asking. To get right to the point. Lizzy and I plan on going back to Wyoming. The girls don't want to go. They like it here and they like the both of you. What we want to know is, would the two of you be willing to stay on and take care of Carleen and Louisa?"

With a big sigh of relief, Anana said. "Yes, Oh yes, we would. How long do you plan on being gone?"

Lizzy said, "We don't know for sure. Life on the frontier is iffy at times. Who knows, it might be forever. That is, if we go under. Somebody might shoot faster and straighter than us. But we will set up a trust fund that will be more than sufficient to run this place and take care of all of the financial needs of the four of you. For life."

"How will that work?" Abu asked.

"We know how silly young girls can be at times. So till the girls reach the age of 25, the two of you will have to oversee their needs. Then their individual trust funds will kick in. We have already took care of the details with the banker. You both will be taken care of for life." Lizzy said. Then added. "If you don't hear from us within five years, the banker has instructions to put this property and funds in his bank, in your names."

They were more than a little flabbergasted at the reversal of their fortunes. Going from being a slave with nothing to running the show. Paradise right? Far from it. Along with affluence, comes responsibility. You see, power corrupts, total power, totally corrupts. The banker also has instructions to keep an eye out for any off the shelf behavior. Any good rifle also has a safety.

But I had every faith in them, or I wouldn't be leaving the girls or the property with them. We left two days later. Amid a flood of tears. Ours, not theirs. Oh, they had misty eyes, or were they tears of gladness? That's unfair, of course they were sad to see us go, who else could they look to for comic relief?

We took the stage back to New York City. Bill Custer met us. We went directly to our coach. It was as we left it. Bill had even had it stocked with fresh food and water. The train left two hours after we got there.

But we did have time to catch up on Bill's life. He had quit Pinkerton's. He had started his own agency. Said he had all kinds of clients and he didn't even have to leave the city. We wished him well. We spent that night wrapped in each others' arms. Pretty soon the clackity-clack of the rails put us to sleep.

We arrived in Philadelphia the next morning. After we made arrangement's for our coach, and before we looked up Charlene, we took a stage to Williamsport. If you will remember, that was where my Father was supposed to be, we would see.

The town was a goodly size for the time. Tree lined streets, a nice settled town. We went to the hotel. Booked a suite on the top floor. We were taking it nice and slow. I had registered under the name of Mr. and Mrs. Buck Gentry, they didn't blink. It was the next day before I inquired if they knew a Sir Phillip Gentry?

Turns out they did. Said he lived on a large estate about five miles north of town. They gave us directions. It was two days later before I got up nerve enough. We rented a couple of Morgans, they had a good gate.

We rode out in mid-morning. Fertile green fields lay beside the tree lined road. Nice...

We came to a high gate with the name Gentry over it. We rode through. A shady lane leading up to a large house. A young girl was playing with a large dog on the lawn. She stopped playing, the dog ran toward us, barking. Then when he got close, I gave a low whistle, he stopped and wagged his tail.

The girl was about six years old, blond and pretty. Lizzy said, "Is your Daddy or Mommy home?"

The girl said, "How did you make Blackie stop barking? He usually tries to bite strangers. But Yes, they are both home, won't you come in?"

We dismounted and tied our horses to the hitching rack. Blackie was licking my hand. I asked the little girls name. "It's Millie, Sir. May I ask yours?"

"I'm Buck, this is Lizzy my wife. We have come a long way to see your Father."

We followed her into the house. She was calling, "Daddy, Mommy, we have company."

A middle aged man came through, what I assumed was the kitchen door, a younger looking woman followed him. Millie said, "Buck and Lizzy want to see you."

He looked at us with a question in his eyes, "Yes, I am Phillip Gentry, how can I help you? Oh, excuse me, where are my manners, this is my wife Phyllis and you have already met our youngest child."

J.D. Oliver

"This is my wife, Elizabeth Drake, my name is Buck."

"What can I do for you Mr. Drake?"

"We are from Wyoming Territory, the south fork of the Shoshone, Cheyenne and lately of Denver. Are you familiar with that area?"

"Strangely enough, I am. I used to travel that area quite extensively. At one time I thought I would live there, but things changed. I was just having some coffee, would you both like some?"

"Why yes, we would." Lizzy said.

"Good, do you mind having it in the kitchen?"

"Why no, that is my favorite room." I said. Phyllis poured us some coffee and set out some bear sign (doughnuts). They were good. As we made small talk, he was looking at me. Finally he said, "Mr. Drake, forgive me, but are you part Sioux?"

"Why do you ask?" I said.

"I used to live with the Sioux, you favor them."

"You have a good eye, Sir. Yes I am part Sioux."

"May I ask your mother's name?"

I looked at my wife, took a long breath and said, "Yes, I guess you can ask me."

He looked confused, "Uh, then, what is your Mother's name?"

"It's 'She Who See's The Light'."

He dropped his coffee cup. "How can that be, she died when she was a young woman, she didn't have but one child, he died when she did?"

"Did he?" I said.

"No, that's not possible, he would only be about thirteen years old, you're in your middle twenties, if you're a day."

"I am afraid it is true, Sir. I am only thirteen years old,

171

in lunar years. And yes, you are my Father. You see, Grandfather didn't like you, he lied when he told you I died. He put me beside the trail, a couple from Texas picked me up. Old Man Coyote told me all about it. I can't explain it any better than that. Because what I am can't be explained. But believe me I do exist, I am not a spirit. Here feel me, I am flesh and blood."

"But, but, all these years. I thought you were dead. I just don't know."

Lizzy spoke up. "Let me make this clear, we do not want anything from you, we do not plan on interfering with your life in anyway, Buck, or should I say Phillip Gentry the second, just wanted to see his Father. I can see by your wife's eyes that she feels threatened. Please do not feel that way. We are on our way back to our country."

Phyllis spoke up and said. "You say that now, but you can see that we are well off, I am sure you want money."

Lizzy said, "No, we don't want any of your property, in fact we could buy and sell all you own. Do you not recognize the name Drake? And besides that your son is rich in his own right."

Sir Phillip said, "Please Phyllis, sit down and be quite, he is who he says he is, I knew it the minute I seen him. It just took me a while to admit it to myself. Please Son, don't mind her." I didn't, but---

To make a long story short, it was the reunion that I had hoped for. And Phyllis came around, after a bit. Besides Millie, there was a boy ten years old, Harold. And another girl, eight, Stella. I think Lizzy was just as entranced with our new family as I was. Our else she was an awfully good actress.

Chapter Ten

A day turned into a week, a week turned into a month, the fall turned into winter. I didn't forget about Charlene Russell, I sent her a message that it would be spring before we left for home. She sent one back, saying, "That would be fine". When we did leave, she would be the only one going. The children would be staying with Charlie's family.

As I said before, Phyllis did come around, of a sort. She accepted us, but you could tell that she wasn't happy about it. I didn't blame her. Most women would react the same. Women are nesters, and anything that disturbed their nest, was suspect. I wondered how Lizzy would react in the same situation? I think she would take it right in stride. It was early December, it was snowing. We were upstairs in our suite. A big bedroom with a setting room with its own pot bellied heater. It was warm and cozy. Lizzy was setting in front of her dressing mirror, nude as usual. I lay in bed watching her brushing her hair. She was humming some tune to herself. Eve could not of been any prettier than she was.

I asked her, "Lizzy, you sound happy and contented, are you?"

She stopped brushing, turning, she said, "How can you ask that, don't you know? Of course I am. I am a woman, and believe me, if I wasn't happy you would know about it."

"I suppose so, but it's just that we have been on the move ever since we got married. Most women would want a home of their own. And I don't mean our railroad coach."

"I have one, in Denver, have you forgotten?"

"Well I haven't exactly forgotten. But it seems so far in the past. Even our house in Elmira, seems unreal. Everything that has happened is as a foggy dream. That is except you and me, that is crystal clear."

She glanced out the window, "Oh, it's snowing harder." She got up and went to the window. I followed her. She was right, the flakes were big and soft, floating down like pie plates. The gas lights along the drive way were a good backdrop for the dancing of the snow fairies. I walked back to the lamp and turned it down, so it wouldn't frame my naked wife in its light.

There was a light knock on our door. Lizzy threw on a red velvet robe and went to the door. The children were there with a tray of hot chocolate and cookies.

Millie said, after we had consumed the treats. "We are going to cut our Christmas Tree tomorrow, you're coming aren't you?"

Stella and Harold chimed in, "Yes, please do. The whole family goes, it's our tradition."

Lizzy and I looked at each other. Christmas? That was something we had not discussed. I could take it, or leave it. But I knew Mee-Ling's family probably didn't observe it. But she said, "Sure, we would be glad to, wouldn't we Buck?"

"Yes, I guess so, Ma always read the story from the Bible on Christmas Eve. Otherwise we didn't do much, but I'm always open to any party."

The five of us walked over to the window and watched the snow. It was mesmerizing. The spell was broken by Dad coming in. Yep, even I was starting to get used to calling him that. Lizzy started calling him that long before I did tho.

"Hey you three, it's bed time. That is if you want to go cut that tree in the morning."

After breakfast, Lizzy and I went back to our room to put warm clothes on. Out of habit I stuck one of those small pistol's of Dunraven's in my coat pocket. Of course my Bowie, as always, was on its strap down on the back of my neck. Habit is a hard thing to break. Now habit can be good, or it can be bad.

Now habit is bad if, for instance, you always took the same trail when you went hunting. That could get you killed, the Shoshones showed me that. What about good habit? Well for instance, that pistol in my pocket, that was good. And Oh yes, kiss your wife every chance you got, now that was really a good habit. Tasted good too!

The snow lay two foot deep on the level. We hooked a four horse team to a large hay sled, that was about one third full. Enough hay to keep us warm. The women and children did just that, snuggled under the hay. We had to go about ten miles to a small forest of Pine trees. Dad drove and I sat beside him. We talked.

I said, "Everything seems pretty peaceful here. Not many criminals around here I take it?"

"No, but there is a prison on the other side of Williamsport. Sometimes they escape, not often tho. But you know people are people. There are bad ones and good ones wherever you live."

"Yes, I know that. But it seems a lot of the bad ones are moving west. Or maybe its just the lack of restraint on the frontier. A lot of times if people think they won't get caught, they are more liable to commit crimes."

"Yes Son, I believe that is true. But if you raise up a child in the right way, it should stick with them. Sometimes tho, kids go bad, no matter how they were raised. They way it looks your foster parents did a good job with you."

"Yeah Ma and Pa did their best, but I think genetics have a lot to do with it."

"Some, yeah some, but who knows, I guess God does." Dad said.

"I think you're right, Old Man Coyote taught me a lot." Dad looked at me funny. "Not just him," I said, "The Great Spirit, Jehovah God is the one who sent him to see me." Dad really gave me a strange look. Yeah, even tho he was my Dad, we were different. He must have forgotten whatever my real Mother taught him. Or maybe he didn't listen too good.

You see, everything was created, and everything has a lesson to teach, if you listen. Funny tho, white people don't seem to be able to hear what the hills have to say. Hell they don't even pay attention to Old Man Coyote. I didn't mind tho, heck, even white folk were created, they must have some purpose.

When we got to the pine trees, there were several sleds already there, neighbors. Turned into a little party right there on the hillside. Along with the hot cider and scones everyone had brought. Lizzy and I got a few looks, but overall they accepted us. Dad introduced us, as his long lost son and his wife. Of course it helped that Dad was one of the biggest land holders around. Like always, wealth talks. Sad, real sad, when used in the wrong way. But a useful tool when used right.

Now what did all that have to do with cutting a Christmas Tree? Oh, I remember, it all started with the looks Lizzy and I got. Now you can see how easy it is to head off at a tangent. But isn't that the way life is, just a series of tangents?

I shook my head and focused real hard. One big old fat lady was coming through the snow dragging a tree that was not quite as big as she was. I asked if she needed any help. She said, "Nope, this little twig ain't nothin, why Son I could drag that tree over yonder with you on top of it." I just nodded, she went tootin' by, I just made sure she didn't run over me.

"Come on Buck," Harold said, "We found the tree we want, we want you to cut it down."

"You want me to murder that tree?"

"Huh? What do you mean, murder that tree?"

"Don't you know that tree is alive?"

"Sure, but not like us."

"You're right, it's not like us, but it is still alive. We will have to ask the Great Spirit's forgiveness for cutting it down." I followed him. It was a nice tree. I said, "Now's who going to do the asking?"

Dad said, "What do you mean, asking?"

"Well for cutting this tree down, someone's got to ask the Great Spirit forgiveness for killing it." They all looked at me. "Ok, then I will." I was sort of spoofing them, just a little, a silent prayer would of done it, but heck, when you have an audience, you might just as well play to it. So I started a chant and dance. Around the tree I went, I would of made a good medicine man. Lizzy was holding her hand over her mouth, to keep from laughing. Dad had a big smile on his face. He knew what I was doing. I stopped, then said, "Ok, now you can cut it down." All the other neighbors were staring at me. I bowed. They all clapped. I guess I wasn't fooling them any. Oh well, it was fun.

The trip home was even more fun. They were all singing, not me or Lizzy, we didn't know any of their jingles. We were snuggled under the hay, now that was fun. We were home just after the noon hour. We had the tree up before dark. It was after supper when the tree trimming got underway.

We used popcorn, dried berries, candles. Just about anything. They had some ornaments that were store bought. The kids had made an angel out of plaster, did a pretty good job. It was put on top of the tree. It was nice to feel like a family again. What do I mean again? I never had a family like this. Lizzy was beaming, I guess she was liking it too.

That night in bed, we just held onto each other, afraid to let go, afraid it would all disappear. Sleep found us, the dreams were good. We spent the winter in our own little fairy land. Christmas came and went. They had the custom of giving presents to each other. We did likewise. Didn't make a whole lot of sense. Wouldn't it be better to give gifts all the year around? Why just at one time of the year? Anyway we didn't upset the apple cart.

There came a day when the water started dripping off of the roof. Two weeks later we made ready. They all tried to talk us into staying, that all included Phyllis. I guess we grew on people. Damn, I hated to leave. But trouble was calling to me and I was its handmaiden.

I thought back to my vision quest, yes there was trouble in our future. Things I could not sidestep. But what I couldn't understand was that my visions only went so far. Could it be that maybe my death was why they ended? I knew what I had to do, but I sure wasn't looking forward to it.

Dad and Harold accompanied us by stage back to Philadelphia. Millie and Stella wanted to go also. But Dad said no. Harold was excited by the trip, as any eleven year old would be. Yes he had a birthday. Now me, I had a fairly good idea when I was born, within a few months. But I wouldn't celebrate my birthday anyway. Age is only relative to your aches and pains.

Harold could hardly sit still. He was up and down, from one side of the stage to the other. Asking questions, galore. It kept Lizzy busy answering. I sat opposite them. I noticed a slight bulge in Dads coat. I asked "What kind of a firearm are you carrying?"

"It's just a five shot, .36 caliber. I never travel without one."

"A good idea, it gives a person a little confidence. And sometimes confidence is all you need. Criminals prey on the weak."

"You've noticed that too, have you?"

"Yes, a quiet, calm, self-assured manner, averts a lot of trouble." I said.

Dad thought a minute and then said, "I have noticed that your speech denotes a good education, you speak as if you graduated college."

"Do I? Well I guess you could blame Ma for that. She was my only school Marm. How did you like that colloquialism? Marm? I am very fond of colloquialism's. Even cliché's. I find a lot of wisdom in them."

"Then you believe life is wisdom?"

"I believe the creator of life showed a lot of wisdom in making man, in fact like the Bible says, we are wonderfully made."

"Yes, too bad we have twisted it so." Dad said, then fell silent looking out the window.

After a while, when I could get a word in edgewise, through Harold's constant chatter. I said to Dad. "You look a little sad, what are you thinking about?"

"The past, your mother, I really loved her, you know? I still dream about her at times. Not that I don't love Phyllis, I do.

But you never forget your first love."

"You don't have to forget her, she lives because you do remember. In the long run, that is all we have, our memories."

"I know that Son, but flesh and blood is still flesh and blood. And it sure feels good to snuggle up to on a cold night."

"Doesn't it tho," I said as I squeezed Lizzy's hand. She squeezed right back. Then the stage took a lurch and slowed to a stop.

"Hands up and throw down that mail bag." A male voice said.

A hold up? In the civilized east?

"All of you in there, get down and hold your hands high." The same voice.

We did as told, for the minute. I had no intentions of letting them rob us. Not that I would miss the money and foo-fa-raw. It was just the principal of the thing. There were three of them. Two big fellows with bandanna's over their faces and one smaller one, she was standing back and shaking, Yep, it was a she and by the curves, not too bad. The little pistol in her hand was shaking so bad, she couldn't of hit the broad side of a barn anyway. I glanced at Lizzy and nodded toward the woman. Meaning, that one was Lizzy's problem.

One of big fellows told the woman to get our plunder. Of course he didn't use the word plunder. The woman came close, Lizzy grabbed her and flicked the gun from her hand, then held her as a shield. I shot through my coat pocket. I got one, then another shot, Dad got the other one. They were both clean head shots. The woman was hysterical. Lizzy pinched the base of her neck. She went limp, between us, we lifted her into the coach and sat her up in the corner.

The stage driver and his shotgun guard got down and pulled them out of the roadway. By their clothes, they were escaped convicts. The stage driver said, "What are you going to do with that one you put in the stage?"

"I don't know, finders, keepers, I reckon. When she comes to, we'll see. What are you going to do with those two dead ones?" I asked.

"We'll let the Sheriff know at the next town, he can come get them."

So, we all got back in and went merrily on our way. For once, Harold was quiet. Lizzy pulled the bandanna from the women's face. She was young and pretty. Her clothes were well worn, but clean. She stirred, then her eyes opened. Lizzy said. "Welcome to the rest of your life. Now it can be short or you can live to see your grandchildren. It's up to you. What were you doing with those men?"

"One was my step-brother. He showed up at the orphanage this morning. They forced me to go with them. The other one said he was going to do me, whatever that meant, kill me I guess. They said that I had to help them."

"Just for your information, 'do me', didn't mean to kill you, he was going to rape you. What's your name? And how old are you?" Lizzy asked.

"It's Cora MacFie and I'm fourteen years old."

"Oh, it's a wee lassie we have here," Dad said. "You two corralled her, what are you going to do with her?"

I said, "I don't know, we're going to have to ponder on that awhile. What do you think Lizzy?"

"Well we could take her back to the orphanage. Or maybe just let the law take care of her. What do you think Cora, what should we do with you?"

"I don't know, I don't want to go to jail, they forced me to take part. I don't like the orphanage either."

Harold found his tongue, "Dad, can we keep her, it

don't look like she would eat much?"

"Harold she's not a dog or cat, she's human. How about it Cora, would you like to come live with us? We have two more daughters at home and of course my wife, Phyllis."

"You mean a real home and family? Yes, of course I will, what would be my duties?"

"Duties? Well you would have to go to school and of course help with the chores, like the rest of the children. You would be a member of the family and would be treated as such." Dad said.

"Yes, yes, I would be more than happy. What would your wife think? Would she accept me?"

"Well she has had other surprises lately, and came around, so yes, I think so. And you have a booster in Harold here. So you have two of us on your side."

"Well," I said, "It's settled then, she goes home with you."

Harold scooted over beside her and she put her arm around his shoulders like a big sister should. He laid his head on her shoulder and went to sleep. We spent the rest of the ride getting getting to know each other. She was some surprised to find out I was a son and brother to Dad and Harold. When she looked at Lizzy and me, there was a question in her eyes. They could explain that to her later.

When we arrived, we found the Coach in good shape. We had written to the railroad in advance, they had it all stocked. When you have the money, service is great. When you don't, you don't. Everything was just as we left it, even the safe. Dad, Harold and Cora spent the night with us in the coach. They thought it was fun. We seen them off the next morning. Dad was reluctant to leave us. He thought he would never see us again, but I assured him that we wasn't due to go under yet.

They were going to do some shopping for Cora, so we said goodbye, they walked off with many a glance back over their shoulders.

We were to leave Philadelphia the next morning, so we had this day to see Charlene Russell. To see if she still wanted revenge. Revenge is a dish better served up hot, when it gets cold, it leaves a bad taste in your mouth.

We left the railroad station ourselves. We found Charlene at Charles Russell's house. She answered the door at our knock. "Come in, come in, I am so glad to see you. I know the children will be also, but they are in school. I am the only one here, Charles' wife is with him at Bible Study. I am afraid they think I am some kind of a pagan. But that is all they do, is study the Bible. They know it, backward and forward."

"Well I guess there is worse things to do with your time." I said. "But have you made up your mind, as to whether you are going back with us or not?"

"Last fall I had, but now, I'm not so sure. I think my place is with my children."

Lizzy said, "We completely understand.""Yes, well, Charles said that I should leave it in the Lord's hands, that revenge belongs to him, do you think that's true?"

"Why yes I do, to some extent. You see, what goes around, comes around. In other words what you sow is what you will reap. Type belongs to type, you can't get around it." I said.

"Are you saying that, they will get what's coming to them?"

"Oh, I am sure of it, sooner or later. In this case it might be sooner. They are still in Indian territory. It was a wonder that it wasn't them that killed your husband, instead of those white men."

Lizzy spoke up, "You can put your mind at rest Charlene, as far as you're concerned, they no longer exist."

"Can you stay for tea?" Charlene asked.

"Of course we can, we're never too busy for friends."

We did a little shopping on the way back to our coach. New underwear and stuff like that. I got a new beaver felt hat, a sort of fawn color. Lizzy got one just like it. But more feminine. I got to pick out her underwear and she picked out mine. The clerks were nonplussed. It was completely not heard of, a man in the women's undergarment department!

We put on our new hats, Lizzy cocked hers to one side. It was an unmistakable fact, Lizzy was the most beautiful woman in Philadelphia. And all of the men that were tripping over their own feet as we walked down the street proved that out. Of course all the women were doing that for me, at least I would like to think that.

Our train was due to pull out in the morning, as I have already said. So that left us with the evening to kill. Now what could we do? What would you do on a beautiful spring evening, in the big city of Philadelphia, in 1873? Why, first of all, we needed to eat. So we found the most expensive restaurant that we could. If you do it right, eating can be entertainment in itself. We did it right, it took us three hours and a big bottle of champagne. Then a surrey ride around their park. Needless to say, by the evening's end, we were in the mood for love.

We awoke the next morning to the clickity-clack of the rails. The champagne of the previous evening was not a good idea, in retrospect. Drinking, never is, is it? Oh well, it was a lesson well taught.

This morning, Lizzy was not the first one out of bed. Even with the haggards, she was beautiful. She was still lying there holding her head, as I brought her coffee to her. I propped her up in bed and held her cup, as she sipped. It wasn't long before the coffee took effect.

She smiled. I said, "Come on lover, I have a hot bath drawn for you." She sighed as she lowered herself into the soapy water. I washed her back, then let her soak as I fixed breakfast. Really it was only toast, with the aforementioned coffee.

I had a large towel ready for her as she stepped out of the tub. She dried off, then came to the table with the towel draped around her. It wasn't long though, before the towel slipped to the floor. She was then in her natural glorious state. She was completely oblivious to her charms. The butter on her chin added to them. She was babbling on about something, I know not what. I sat, as a man in a trance. Just drinking in the whole essence of her.

A knock on our coach's door, brought me back to my senses. Lizzy scurried into the bedroom. I answered the knock, it was the conductor.

He said, "I was just checking to make sure everything was satisfactory?"

I said, "Won't you please come in? I have the coffee on, would you like some?"

"Why, I don't mind if I do. I must say that is uncommonly nice of you. Most rich people are quite standoffish, you seem to be the exception."

He was a man in his early forties. And Irish, I would say. That in itself was unusual. In this day and age, it was hard for the Irish to get a job. I said, "Let me introduce myself, although, you probably already know our names, I am Phillip Gentry, my friends call me Buck."

We shook hands, he said, "My name is Clancy Boyle, lately of Dublin. May I call you Buck? Mr. Gentry."

"Sure, you see, being rich is just a state of mind. Money comes and money goes. It's what's in your heart that counts."

"Aye, that be so, Buck. Then by that standard, I be rich, also."

"That you are, Clancy. So what can I do for you?"

"Well it's like I said, I was just checking to see if everything was alright. And the truth be told, I was a might curious to see what a rich bloke looked like. And you didn't meet my expectations. You far exceeded them."

Lizzy came out of the bedroom. She was dressed. I said, "Clancy, this is my wife, Lizzy."

Clancy stood up and bobbed his head, he was speechless. Now that was unusual, an Irishman being speechless. But who could blame him? She even affected me that way at times.

"Lizzy, Clancy here was curious as to what us 'rich folks' looked like, how do we? My love."

"Why, I expect we look like most everybody else. Don't we?"

Clancy found his voice, "No Ma'am, you don't. You look so much better than anyone I have seen in this lifetime." His face was turning red.

"Oh, thank you, Clancy. I can see that you are not married. Otherwise your wife would be the one to fit in that category."

He bobbed his head again and said, "Yes, Ma'am." Funny thing about women, they could turn big strong men into bumbling fools. "Well, I must be getting back to my duties, if you need anything, just ask." Clancy said, as he backed out of the door.

"He sure beat a hasty retreat, didn't he?" Lizzy said.

"It was understandable, you do tend to intimidate men.

Not me though."

"Oh, are you saying that you're immune, or that you are not a man?"

"I think you know the answer to that question, or do you want me to reassure you?"

"Well I did just get dressed, but it wouldn't take but a second to drop these clothes."

It was lunch time, my how time flies when you're having fun. We spent the afternoon visiting with the other passengers on the train. Some of them were moving west. In fact most of them. Have you ever gotten tired of talking? I have and am. So I left Lizzy flapping her lips and I went back to our coach. I hadn't finished Moby Dick, no time like the present.

Two hours later, she, my veracious wife, came home.

"That wasn't nice, you leaving me by my lonesome, someone could of done me harm."

"Done you harm? I think you should put the shoe on the other foot. I was more afraid of you doing them harm. Really love, you are perfectly safe on this train. Or don't you think so?"

"Yes, Sweetheart. I don't think there is much danger on the train. But some of them, three in particular, are different, you'll have to see them yourself."

She got my attention. If she thought they were different, then they must be. "I tell you what, after supper, why don't you show me these three, different people, as you call them."

Clancy came by and ate supper with us. "Clancy, my wife thinks she seen some 'different' people on this train. Do you think there are some, that are 'different'?"

"Too many to count, but aren't we all? Who in particular, do you think are 'different',
Mrs.Gentry?"

"Oh, you know, that older woman, that just sits in her rocking chair by the stove and her two children, that won't let go of their rifles."

"Oh, you mean the hill people. There are five of them altogether. The two oldest boys stay with their livestock. They have some purebred horses, they don't let them out of their sight. The younger boy and girl are very protective of their mother."

"They do sound interesting, maybe after we do the dishes, you will introduce me to them?" I said.

"Aye, that I will, their name is Langhorne. I believe the mother's name is Victoria. The daughter's name is Hallie. The young boy is Daniel. The two older boys are Edward and Edric. Anyway, that's what it says on their tickets."

"Victoria Langhorne, a pretty high-toned name, if you ask me." I said.

Lizzy said. "Well sometimes names can be deceiving, wait tell you see them."

"Yeah, could be. But at the same time looks can be deceiving. Maybe there is more to them than meets the eye. We'll see."

"Of course, you're right, Sweetheart. Look at us, our names sure don't match us, do they?"

"Well, our nick names do, Lizzy fits you and Buck fits me."

We finished drying the dishes. I said, "Let's go see these famous people."

"Right," Clancy said, "They are in the coach closest to the livestock car. They have taken over the whole end of the coach, around the pot belly stove. Everyone else leaves them alone."

Now you would think the stove would be located in the

center of each coach. But, due to having to take out ashes and bring in wood, the stoves were located in each end of the coaches. Yep, they had stacked their claim alright. Sitting in her rocking chair, was a woman in her late forties, she was reading. They had Their clothes hanging from the windows. The girl was just finishing the dishes. They had converted the whole end of the coach into their private living quarters. And no one dared to challenge them. Daniel was cleaning his squirrel gun. A Kentucky long rifle. I bet he could shoot the eye out of a squirrel at two hundred yards. Clancy walked up to her, "Mrs. Langhorne, I have some people who would like to meet you. Is that all right?" Clancy was even walking on eggs. She looked up, smiling, she said, "Of course, I'm always glad to meet anyone." She stood, laying her book on the chair seat, she came over and took Lizzy's hand in hers.

"I seen you yesterday, when you were staring at us. I knew you would be back I'm Victoria, and you are?"

"I'm Lizzy, I mean, Elizabeth Drake-Gentry. This is my husband, Buck, or Phillip Gentry. To be honest, yes, I was staring. The way you have made yourselves at home peaked my interest. Am I being too bold?"

Victoria looked from Lizzy, to me. "It is I that should have her interest peaked, you two are the ones that are different in our eyes."

Her speech belied her appearance. She was almost the spitting image of Ma. In both form and manner. I was suddenly very homesick. Victoria turned her attention to me, "Yes, and you young man. You are certainly a conundrum, a contradiction in appearance and manner. Is it Sioux? Yes, I think it is. And your beautiful wife is Chinese. Of course the other halves of the both of you are Anglo-Saxon. What a war must be going on inside the both of you."

189

I said, "Not really, we have made peace with ourselves. But enough about us, I would like to know your story, if I am not being too bold?"

"Come, sit down. Hallie, would you pour them some tea? Daniel, clean up that mess, so they can sit down."

Daniel made haste to do as he was bidden. Hallie, likewise. We sat, holding the fine china tea cups in our laps.

"Our story? Let me see. Yes, we are from Tennessee, originally. My husband, Howard, left last year for the frontier. We have not heard from him, since. He was to find a place suitable for raising horses, then send for us. I am afraid he has run afoul of something."

"If you wanted to go west, how come you came so far east?

"We got a letter from a lawyer, it turns out, we had a inheritance coming. We collected it. It took a little persuading, but he gave it to us."

"Yes, I just bet he did." I said. "So just where do you plan on going?"

"Howard said, he was going to look around in Montana or Wyoming Territory. So I guess we'll get off in Cheyenne."

"By a strange coincidence, that's where we are going, also. But you know, how you are camped out here, its awkward, to say the least. I am sure Clancy has some sleeping births open in the Pullman car. Isn't that right Clancy?" I said.

"Yes, I have one open, the ladies are welcome to it. Of course, I would have to charge for it."

Lizzy said, "We will pay the extra fee, I know how women need their privacy. Will, Daniel and your other two son's be alright here?"

"Sure, they spend most of their time in the woods anyway. And we'll be here during the day, to make sure they eat right." Ma said. There I went, calling her Ma. But she sure reminded me of Ma. Victoria and Hallie gathered up their needfuls, and followed Clancy to the Pullman Car. We told them we would talk more in the morning. Now you probably think we should of taken the women to our coach. But shucks, we wanted a little privacy too. You might just as well run around naked, while naked still looked good.

The next morning dawned with the clickity-clack of the rails keeping time with our heartbeats. I lay there watching her breasts swaying with the movement of the coach. Quite entertaining, to say the least.

Lizzy opened one eye, "Having fun?" she said.

"Yeah, I reckon. How about you?" She had the habit of holding me, you know, down there, when she slept. She relaxed her hand.

"I'm sorry, but it's sort of like a security blanket, I sleep better. But you know that."

"Yeah, Sweetheart, I do. After all, it belongs to you."

"Doesn't it though?" She said, then rolled over and got up and padded to the toilet. That was an 'even better' sight.

I made breakfast, that meant Lizzy had to do the dishes. We did all of our chores, then went to see how the Langhorne's were doing. Victoria and Hallie had just finished their breakfast tasks. They were still dressed in the same clothes as yesterday, of course. But watching them, I thought, Victoria wasn't that old, she just thought she was. Sometimes life can get you to thinking that way.

I got Lizzy aside, "You know, I bet if you got them cleaned up a might, and new dresses. Why they would be almost new women." Lizzy glanced over her shoulder at them.

"Yes, you are right. I will see if they would like a bath. And there are plenty of dresses in our coach. But you know how prideful some of these hill people can be."

"Sure do, but give it a try, we'll see."

"You think we stink?" Victoria said, with a twinkle in her eye. Hallie spoke up.

"Ma, I would like a bath. Especially since, you know." She looked down. Now Victoria was one of those people who didn't pull their punches, sort of like me.

"Yes Honey." Then she looked at us, "Hallie has just started her first time of the month. She is a little shy about it. But yes, we would both like to get cleaned up."

Lizzy took them in tow. Daniel was still cleaning his rifle. He looked up at me. I said. "Well Daniel, I think it's time for me to meet your brothers'."

"Sure, I told them about you, they are a might curious. They think you might be a confidence man. But I told them that I didn't think so. But, I rightly don't know just what you are."

"Well, that's good, keep people guessing, Ma always said. That way they can't get a clear shot at you. But lead on McDuff."

"It's Daniel, do you have a bad memory, or are you a little slow?"

"No, that was frivolity, you are familiar with humor, aren't you?"

"Yeah, I reckon, I like a joke as much as anybody else. But haven't seen too much to joke about lately."

"Well maybe, things just might be changing. How old are you Daniel?"

"I'm fourteen, but I can hold my own with any man."

"I just bet you can, and that's good, cause where were going, that's needful."

As we opened the door to the stock car, two lanky boys stood up and pointed their long rifles at me. "Whoa there, point

J.D. Oliver

Bessie and Betty some other direction, I'm right peaceful."

Daniel said, "This is Buck, you know I told you about him. Buck, these are my brothers, Edward, the oldest, and Edric, he's a year younger than Edward."

I held out my hand, they lowered their rifles and held out their hands. We shook. Their grip was as iron. I gave back as good. I reckon it was a little test they liked to give. I must have passed, anyway, they broke out in smiles.

My eyes went to the horses. Yep, they were impressive. Thoroughbreds, but they looked to have more bottom then the ones I had seen before. No wonder they kept a close eye on them. I looked at Edward,

"What are your plans, when we get to Wyoming Territory?"

"Didn't Ma tell you? I reckon we'll look for Pa. Then get us some land and raise these horses."

"Well, I can see that you're not big on details. Really how could you be, for details have a tendency to blow around in the wind."

"Ain't that the truth, them details can be pesky things, best left to providence." Edric said.

These boys' would do, yep, they would do. We sat and jawed the morning away. I called them boys, with me not much more than one, in age anyway. But, like I told you before, the ancients, were in my bones. There was some reason, I didn't die at berth.

I left them fixing their lunch. I would of asked them to come and eat with us, but they wouldn't of left their horses anyway. So, I meandered back home, talking to this one and that. It was an effort, but I was sociable. I guess you could say that I was an introvert, a smart-alec one, but still an introvert.

Chapter Eleven

One thing I was thankful for, as I walked in, they were all dressed. And I was right, Victoria was an eyeful. Once you got her out of that gingham dress and into one of Lizzy's creations, she was a different woman. She filled the dress out almost as good as my wife. I said almost, no one was as good as my wife. Hallie was even smiling, a bath and pampering had done wonders for her.

They had lunch ready. I told them the boys' were already eating. Victoria said, she wasn't worried much about them, they would do. After lunch, I asked her, "Do you think your husband, Howard, is still alive?"

Lizzy gasped, "Buck, really, what kind of a question is that?"

"No, that's Ok, I don't mind. One can only hope, can't one? But in truthfulness, I don't know. It's been a little over a year. I still have hope."

"Well hope reigns eternal in man's soul, they say. As long as there is still respiration." I said.

Victoria looked at me and said, "You speak as if you are a college educated man, Buck. Are you?"

"No, no I am not. I guess you could say that I was home taught. Ma put many a long hour into teaching me. She thought the investment was worthwhile, I hope she was right."

Lizzy put her hand on mine, "I am sure she was right, I love you so much." She leaned over and kissed me.

Victoria said, "Now, now, you two can wait till tonight, I have one more question, Buck, just how old are you?"

"Why do you ask?" I said.

"I don't know, call it a mother's instinct."

I looked at Lizzy, she nodded. "Ok, I am going on fourteen." I said.

"I thought so, how?" She said, gesturing with her hands.

Lizzy said, "We don't know, do you believe in God?"

"Why yes, I do. What does he have to do with it?"

"I suppose, everything." I said. "Like Lizzy said, we don't know, but we do know there is more at work in us than meets the eye. You see, I know the past as well as what the Great Spirit has told me about the future. Why? we don't know."

"Well, each one of us has their purpose, I guess. It's the wise one who can figure out what that purpose is," Victoria said, then changed the subject.

It was decided, that Victoria and Hallie would use a couple of our spare bunks. And that Daniel would use the Pullman birth. Maybe trade off with his brothers. Victoria had noticed the many books we had. She started an impromptu school right then and there. She made Daniel attend also. I contributed where I could.

So went the time till we reached Chicago. They pulled our car out of line, as well as the stockcar. It was two days, setting on the side, before the Union Pacific's next train out. George was the conductor.

He was overjoyed to see us. He and Louisa had been in contact by mail. He couldn't stop thanking us. Needless to say, we didn't have any problems getting restocked. Or even getting births for the brothers'. Of course the women would continue to stay with us. I didn't mind, really. Even though we had to contain our libertine ways.

West of Chicago, the ambient changed. I started to wear my guns again. Lizzy had her knife and a small .32 strapped to her thigh. She felt the atmospheric change also. We were coming home.

It was the dark of night, when we pulled into Cheyenne. Our coach was set on the same siding as it used to sit. It was daylight, when the horses were unloaded. We put them in Carl Hatfield's stables'. The town was just coming awake when we knocked on Chen-Lee's door. He pumped my hand and hugged Mee-Ling, tears running down his cheeks. I don't think he ever planned on seeing her alive again.

"Sister of mine, you look so well," He looked her up and down, "I see you are not with child, as of yet."

"No, not yet. Although it's not for lack of trying." Everyone laughed, all except me. I didn't know we had been trying, I thought we were just having fun. Stupid me.

After breakfast, I went to see John. I wanted to find out if there were any places, ranch's that is, for the Langhorne's'. Turned out, there was. A small place just outside of town. The former owner had went chasing some rustler's and never returned. Never let your ambition overload your abilities, was the morale of that story.

We moved the Langhorne's and their stock out there the next day. The previous owner had been a bachelor. It would take them awhile to clean up after him. Most of the stock that he had left, were long since gone. All except his Dog. A large shaggy animal, that took to Hallie right off.

J.D. Oliver

The sun was a thumb above the horizon as Lizzy and I rode back to town. We dropped off our horses at the stables. Then walked to our coach, that was sitting on the rail siding near the depot.

We stripped and took a bath. Both of us were fairly silent, for some reason. Lizzy had a little sunburn on her neck and arms. We both had paled a little from our life in the east. I rubbed some lotion on her sunburn. Of course one thing led to another. The sun had set by the time we got dressed.

"I don't feel like cooking, do you?" Lizzy said.

"No, let's go to the Cheyenne Supper Club. I could do with a thick steak."

We walked hand-in-hand, through town. People would stop and look at us. Strangers to us. A lot of new people had moved in. And a lot of the older ones had moved on. But the so called pillars of the community still held sway. I held the swinging doors open for my wife. They had remodeled the eating area. It was walled away from the main bar area. That was good. But the hustle and the bustle was still very evident.

We found a table in the corner, where I could put my back to the wall. Otherwise I would have that creepy feeling up and down my spine. You know the one, where you expect a slug to rip through you any second.

We sat there staring at each other, while waiting for the waitress. Lizzy was auspiciously beautiful this evening. She wore one of her riding habits, with that new fawn colored hat cocked to one side. Every eye in the room was drawn to her, even the female ones. I was sure they weren't looking at me. After all, I was nothing special. But by the look in Lizzy's eyes, she thought I was.

There were four chairs at our table. I heard the click-click of paws on the hardwood floor. Old Man Coyote hopped into one of the empty chairs. I glanced around at the other tables, no one seemed to notice him.

"Don't worry Phillip, they can't see me. Only the two of you can."

"Did you come to eat with us? Or are you just slumming?" I asked.

"Don't be factious, Phillip. You have enough troubles without making anymore enemies. Look around you, half of these men in here, think killing an Indian is akin to killing a rattlesnake. And the other half, think that way about the Chinese. But they don't know quite what to think about you two. So you are wise to sit with your back to the wall."

The waitress came before I could answer. I ordered three steaks, with all the trimmings. The waitress said, "Three? There are only two of you."

"That's Ok, just bring the three, they will get consumed, my husband is a big eater."

"What are you doing here? Did we do something wrong?" I asked.

"No, nothing like that. I just came to give a little advice. And maybe comfort. Have you noticed Buck, that your internal conflict has lessened? I am sure you have. You have come to grips with yourself. You know, what is happening within yourselves, is what is happening to this country. It is going to be a melding of all of the nationalities. They are going to have to come to realize that. Of course, it will take hundreds of years, to fully jell. But this country's strength is in its diversity. Just as both of yours are."

The food came while we were pondering that. Lizzy leaned over and cut up his steak. After all, it would be kinda hard for Old Man Coyote to use a knife. Think how funny that would of looked for a steak to be flopping around in mid-air.

He said, "That does look good, thank you. I very seldom get cooked meat."

In between bite's, I said, "So you think this country has a future?"

"Oh, it definitely does. After all it and England will be the seventh world power."

"Huh? How come? Where do you get that?"

"Read your Bible, Phillip. It's in the book of Daniel."

"If that's true, how long will that kingdom last?"

"Till it self destructs. I'm afraid mankind is doomed to repeat his failures. But not for you to worry, because no man will know the day or the hour."

"Well that's not much comfort."

"Really it is, leave it in the Creator's hands, he knows best what to do with his creation. You have to trust him."

"I heard some of them pulpit pounders say that we all are going to either heaven or hell, what about that?"

"Is there a heaven? Is there a hell? Oh, that is the question, isn't it? Don't worry, the light will get brighter as the day nears." Old Man Coyote said, as he gulped down his last piece of steak.

"Well of course it does, as the sun is about to rise." I said.

"Yes, now you understand. As the son is about to rise." He said, as he got down from the chair. He sat down and scratched behind his ear and padded off. Sometimes I could just strangle him.

The waitress came back, she looked at all three plates. "Well he did eat it all, didn't he?"

"Oh, he can be quite the pig. Would you bring us some after dinner wine?"

"Yeah sure, what color?"

Now I knew there were a lot of different wines', but in the Wyoming Territory of 1873, You were fortunate if you got to pick the color, much less the vineyard or the year. So I said, "Make it red, like me."

She looked at me and said, "You have a nice tan, but it don't look red to me."

I said, "It sure is nice that some people are color blind. Thank you." She gave me a wink. Lizzy kicked me under the table. "Hey, I didn't do anything, she was the one that winked."

"Yeah, and you just keep it that way. Or I will do more than just kick you. I'll cut it off."

"What, my leg?"

"Yes, that's right, your 'leg'." She said with an evil smile.

I let it drop. Besides the place was starting to get noisy. There were four men at the next table, they were deep in their cups. Would you believe they were arguing about who had killed the most men? The booze had oiled their tongues and put them to wagging.

One of them said, "You can't count, Nigger's, Indian's or Chinamen. Hell, if that were the case, then I've killed at least ten." Then he burped.

One of the other's said, "Keep it down Charlie, that comment was way out of line. In fact I'm getting tired of the like's of you, I'm going back to camp. Any one going with me?"

One of the other men got up, they tossed some money on the table and left. "Let them go Charlie, the Yankee cowards." He said, then yelled, "Waitress, more whisky." Now sometimes people blame liquor for their actions. But I have found that all whisky does, is bring out what is already there. If a man's soul is dark, liquor just brings it to light.

J.D. Oliver

She brought them another bottle. They pinched her butt. She slapped the one called Charlie. I was already out of my chair. Charlie got up and took a swing at her. I caught his fist in my hand.

"Now, now, you are being a naughty boy. We don't hit women, now do we?"

"Who the hell are you?" He said, as he got a good look at me. "Hey, you're an Indian, let go of me, you stinking red skin." I did so. He stumbled backward. Regaining his balance, he set his feet, "I'm going to blow your fucking head off." He reached for his gun, I let him clear leather. Even though my wife said for me not to let them do that.

The roar of my .44 blew him ten feet backwards, he bounced off the wall and lay there, in his own gore. I turned to the sound of gurgling. The other one had dropped his gun and was clutching at my wife's knife sticking through his throat and out the back of his neck.

I punched out the spent cartridge and filled the emptiness with another coffin nail. Lizzy bent over and pulled her knife out and wiped it on his shirt.

Her eyes were impassive, a reflection of my own, I suppose.

"I'm sorry I was late. I was told they were here, sitting at the next table to you. I tried to hurry. Oh well, I suppose some people are just too dumb to save." John Wesley Harden was standing there. Two of his Deputies were with him. They dragged the bodies away.

"Would you like a glass of wine John, we were just about to have some." Lizzy said. As the swamper came with a bucket and a mop and started to clean up the mess.

"I think I would like something a little stronger. I would say it's nice to have you back, except it isn't. Oh I know it

201

wasn't your fault, it never is. I would like to think that it had been quiet since you left. But it hasn't. You notice that I have two deputies now. It keeps us all busy."

John was rattling on, he was nervous. I looked into his eyes. He was scared of us, both of us. Now why in the world was he scared of us? "John, slow down, what is your problem?"

"I suppose part of it is you two. I know you were just defending yourselves. But the town fathers are a bunch of bigoted bastards. And if you two stayed here long enough, I know you would have to end up killing them. And oh, they would deserve it! But believe it or not, I have a solution. The U.S. Marshall got killed last month, they need a new one. I recommended you Buck."

"Me? Why in the world would they want me, a half-breed?

"They don't know that. The main office is in Chicago. I just wired them that Phillip Gentry was available. They said they knew who you were. The Union Pacific gave you a good recommendation. Plus also the Pinkerton's. So if you want it, you have it."

"I don't know, Lizzy and I would have to talk it over. What about Deputies? Did they get killed too?"

"No, they just quit, you would have to hire your own."

"This would be for the whole Wyoming Territory?"

"Yes, mostly just the southern half, the north is still mostly Indian territory. The previous Marshalls stayed pretty well clear of there. But I guess you wouldn't have any problem. No offense, you being Indian and all."

"Squaw and me, we go, have powwow, let you know morning." He turned red, we got up and left. That was mean of me, I know. But sometimes, its just plain fun, being mean.

Lizzy was wide awake, her breasts rising and falling in the moon light coming in the window. She was thinking, I wasn't. Why should I? When she was doing enough for the two of us.

"Well wife, what are we going to do?"

"I think we should take it. After all, isn't that what we are doing now? But if we took the job, we could do it, legally. Now I say we, cause I am going to be your deputy. No arguing. That's final."

"I wasn't going to dispute that. I had that in mind also. You have always been my backup. Tomorrow we'll go see Chin-Lee and get you some proper pistols. Something with some punch."

She turned on her side, they brushed up against me. She said, "The first thing we should do, is, see who killed that man who owned the Langhorne's new place."

"You're right, I never argue with a woman who has her weapons drawn."

"Huh? You mean-?"

"Yeah, fire away!"

The morning dawned with a new purpose. We met with John and the District Judge that very morning. He was a pompous little fellow. I don't think he liked what he saw. But it wasn't up to him. He had his orders from Chicago. He swore us in. As he handed us our badges. He said, "Now I expect you to bring any miscreants in for trial. No killing them unless you absolutely have to. I pride myself on everyone getting a fair trial."

"Oh, they will Judge, they will." I said, as I sat down on the corner of his desk and helped myself to one of his cigars. I lit it and blew the smoke in his face. He coughed, his eyes watering.

Lizzy said, "Stop that Buck, you know you don't smoke. It's bad for your health."

I said, "Yes Dear," then I crushed the cigar out in his empty coffee cup. His face was turning red. I said, "Are you Ok Judge, you're not having a heart attack are you?"

Lizzy said, "Really Phillip, that was over the edge. Apologize to the Judge, that was just nasty. Do it now!"

She wasn't joking. "I'm sorry Judge, sometimes I do go overboard. But I always get the job done. I won't mess with your cigars anymore." I stuck my hand out. He shook it, reluctantly.

"That's Ok, Marshall Gentry. I have here a stack of outstanding warrants. Work them in any order you wish. Your pay is one hundred dollars a month. Your Deputy gets sixty. For each warrant you clear, you get a two hundred dollar bonus, your Deputy gets one hundred and fifty. Are there any other questions?"

"I have one," Lizzy said. "What do we get for bringing in those not on your list?"

"That depends on the severity of their crimes. For murder and rustling, you get full price. And so on down the line."

"What about those that put up a fight and we have to kill?" I said.

"That's the same as bringing them in. But don't kill them to just save the trouble of bringing them in."

"Judge, what you just said, was like calling us murderers. One thing you must realize is that we don't need your blood money and we don't want it. In fact, we want that money put toward helping the poor. And we want you to live a long life, so don't ever make a derogatory remark about us again." With that, we turned and left.

We went by Chen-Lee's. He had a matched pair of .41 caliber Navy Colts. It didn't take him long to fit Mee-Ling's gun belts to her luscious hips. We had all the rifles we needed. She strapped them on. She walked over to the mirror, her hands streaked down. They seemed to just jump into her hands. I had never seen a faster draw. And from experience, I knew her aim was just as deadly. I would not want to get on her bad side.

We went to the Cheyenne Club for lunch. It was quite, just the local merchants, eating their lunch. Of course every eye was looking our way. They did a double take when they seen our badges, especially Lizzy's. Then their eyes dropped to her guns. They had better be looking at her guns and not anything else.

As we were eating my thoughts turned to my jealousy. Now I knew the green eyed monster could get a man in trouble. So perhaps I had better turn the fire down a bit. Jealousy was not an attribute to have. It showed a lack of trust of your loved one. I trusted her implicitly and I knew she did me also. Yep, jealousy is a childish trait. Common sense isn't, though.

The owner of the General Store came over. You remember he was one of the city fathers that hired John. His name was Gustav Steinmetz. I think he was one of those that wanted me out of town. He said, "I see that you are the new U. S. Marshals. I suppose we won't be seeing much of you. Hunting down all of those bad people and all."

I turned and looked him up and down. "I don't know, I might just stay right in town and Hire my work done. I am rich you know. In fact I just might start another store, right here in town. What do you think I should do?"

He swallowed hard, then said, "All right, I deserved that. I must apologize. We thought you were just a kill happy gunslinger. I learned a lesson. Appearances' really can be deceiving. Again I am sorry."

I looked at my wife, she nodded. "I, that is we, accept your apology. I can see by your name and your appearance, that you are a Jew. So you, more than most people, know what prejudice is. Just remember that, the next time you make a snap judgment. You see we all are guilty of being bigot's at times."

He said, "Your wife looks quite deadly, if I may say so. Somehow I think that is more than just looks." I slapped him on the back, "And I would say that you are right Gustav. In fact she is faster than me and shoots just as straight. Anyone who thinks she isn't will spend eternity digging his way to China." It never hurts to do a little advertising. Perhaps it will scare the weak at heart. More than likely though, we had better watch our backs all the more.

We spent the rest of the afternoon getting our traveling outfit together. We would use Jill and Lil as our packhorses. Lizzy would ride Jim. I would ride the black. We looked through the stack of warrants. Low and behold, there was Artus McNally and his three sons. You remember, they were the ones who killed Charlene Russell's husband. And they weren't even a day's ride away, close to Laramie.

We were walking towards the bank to check on our account, when Felicity saw us. She rushed up, gushing. She had turned into quite the housewife. To make her long story short, she invited us over for supper that night. Of course we accepted, or I guess I should say, Lizzy did. As we parted, Felicity glanced at our guns. She said, "I'm sure you won't need those tonight."

"Oh, on the contrary," I said, "We need them more than ever now, or didn't you hear? We are the new U. S. Marshals."

"Both of you?"

J.D. Oliver

"Well yes, I am the Marshal for the Wyoming Territory and Elizabeth is my deputy."

"I guess in that case, you will need those guns. It seems they don't live very long."

Lizzy spoke up, "We plan on changing that. In fact we need to see your husband, we need some posters printed up. You know, wanted posters. We want to make it safe for every law abiding citizen in the territory of Wyoming. And just the opposite for those who don't abide by the law."

That's where we went next. We left the stack of warrant's with him. Told him to deliver them to our office in the Federal Court House, when he got them printed up. Then we finally made it to the bank. The same clerk was on duty.

He came over and shook my hand, "Hello Mr. Gentry, it's good to have you back. I was so glad to hear that you were the new U. S. Marshal."

"Yes, well, how are my finances coming? What was that rate of interest the bank pays again?"

"It's four percent, you are richer now than when you left a year ago. Do you need to withdraw some money?"

"No, we have plenty. I was just wondering. Keep up the good work. Say, I completely forgot your name?"

"It's Perceval Hightower, Sir. If you ever need anything, feel free to call on me."

Yeah, it was time I started acting like a 'civilized citizen'. You know, being nice to people. Its not that I wasn't nice to people. But I wasn't 'politically' nice to them. You know, blowing smoke up their ass. Now I suppose I would have to start.

Lizzy looked at me, "Buck, it's Ok to be nice, even when you don't feel like it."

"Huh, how did you know I was faking it?"

"Sweetheart, I know you front, back or upside down. I'm a Geometry whiz, when it comes to you."

"Oh, you do, do you? Ok, what am I thinking right now?"

"That can wait till tonight, you can't do it right here on the street. Oh, I know you would like to. And you know what, so would I. But decorum prevents us."

"That's a terrible word, 'decorum'. It's almost as bad as the word 'work', but not quite."

"Since when have you hated to work?"

"It's not the work itself, just the thought of it. Like when a person says, I have to go to work. Why do you have to? You see, the ability to work is a privilege. We shouldn't have to do anything."

"For goodness sake Buck, you do rattle on, or is that Phillip talking?"

"No, its not Phillip. It seems we are one, now. All though at times I would sure like to blame him for some of the things I say. Everyone needs a scapegoat."

We verbally bombarded each other all the way back to our coach. We were almost late for our supper with the Oglethorpe's. Not due to the talking, but you know, due to the other thing.

Felicity and Walter met us with big smiles on their faces. Why they were so happy to see us, I have no idea.

Turns out they credited us with getting them together. Well, not so much us, more me. They did have some good news they wanted to share with us. Felicity was pregnant. Now I thought for sure that announcement would get Lizzy to wanting a child. But she took it right in stride. We finished out the evening and left with good cheer.

They were some surprised that Lizzy was my deputy.

On our way out, Walter said, "Now you be sure no harm comes to your beautiful wife."

I said in return, "I'm afraid it's me you will have to worry about. Lizzy not only takes care of herself, but she has saved my bacon a few times."

Lizzy said, "Oh Sweetheart, you know you always return the favor. Don't you pay attention to him Walter, he is my protector and will always be."

Felicity came over and gave us both a kiss. The little vamp stuck her tongue in my mouth. As we were walking home, I said, "Did you see what she done, she stuck her tongue in my mouth."

"That's Ok, Dear, she did the same to me."

"She did? Well, I guess she is an equal opportunity kisser."

"Oh, is that what it's called? You know, I've heard, that when some women get pregnant they really get horny. Something about they don't have to worry about getting pregnant, since they already are. They sort of feel free."

"Then I would hate to see you pregnant, you would wear me to a frazzle. You're all I can
handle right now."

"Well, satisfaction is my aim. For both of us."

"Well, I think you hit that target every time."

Later that night in bed, the specter of work raised its ugly head. I said, "Lizzy, there must be a better way to get Artus McNally and his sons. I mean than just going in and blasting them."

"Funny you should bring that up, because I was just thinking about them. And I do have an idea. They hate so called 'nesters'. So why don't we let them come to us?"

"Come to us? I don't think they are just going to come

and give themselves up."

"No, of course not. But if we became 'nesters', say on the Russell place. In fact, we could go to the land office and file on that place ourselves."

"Oh yeah, they're that stupid. I am sure they have already filed on it."

"I don't think so. Men like that think they're above the law. They think they can just take anything they want."

"Alright, I bet you a roll in the hay, anytime you want it. That they have filed on that land."

"Ok Buck, you're on. Now it's anytime I want it, no matter where or when?"

"Sure, cause I've already won, I bet."

"Now don't forget, it's anytime I want it, not you."

With that delightful thought in mind, we went to sleep.

We made breakfast at home. The railroad coach had become our home. We had it sitting on the same siding where it used to set for so long. We had paid the station agent to keep us supplied with water and ice.

The man at the land office studied through the plat's. Lizzy won the bet. Shucks. Now she had quite the imagination. I can hardly wait to see how and when she collects the bet. We paid the filing fee. He said it had already been proved up on. That means the required buildings and plowing had been done by Russell. He looked at both of us and said,

"You two don't look like you're the homesteading type. I know who you are, Marshal. You aren't trying to pull a fast one here, are you?"

"Don't we have the same right to homestead, as anybody else?" Lizzy said.

"Sure you do, but just make sure it's you two that do it. And not sell it off for a profit."

"You mean to say, that we don't have the right to sell it, if we want to?"

"Sure you do. But it's just the idea, most people at least try to make a go of it."

"Don't you worry about that," I said, "We will have that place ticking like a Swiss watch."

"Well, just don't forget to wind it, every once in a while." He said, as he slammed the Plat Book closed.

My, my, me thinks he doesn't like Indians. He probably thinks we are all lazy. Some people get that impression of us Indians. But that's not the case. It's just that we dance to a different drummer. It's just like the principle of building a campfire, why build a big one, when a small one would do? We took our paper work and headed for the door. I couldn't resist, I did a chant and a little dance before I went out the door. Lizzy burst out laughing at the expression on the land agent's face.

"Buck Dear, you have a weird sense of humor, but I like it." then she kissed me, right there on the board walk. We went to see Carl Hatfield. He had a covered wagon that would do. We had our four horses and then we bought two more. "Carl, do you know of anybody that has a few cows and maybe some goats for sale?"

"It just so happens that I might have some for sale. I have this goat, that my wife says, either me or it, is going to go. Plus I can spare a few cows."

"How about some stuff that homesteaders usually carry? You know, pots and pans, plows, anything like that?"

"You can go see Gustav at the General Store, I bet he can fix you up."

"Yeah, I forgot about him. I will do that."

Wail Not!

That's what we did. By the time we got all outfitted, it would take six horses to pull the wagon. When we headed out at noon the next day, you couldn't tell us from any other homesteader.

Now that goat was a pistol. I could see why Carl's wife wanted it gone. It thought it was human. I called it Bub. For Beelzebub. Because it sure was full of devilry. I didn't need a dog, that Goat kept those cows herded up right behind the wagon.

When we stopped to eat, Bub came right up for his share. Now he wasn't pushy, he was polite about it. He sat there on his haunch's waiting. I filled a plate and sat it before him. He waited till we started eating, before he did. Yep, a right polite goat. Too bad he couldn't talk. At least I don't think he could. But he seemed to understand everything we said.

We stopped overnight on the trail. Bub let the cows graze out-a-ways. Then before dark he herded them in close to the wagon. I never seen the beat, the cows seemed to understand him. I said, "Bub, what's your story? I bet you have a doozy."

He just looked at me and bleated. That night he slept under the wagon, close to us. I didn't even have to hobble the horses, they all stayed within shouting distance the whole night.

The next morning they all were standing there waiting to go. We pulled into the homestead in mid-afternoon. The house was burnt. The barns and corrals were still standing. Of course they wouldn't have burnt the barns and corrals, they were useful. Someday they might want them.

I could see why they wanted the place. There was not only a live stream, but a spring coming out of hill in back of the house. (Or where the house used to be.) Yep, Russell had chosen well, well enough to get himself killed.

J.D. Oliver

We unloaded most of the stuff into the barn. Then pulled the wagon close to the spring. Un-hitched the horses from the wagon, then drove them over to the barn. Where I took the harness's off and hung them in the tack room in the barn. I turned the horses loose. Bub and the cows were already muzzle deep in the grass. Now goats like weeds, in fact they prefer them over grass, Bub was busy ferreting them out.

We fixed the wagon up, like we were staying in it. But we had no intention of sleeping in the wagon. Back away's in the brush, I made us sort of lean-to. It couldn't be seen, but we had a good command of the whole ranch yard.

The next day we saddled Jim and Jill and rode to Laramie. We needed to let everybody know we were there. One good way was to buy lumber and such and hire someone to rebuild the house. Bub wanted to go with us, but I told him he was needed there. I'll be dammed, but I was sure he understood.

At the General Store, I told them we were homesteading the old Russell place. After calling me a dam fool, they agreed to sell me what I needed. They even put me on the trail of a good carpenter.

I found the carpenter in the local Café, eating lunch. His name was Jesus Romero, what better name could there of been, for a carpenter. After bribing him with a much too big of a fee. He agreed to build us a house. Turns out, he had a large family, brother's and cousins. I told him to get what he needed at the store. I had already made arrangement's. Then we went by the local Marshal's office.

I showed him the wanted posters of Artus McNally and his boys. His face turned pale. He looked at us, "Just the two of you going to do this?"

"Yep, I reckon, why? Do you think that's an overkill? Maybe my Deputy here, can handle it all by herself. What do

213

you think, Marshall?"

"Oh, you think you're funny, those men are killers. They'll kill you two before breakfast and drink a toast to your souls."

"If they did, what would you do about it, Marshal? Nothing, right? Just like when they killed Russell. And I don't know how many others. But I bet you do, am I right?"

"Hey, I am only one man and I have a family, what would you have me do?"

"Just be a man, that's all. That's all one man can ask of another." Then we turned and left.

"You might have been a little harsh with him." Lizzy said. "There probably isn't one man in this town who would back him up. Some towns are that way, they have never grown a backbone."

"Yeah, they usually don't last too long, without one. But maybe this town can be saved." We went back to the café. We didn't feel like cooking. We had not put our badges on, the Marshal was the only one who knew that we were U. S. Marshal's. As far as everybody else knew, we were just a couple of hapless homesteaders.

The woman who ran the café was a middle aged widow. We were the only ones in there, being that it was mid-afternoon. She sat down and jawed a while with us. Turns out the McNally's had killed her husband. Lizzy asked her, "Why didn't you leave and go back east?"

"Cause, I'm just too blamed stubborn. Those no-account vermin are not going to run me out of here, they'll have to kill me first."

"How come they haven't killed you?"

"Because they know this town wouldn't stand for it. Women are a prime object here in the west. You can do a lot of things, but you can't go around killing women."

"I suppose they can create some kind of an accident to get it done."

"I've thought of that, I don't go out much, at least by myself. They just haven't had the opportunity, as of yet, anyway. But enough about me, what about you two, out there by yourselves?"

"Don't worry about us, Ivy. We can take care of ourselves." Lizzy said, then pulled her badge out. "We're U.S. Marshal's, sent here to take the McNally's in. Keep this under your hat, tell no one. And I mean no one, not even your lover, if you have one."

"Goodness gracious no, I won't even tell my cat. I want those killers brought to justice. You can count on me."

Well so far two people in Laramie knew who we were. Let's just see who has the biggest mouth. Maybe neither one, huh?

Jesus was going to be out in the morning. We paid the storekeeper for all the materials. I made sure he seen the roll of bill's. When you're trolling for the big fish, you want to use lot's of bait. Who knows, we just might snag some small ones along with the big ones.

When we got back to the homestead, Bub was waiting for us. He ran up and nuzzled our hands. I had picked up some candy at the store. He really liked that. We spent the rest of the daylight hours going through and raking the ashes. We found some of Charlene's trinkets. We saved what we could, we knew she would want any keepsakes that we found.

Then we bathed in the stream. Someone had dug out a pool of sorts. We had brought some store bought soap with us. I washed Lizzy's hair, it was getting long, almost down to her hips. Mine was not near as long. It was just getting dark when we went to our lean-to. We didn't make love, we didn't want to be distracted, abstinence sometimes can save your life.

This night, nothing happened. Jesus and his relative's showed up shortly after dawn. They had the foundation up by mid-morning. The walls were up before they left. They knew what they were doing. I knew the word that we were here, had surely reached the McNally's by now.

The sun was low on the western horizon, when I seen a glint on a hill to the east. Someone was glassing us. I guess they had never heard about reflection. So we played the part. I built a fire and we put some food on. We sat around and ate. Washed the dishes in the stream. Then made sure they seen us get into the wagon.

After the shadows engulfed the land, we crawled out the far side. There was nothing of value in the wagon. They could burn it, no big loss. We made our way into the brush. We had stashed our weapons there. I told Bub to take all of the stock back into the hills. Of course Jim understood what I said anyway. They disappeared.

I knew they would wait till they thought we were sound asleep. So we went to check them out. Lizzy was like a panther, she took to the shadows as if born in them. We came within fifty feet. There were ten of them. "Look, we can kill them now, you take five and I'll take the other five." Lizzy said.

"Lizzy, do you really want to? We don't know which ones are the McNally's. And if we Kill all of them before they attack us, can we really claim self-defense?"

Lizzy didn't say anything for several minutes. "I'm sorry, I guess I got caught up in the heat of the moment. I guess you are right, but hell we know they are going to, it's only common sense to strike first."

"Yes, of course you are right, but when did the law ever

show common sense?"

"Shit, come on, lets go back and get ready. I get six of them then. Alright?"

"That depends on how fast and straight you shoot." I said. Then we faded into the ambient. Lizzy was starting to talk in the vernacular of the day, using colorful metaphor's. I was probably rubbing off on her.

Bub met us by the barn. He was by himself. Bub's horn's were a little different than other goats. His were almost straight, with just a gradual curve. I bet he knew how to use them. He stayed in the barn, while we went into the underbrush.

The stars said it was almost mid-night, when we heard them coming. They thought they were being quite, if they were a herd of bison they were, but they were on foot. I was glad of that, I didn't want any horses to get killed. In my mind, one horse was worth all ten of them.

I whispered to Lizzy, "Stay down, don't skylight yourself against the stars. After you shoot once, change position. That way they can't shoot at your muzzle flash. Be a wraith in the night."

"The same goes for you lover, if you get killed. I will kill you again, just for spite."

"I think that's called double jeopardy, isn't it?"

"You read too much, just you shoot straight Buck, I love you."

We fell silent. They arranged themselves in a semi-circle around the wagon. One of them raised his hand and said, "Now!" They all started to shoot at once, they were making kindling out of our wagon. We got four of them before they even knew they were being shot at. They looked around, confused , they started to run in circles. We got four more.

The last two broke and ran for the barn. Lizzy said,

"They're mine." She stood up and got the hindmost one. The other one made it inside of the barn. We heard a loud scream, then silence.

Bub came out of the barn, the moon came out from behind a cloud. It's rays were shining off of the sheen of blood on Bub's horns. He bent down and cleaned them in the dirt of the barn yard. Then he trotted over to us, he checked us both out. Then he went to the stream and jumped in. I guess he wanted to wash the rest of the blood off.

We dragged all of the bodies into the barn yard, lining them up in a row. Then we turned all of their horses loose. Then we took a swim in the nude, and went to bed in the lean-to.

Jesus Romero and his troop woke us up in the morning. They seen the bodies and started to babble in Spanish. We slipped on some clothes and went out. I walked over and said, "Do you know them?"

"Yes, this one is Artus McNally, these three are his son's. Those other's work for him. It's his whole crew, all except the cook. You've killed them all. Who are you people?"

"We're the U. S. Marshal's for the Wyoming Territory. Did the McNally's have any other relatives?"

"No, not that we know of. I guess his ranch will revert to the government."

"We'll see. Will you haul the bodies to town and turn them over to the coroner. Then you can come back tomorrow and work on the house."

"You still want the house finished?"

"Sure why not? Do you have a place?"

"No, we rent a small house in town."

"Well maybe we can work something out on this place, we'll see. In the mean time we are going to ride over to the

McNally's place. We'll meet you in town."

We rode into the ranch yard. The cook came out to meet us. He said, "Mr. McNally isn't home, he's been gone all night."

"That's Ok, we know where he is, are you the cook?"

"Yes, I'm Harry Mcfab. And you're?"

"I'm the U. S. Marshal, my name is Phillip Gentry, this is my wife, Elizabeth. She is my Deputy. The McNally's won't be coming back, nor the rest of the crew, they're all dead. I need to look over the books. Would you show me where they are?"

He threw up his arms and went down on his knee's, saying, "Thank you Lord, you finally answered my prayers'." Then he stood up and said, "Sure, right this way."

One strange thing about the books. It seems the McNally cows gave birth several times a year. Lizzy was looking over my shoulder, I said, "Just how are we supposed to get these cattle back to their rightful owners?"

"I don't think there is an equitable way. Have you ever heard of 'poor farms'?"

"I've read about them, why?"

"Well, I was thinking, have you heard of 'Share Cropper's? Anyway, what if people in need could run this place on shares? Everyone who works here could share in the profits. Sort of a government ran 'poor farm', how does that sound?"

"Ok, just who would manage the operation?"

"I was really impressed with Ivy, you know the restaurant owner in town. Also, what about Harry McFab, he is familiar with the place?"

"As long as you're solving problems, what about the Russell homestead?"

"I even have an answer for that, why don't we sell it to the Romero's for one dollar?"

"Let's run it by Harry and see if he would be willing. He might not want to. Or he might not like to share the management with Ivy." I said.

"Alright, I'll go ask him." She turned and left. I continued to peruse the ledgers. I knew anything that was done, would have to be approved by the Judge in Cheyenne. Lizzy came back.

"He was very interested. Especially in Ivy. He has a crush on her. He has lunch ready, do you want to eat?"

We rode into Laramie in mid-afternoon. Going directly to the café, we broached the subject to Ivy. She said she was tired of running the café anyway. And she knew Harry, she liked him. Since that was settled we went to see the town marshal.

He was a little perturbed about the town having to bury the ten dead bodies. Said the Federal Government should pay for the burying. So we did. I got death certificates for all ten of them. The Judge would need proof. Then we went back to our homestead.

They had pretty much ruined our wagon. It was a good thing we were weren't in it, we would of had more holes in us than Swiss cheese. We built a fire and cooked our supper, then went for a swim. Bub was glad to see us. What in the world were we going to do with a goat?

We did get a good nights sleep. Of course a little after dawn the Romero's were there. The pounding woke us up.

"Jesus, you sure get up early." I said, as I stumbled out half dressed. A couple of his daughters were sharing a Tortilla with Bub. One of the girls had her arm around his neck. Maybe the problem of the goat was solved?

I said, "You're doing a good job on the house. And you know that's good, since you're going to be living in it."

"What do you mean? Patron." he said, dropping his hammer.

"I mean, we have no use of this place. You can buy it, for one dollar. You have a dollar, don't you?"

"Si, I do." He hurried to reach in his pocket and handed me a dollar. I went on,

"You can also have the cows and that goat, your girls seem to like him. Plus there are ten head of saddle stock running around here someplace, you can have them too. We will take our six horses with us. With all of the farming stuff we bought, you should be all set-up to make a living."

"Si, how can I ever thank you? If you ever need anything just call on us."

"You never know, I just might need a favor someday. It's good to have friends. Don't you think so girls?" Their smiles were bright, as they stood there with Bub.

"One thing, Patron. All but one of those men were shot through. But Artus McNally had two puncture wounds, that did not go all the way through. What killed him?"

"Well, your girls have a good protector, it was Bub that got him. Bub was in the barn, Artus ran in there and surprised him. When you play with the Devil, you're bound to get burned."

"Si, Si, I will remember that."

It was just after lunch when we left. We had packed our possible's onto Jill and Lil. We rode the black and Jim. The other two horses followed along behind. We didn't have too much to say. We were in no hurry. We were riding stirrup to stirrup, we'd glance at each other and smile. We did not need words.

Cheyenne was too far to make it before dark. So we found a nice spot to camp, back from the trail along side of running water. We unsaddled and took the pack saddles off of Jill and Lil. We didn't bother to hobble any of the horses, they'd stick around.

The moon was up, he had a sky full of stars for company. We lay on our backs beside our small camp fire. We were almost dry from our swim in the babbling brook. I said, "You had better sit up and let me comb your hair before it dries." Lizzy sat up. We had an Ivory Comb from Dunravens' coach. The handle was inlaid with gold. Lizzy was perfectly capable of combing her own hair. But it had got to be sort of ritual, me combing her hair. Not all the time, but just on special occasions, like this night. But then again, every night with Lizzy was special.

The next morning we dressed for the city. Of course we each had our twin guns strapped on. But somehow, mine just didn't look as good on me, as my wife's did on her. Must of had something to do with her shape.

We stopped at our coach first and unloaded the horses. Then took them to the stables. Next came the part I was dreading. We went to see the Judge.

"Ten!, you killed ten men?" He was starting to get his dander up.

"No, not really, we only got nine of them, our goat killed Artus McNally. But you're missing the point, it was all in self-defense. They were shooting our wagon to kindling, thinking we were in there. Here we have the death certificates' on all of them, saying the cause of death was stupidity. Or anyway it should say that." Lizzy said.

I didn't say anything. I just sat there looking at him. He was getting red around the collar. He couldn't meet my stare, he kept looking away. Finally he gave us voucher's for the blood money. We left and went to the land office.

The land agent was more affable. He didn't give us any trouble a'tall about transferring the homestead into Jesus name. I wonder why he was so nice. Last time he was a little snotty. Our office was in the same building as all the government office's were. So we didn't have far to go, just down the hall.

So down the hall we went. Lizzy got to the chair behind the desk before I did. She leaned back and put her boots on the desk. There was an adjoining office. Turns out we had a secretary that we didn't know we had. She came in and said, "Would you both like a cup of coffee?"

We looked at each other, then back to her. "Sure." Lizzy said. "But, just who are you?"

"Oh, I am sorry, my name is Othello, but everyone calls me Tella. I am your secretary."

She looked to be about the same age as my wife. A good figure, but not as good as Lizzy. "How come we didn't know you existed?" I said.

"I don't know why. This has been my job for two years. The marshal before this last one hired me. Seems they don't last too long."

"Ok, just what do you do, besides making coffee?"

"I sweep up and keep up with the filing and correspondence from the main office in Chicago. I fill out and send the weekly reports. Also keep track of all the wanted bulletins they send us. The Judge gave me the death certificates you brought back, I will forward them to Chicago."

"Ok, what if, from now on we just give you the paper work? Do we still have to check in with the Judge?" I said.

"Well he has a super big ego, he thinks he is in charge. But really the Chicago office is. But if I were you, I would continue to let him think he is."

"I bet I know who really is in charge, and I bet its you!" Lizzy said.

"Well I do like things neat and orderly, Uh, would you please take your feet off of the desk? I just polished it."

Lizzy put her feet down and sat up. I thought Tella was going to get it now. But Lizzy just smiled and said. "You're right, I'm sorry, it was rude of me. You never put your feet on the furniture in someone else's house. And I believe these offices are your domain."

Tella smiled and went to fetch the coffee. Lizzy looked at me and said, "You never mess with cooks or secretaries. They both can make your life miserable."

"Yes dear," I said. I knew one more person you never mess with. That's my wife. Or any wife, they can make your life miserable also. I was no dummy, I knew that even before I was married. Because I was very observant, Pa never contradicted Ma. And I never either.

Tella came back with the coffee, "Cream or sugar?" she asked.

"I like a little cream with mine," I said, then added, "Lizzy likes hers black, no sugar."

Lizzy said, "Tell me Tella, are you married or have any other family here?"

"No, to both questions. I was on an orphanage train. I was sixteen. I was supposed to go to a family on down the line. But I jumped train here. I always looked older that I am. I was hanging around the saloon door, when the marshal who hired me, found me. He was a nice man."

"You say you're only eighteen?" I said.

"Yes, that's all I am. But if you count experience, I'm much older."

"Yeah, the same with me." I said. I didn't go into details though. I didn't need it getting back to the Judge, how young in years I was. Lizzy and Tella fell into women's talk, I suddenly became invisible. They were yakking on about dresses and cloth and I don't know what all. I went and sat down by the window. Lizzy was dark, whereas Tella was a blonde. Tella was in a homespun dress. While Lizzy had on one of her riding habits, with crossed six-guns. Damn, but my wife was good looking. I could set here and stare at her all day. There is a saying that love is blind, well my love didn't need to be blind, cause everyone who had ever met Lizzy, knew she was a knockout.

I guess I dozed off, cause, "Hey Buck, wake up. It's time to go to lunch. You're buying us all lunch, we flipped, you lost." Lizzy said. I got up and checked my guns. It was starting to be a habit with me. Every time I came awake, to check my guns. I don't know why, I never sleep that hard, if anyone messed with my guns, I would know it. Survival was becoming a habit I didn't want to break.

I followed the two women down the stairs. The view was fine. Lizzy did not carry a purse, Tella did. It looked heavy. I knew what was in there. A woman couldn't be too careful in Cheyenne in the summer of 1873. On the street, I fell further back, they were almost a half block ahead of me.

Why I was walking so slow, I had no idea. But I found out fast enough. I heard the report the same time as I felt the slug. It hit me a glancing blow in the ribs. The impact knocked me down to one knee. My guns were in my hands, but I was facing the wrong way. No big deal, cause I heard Lizzy's guns banging away. I got turned in time to see a figure fall from the alleys' mouth.

Lizzy ran up, "What were you doing so far behind us?

Are you alright?"

"Yes, thanks to your cloth, the slug just bounced off of my ribs. Why I was so far behind you I don't really know, except maybe providence. If I was up beside you both, they might have hit you women. Did you see if there were anymore of them?"

Tella spoke up, "Yes, I saw two more, I think I recognized them. I think I have a poster on both of them back in the office."

Lizzy walked over to the dead man and turned him over on his back, she reached down and picked up his gun and tossed it to me. Then stripped his gun belt off and hung it over her shoulder.

John came running up. "What happened?" He said.

Lizzy looked at him and said, "You're a day late and dollar short, my friend. This fool tried to dry gulch my husband. There were two more of them. Tella knows who they are. We'll get them."

"If there in the city limits, its my job, my jurisdiction." John said.

"Only if you can draw faster and shoot straighter than me," Lizzy said. "But you can take care of that carrion. Have the coroner get a death certificate over to Tella, will you?" Then they, Lizzy and Tella turned on their heels and left. I looked at John and shrugged. Then I hurried after...

We reached the Cheyenne Supper Club with no further hindrance. Sitting with my back to the wall, I felt my ribs. It felt like I got kicked by a mule. Lizzy leaned over and felt around, "Nope, they're not broke. You'll be Ok." Then she turned to Tella, "what do you think? Here feel, that's just swelling, not a break, right?"

Tella did the same as Lizzy. She looked concerned, "I don't know, can you breath alright?"

"Well it does hurt when I breath, they could be cracked."

"Ok," Lizzy said, "After we eat, we'll go by the Doctor's and get him to look at you."

"If you think that's best, but I'm like you, food first. Besides, I've had my ribs wrapped before, I don't know what's worse, the wound or the cure."

Really, I was reveling in the attention, after being ignored all morning. It's funny how childish men can be at times. I even got them to cut my steak up for me. I know, I know, that's pushing it, but hell, how many times a day does a man get shot?

The doctor said, that two of them were cracked. Shit, I could hardly move after he got done. He said I had to keep them wrapped at least for a week. We all went back to the office. Tella found the poster's on all three of them. They were escaped convicts out of Kansas. Why in the holy hell, didn't they just keep on moving? Why draw attention to yourselves by taking a pot shot at me?

It takes a stupid man to be a crook in the first place, and stupid is as stupid does. So now I couldn't get any rest, I had to go after them. We picked up their trail on the other side of the tracks. Heading north. We didn't bother to take a pack horse with us. We could use their horses to carry their dead bodies back on. That is unless they would come peaceable.

They were really fogging it. If they didn't take it easy, they would kill their horses. They had a two hour head start on us. But I wasn't worried. They were heading right for Indian territory. It wasn't long before their tracks slowed down to a walk. But they were still heading north.

I wonder where they think they are going? We kept up a slow steady pace. I didn't want to push them to hard. It was coming on to dark. We stopped and made camp beside a small creek. I built a small fire out of dry wood. Lizzy reached in her saddle bag and got out a sling, bending down she found some small smooth stones. She wondered off and ways, then came back with two rabbits. Was there anything she couldn't do? Yeah, I had to clean the rabbits. But she cooked them.

Just before dark, we seen the smoke from their campfire. They were about ten miles ahead of us. Too lazy to find dry wood, they probably broke some branch's off a tree, green wood smoke.

I had built the fire in the lee of a large stone, so it reflected the heat back on us. Being that we were also under the lower branch's of a pine tree, we were quite cozy. We had Jim and the Black, they had finished grazing and were close around us. The temperature would get down in the lower forties, in this high desert atmosphere. But like I said, we were pretty cozy, so we could sleep in the altogether and not be cold. Our guns were close at hand though. Of course when we got closer to our prey, we would have to stay dressed at night.

We awoke before the dawn, after completing our absolution's, which we did by bathing in the creek. We ate a handful of pemmican and saddled our horses and got underway.

We were closing on them. But not too fast. In the back of my mind, was the thought, that maybe if we just loly-gagged around, the problem might take care of itself. After all they were heading for Indian county.

Chapter Twelve

About mid-afternoon we swam the Platte River. It was moderately high. It was coming on to supper time when we made an early camp on the Dry Fork of the Cheyenne, in what was called Thunder Basin. What water there was, was clear and cold.

Their tracks were heading a little northwest. The only thing was, that was Sioux Territory. The Laramie Treaty of 1868 gave the Sioux "that country north of the North Platte River and east of the summits of the Big Horn Mountains." Sitting Bull, the medicine man of the Hunkpapas was there in this unceded territory. The Northern Pacific Railroad had sent survey parties in there last year and again this year, I had heard back in Cheyenne. The wound had already started to bleed.

I told this to Lizzy. "I know all about it. And I don't like it any better than you do. Our government has broken almost every treaty they ever made."

"Anyway those fools are heading straight into trouble. I could say that they deserve what will happen to them, but, hell, stupidity is no sign to torture and mutilate them." I said.

"Isn't Fort Phil Kearny up that way? They could be heading for it." Lizzy said.

"Yeah, it is. But they will never reach it. We brought

our buckskins, didn't we?"

"Yes, I packed them like you asked. Why? Do you want to change into them?"

"Yep, I think its time. Let your hair down and tie it in two braids down your back. I will tie mine in one. Put your guns on under that squaw dress, its loose enough, isn't it?"

"Yes, I'll cut some slits on either side, so I can reach them fast."

"Good. Do you know any Sioux? I mean the language, not people."

"Yes I do, I had some Sioux children stay with me one winter. I picked it up fast, I probably know more than you do. I know you speak Shoshone."

"I know some Sioux, enough to get along. But if you are fluent, I will let you do most of the talking. Only sometimes. Now I said sometimes, women aren't allowed to speak. Like in counsel. So don't get pissed. You have to act the part, not only look it."

Lizzy got the buckskins out of the saddle bags. She pulled her clothes off and walked into water. I did the same. It was an hour later before we got dressed. When we did, you couldn't tell us from members of the Sioux tribe. Now I said you, the Sioux probably could.

We made the Belle Fourche by the time the sun stood high in the sky. We were only an hour behind them, the tracks were fresh. We continued northwest, toward the Powder River. We saw the tree line along the Powder, then we heard the yipping and the yelling. We were too late, the Sioux had them!

We pulled up in a stand of Juniper. We unsaddled the horse's. It would be dark soon. At full dark, we took our weapons and walked toward the encampment. A dog seen us coming, he didn't bark. He ran up, stopped and looked at us. He

J.D. Oliver

whined, I patted him on the head. He was a hybrid, half wolf and half some kind of dog. I bent down and looked into his eyes, then said, "I tell you what boy, you see those Juniper's? Our horses are over there, you go on over and wait for us, we'll take you back with us."

Lizzy looked at me, "I will never figure out your rapport with animals. You must be part wolf yourself." I looked at her and bared my fangs. She giggled.

We simply walked right up to the edge of the camp. They were too busy hassling their new captives. They were naked and tied to stakes. The squaws and children were tossing hot coals at them. We continued on till we were at the edge of the firelight.

"Lizzy, what we were these two in prison for?"

"Rape, torture and murder. Among a few other things. They were part of Quantrell's raiders. Why?"

"I was just thinking on how hard I wanted to try and get these two out of their clutches."

One Indian got up and threw more wood on the fire, it flared up. In the increased light, we became visible. The whole camp got quite. Deathly quiet. They all were staring at us. One big fellow stood up in a feline move. I knew instantly who it was: Tatanka Lyotanka. Or in English, Lyotanka Tatanka Sitting Bull. The Medicine Man for the Lakota tribe. He had the most piercing eyes. They seemed to be burning a hole right through us.

Walking toward us, he said not a word. He stopped not three feet in front of us. Lizzy said to him, "I'yotankahan Tatankabdoka?" Which was Sitting Bull, but in the Dakota dialect. Then she whispered to me, "That is Sitting Bull, right?"

He smiled, looking back and forth between us, he said in English. "Yes, I am Sitting Bull. I know who you are 'Son of

231

She Who Sees the Light,' but your woman I do not know. She speaks Dakota, but she is not Sioux."

"No, she is not Sioux. She comes from China, a land across the big ocean. She is my wife, therefore Sioux by marriage. My name is Tamdoka, or Buck in English, Son of She Who See's the Light. My wife is called 'Lizzy"."

"Why are you here, Tamdoka?"

"Since you knew I was the son of 'She Who Sees the Light', why do you not know our reason for being here?"

"I know, you came for the White Creatures. Their skin is white, but their hearts are black.."

They (the Indians) had got over their surprise in seeing us appear out of the night and had went back to the pastime of torturing their captives. Now, they had made small spears out of willow branches. They had feathered the ends and put pine pitch on them and lighting them in the fire, they would run by the captives and toss them into their flesh.

Sitting Bull said, "Would you come and Cannonpa?" Or (Smoke the Pipe?)

We both nodded and followed him back to where he was sitting when we first seen him. The screams were getting louder. At each blood curdling scream from the two, the Indians would roar with approval. He lit the pipe, handing it to me first. I took a puff and handed it to Lizzy. Now women did not usually smoke the pipe with the men. I could tell by his eyes, that he was surprised when I handed it to her.

I said, "My wife is not only my wife. She is a Warrior. As such she is my equal in battle."

He smiled, I could tell he didn't believe me. The screams were starting to bother Lizzy. I said to Sitting Bull. "These men are wanted by the White Man's law. They are bad men. We want to take them back to be hanged. Will you give them to us?"

"I cannot, for they are not my prisoners. They belong to the women who have lost husbands in battle against the white man. It is their right to kill them as they wish. We men cannot interfere."

I hadn't noticed it before, but it was only the women who were torturing them. Lizzy looked at him. Then she stood up, she undid the tie on her dress. The dress dropped to the ground. She was naked, except for her crossed gun belts. She turned, in a lightning fast draw, she drew both pistols and put a slug threw both their heads. Then she punched two new rounds into her guns. She holstered them. Then reached down and put her dress back on. She sat down.

The camp was quiet once more. Everyone was staring at her. Then they started to laugh, some came over and patted her on the back. Now if I would of shot them, they would of been pissed. But being a woman, Lizzy had the right to kill them.

The women brought us some stew to eat. We were accepted. We smoked the pipe some more. I said to Sitting Bull, "How much of your future do you know?"

He sat, not saying anything for five minutes. He said, "I have seen a victory that we will have over the white soldiers, they will fall into our camp."

"Yes, I have seen that also. But a battle does not the war make. We were doomed from the time the first white man stepped ashore from where the sun rises. They are many, we are few. This land will be a land populated by people from the four corners of the world. Our only hope is to stay alive and become part of it. Fight your battles as you must. Then make peace with destiny." I said. Then we stood up and hand-in-hand we disappeared into the night.

Dog, our new pet was waiting for us. He licked our

hands. We tightened our cinches and rode slowly away with the Dog following us. It took us three days to get back to Cheyenne. We sort of turned it into a mini-honeymoon.

Would you believe that the Judge wouldn't pay us for those two? He said we had no proof they were dead. Lizzy stayed my hand, or he would of joined them. Not because I wanted the money, but because he inferred that we were liars. I said, "Honey you only delayed the inevitable. You know sooner or later, we are going to have to kill him."

"Maybe not, maybe somebody else will do it. You know nobody likes him. Just be patient. I am sure somebody else will do for him."

It wasn't a week later that a rancher did just that, when the Judge turned a rustler loose. Said there wasn't enough evidence. The rustler was caught with a running iron and it was hot. I would say that was enough. I didn't arrest the rancher. Figured it was justifiable homicide.

No one really missed the Judge. Tella kept right on running the show. She had sent a telegram to the Chicago office. They said they didn't have anybody available right now. Really no one wanted the position. They said as soon as they had anybody they would send him on. Tella was to be the acting Judge. An eighteen year old female Judge? Oh, well, she was just as qualified as most anyone else.

She was just as capable as our old Judge and a lot easier on the eyes. And a lot better to get along with. Our work fell into a routine. Most of the felons just gave themselves up when we approached them. I guess our reputation proceeded us. In fact we were getting a little bored.

But who could be bored with Lizzy in their life? She was a delightful surprise every minute every day. Dog had taken to sleeping under our coach, no one could approach without his alerting us. During the day he shadowed our every step. So went the summer.

By September Tella had been appointed a full fledged Judge. Her and Lizzy were great friends. We spent a lot of time swimming in the warm springs, all three of us. Of course Dog enjoyed it too.

But with the first wind of fall, our spirits grew restless. We were laying in bed with the morning breeze blowing on our naked bodies. When Lizzy said, "I think its time we moved on. I want to go see how the girls are doing. Also I think its time we checked on our business interests in Denver."

"Alright, but how do we get out of this Marshal business?"

"I have been talking to Tella, she has already put out feelers. The office in Chicago says there is a man that wants the Marshal job. It's up to you though. All you have to do is say yes, and he can be here on the next train."

Of course I said yes. I was restless too. But even if I wasn't, I would of said yes. Because when your wife wants something, you had better satisfy her, or your life will be miserable. I guess it's the same in reverse also.

We met the train. The new Marshal was a man in his late twenty's. He was wearing a Derby Hat. It was cocked to one side. He was about five foot ten. And he spoke with an Irish brogue. His name was Shamus Lafferty. He was wearing a short barreled .45 on his left hip, rigged for a cross draw.

Tella held out her hand, he took it, holding her hand while looking deep into her eyes. Then he bowed over it and kissed her hand. She turned a bright red. Well, I could see we wouldn't have to worry about her being lonely.

He turned to us. "Tis the famous Gentry's I have thy honor of meeting?"

I said, as I took his hand. "I don't know about the famous, but yes, we are the Gentry's." His hand shake was firm, perhaps a trifle too firm. I gave back what I received. He winched. I hoped he could still use his shooting hand.

Lizzy took his hand and massaged it a little bit, he smiled. She gave me a dirty look. Well, what the hell, he started it. I said, "Do you have any other baggage, Shamus?"

"No, just this carpet bag. I travel light."

"Alright, we have a room reserved for you at the Hotel. We plan on staying for the next week, so you can get both feet on the ground. I am sure you will enjoy working with Judge Othello."

"Aye, that be the God's truth, Mr. Gentry." He held his arm out for her. She put her hand in the crook of his elbow, they walked off smiling at each other.

We made arrangements for the railroad to take care of our coach. We paid them a year in advance. We also had Carl Hatfield get our custom made carriage out of mothballs and oil and grease everything up. We would be using four horses to pull with two spares following behind. Our friends, including my brother-in-law, Chin-Lee, were giving us a party the night before we were scheduled to leave. Victoria Langhorne and her children were also coming. They had made a success of their horse breeding farm.

Shamus Lafferty and John Wesley Hardin, had become good friends. Was that good or bad? Who knows. Only time will tell the tale.

Oh, I think I might of mislead you. About the Judge's death. That rancher didn't kill him in cold blood. You see, they got into a yelling match over that rustler. It was the Judge who lost his temper and pulled his hog-leg and took the first shot at the rancher. The rancher was just defending himself. The way I explained it the first time, would make you think I wasn't doing my duty by not arresting the rancher. It was Lizzy who drew that to my attention, as she was perusing my daily journal.

The party was well attended. I was surprised by the number and quality of friends we had made in the Cheyenne area. Friends are sometimes a iffy thing. They are like a garden, you get out of it what you put into it. That is if the Devil's hailstorm doesn't come along and wipe your garden out. But why worry about the future?

You see, some people exist in a vacuum between the past and what they hope the future to be. But instead we should take a lesson from the animals, they worry not about the past, nor the future. They're happy just being alive in the present. As I definitely am, because my wife just woke me up to make love......!

We said our goodbyes to Chin-Lee and his wife and were on the trail by mid-morning. It was the fall of 74' and the morning was crisp. The horses were anxious and happy to be on the road. Most people think animals don't get bored, but they do. Why else do horses crib on the corral posts? If you were left hours on end in a small enclosure, you would start chewing on things too.

Lizzy had her hair tied back in a pony tail. She was driving with a big smile on her face. I guess she must have been bored also. We were well suited to each other. Neither one of us could stand to stay in one place too long.

The traffic was light. A few lone horsemen, ranchers, heading to town. And of course freight wagons coming up from Denver. At this rate it wouldn't take long to settle this country. And then what would we do? Here I was violating my own rule, worrying about the future. So I busied myself, shooting at inanimate objects along the trail. The horses didn't like it at first, but they got used to it. But finally Lizzy made me stop it. Said she was getting a head ache.

We didn't stop too long for lunch, just time enough to water the horses and change two of them out. We just ate an apple apiece. When we stopped for the night, there was already a wagon at our favorite spring. I thought about going on, then changed my mind. There was enough room for all.

Turns out they were Mormons. Now I didn't know too much about Mormons, but I always believed in letting sleeping dogs lie. I mean to each their own. The man looked to be in his middle forties. He had two wives. One wife seemed to be about his age and they had a couple of little ones. The second wife was young. And she wasn't happy. How did I know? Well if you don't know when a woman's unhappy, I feel sorry for you.

Now the way I looked at things, it was mighty unfair to a woman to have to share one man. And the way he looked to me, he would have trouble satisfying one woman, much less two. I know one woman was all I could handle. Now the older ones were a right sociable bunch, but that girl didn't say a word. But when she went to find a bush, Lizzy followed her. They were both gone longer than it takes to pee.

Now I'm not too stupid, but some, when it comes to women. But I knew enough that Lizzy wasn't going to let that dog sleep. They came back, Lizzy leaned over and said in my ear, "Her name is Louisa Lou, they bought her just this morning from her parents, she's still a virgin, as of this minute. He plans on changing that status this night. Lulu hates him. What are you going to do about it?"

"Me? Why me? Why don't you just shoot the son-of-a-bitch?"

"We can't do that. He has a wife and kids to support. You are going to have to do it, without killing him."

"Oh, alright. I'll take care of it." I said, not really knowing how I was going to do that. So I decided I would be sociable. So I went over to their fire. On the way I picked up a chunk of wood. Sitting down, I pulled out my Bowie Knife and went to whittling on it. I'd glance up at him from time to time. Then I would just smile real big and grunt, you know Indian stuff. This went on for about a half hour. He was getting nervous.

Finally I said, "You have a right nice family there. You love them?"

He said, "Well of course I do."

I said, "Sure would be a shame if they got scalped. That there big girl - is she your daughter?"

"No, she's my second wife." He said, sort of turning pale.

"Well, well. How about that. Now if it was me, I would pay more attention to my wife and children, yeah, those that are setting over there. There are a powerful lot of Injuns around here, now some of them don't have any wives at all. Much less two. Did you ever hear that old saying, 'a bird in hand is worth two in the bush.'?"

"No, can't say that I have. What are you trying to get at?"

"Man, you sure are dumb. They say that if a man has one wife, that he is monogamous. And that's good. You see, when God created Adam, he didn't create two Eves, now did he? I see that you agree with me. Now if a man has two wives, that's Polygamy. Now that's bad. Now, let me ask you this, do you know the difference between good and bad? You're nodding, now that's good. I think we're getting somewhere. Now do you think you should divest yourself of this second wife?"

"But, but, I paid a hundred dollars for her."

"Oh, I see that you are a little materialistic. Well that's no problem. Lizzy, give this man two hundred dollars, will you? You see, you've made a hundred percent profit. Now do you know that being materialistic is also a sin? You do? Good. Now I am going to tell you one more thing, you are not going to have a second wife. You are going to be faithful to just this one. Do you understand? Good." I looked at Lulu and said, "Do you have any baggage?"

"Just one suitcase, it has everything that I own in it."

"Good, get it and take it to our carriage. You are now a free woman. To come and go as 'you' please. How old are you anyway?"

"I am thirteen."

"Shit, I thought so. Ok, Ok, I'm not mad. Don't cry. Lizzy, you had better keep that creep away from me, I just might plug him for fun."

"That's alright, looks like they're breaking camp and moving on. Good riddance, I say."

Lulu had her suitcase, she still had a tear running down her cheek. Lizzy put her arm around her and hugged her. Can you imagine how she must feel? Her own parents selling her to be a second wife. And her not much more than a child herself. I had better not run across those parents. I might just plug them.

As they were pulling out, the woman gave me a big smile and mouthed 'thank you'. I smiled back and winked. It seemed like we were always taking in some waif. This was bound to put a crimp in our sex life. Oh well, absence makes the heart grow fonder. Anyway that's what I was going to keep telling myself.

Lulu slept in the carriage, we slept under it. It wasn't me that had to restrain himself. It was Lizzy who had to constrain

J.D. Oliver

herself. She whispered, "I'll be real quiet."

I whispered back, "It's not you, you know how noisy I am?"

She said, "Damn, you're right." Then she turned over and we went to sleep.

The next morning the women went to the spring to take a bath, Lizzy was still pissed, she pulled her clothes off before she left the wagon and walked to the spring naked. Thankfully Lulu did not follow suit. When Lizzy got there, she turned and stuck her tongue out at me. I hurried and went to see about the horses. Everything Lizzy did, just made me love her that much more.

When the Mormon's left last night they were heading south, toward Greeley. When we got there just after mid-afternoon, while we were stabling our horses for the night. The town Marshal came up. He looked us over and said, "Hi Buck. Good to see you both again. Looks like you have a passenger?"

"Yep, what about it?"

"Oh, nothing. Just that a crazy Mormon came by this morning, said you had kidnapped his second wife. I threw him in jail. It's illegal to have two wives. He's still there, what do you want me to do with him?"

"Can you hang him?"

"No, don't think I can rightly do that. Might shoot him trying to escape, though."

Lizzy said to me, "You didn't change his mind about polygamy at all did you. Let me give it a try. You take Lulu and get us two rooms over at the Hotel, now make sure you get two rooms. You think you can handle that?"

I took Lulu by the hand and stuck my tongue out at Lizzy. Lizzy and the town Marshal headed toward the jail. I didn't find out till later what Lizzy had done. She had the

241

Marshal let her into his cell. The first thing she done was string him up to the bars by his wrists. Now he was a pretty big man, but she done it. Then she cut his pants off, then his underwear. Then she took her knife and started making little curlicue's on his belly, getting ever closer to his jewels. Before she got there, he passed out. No, she didn't castrate him, but he thought she did. After he passed out, she wrote 'Shit head' on his forehead, with her knife. So when it healed you would still be able to read it.

I guess when he came to and seen he was still whole, he got down on his knees and thanked his God. The Marshal turned him loose then. No one every seen hide nor hair of him again. He lit out and left his wife behind. We heard later that she remarried. He was an atheist.

That night, was I ever glad I got two rooms. I could hardly move the next morning. It was like she had something to prove. And I was more than happy to let her prove it. We were woke by Lulu knocking on our door.

We spent two more days in Greeley. They had a good General Store. We bought Lulu a complete outfit. There weren't the best of quality, but would do her till we got to Denver. She was some shy and a little backward. And would you believe, she couldn't read. Her parents didn't believe in teaching girls to read and write. But that could wait till we got to Denver also.

This was the second day, and Lulu still hadn't taken a bath. Lizzy told her, "Lulu, this shy bit goes only so far. We have bought you new clothes. Including underwear. So, no excuses, get those clothes off and get in that tub." Nobody argues with Lizzy when she gets that tone in her voice. I was in our room with the connecting door open. I could hear her clothes hitting the floor.

I heard a gasp, then, "Buck, get in here, look at this."

I rushed in, Lulu's body was covered in bruises. She tried to cover her small breasts with one arm and her other with the other arm. I said, "Lulu, who did that to you? Was it that Mormon?"

"Nooo, he didn't hit me," she sobbed. "It was my Father. He didn't like the way I did the chores. I was too slow." I was seething. Pacing back and forth. "Lulu, can you take us to your old home?"

"I don't want to go home, I want to go with Lizzy, don't you like me?"

"Yes, we like you. And you can go with us, you don't ever have to go back to them. But I just want to talk. We need to get your health history. I tell you what, you just tell me where they live, you can stay here with Lizzy, I will go talk to them by myself. Uh, you can get in the tub now."

Lizzy and I went in the other room to talk and let her have some privacy while she washed. We gave her about fifteen minutes'. Then Lizzy went back in. I sat in the chair looking out of the window, thinking. Lulu was a natural blond with blue eyes. With the proper food and loving parents she would blossom. I intended to make sure she got her chance in life.

Lizzy came back in. "I put her to bed. She did tell me where her old place was. It is only about thirty miles northeast from here. It's on Crow Creek. You can't miss it."

"Good, I want you two to go on to Denver in the morning. I'll get a horse from Festus and meet you at your house in a few days. Do you want someone to ride shotgun for you?"

"No, I don't think so. I'm feeling mean. If I have someone riding shotgun, the perverts will leave me alone and if they leave me alone, I won't get a chance to kill them."

"You know of course, that most women would want to be left alone. But then again, you're not most women. You're all woman. You keep that revolving shotgun handy."

I saw them off the next morning. Lizzy had her .41 caliber revolver's crossed over her lovely hips. The shotgun was propped up on one side and her .44 caliber Henry on the other side of her. I pity the poor fool who messed with my wife. She had a complete arsenal and knew how to use it. Plus she was in our armored carriage.

Festus had a big strong gelding saddled for me. I slipped my .44 Henry in the scabbard. I had two hundred rounds in my saddle bags. I pulled each revolver out and checked the .44 loads. It made things simpler to have both your rifle and pistols the same caliber. I had enough food in the other saddlebag to last me for a couple of days. I was wearing my buckskins.

I was in no hurry. I wanted to get there just before dark. This was one Indian that liked the dark. It was the dark that brought out the fear in men. And fear was a weapon that I loved to use.

Lulu wanted Dog to go with them, but Dog wanted to go with me. Strange, most times Dog preferred the company of children. But I think he knew I would need him. Now why would I need Dog? Ah, yes, fear. And what's better to strike fear in a man, than a large wolf looking dog? Dog was pretty independent. He had disappeared the morning after we got Lulu, he had shown up just this morning. I wonder where he had been?

I swung up in the saddle, Dog trotted off a ways and looked back at me over his shoulder. Then gave a small Yip. I think he wanted me to follow him. Since he was heading in the direction I wanted to go anyway, I did so.

We arrived one finger before sunset. The place was set

in a small valley beside a lazy creek. Nice layout. We had stopped in a little stand of brush on the hill side, where we could look and still not be seen. The place was fairly well kept up. Looked like the guy wasn't lazy anyway. That was one thing about the Devil also, he isn't lazy.

Since we had about fifteen minutes before the sunset, and a good half hour before dark, I decided to take a short nap. When I awoke, it was dark and Old Man Coyote was sitting beside Dog, watching the house.

He said, as I sat up, "Did you have a nice nap, Buck?"

Now, I don't think he said it out loud, I just heard it in my head. But I did say, "What are you doing here?"

"You aren't the only one who likes to set matters right. The Great Spirit does also. In fact, this problem is his. I am here to stop you from interfering."

"Interfering? I was just going to go down and let some daylight into his innards."

"Let those without sin, be the first to cast a stone. I don't think you qualify, do you?"

"No, I guess I don't. But then again, I don't think anyone can fit that bill."

"Exactly, that's why he will take care of it. Watch, it will happen this night."

So I got up and got some pemmican out of my saddlebag. Gave some to Dog, then offered some to Old Man Coyote. He said Thank you, and accepted some. We sat there munching away. It must of been going on to nine o'clock when the yelling and screaming started.

They were having a fight, the man and his wife. As far as I could see they didn't have any hired hands, just the two of them or so I thought. We could see them at the kitchen table. They were quite the pair. She gave as good as she got. Such language I had never heard. We could see a bottle of whisky on the table. Nothing like alcohol to fan the flames.

She slapped him, he picked up a knife from the table and stabbed her. She stumbled back, out of sight. There must of been a shotgun close to hand, because there came a blast that hit him in the chest. He was dead before he hit the floor. She came into view again, she sat down in a chair, holding her chest. Blood was seeping out between her fingers. She leaned forward on the table and didn't move again.

We sat there for about ten more minutes. Old Man Coyote said, "You wanted a little history on the girl, Lulu? As you call her. They were not her parents. As you can plainly see, they are both dark complicated. Your girl is blond and blue eyed. They found her beside a burnt wagon when she was only three. Some of your people killed her real parents. She had hid, they missed finding her. Too bad they didn't, she would of had a better life. So now, if you would, go down and collect the little Indian boy that is locked in an upper room. Don't disturb the dead, when you have the boy, set fire to the house. Then turn all of the livestock loose, all except one horse for the boy. You will take him with you, to raise as your own. He already thinks Lulu is his sister."

After saying all of that, he just got up and disappeared into the night. I didn't move immediately. It's strange how evil, when left to fruition, will implode on the Devil's own. I got up and stretched, with Dog and my horse following me, I went down the hill.

I went to the barn and saddled a nice pinto. I turned the rest of the stock loose. I felt for a pulse in the woman's neck, just to make sure she was dead. She was. Dog was ahead of me, he went up the stairs. He stopped before the attic door. It had a big padlock. I shot it off, making sure the bullet did not go into the attic room. Sitting on a makeshift bunk was a Indian boy about eight years old.

He looked at me, smiled and got up and hugged me. Then he bent and commenced to pet Dog, talking to him in Sioux. I pointed to myself and said, "Tamdoka" (Buck). He said, in the Dakota dialect, "Ioyomya Ideya" or in English, 'He Who Lights The Lamp'.

I asked him, "Do you speak any English?" He nodded assent. And then said,

"I have been here two years, I am a fast learner."

"It is good to know the language of those who would take our land. For they are many and we are few. And in order for us to survive in their culture, we have to adapt. And fight the fight in the white man's way. They fight most of their battles with the sword of the mouth. And we have to become fluent in their ways."

"Tamdoka, you are 'Ska San' of light complexion."

"Yes, that is why I know what we have to do, because I am half 'Wahsicun'. We will have plenty of time to talk. Now please, gather up any belongings that you might have, we have to leave this evil place."

He made up a small bundle, that he wrapped in deer hide. Then he took some blankets and made a bed roll, that we could tie behind his saddle. I found a can of coal oil in the pantry. I splashed it all around the house. Then as we went out the kitchen door, I took the lantern from the table and tossed it on the floor. The light from the fire ushered us into the comfort of the night.

We made a dry camp amongst the purple sage of the prairie. I decided to give him a nickname, 'Lad'. You know, from Aladdin and the lamp. Come on, you know, from his name- 'He Who Lights The Lamp'. I know, I know, it's a stretch, but give a guy a break.

Lad started to gather sticks for a small fire, but I told him no. It was a clear night and the light would be seen for miles. I didn't want anybody to know that we had even been to that house. Besides the stars and the waning moon gave us plenty of light. In the high desert in the month of September, the nights were a might crisp. The horses had finished grazing and came and laid down close to us. Their body heat helped.

We were saddled and ready to go shortly after dawn. I wanted to bypass Greeley, didn't want anyone to recognize Lad. Someone might have seen him at their ranch in the past. We didn't do anything wrong. But to some people that wouldn't make any difference, we were Indians to them. Not that I was scared of them, but shoot, after awhile you get tired of shooting fools.

There was Fort Vasquez that a had a little town, sort of, that had grown up around it Figured we could stop there. I wanted to get some clothes and such for Lad. The people up around Cheyenne knew me as Phillip Gentry, U. S. Marshal. But down this way, I don't know. Some do, some don't. Some of them, just knew me as Buck Gentry, gunfighter. Some of them didn't know me at all, except as a damn Indian.

It was late afternoon when we got there. The town was about two hundred yards from the Fort. It did have a General Store. The woman who waited on us, was a white middle aged woman. She looked at us funny, but was nice enough. She even gave Lad a piece of Licorice. I outfitted him from top to bottom. The woman smiled when I paid in gold coin.

We came out and tied our purchase's on our saddles. There was a combination saloon and eating place beside the store. I thought we might as well get a warm meal, thought Lad could use it. The bar and café was in the same room, but at different ends. We went in. It was a little early for supper. But there was a few people already eating. I found a table that I could put my back against the wall. It always gave me a creepy feeling if I didn't.

The waitress came over, she gave us the same strange look, but she was nice enough also. She asked what we would have, I said, we weren't picky, that we would have whatever she had the most of. She said, "Beef Stew it is then. What would you like to drink?"

I said, "Just bring me a beer, and maybe a Sarsaparilla for the boy." She nodded. Then she leaned over and whispered in my ear. "It's not safe for the two of you to be in here."

I looked at her, startled, "What do you mean?" I whispered back.

She whispered, "There are some who don't like Indians, not me. But some of the soldiers from the Fort. They're bullies. They not only don't like Indians, but just about everybody. If they come in, I will let you know, so you can slip out the back door."

I smiled at her. "Don't worry Miss. But yes, if they come in, I would appreciate you letting me know who they are." She walked away, she did have a nice sway in her get-along. Now I just mentioned that in a academic way. Because there was only one woman in my life, but that was no sign I was blind. As I was sure that Lizzy wasn't blind either.

She brought the food and drink. Lad liked his drink. He said, he never tasted that before. But like a good boy, he ate his food, while just sipping his drink. He was making it last. We were just finishing up, when the front door was thrown open with a bang.

In came a half dozen soldiers from the Fort. They were a rambunctious lot. We were sitting in the corner, so they didn't see us, right away that was. The waitress came over and sat down in the chair next to Lad. The soldiers had bellied up the bar, with their backs to us. The whooping and hooting went on for about fifteen minutes before one of them looked around and saw us talking to the waitress.

He was busy telling his comrades. They all looked our way. Our waitress was turning pale. "Miss," I said, "I think you ought to get out of the line of fire, take my son with you and go in the kitchen. Don't worry about me, my name is Buck Gentry." Her eyes opened wide, she knew of me.

One of the soldiers was trying to talk the rest out of committing suicide. Maybe not that, but he was trying to dissuade them. Good for him, he might live to see the sunrise. He pulled away from them and ran out the door as they came toward me. The vision I had on the South Fork of the Shoshone came back to my mind - The atrocity's of the future massacre at Wounded Knee came blaring into my mind, the screaming of the women and children, the calls for help.

Yes, I was showed all that day by the Great Spirit. I tried not to think of it, but at times like this, I could smell the rotting flesh. They came up to my table, calling me and my ancestors all of the crude and vulgar things they could think of. Each invective dropped another shovel full of dirt on their unseeing eyes.

They reached as one for their holstered revolvers. I let them get almost level. Then flame and death from my twin .44's spat lead from under the table. When the smoke cleared their broken and bloody bodies lay strewn on the rough board floor.

I looked around at the white faces staring at me. I said to them. "Is there anyone here who thinks that I did not fire in self-defense?" No one said a word. I was still waiting when the door opened and the soldiers who ran out, came back with the Commanding Officer from the Fort.

He looked at them laying there. Then he looked at me. He said, "Marshal Gentry, is that you?"

Yes, I knew him. We had drinks together in Cheyenne a couple of times. "Yes, Major, it is I. I am sorry about your men. Well maybe not sorry, just irritated that they made me kill them. Do you have any other such that need killing?"

"Perhaps, but I am sure they will get that way soon enough. These were the worst of the lot. I guess I owe you a debt of gratitude. You saved me and the Army a lot of trouble by doing away with them."

I was staring at him with a lop-sided smile, as I punched fresh cartridge's into my .44's. I twirled them and stuffed them in my holsters. He gulped. The waitress and Lad came out of the kitchen. Lad came over to me and I put my arm around his shoulders.

"Major, this is my son, Ioyamya Ideya, 'He Who Lights The Lamp'. I call him Lad. I suppose you know our Waitress? Yes? Good. I seem to remember that you are single, so is she. Marry her and live a long life Major. She will give you many sons."

Then we simply walked out and rode away. We made another dry camp that night. But the following day we rode to Denver.

Standing at the gate of the white picket fence with her hand on the latch, was my beautiful wife. Standing beside her was Lulu. It had only been a little over two days since we parted, but it seemed like an eternity. To her also, because my feet had no sooner touched the ground, then she was in my arms. We came up for air to see the children babbling to each other. They truly had become brother and sister.

"What took you so long? And where did you get the

boy?"

"Turns out he was locked in the attic. Old Man Coyote told me about him. As you can see he speaks English as well as the Dakota dialect Sioux. It appears that Lulu can speak Sioux also."

Lulu and Lad had changed from English to Dakota. I told Lizzy what his name was and how I was instructed to burn the house after they killed each other. Also about our little run in at the Fort.

"What about your trip? Anything exciting?" I asked.

"Not much. There were a couple of men who thought we were easy pickings. I shot one in the shoulder, they lost interest. And Oh yes, I got a telegram from Chicago. It turns out they didn't accept our resignations. They just put us on leave. They are sending us two new badges by mail. They want us to just be on call, anywhere we are needed. I knew we did too good of a job."

"Well, they have to find us before they can use us. I think at times we are going to be pretty hard to find."

"Not this winter we're not. I want to stay put for awhile. Did you know they built a new school house? No, I suppose you don't, you just got here. Anyway, now we have two children that can go to school."

"How are Yin-Li and Yang-Su? And Pike and the bank? And the Clifford's and Mr. Peters?"

"Whoa, slow down. I have only been here a day myself. The girls are out at the ranch. Pike and the bank are fine. It seems like we get richer by the day. The girls don't know we're here, the housekeeper expects them back tonight. Look over there, the girls had another wing built on the house. More bedrooms and a bath house. It has a big pool or tub, its heated from the kitchen. You are going to like that, its big enough for everybody at once."

"Everybody, what do you mean, everybody?"

"I mean the family, not the whole town, silly. You know how the girls enjoyed those hot pools at Cheyenne and of course we did too."

"Yeah, but now we have two children. We have to set a proper example."

"Well, of course, but they have to learn not to be ashamed of their bodies also, right?"

"Yeah, but I think when the children are in there, you can count me out."

"Oh, you big prude , you."

"No, its not that. I am just uncomfortable with a grown man being nude around children."

"Yes, I suppose you're right. It does seem a bit too much, doesn't it? Anyway enough said on that. The dress shop is going good, they have been importing clothes from Paris, isn't that grand?"

I looked at her, "Grand? That's pretty hi-falutin isn't it?"

We had been walking to the house, she stopped. "Yes, I suppose it was. But don't you think it would be fun to just put on airs at times? We have been dealing with the scum of the west so long, that I would just like to think flowery thoughts. Can't we just pretend, just for little while?"

"Yes Honey, we can. In fact why don't we have a party. You and the Girls can get one up, can't you? Invite everyone we know, maybe even some we don't, let's have a shindig."

She was overflowing with ideas as we went on toward the house. The Children had taken the horses to the barn. We didn't even have to tell them. I was starting to feel the two nights we spent on the hard ground. And I needed a bath. So before supper, I tried out the new tub. She was right, I did like it. Especially when my wife joined me.

Chapter Thirteen

Yin-Li and Yang-Su arrived before we got out of the tub. Yeah, you're right, they got in, I got out, I couldn't stand all that chatter. It really wasn't that, it was that those girls had really matured. That was going to take some getting used to. It was all too overwhelming for me. You know what? Maybe I was a prude. Nawww, I wasn't. I thought, as I glanced back over my shoulder.

Dog had made himself at home, laying at the children's feet under the supper table. The housekeeper didn't like it, but what the hell, whose house was it anyway? Whose house? Well the teepee always belongs to the woman. They just put up with us men. And you damn well better follow the rules. Ma had taught me that.

Everyone liked the party idea. It would give us the chance to get reacquainted with everybody. After supper we sat up for awhile, drinking some kind of fancy wine. The children had their own bedrooms and went there by eight o'clock. We weren't too far behind, Lizzy and I, we had some catching up to do.

Party night came. All of our friends showed up, even some that we didn't know we had. It was wall to wall people. Now I could give you all the details, but it would only cause you to flip pages, looking for something interesting to happen. Well there was one thing that was interesting, one of the friends that I didn't know, said, that they had got a new shipment of girls in at the local whore house.

Why was that interesting? Because he said they were young Chinese girls. He told me this. I got Lizzy aside and told her. She was sure they were not there under their own violation. She wanted to go over there right now. I told her she was the hostess of this party and couldn't leave. But that no one would miss me. So I was elected.

I didn't take my .44's. But I did slip a twelve shot .36 in my pocket. Of course I always had my knife. I never went anywhere without it. The whore house was on the seedier side of Denver. I tapped on the door. A large man opened it. I laid him out cold with one blow, then dragged him outside. I took his belt and hogtied him. No one noticed the small disturbance.

There was a black man pounding on the keys of a piano. The Madam, asked me what my pleasure was. I motioned for her to come over in the corner, she came over. I laid my knife along side of her throat.

I said, quietly in her ear, "I hear you have some Chinese girls here, how much did you pay for them?"

"I gave five hundred a piece, why, what business is it of yours?"

"Do you know who I am?"

She looked in my eyes. "Yes, I think so, you're Buck Gentry, the gunfighter."

"Yes, you are partly right, but I am also a U. S. Marshal. And the slave trade is illegal. I could arrest you right now. But since you provide a service that keeps decent women from being bothered, I am not going to. You just trot out those Chinese girls. And Oh yes, any others that you have obtained illegally. Don't leave any out, because I 'will' find out."

I applied a little more pressure to the tip of my knife, a small drop of blood appeared and ran down her neck. I followed her up the stairs. She was in her middle forties, looked like she would have to go back to work after I took some of her girls.

I left with three Chinese girls and two Irish girls, in various stages of dress. I went in the back way, straight to the big tub. "Ok, girls, shuck those clothes and get in the tub." The Irish girls had to help the Chinese ones, they didn't understand English. I left them there and went to get Lizzy.

She was the belle of the ball. I finally got her aside. "Liz, there are five girls in the tub. You can take care of them. They will need clothes. You might want to get the twins to help. No I don't want to help, you think I'm crazy?"

I went back to the party. I wondered how the Madam got these girls. I forgot to ask. Lizzy would find out. I was sure this wasn't over yet. Lulu and Lad were still at the party, I sent them off to bed. Dog went with them.

The party broke up, long after mid-night. Pike and I went into the kitchen and made a pot of coffee. I found some cream in the icebox. I poured our cups half full of cream and topped it off with the thick coffee. It was delicious.

"Well Pike, how is married life treating you? You look fat and sassy."

"I am very happy. The widow lady is a Tiger in bed and even better than that, she is not a shrew. She is everything a wife is supposed to be. And smart, she practically runs the bank all by herself."

"I sense a 'but' in there somewhere."

"Well, maybe it's too perfect, we never fight. Sometimes I wish she wouldn't agree with me all the time. It's not natural."

"Well what about you, do you ever do anything she doesn't like?"

"No, I try not to, you see, I love her."

"Well of course you do, but just for a change, why don't you track mud across her just scrubbed floor? See if she gets mad. That's one thing most women really don't like. You see, its better to fight about small things that you can do something about, than the big things, that you can't do anything about."

"Is that what you do?"

"Yeah, of course, she does too, we both enjoy the make up sex. We'll pick some small thing, then fight like hell, then spend the night making up."

Lizzy came in the room, "I heard that. But I'm too tired to fight tonight. We got the girls to bed. I found out where she got the Chinese girls, they were bought in San Francisco. Come spring, we'll have to take care of that problem. Have you looked outside? It's snowing. Pike, your wife is waiting to go home."

Pike jumped up and hurried out. Lizzy smiled and said, "I guess he's going to have to wait till tomorrow to try your advice, I think he's pretty well pussy whipped."

"Oh, and I'm not, huh?"

"Oh baby, you are, you most certainly are." I guess she wasn't that tired.

When we awoke the next morning it was still snowing. It was a wet heavy snow, you know the kind that breaks tree limbs. Especially since the leaves were still on the trees. There wasn't anything we could do outside. Our hired help took care of all the animals. I did get up and let Dog out. Then I hurried back to bed. We played slap and tickle for awhile. That is till the twins and Lulu and Lad came in.

They said that they were bored. I said. "How can that

be? You all have a brain, don't you? And besides, didn't I hear someone say that they had a good school here?"

Yin-Li spoke up. "Yes, and it starts on the morrow. Yang-Su and I can take the children and register them today, if you want us to?"

Lizzy sat up, pulling her top together, and said, "Yes, we would like you to. How are our other guests doing this morning?"

Yang-Su said, "They are all up and in the kitchen. The Chinese girls are a little shy, those Irish girls aren't. In fact they were running around half naked, till we made them put more clothes on. What are you going to do with them?"

Lizzy got out of bed and slipped a pair of breeches on. While she was combing her hair in the mirror, she said, "I think I know some Chinese families here in Denver that will take the three in. But as to those Irish girls, I just don't know. What about you Buck, do you have any ideas?"

"Me, no I don't, the twins should have some though. They know most of the town's people. Maybe there are some Caucasian families that will do the same?"

Yin-Li said, "I don't know. Those two aren't bad girls, they are full of ginger though. We'd have to screen the families pretty closely."

"Alright its settled then. Lizzy will take care of placing the three girls. You two will put out feelers on the Irish girls. But I will be the final judge on who they go to. I keep thinking about something Sam said back in Elmira, 'you can pick up a starving dog and make him prosperous, he will not bite you: that is the principal difference between a dog and a man'."

Yang-Su asked, "Sam who?"

"Mark Twain, his name is Samuel Clemens. A pretty wise old duck. You see, there is also another saying that I like, 'a good deed never goes unpunished'. Another one is, 'never leave a rattler for dead, unless you cut his head off'."

"That's enough, just stop it with the colloquialism's. Come on get out of that bed, aren't you hungry?" Lizzy said.

"I can't get up till everyone leaves, you know I don't have any clothes on. And yes I am hungry, all the time. You should know that." The twins started to turn red, the children didn't pick up on the double meaning. Lizzy threw her hairbrush at me. Anyway they all left, so I guess I had to get up.

I got up and was peeing in the night pot, when I heard the door open. I thought it was Lizzy coming back for some reason. I shook it off and turned around. Damn, it was those two Irish girls. They stood there, staring, so did I. "Are you girls lost, what can I do for you?" I said.

"We were just wondering, what do you plan on doing with us?" Said one.

"I guess we're going to try and find a good home for you both, by the way, what are your names?"

The one that spoke first said, " I am Aileen and this is Aislin, we are cousins from the county Cork. Are you an Indian?"

"Yes, I am half Sioux and half English."

"We thought you must be, cause your thing is bigger than most Englishmen." One thing about these girls, they were not shy. It was not just because they had been abducted into that whorehouse. It was also because they were raised in poverty in Ireland, their whole family probably shared one room. Lizzy came back in the room.

"Yes, he does have a nice one, doesn't he? Get dressed, you lunk head," she said, as she tossed me a pair of pants. "You girls come on downstairs, lets let Grandpa get his clothes on."

Lizzy had put her arms around their shoulders, they

were laughing, and I heard her say on the way down the hall, "Its not always so big, sometimes its this small." Now I know she said that for my benefit, cause she had raised her voice so I could hear it. Lizzy was a wonder, she didn't get mad at the girls, she just made a joke out of it. I loved her more and more as each day went by.

As I was buttoning my shirt, I glanced out the window, the snow was getting worse. It wasn't so wet now. The flakes were smaller, the temperature must be falling. Looks like we were in for a blizzard. I had noticed that the barn loft was full of hay. Also that the wood shed was full of wood. We had got a load of coal just yesterday. I remember hearing it going down the coal chute into the basement.

I went to the kitchen door and opened it, a swirl of snow came in with the dog. Dog padded directly to a warm spot behind the kitchen range and went to nibbling at the snow packed between his toes. He looked up at me and winked. I swear, he winked. Everyone was in the kitchen. A good thing it was so big.

Lulu and Lad were seated beside each other at one end of the big table, stuffing large fork full's of hot cakes down. Butter and syrup was running down their chins'. You would think that they had been starved. Could be, because they had been. There was a large pitcher of cold milk in the middle of the table. But I went for the Coffee, with half milk though.

The cacophony at the table was almost deafening. The babble of different language's and dialects was a delight to hear. Ah yes, this country would be a great one, one day. How could it not be? Look at all the talent these immigrants were bringing to it. Of course to me, they were all immigrants. How could they not be? But really in the long run, weren't we all?

I leaned my chair back on its hind legs, sipping my

261

coffee, just enjoying myself. Then shit, I fell over backwards. I lay there on my back, holding my empty coffee mug. Of course the coffee was all over me. Lizzy's pretty face came in view. "Are you alright?" she said, with a tinge of worry in her voice.

"Yes, but I thought I would just lay here awhile and contemplate my stupidity, do you want to join me?"

She got down on her hands and knees and gave me a kiss. "Come on, Honey, I will help you up. And by the way, you're not stupid." You see why I loved her so much?

From that day forward, I never leaned back in my chair, that was of course, unless I had the wall at my back. And of course, I was never to live that down. Every time we had a snowstorm that story came up.

Lizzy helped me up. Then went with me back to our room. "You take those clothes off, I'll have some hot water brought up, if you're good, maybe we'll get in the tub together." I was good, but she was better.

The blizzard lasted three more days. Then a period of Indian Summer set in. Lulu and Lad finally got to school. We found homes for the three Chinese girls. But so far none for Aileen and Aislin. So they were with us when we went out to the ranch to check on things.

Lizzy had made riding pants for them. They had never rode before. It was quite comical. But they were good natured about the kidding they took. Before we were half way out there, they had come to terms with their horses. The horses agreed not to buck them off, if they would stop bouncing.

On the way out there, the twins, filled us in on how the ranch was run now. They, the twins, handled all the financial details. Including the payroll. You know how most ranch's hire extra hands in the summer? Well the twins had set up a policy of keeping a full crew the year around. Why lay off good hands, then have them move on to somewhere else in the wintertime? Then come spring have to hire and train new hands? It was counterproductive, they said.

Of course Mr. Peters and Hank Clifford still ran the ranch, that is, all except the money. The twins weren't skinflints with the money, but they were fair. They sure weren't wasteful though. We had brought extra clothes with us, we planned on staying for two days. The housekeeper would look after Lulu and Lad.

The first thing I noticed that was different, was the new bunk house. And a cook house. It not only held the kitchen but a large dinning room. And there were three more cottages just for guests. I guess that was where we were supposed to stay. The barn had been enlarged and I noticed the loft was full of hay. Plus many other haystacks in the meadows. There were still some drifts that the sun hadn't melted. But the yard wasn't too muddy. Someone had landscaped it, so that the water would run off into the creek.

I was well pleased with the layout. We rode up to the hitching post. Two cowboys came to get our horses. One was Henry, Hanks boy. The other was Victor Wade, you remember him, from the stockyards in Chicago?

Well, we said our howdy-do's, but those two boys only had eyes for our two little dudes. And I think it was mutual by the come-on looks Aileen and Aislin were giving them back. Aileen made like she was falling off, right into Victor's arms. Aislin wasn't quite so forward, she let Henry help her down. Did you ever see a black man blush. Well I did that day. Need I tell you how it turned out?

Well, if I must. To jump ahead, the double wedding was held two weeks later. Of course that necessitated the building of two more houses. But that didn't happen till spring, good thing we waited to build them, because they had to enlarge the plans to include a nursery. But to get back to the present.

The P Bar P was now the largest ranch in Colorado. In the two years we had been gone, the twins had been buying up any land they could. Anytime a homesteader failed they were there with the cash to buy him out. And they were generous with the money. I was proud of them.

I wondered when they would find some man and settle down. I think most men around there were in awe of them. I know I was at times. Even though they were my kin. You know most men have the habit of putting women up on an ivory pedestal. They put them up there and then are afraid to touch them. Oh, it would all come out in the wash.

The next day we rode all day and never reached the end of the ranch. Yep, they were in the big time now. It just wasn't me though. It was way after dark when Lizzy and I got back to the ranch. We put our horses in the barn and grained them. Then went to our cabin. Our table was all set with food. That was nice of them. We ate and then went to bed. Someone had put hot water bottles at the foot of our bed. We crawled in. Lizzy snuggled up close, I put my arm around her. "Liz?" I brushed the hair back from her face. She looked at me. "Are you happy?" I asked.

"Sure, is there some reason you asked?"

"Hell, I don't know. I mean we have all the money we will ever need. Is that what makes you happy?"

"No, it's not. You are what makes me happy. But I think I know what's bothering you. It's all these material possession's isn't it?"

"I don't know, I guess. I mean I like them. And am thankful for them. But, I guess what bothers me is, that I feel I don't deserve them."

"Do you feel you deserve me?"

"Oh yes, you I deserve and need. But 'things' come and go. And I am afraid I will get to thinking that I do deserve them. And to me, that would be worse than death."

"I promise you honey, if you start to get the big head, I will deflate it real quick. But knowing you, I don't think that will ever happen." She snuggled closer. Then said, "I forgot to tell you, those Marshal badges and I.D. came the other day. And since we're talking, I was thinking, if the weather holds, that we should go to San Francisco and take care of those slavers."

"Yeah, I know that is really bothering you, me too. Ok, when we get back to town, we'll set things in motion. And talking about motion, do you want to, or go to sleep?"

"Aren't you tired?"

"Come to think of it, I am. So lets just go to sleep. Maybe we're getting old. No, I don't think so. There's nothing to say we have to have sex all the time is there?"

"No, honey, there isn't, go to sleep."

We awoke the next morning with a light rain falling, it didn't wake us up, the twins did. Of course we didn't bother locking the cabin door. Fact is, I don't think it even had a lock on it. Anyway, there they were, each sitting on either side of the bed.

"Are you awake?" Yin-Li said.

"We are now." Lizzy said, as she set up in bed. "What can we do for you girls?"

"Nothing, we just wanted to let you know that breakfast was about ready. And to tell you that it was your turn to ride herd on those Irish girls."

"Why, what are they doing?" I asked, as I pulled the covers over my head.

Yang-Su said, "They're chasing after Henry and Victor, I am afraid they will catch them."

"Yeah, I guess we had better head back today. We've seen what we came to see, anyway." I said, as I tossed the covers back, forgetting that I slept in the nude. The girls didn't bat an eye, though. As Yin-Li tossed me my long underwear, she winked.

"Alright girls, give us ten minutes and we'll be with you at the cook shack." Lizzy said, as she stood and stretched. Yang-Su tossed Lizzy her long underwear.

As we walked to breakfast, the rain was still falling, with some small snowflakes mixed in. Lizzy looked at the sky and shook her head. "It doesn't look good, does it?" She said.

"No sweetheart it doesn't, it will be a cold wet ride back to Denver. One good thing about it though, it should cool those girls ardor."

"Don't bet on it, the only thing that will cool them off, is their wedding night." Lizzy said, as she hopped over a puddle.

It was a good thing that all of us had oil slickers tied on behind our saddles. By the time we got home it was not only getting dark, but the rain had turned to all snow. I told the twins to go ahead and take the girls into the house. That I would take care of the horses. It wasn't a chore for me, I enjoyed unsaddling them and rubbing them down. Of course Lizzy stayed to help. She liked it also. As I was putting them in their stalls, Lizzy was forking hay down from the loft. She had already put grain in each stall.

We stood in the barn door, watching it snow. Lizzy said, "Well, it looks like there goes our trip to California. I have mixed feelings, one part of me wants to go and take care of those bastard's. The other part would like to stay right here for the winter. But I guess old man winter has settled that question for us."

I said, "Are you ready to go in? If you are I will turn the lamp out." Lizzy nodded. As I turned the barn lamp out, I couldn't help but notice the comforting smell of a clean barn. Some people don't like a barnyard smell. There is a difference between a dirty neglected barn or barnyard, then when it is kept clean and dry, then it just smells like home. I guess I was feeling a little homesick for Pa's place on the South Fork of the Shoshone.

As we walked to the house, Lizzy glanced at me, "What's wrong, you look a little wistful?"

"Some, I was just wondering how Pa was doing. And cousin Penny. She was some upset when I left. But I guess no news is good news."

"Not necessarily. But in this case, unless we know different, we will have to wait till spring for that also."

We were met by the gaiety of the family as we went in the back door to the kitchen entry. My dour mood was soon dispelled.

The double wedding came and went. Then we settled down for winter. We had a big gathering for Christmas. The new year of 1875 was duly celebrated. January was bitter cold with lots of snow. But a Chinook came through in February. The last week in February another storm hit.

Does it seem at times that winter is just a series of weather reports? It was the middle of March before we got another Chinook. But it looked like this one was going to stay awhile. But the weather wasn't the only thing, the twins were being sparked by another set of twins. Two big, blond, blue eyed Swedes. I couldn't quite get my mind around what they're offspring would look like.

But, like I said, they were being courted. Yin-Li and

Yang-Su were no push-overs. They were going to make the Swedes work for their hands. But even if they did get married, I know who the boss's in those family's would be. After all, who was the boss in my family. I know, I know, if you would ask the women they would say I was. But come on, do you really believe that?

We were making plans for our trip to San Francisco. We decided to take the stage to Cheyenne and catch the Union Pacific to San Francisco. As of yet it was the only railroad to the west coast. Although there were rumblings of another line being built through Montana. Some guy named Cooke, had lobbied for Congress making Colter's Hell into a national park, they called it the Yellowstone National Park, they did that in March of '72. I personally think he did it, just to get government help to build a railroad. Of course the railroad came with free land from Congress.

I was fast becoming disillusioned with the political process. There was a saying that I read somewhere, "Power corrupts, and total power, totally corrupts." The more I was around any of man's governments, I found it to be true. I think I read it in the Bible, not to put your trust in earthly man.

Oh well, I did put my trust in my wife, though. And I think she does the same with me. Really I don't think, I know she does. Without trusting our loved ones, we would be pretty miserable creatures, wouldn't we?

Lulu and Lad were to stay here and continue on in their studies. We told them that we would take them with us this summer, when we went to the South Fork. The Swede twins were coming over almost every night. I was getting tired of the 'Yah, sure.' But Yin and Yang weren't, so I kept my mouth shut. They were nice young men and you could tell that they adored our girls. So I guess I could endure their jovial demeanor. How could anyone be happy all the time?

Every time I came in the room they would jump up and great me. Finally I told them to knock it off, they were going to get a hernia or something. Anyway they sure were afraid of pissing me off. I think they were listening to too many stories about me.

We packed light, taking only one suitcase apiece. We figured if we needed anything more once we reached San Francisco, we could buy it. It was the last week of March and it was going out like a lamb, when we boarded the stage. Of course Yin-Li and Yang-Su were there with their beau's. Lulu and Lad had skipped their studies to see us off. They were crying. We assured them we would be back.

If you're from a broken home, or ever been abandoned, like they were, then you know how they were feeling. After awhile you start not trusting what people say. We would have to earn their trust. Yin-Li and Yang-Su put their arms around them and hugged them close as the stage went from sight.

I glanced at Lizzy, a little tear was running down her cheek. My eyes felt a little misty, also. "Hon, don't worry, they'll be Ok." I said.

"I'm not worrying about that, it's, shit, I don't know, I miss them."

"Yeah, strange isn't it? Two tough hombre's like us, missing our children, even before they get out of sight."

"Yes, I guess we'll just have to take good care of ourselves, to make sure we get back safe. That's why I made us new vests. They're made out of triple layers of my special weave."

We were talking in whispers. Cause there were three other passengers. A fellow who looked to be a drummer. And a Preacher of some sort and his wife. He looked like a self-righteous twit. Probably in his middle thirties. His wife in her early twenties. She wasn't bad looking. In fact too good for him. She tried to talk a couple of times, but he shushed her up. She spent the rest of the time looking down at her hands.

I looked at Lizzy and inclined my head at them. Lizzy nodded. The drummer was falling asleep, strange most times that ilk likes to talk. Maybe he had talked himself out in Denver. Lizzy made another attempt to talk to the woman. She asked her if she would like a little sip of blackberry brandy? You know to help settle her stomach, from the constant movement of the stage.

The woman smiled and nodded yes. Her husband butted in, "No, she would not, and I thank you not to talk to my wife."

Now I am a student of physics, every action, requires a reaction. Before I could help myself, I reacted. We were setting across from them. My fist lashed out, his head banged against the back of the seat. He was out. The girls hand went to her mouth, she was more of a girl, than a woman. She looked back and forth from her unconscious husband to me. She smiled and held her hand out for the brandy.

After she handed the flask back to Lizzy, Lizzy took the brandy and holding the unconscious fellows mouth open, she poured a goodly amount down his throat. He snorted and slowly came awake. "What, what happened?" he gasped.

"Don't you remember, we were passing the brandy back and forth and you must have over imbibed. You passed out." I said. "Do you always drink too much?" I added.

"No, I don't think so, my jaw hurts, did I fall down?"

"Well you did fall against the stage door, but your good wife picked you up. You know you are very lucky to have a wife that will put up with your drinking. If I were you I would listen to what she has to say from now on. She tried to warn you, but you wouldn't listen."

The girls eyes were getting larger and larger, she leaned forward and said, "That's ok, Dear, but from now on, when I say something, you had better listen. If you don't you will have to sleep by yourself, because I will have no drunkard in my bed."

He took her hand and said, "I am sorry Dear, from now on, I promise I will drink no more, please forgive me?"

The drummer had listened to all of this, he could hardly contain himself. He said, "Yes, and that goes for me, I don't want to share a stage with a hypocrite, you being a man of the cloth, and all."

The Preacher said, "Oh my, please forgive me friend, it will never happen again."

"Just see that it doesn't, in fact I am going to give your wife my address and if it ever happens again she can write and tell me, you see I am a Judge in Greeley."

Boy did I miss on that one, I could of swore he was a drummer. The Judge looked at me and winked. It turns out they were on their way to Greeley, to take over the Methodist congregation. I don't know what the law can do about self-righteous idiot's, but I do know that everyone needs their outlook on life adjusted every now and then.

When we arrived in Greeley, the Preacher Man stepped down first, then he helped his wife down, he was almost groveling. She was almost embarrassed he was so attentive. When he turned to get their baggage out of the boot, she came over to us and said,

"Thank you both, you don't know how much I appreciate your help. I was about ready to kill myself, you saved my life."

Lizzy said, "We were glad to help. Just don't let him

revert. Remember you are in control of your destiny. No one can make you feel worthless unless you let them. If he so much as looks cross eyed at you, let him have both barrels. If words don't help, use the literal barrels. Blow his damn head off."

Let me jump ahead here. Two years later he did revert, she blew his head off. She was arrested but let go the next day. Two weeks later she married the Judge. I thought I would tell you this, before it got lost in the wind.

Anyway, to get back to the present. We went to the Hotel, they remembered us. They gave us the best room. Every time the desk clerk looked at me, he broke out in a sweat. I asked Lizzy as we went up the stairs, "What's wrong with him? Do we know him?"

"We don't know him personally, but I know the type. He's a small time grifter, a petty swindler. He knows who we are. That makes him nervous. We'll put a chair under our doorknob tonight."

Later that night, every time we started to get amorous someone rattled the door knob. Now I can put up with a lot of things, but interrupting our sex life, I would not put up with. So I took the chair away from the door. The next time they rattled the knob, I jerked the door open. It was the desk clerk, I broke both of his arms, it would be a long time before he lifted anyone's poke.

We had no more trouble in Greeley. We were the only ones on the stage to Cheyenne. It was sorta nice to let someone else do the driving. And it was especially nice not to have to whisper, when we talked. Although we did think it was unusual that there were no other passengers. And about twenty miles out of Greeley we found out why.

The stage slowed up and we heard the driver say something about a tree in the road. Red Flag! We had our guns out and cocked. We had no sooner stopped than a slug came through the side of the stage. Then another one from the other side.

I kicked the left stage door open and jumped out, rolling on impact. I came up with both .44's blazing. Sounds hokey, doesn't it? Well, whether it was or not, it was effective. There were two of them half concealing themselves behind some boulders. Well really they were more than half concealed, only parts of the craniums were sticking out. It was enough.

I twisted around and ran behind the stage to get to those that were trading shots with my wife. I came around the back, then something hit me in the chest, knocking me backwards. It felt like a horse kicked me. I picked myself up and felt my chest, I'll be damned, those vests really worked.

Of course by the time I got up, Lizzy had finished her tasks. It seems when they hit me, they were so happy they stood up. Big mistake, Lizzy doesn't miss. Lizzy got out of the stage, coming up to me, she said, "Thank you Dear, for distracting them. It was nice of you. I would of really been mad if you would of killed them all and left none for me."

I was still massaging my chest, "Who were they? Have you ever seen them before?" I asked the Stage Driver.

He walked around and looked at them all. "Yes, I have seen them, they usually hang around the Silver Spur in Greeley. I have never seen them work one day in their life."

"Well they missed their chance for a productive life, maybe the Devil will work them hard." Lizzy said. "Or maybe not, maybe he will just shitcan them." She added.

"I don't care where they go, I'm just glad their gone. I don't like people shooting at me." I said, as I picked up their weapons and went through their pockets. Strange, they had some new silver dollars, with the date of 1875 on them. And they were from the San Francisco mint. How did they get clear out here so quick.

"Lizzy, who all knows we were going to San Francisco on the slave thing?"

"Well our family and of course the main office in Chicago. I sent them a letter. They sent one back and said they were going to let the office in San Francisco know we were coming."

"Well being forewarned is to be forearmed. At least we know what to expect now. There must be a bad one in the San Francisco office. Come on Driver, lets get going, you can go around that tree."

"Well, what about those guys you killed, aren't you going to bury them?"

"Hell No! Let the Devil bury his own." Lizzy said. I glanced at her, she had her jaw set. My wife was pissed. Watch out San Francisco, here we come. The driver looked at her too, then made hast for his seat.

We only lost about twenty minutes, death doesn't take long, does it? A spring snow squall came blowing in. We put the side curtains down. It was rather cozy, just the two of us. Lizzy said, "Take off your jacket, shirt and vest, I want to look at your chest. Did that bullet break the skin?"

I did as I was told, she started poking and prodding. "That's going to be a good bruise, but I don't think any ribs are broke." As she was doing that to me, I was unbuttoning her clothes.

"Hey, I wasn't hit, what are you doing?"

"Well, how often are we going to be in a public conveyance by ourselves? It's a perfect opportunity to mess around a little bit. Don't you think?"

Evidently she did, because it didn't take her long and

she was completely naked. I had to hurry to catch up. It was quite a ride, the bumpy road helped a lot. Thinking on it, as we got dressed, it was more of an emotional release, than a physical one. But the physical was right up near the top.

You might think that we were rather callous about killing. That couldn't be further from the truth. I and my wife, remembered each one. And we regretted the bastard's making us kill them. We never killed unless we had to, to save our lives or someone else's. We couldn't help it, that the constant practice made us good at it.

When we got to Cheyenne we went to the Hotel, it would of been too much trouble to get our coach ready for just one night. Since we weren't going to take it with us. This was not a pleasure trip. Although there was no reason we couldn't have some fun along the way. We had made our train reservations ahead of time, so there was no worry there.

Again the Hotel was glad to see us. Lizzy told the desk clerk to have some hot water brought up for bath's. It was a good thing that the one's who brought it up were women. Cause we had no sooner got in our room and she started to shed clothes. Lizzy was standing there tapping her foot when they arrived. Even though they were women, you could tell by their looks that they appreciated what they saw. And there was no reason why they shouldn't, I did.

Usually, I would of got in the tub with her, but being forewarned, I thought it best that one of us, at all times, be ready for the unexpected.

The water was still warm when Lizzy got out. So, no use getting fresh, I got in. She dried off and instead of getting dressed, she just buckled her guns around her waist. Now that was quite a site. That was what I loved about her, she always did the unexpected. As she did when I got out, and she never even took her guns off.

J.D. Oliver

Chapter Fourteen

Our train was due to leave by eight, so we were there by seven-thirty. We had procured a Pullman Compartment. We had brought several books with us. We planned on keeping to ourselves. Just venturing out at meal times. Who ever it was that wanted to kill us, would have to come to us. We didn't need any collateral damage. If they were as inept as those first four, innocent bystander's might get killed.

Lizzy tapped me on the shoulder, I looked up from my book. She pointed out the window. I knew they were killing the Buffalo, but I wasn't expecting what I seen. Piles of bones, whitening in the sun. If you can't subdue the Indians by killing them, then remove their reason for living. A tear ran down my cheek.

I knew it was coming, I had seen it in my vision. But that didn't make it any easier to take. I knew also, that we would never fully recover from it. I knew they would herd us to reservations, as they called it, and try to starve and kill us. I say us, because even though I was only half Sioux, my heart was all Sioux.

I leaned my head back and closed my eyes. The visions of the past and present, also the future came before my eyes. The battles fought came clear. I had warned Sitting Bull. But he

277

could not change what was to happen, any more that I could. He would win the battle of the Little Big Horn. But a battle is not a war. My heart was heavy in my chest. The only consolation was knowing that the same thing would happen to the conqueror, as to what happened to the conquered. Yes, my vision went far into the future.

I went back to my book. Lizzy was playing a game of solitaire, she was not winning. I glanced down at the floor. There was a one card laying beside her foot. No wonder she wasn't winning, she wasn't playing with a full deck. I let her go through them a couple of times more. Then I cleared my throat and pointed to the floor. She glanced down, "How long has that been there? Has it been there all the time and you didn't tell me?"

"I refuse to answer, because if I do, you are going to beat the hell out of me."

She pounced, the battle was on. We were having a great time. Of course, you being a smart person, you know how it ended up. We got our clothes back on by lunch time. We didn't bother picking up our mess, till after lunch.

I was reading and she was playing with a full deck, and winning by the way. When there came a commotion out in the passage way. We glanced at each other. Sounded like a man and woman having an altercation. Now we weren't stupid, at least I didn't think we were. I got up and opened our door.

A man and a women, they looked to be in their middle thirties. Were going at it. He slapped her, she punched him back. Funny thing about it, neither blow brought any blood. They seen me, this time he slapped her pretty hard, she fell down. Well, hell, maybe this fight was legit. I said, "Whoa, there pardner, take it easy." He looked at me and I seen triumph in his eyes. He snaked out a small Derringer from his vest. It was a double barrel model. His first shot missed me. He never got a second. My knife was through his throat and pinning him to the wall. I had forgot about the woman, stupid me.

She was up and tried to stab me in the back. My vest stifled her effort. She never got another chance either, Lizzy's knife had no trouble penetrating her bodice. It was all over so fast, it didn't draw anyone's attention. But what a mess. I for one, was not going to clean it up.

"Lizzy, will you ring for the Porter, please?"

He came, it was an older black man. He looked at them, then at us. I showed him my badge. "They tried to kill us, do they have a compartment?"

"Yes, they surely do. In fact its right next to yours."

"Would you open it please, we need to see who they are and why they wanted us dead."

He opened the door, I handed him a twenty dollar gold piece, "Can you get someone to clean up that mess, then tell the conductor to stop at the next town, they should be buried as soon as possible."

Lizzy had already gone through their pockets. She put everything in the woman's purse. I went in and went through their luggage. She was what some called a 'soiled dove', they both worked for a brothel in San Francisco. He was a bouncer/enforcer. Would you believe, they were married? A Mr. and Mrs. Ed Kraft. Her name was Mabel. We kept all of their personal belongings. We would give them to their employer, just before we cleaned his clock.

We stopped at a little town called Rock Springs. The Sheriff and Undertaker came aboard. The undertaker wanted a hundred dollars to bury them, I gave it to him. The Sheriff wasn't to be outdone, he wanted the same for administrative fees. Oh well, what the hell, these little towns had to make their money somewhere.

The Sheriff was a cagey little fellow. He had asked to see our Badges. We handed them to him. That was when he first got there. When he turned to go, he had not given our badges back. As he started through the door, I grabbed him by his collar, lifting him off of his feet, I said, "I believe you have something that belongs to us, our badges?"

"Oh, yes, I almost forget, here they are, they look to be pure gold." he said, as he handed them back to us, with a small embarrassed laugh. I sat him back down on his feet. I guess you couldn't blame him for trying. But I did make up my mind, the next time someone tried to kill us, I was just going to toss them off of the train, save a lot of trouble.

It was full dark by the time we got underway again. We went to the dinning car. The word had got around, everyone was staring at us. Idle curiosity didn't bother us any, as long as it remained idle. One thing about people, they are all different, some bright, some stupid and some fools.

One fool came over and started his fool routine. Asking questions that were none of his business. Finally Lizzy brought her boot heel down on his instep. He limped away, looking back over his shoulder. I guess he got the message.

Now a strange thing about fools, there are different kinds. Some are really fools, some only act the fool. Now I hope for his sake, that he is a genuine fool. He will live longer. But I guess, time will tell, won't it?

We finished our meal without anymore interruptions and then went back to our compartment. Lizzy sat down and looked out the window. Weren't much to see, being dark and all, but there were a few lights flickering a ways off. She looked sort of melancholy.

"What's the problem Lizzy?"

"I don't know, but, it's sure a shity world, isn't it?"

"Well, I think we've know that a long time haven't we?"

"Yes, I suppose you're right. But, Buck, do you think it will ever get any better?"

"Get better? Well it might appear to get better, but it won't. Because people are people. And the further they get away from their creator, the worse they will get. That's why it pays to live in the present, you know take advantage of what you have, not what you hope to have."

As we were talking Lizzy had gotten up and was putting our bed down and making it. Then she started taking her clothes off. We both have never used night clothes. Saved our having to take a lot of baggage with us. Then she went to the sink and took a spit bath. Of course I followed suit.

Now our bed was level with the window, so we could lay and look out. We turned the lamp out. The stars were bright this night. The moon was late in making its appearance. Late? No the moon wasn't late, our expectations were too early. How can the celestial bodies be late? Lizzy wasn't sleeping, she was counting the shooting stars.

I was cuddled up behind her doing the same thing. I got to thinking about what I said, you know, about our expectations being too early. Man is an impatient being, they want everything right now. We ought to take more of our lessons from the animals. They're happy most of the time, that is as long as man isn't mistreating them. Well one thing for sure, Lizzy sure wasn't mistreating me.

When we awoke the next morning we were deep in the Utah Territory. Not far from Salt Lake City. We were due for a crew change there. Now that there Salt Lake was something to see. They say you could hardly drown in it. They say the salt was so strong, it held you up. Now I didn't know for sure, since I never went swimming in it. So I believed it, why would they lie about something like that?

We had a four hour lay over, while they restocked the train. So we went into town. People were friendly enough. We bought some fresh fruit from some street vendors. We got a few stares. But I suppose no more than we gave. I had forgot about polygamy. Didn't bother me any, in most of the tribes, men had more than one wife. Now I didn't hold with it. And I know Lizzy didn't, because she looked at me and said, "Don't get any ideas."

Now I got to thinking again, that sure is a curse, isn't it? I mean thinking. Anyway, why in the world would you want more than one wife? Now I didn't have a mother-in-law, but I had heard stories. If they were as bad as all that, one would sure be enough.

The rest of the trip was quite uneventful, no one tried to kill us. Or for that matter, even speak cross to us. Of course, those that were on the train, when we had to kill those two, every time we came in sight of them, they ran. I guess we were some kind of ogres. Well, I never did like to talk too much anyway.

It was coming on dark when we got to Sacramento. They did have a spur line into San Francisco, but we decided to take a ferry at Knights Landing. We spent the night at a Hotel close to the Railroad Station. Then caught a ride to the Landing the next morning.

The trip down the Sacramento River was enjoyable. A lot of wildlife all along the way. The closer we got to San Francisco, the darker Lizzy's face became. I didn't know if it was the thought of our upcoming task, or some kind of bad memories, causing the clouds. I figured she would tell me when she got around to it.

When we got to San Francisco, the dock was teeming with the business of commerce. Lizzy turned to me and said. "Keep your eyes open. There are more scum running around lose here, than there is in the sewers. And they stink just about as bad too."

I was carrying both of our suitcases, that left her hands free. I seen her check her knife, that if it was loose in its sheath. Then reach into her skirt and check her pistol. I smiled a little bit, I thought she was over doing it. But I guess she wasn't. Cause we weren't even a hundred yards down the quay, till some low life tried to snatch one of the suitcases from me.

Lizzy didn't mess around, she could of just broke his arm or something, instead she slid her blade in and out between his third and forth rib. He fell, he was dead before he hit the boards. No one took any notice of the little fracas. Lizzy wiped her blade off on his shirt and stuck her knife back in its sheath. I leaned over and gave her a kiss.

We went to the Palace Hotel. It was the best one in town. It had a lift to get you to all the floors. A small moving room that went up and down. I was a little bit leery of it. But Lizzy took it right in stride. We had rented the whole top floor. At first the clerk wasn't going to let us have the whole floor, we had to ask for the manager. He acquiesced fast though when he seen the color of our money.

After we got settled in, and our bath taken. Lizzy wanted to go shopping, so I tagged along. Once you got off of the water front, San Francisco wasn't that bad. When it came to shopping Lizzy knew what she wanted. And I guess what I wanted also. She didn't ask me, she just pointed and I picked up. Of course our suits would have to be tailor made. I even stood still as they measured me. But when he started to take measurements of my crotch, I balked. But it turned out he had to know how much room to give me. But Lizzy had to do that measuring. With her doing it, it was sort of fun.

You remember, I mentioned 'our suits'? Lizzy had one special made for her. With the curves in the right place. Also with room for weapons. My suits were made to accommodate all of my weapons also. They said they would bring them to the Hotel when finished for the final alterations.

While we were eating our supper in the Hotel dining room, Lizzy explained a few of things to look out for while we were here. Like for instance, being Shanghaied. She explained that a lot of sailors jumped ship when they got to the United States. Especially here in California, looking for that pot of gold. But in order for the ships to get back to sea, they needed hands. So a lot of times they just knocked them over the head or got them drunk and kidnapped them. And they would be far at sea before they woke up.

It was the second day, before we got around to going the Federal building. We had our new suits. We had ordered the suits without vests, so we could use our own. Now women in 1875 didn't wear suits or even pants, but Lizzy was a knockout in hers. I had a hard time keeping my eyes on her face when she talked, they kept wanting to stray.

We were directed to the U.S. Marshal's suite of offices on the second floor. In the outer office sat a receptionist. Her desk was big enough to sleep on. Or do anything else, if you had a mind to. She looked at us and sniffed. A bitch if I ever seen one. Lizzy was being cordial.

"Is the Marshal in?" she asked, very nicely.

"Do you have an appointment?" She said, looking

J.D. Oliver

down her nose. Now I knew my wife, trouble was brewing.

"No, but I am sure he wants to see us, we are Mr. And Mrs. Phillip Gentry."

"I am sorry, but without an appointment, I'm afraid its quite impossible."

Lizzy smiled sweetly, then leaned over her desk. Her hand snaked out and got a fist full of her hair, then Lizzy banged her face into her desk. Lizzy looked at me and said,

"I made sure her forehead hit the desk and not her nose, I didn't want to spoil her looks. I am sure she will turn out to be a nice girl from now on."

We opened the door to the inner office and went in. He was right in the middle of banging a woman on his desk.

I said, "That's Ok, we'll wait, you just go right ahead and finish, we'll just set down here and watch."

He jumped up, yanking at his pants. The woman just laid there. "Who the hell are you, you have the nerve just walking in, I'll have you both arrested."

I looked at the woman on his desk, she was a young Chinese girl. Lizzy spoke to her in Cantonese. I guess she told her to get up and get dressed, and to wait in the other room. Anyway that's what she did.

"No, no you won't." I said. Lizzy was speaking to me in Sioux. Turns out our hunt would be easier than we thought. The dross had risen to the top. Turns out he was the head honcho of the slavery ring. It didn't take much torture to get the rest of their names. I only had to nail one of his balls to the desk. Really not even that, it was just his sack. When he came to, he spilled his guts.

I put him back to sleep and we went out to the other office. The bitchy receptionist was just waking up. She seen the Chinese girl sitting there. Then she seen us. She said, "I had

285

nothing to do with this, he said if I didn't keep quiet, he would sell my sisters into slavery. Honest, I knew what was going on, but if I talked he would do the same to me. Besides who would I tell? He was the law, even above the city police."

I looked at Lizzy, "Do you believe her?"

"Yes, I do. What is your name?"

"Jane Tavel, please don't kill me."

"We are not going to kill you. We are U.S. Marshal's from the Chicago office. Sent here to clear up this mess." Lizzy said.

I went over to the water cooler, a stone jug turned upside down with a spigot. I ran some water on my handkerchief. Then handed it to her to put on the bump on her forehead. She took it and did so.

"So Jane, are there any honest police in San Francisco?"

"Yes, Mr. Gentry, there are. In fact I know the city attorney, he's honest."

"Good, then after we get rid of the garbage, maybe all hope isn't dead." Lizzy said.

"What I want you to do, Jane, is to go home and get a good nights rest, then come back tomorrow and get everything up to snuff. Can you do that?"

"Yes, Sir, I can. What are you going to do with that girl?"

"Don't you worry about that, we will take care of her. Just go home and keep your mouth shut."

After Jane left, we went back in the inner office and tied the Marshal up and gagged him. Then we took the girl and went to our hotel room. Lizzy and her were talking the whole way there. We left her in our room to get cleaned up, we went back out.

J.D. Oliver

Lizzy headed for China Town. She knew just where to go. In the back of a restaurant, she found the Tong. "Give me that list of names, and you wait out here." She went behind the curtain.

When she came out, she was smiling. The clouds had lifted. "Come on, sweetheart, we have some unfinished business at the Federal building. I know what we can do with him. We'll take him down to the docks and sell him into slavery. When he wakes up, he will be on his way to China."

We waited till dark, then we did just that. Shucks they only gave us two hundred dollars for him. We went back to our room and got the Chinese girl. Then we went down to the dining room. After we ate, we took her to China Town, the Tong would make sure she got back to her relatives.

The next morning we went back to the Marshals office. Jane was there. We got a telegraph message off to Chicago. They wanted us to find a replacement for him. Jane's bump had went down.

"Jane, do you know of anybody who would make an honest U.S. Marshal?"

"Yes, that City Attorney I told you about. I know him pretty well, he is always asking me out. But I was afraid to say yes, till now."

"Alright, can you run and get him and have him come over and talk to us, that is if he's interested in the job?"

She was already out the door. Ten minutes later she was back with him in tow. By noon he was the new U.S. Marshal. We spent the next two days indoctrinating him. I think he understood the importance of the job. Especially after he found out what happened to his predecessor. That night we relaxed.

My dreams were in color. Which made them all the more frightening. I seen an earthquake and fire. I seen a large bridge being built over the inlet to the harbor. I seen much, much more, things I didn't even want to remember. I woke and got out of bed and went to the window. The city was asleep. I kept seeing the buildings falling down, the fire spreading.

I felt Lizzy's hand on my shoulder. "What's the matter, you been dreaming again?"

"Yeah, did you know they are going to build a bridge over the harbor inlet?"

"No, really? When are they going to do it?"

"I don't know, maybe fifty years from now. But there is a big earthquake coming and I do know the year on that. Do you want to know?"

"I don't know if I do or not. Is it just here in San Francisco, or will it be in other places as well?"

"This one is just here, but it will cause fire also. Most of the City will burn."

"Are we in danger now?"

"No, it is years off. If we were in danger I would tell you. I wonder if people would listen if I were to tell them?"

"Probably not. Some might though. Why don't you tell the people at the college?"

"Yes, I might just do that before we leave. Anyway then, their blood won't be on my head."

"It wouldn't be anyway, would it?"

"I don't know, just how much are we our brothers keeper? If we see them about ready to fall into a pit and don't warn them, are we blood guilty?"

"Yes, I see your point, but if we warn them and they don't listen, then their blood is on their own heads." We were still standing there looking out the window. I felt her hand tickling my lower hair, then she took hold and started to work it. We hardly made it back to bed.

We were up before dawn, the mist was hanging heavy over the harbor. We went for a walk before breakfast. We went toward the hill overlooking the harbor inlet. We sat down to watch the swirling mist play with the seagulls. We were setting about two feet apart. All of a sudden we felt another presence. Old Man Coyote sat down between us. The wind had freshened. A storm was brewing.

His words came into our minds. "Euroaquilo."

"What was that, what does that mean?" I asked him.

"The storm, at sea, that is what it is called in the Mediterranean Sea two thousand years ago. You remember when Paul was shipwrecked, a Euroaquilo blew in?"

"Yeah, I guess so. I remember reading about it. In the Bible, but some how I missed that word."

"It doesn't matter. It's just a word. But words make up what we are, don't they?"

"No, I don't think so, I think our actions make up what we are."

"You think so? Good, I'm glad that you do. But words are what gets us in trouble most of the time. The tongue is like a rudder on a ship, small, but Oh, how it can get you shipwrecked on the rocks."

"I don't understand what you are trying to say? What do you want us to do?" I said. Lizzy was just as puzzled as I was.

"Euroaquilo, the storm at sea. You see mankind is like the sea, being blown about by every wind that comes his way. The storm is only going to get worse. The sea's agitation is going to get much, much worse. Until he comes to quite it. We have no control over the pain of the sea. Only the Great Spirit can control the sea. And its time is not yet. What I'm trying to tell you is: Enjoy the ride, because the end will be more terrible than the beginning.

Then he simply got up and trotted off. I looked at Lizzy and said, "What the hell?"

"Exactly, hell, it's on its way." Lizzy said. "Do you know when its coming?" She added.

"Yeah, I guess. I know when the Devil will be confined to the earth. I suppose that's the beginning of the end. One of the dreams I had years ago, something about the end of the Gentile Times, in 1914. But I suppose it will take years after that to get so bad the Great Spirit will bring it all to an end."

"Shit, I don't want to think about it, didn't he tell us to enjoy the ride? Why don't we just do that?" Lizzy said.

"Alright, he didn't tell us to do anything else. I suppose if he wanted us to say anything about it, he would of told us. I suppose he has someone else to do that. I think he just wants us to take care of the more physical things."

"Well, that we can take care of. The physical. In fact I'm feeling pretty physical right now. I'll race you back to our room."

She won.

The next day we went to the college. They knew about the fault that ran beneath the city. They took me seriously. But when I told them the year it would happen, they laughed. Some people had shit for brains.

We left the next day. I'd tell you about the trip back, but I don't want to bore you. I hate travel logs.

Chapter Fifteen

Coming home was the highlight of our trip. It was the first week in April. Lulu and Lad were bored with their lessons. Turns out they were sort of gifted. Anyway they were ahead of the rest of the children their age.

"You promised us a trip to the Shoshone." They said in unison. They must of been practicing.

Lizzy chimed in, "That's right, you did. Not only them, I have been looking forward to seeing your home country. I think we can take them out of school and go on a field trip."

"Well since you put it that way, we can make it a true learning field trip. They can take notes on everything they see and do. They can write it down in a journal."

"Ah, do we have to do that?" Again they said in unison. Boy, they had been practicing.

I just looked at them. Didn't have to say a word, "Ok, Ok, we'll do it, anything to get out of school." Lulu said.

Now lets get back to Yin-Li and Yang-Su and the Swede twins. The courtship was still going strong. I turned to them. "Well, when's the wedding?"

They looked at each other. "We haven't made up our minds yet. Oh, we love them alright. But, you know how the law looks at marriage. We marry them and they automatically get at least half of everything. We have the two of you to think about also. You know how our finance's are all intermingled."

"Yes, we do. And we trust you both. Say, I had a thought. Why don't you make up a legal document, like say, maybe- if you break up, you can only take out of it, what you brought into it?" I said, feeling well pleased with myself.

"That might work," Yin-Li said. "We sort of feel bad, even thinking about material things, but, isn't it true if you get everything clear in a marriage, things will go much smoother?"

"Yes," said Lizzy. "Buck and I, though, have no need of such an agreement. We live in each others minds and hearts. We know what each other is thinking all the time. Yes, Honey, I know what you're thinking, and that can wait. I know, I know, I'm thinking it too. But I can also wait."

Yang-Su said, "Yes, that's the kind of marriage we want, but we're just not that close to them. Does that mean we shouldn't get married?"

"No, not in the least. You see, Buck and I are unique. I don't know, the stars must of crossed somewhere when we were born. We can't explain it, we just know how we are. And you two are mixed up in it somewhere. Not in our marriage, but our lives. You two are part of us also."

"Yes," I added, "you two are flesh and blood and have needs also. And in the marriage bond is where to get those needs satisfied. So I guess, if you have an itch, you had better scratch it."

"Well," Yin-Li said, "I think we'll think long and hard before we take the leap, because when we do, we want it to last forever."

With that, we went to bed. I awoke in the middle of the night. Thinking about Phillip and Buck. I hadn't realized it, but they had completely merged. Lizzy turned over and said, "Yes

Honey, that happened a long time ago. I would of told you, but I thought you knew."

"You know, this knowing what each other is thinking, I guess I knew we did that. But it was so natural, I didn't pick up on that either, till we talked about it last night. Oh, Wow! I like that thought, how do you like this one?"

After that, we went back to just doing it natural, not thinking about it.

It took us a week to get ready for our trip. We were going to take our armored carriage to Cheyenne, then get our pack string together there. We had a family meeting before we left. The twins filled us in on financial matters. Seems we were getting richer by the day. We told them that they had better start giving some of it away, you know to charity. They said they would set up a foundation for that purpose. For us not to worry. That's the shit's isn't it, worrying about having too much money?

They didn't even know the half of it. I still had a lot of gold stashed, from Bannack to the Shoshone. Lizzy came into my mind, "How much?"

"I don't know, several hundred pounds, I guess." I showed her where they were. Just in case something happened to me. "Oh, nothing is going to happen to you. I thought you knew the future?"

"Yeah, I know the big picture, but I'm just small potatoes. Expendable, you might say."

"Like Hell, you are. Not to me, I need you every minute, every day."

"Alright Honey, relax. Remember it's the ride not the destination. Come on, help me pack this box out to the carriage."

As we were loading the carriage, Lizzy said, "I'm not

through with that gold, how did you, being just one kid, get that gold?"

"The Shoshone children helped me, they knew where it was and helped dig it and pack it."

"Then its not just yours, is it?"

"No, I guess not. When they need some, they can have it."

"Well, I should hope so. I know they think they don't need money right now, but in the future they will. Anyway it will be there for them." Lizzy had her thoughts in the outgoing mode, I said, "Hey shut it off will you?"

"Oh, sorry, I guess we'll both have to watch that."

You see, that was the thing, we could keep our thoughts private, if we wanted to. After all, there are some thoughts you don't want anybody to hear. Like maybe, 'my but you're putting on weight.' That would be a good way to sleep alone.

Not that Lizzy was putting on weight, because she wasn't. But even if she did, I would still love her.

"Thank you, dear. That was sweet."

Shit, I had forgot to turn mine off. "Ok, Ok, lets make a deal, we only use this silent stuff when we really need to, otherwise lets keep it verbal."

"How about when we make love, can we use it then?"

"Yeah, like if we're in a public place. Otherwise I like the noise you make."

"Well you aren't very quite yourself, and you're right, its sort of a turn on."

"Here come the kids, with their clothes. Do they have clothes for inclement weather?

"Yes, sweetheart, I made them some just like ours, rain, snow and bullet proof. It being only April, we will still have storms aplenty."

"Yeah, and bullets know no season, they come year around." I said, as I stowed our weapons and extra ammunition away. We were underway by mid-morning. The twins wanted to go, pretty bad. But, but what? I hauled up on the reins and sawed the team around.

"Do you both want to go with us?"

"Yes, Oh yes, we do. Give us two hours to make arrangements and pack our stuff. Our Beau's can wait." The Swede twins weren't too happy, but they agreed. The girls had been working hard for the last year and deserved a good long vacation.

Pike was to watch over everything, you know, the financial matters. Since the twins were going, Dog decided he would go also. We ended up with ten head of horses going. Four to pull the carriage, with two extra. And then the twins were riding two. And since the twins were riding, the children insisted they wanted to ride also, so that made ten.

Dog would run with the horses, till he got tired, then he would get in the carriage with us.

We decided to bypass Greeley. We made camp beside a small stream. The weather held, that was good. It didn't take long to set up camp, cause everyone pitched in. Lizzy and I, took the smaller tent. The twins and children slept in the larger wall tent. It being only April it would get down to freezing in the night.

When we got to Cheyenne, we stored our carriage at the stables. We stayed there two days, in the Hotel. While we got our pack string and gear gathered. The twins and the children though, stayed at Chin-Lee's.

Cheyenne was growing by leaps and bounds. But not as much as Denver. Of course with fast growth, comes a sort of organized chaos. John had several deputies now. The jail was sort of a hotel for the disorderly. It was full every night.

We had dinner the first night at Felicity's. John was there also. It was good to catch up on all the local goings on. Every once in awhile I caught Felicity looking at me with a wistful look in her eye, probably remembering things she shouldn't. It made me uncomfortable. Lizzy's eyes sparkled with glee. She was enjoying my misery.

The night before we left, we had dinner at Chin-Lee's. Chin-Lee was looking older. Watching him, I decided he was working too hard, for his age. Why should he have to work? After all, he had rich children. I got the twins aside and told them to set up a retirement fund for him. They sent a telegram off to Pike the next morning before we left, it was done. Of course, knowing him, I was sure he wouldn't slow down.

When we left the next morning, we were riding six horses, including Jim and Lil, and the black that I had rode before. Plus we had six pack horses. We headed northwest, across country. John had asked me if I was sure I should be taking four women and a child into Indian country?

"John, these women are worth more in combat, than a company of regular soldier's. And as far as Lad goes, he can read sign better than most scouts. And as far as my qualifications, I think I don't need to say any more on that." He looked at the expression on my face and swallowed hard.

"I'm sorry Buck, I know that. But I'm so used to warning people, that I sort of forgot who I was talking to. Keep safe, we'll see you all when you get back."

We had been on the trail for a couple of hours. Lizzy and I were riding side by side. Lizzy said, while looking around, "Are you sure we're going the right way?"

"I've been this way before you know."

"Oh, then this is the proverbial road twice traveled?"

J.D. Oliver

"I think you mean, the road less traveled, don't you? But as far as twice traveled, they say the road twice traveled is boring. But I say, it could be if love was not your passenger."

"Oh! That was sweet, you know you don't have to woo me, I am a sure thing. But if you keep that kind of talk up, we're going to have to find us a secluded spot."

I kicked the black up, "I'm going to scout the trail ahead. Keep those britches on till tonight, our tent will be secluded enough." Then I spurred ahead.

But I wasn't alone, Lad had seen me take off and was hot on my horses heels. That was Ok, maybe we needed a little man time alone. We slowed down to a trot. We talked. I thought he was about eight years old, but he was closer to twelve. Just a little small for his age. And I hadn't lied to John, he did know how to read sign.

This was really about the second or third time we had spent time alone. When he was around the women, he never said much. But he was talking plenty now.

He said, "Ate." (Father), "How old are you?"

"How old am I? Well, you see those hills over there? I am just a little younger than they are. But if you ask how long have I had this body, I have seen the grass green up fifteen times."

"Only fifteen? How can that be, you look old enough to be a grandfather?"

"I don't know how that it came to be that way. Or even why. I just know that is the way it is."

"Then how old is Ina?(Mother)"

"Her body is around twenty-eight seasons. But like me, she comes from the ancient ones."

"I have heard of you people. They say Old Man Coyote guides you."

"Yes, that is so. But he is just a messenger from the Great Spirit, Jehovah God."

"Jehovah God? I have never heard of him. You say he is the Great Spirit?"

"Yes, have you ever heard of Jesus Christ?"

"Ah, yes, the Black Robes talk about him."

"Well he is the son of Jehovah God."

"The Great Spirit has a son? Where is he now?"

"Sitting at his right hand, the Bible says. Have you ever seen a Bible?"

"I seen one, the Black Robes had one, but they said that we could not read it, it was some kind of a secret. Why would they say that?"

"Why? I have no idea, perhaps they have something to do with the Devil, the Devil doesn't want anyone to read it."

"I will think on what you have told me Ate. But right now, there is a Crow Indian watching us from the back of the ridge. I think they will try and steal our horses tonight after we get asleep."

"Yes, I seen him some time ago, Son. I am glad you seen him also. We will have some fun this night. Should we kill them or just count coup?"

"Crow's are good horse thieves. I think we should just count coup, that is unless they make us kill them. Sometimes they get stupid and make us kill them."

"Your wisdom is far beyond your years, Son. We will do as you say."

We circled around and came in behind our pack train. Of course the women seen us coming. There was no way anyone was going to surprise them.

I jogged up beside Lizzy, she said, "Did you see him?"

"Of course we did. Lad spotted him also, he is going to

make a good hand. He was full of questions about us."

"I know, you were transmitting. I guess you turned it on cause you wanted me to hear. That was nice of you. You answered him just right. Very ambiguous. Cause how can we tell the exact truth, when we don't know it ourselves?"

"You used the word 'transmitting', where did you get that?"

"You aren't the only one who has dreams. Ever since I hooked up with you, I have been having all sorts of dreams. Sometimes they scare the hell out of me."

"That's good, I mean good that they scare you. You should be scared. We all should be. The only way I can stay sane is by concentrating on the ride, not the destination."

"Yes, I know you keep telling me that over and over, 'it's the ride, stupid'."

"I have never called you stupid, and I never would."

"Cool down, that was just a figure of speech. Of course you wouldn't, or I would clean your clock."

"Ha, ha, the jokes on you, I don't own a clock."

"You know at times, you have a piss poor sense of humor." She said, as she leaned over and gave me a kiss. Then she spurred ahead.

"Ha, the jokes still on you," I called out, "I don't have a sense of humor." She turned in her saddle and stuck her tongue out at me.

That night we picked our camp spot carefully. Just enough cover, but not too much. We wanted them to think we would be easy marks. Four women, one small boy and one lone man. Surely they would be able to take us easily. Beside's that Lulu's blond hair would be a big attraction.

There was a small stream running through our camp

spot. We kept the horses hobbled, they could still feed and drink, within feet of the camp. We wanted them to come in close. Make them work for their plunder. We made a show of fixing our beds beside the fire. We didn't set up tents'.

I didn't want the sides slashed.

As soon as it got dark, we fixed the beds to make it look like we were in them. Then faded into the shadows. I had told the horses what to expect. Most of them understood. Shortly after the Big Dipper said it was mid-night, I could hear them sneaking up. There were five of them. Why so small a bunch?

The first one reached for Jim's halter rope, he got kicked. It was a slight blow to the head. He was out like flaxen wick in a wind storm. Jim just went back to grazing. Another one bent over the fallen brave. Yin-Li laid him out with a blow over the head with the butt of her pistol. She went to work binding them both and stuffing rags in their mouths.

Two of them out of the action. Lizzy did for another one, Yang-Su for another. I got the last one. They left the smallest one for me. He must not of been over 5'6". He didn't even struggle, I didn't have the heart to hurt him. I grabbed him and put him in a hammer lock. There was a slight yelp, so I eased off on the pressure. Why was I going so easy on him, I had not the slightest idea.

Lad threw some wood on the fire, I dragged my prize over to it. They dragged the rest of them over closer to fire. The twins stripped off all of the horse thief's clothes. They were young ones.

Lizzy came over to the one I was holding and jerked his clothes off.

We gasped and I let go. He was not a he, but a she. She turned around and looked at me. She said, "Tamdoka, do you not recognize me? It is me, Happy Otter. You remember, when we were children, in the Shoshone camp. When all the children used to swim together."

I pulled her closer to the fire. "Turn around, left me see your left cheek. It is you Happy Otter. You still have your Strawberry birthmark on your hip." She was jumping up and down with glee.

"I am so glad it was you, I thought it was, but the distance was far from the ridge top. I could not be sure. I was taken captive by these Crow dogs two years ago. That one over there wanted to marry me. I would of been his fourth wife. But I convinced them I was a Ozuye Wicas`ta (Warrior). I had to hide my time of the month for them to believe me."

Lizzy said, "Alright, stop jumping up and down, we can see that you are a woman. And not a bad looking one either, I might add. But for your information, Tamdoka is my husband now and he doesn't get more than one wife. That is if he wants to keep his balls."

I looked at Happy Otter and shrugged, "I'm afraid that is true. She is my wife and I love her. But we are heading back to your country. You are welcome to go with us."

Lizzy spoke up. "What are these Crow doing so far south?"

"They thought they were big men. They wanted to show the elders how big they were. It was me that suggested we raid south. You see the Crow are friends with the white man. Every time they steal horses from the white soldier, they get in trouble. So I suggested we go south, where they are not known. I thought I would stand more of chance to get away."

Yin-Li spoke up, "What are we going to do with these four, kill them or what?"

Lizzy said, "Why don't we let Happy Otter decide?"

"We could kill them, but that is too easy. They are

proud young men. I think if we hurt their pride, it would be better than killing them. Ridicule hurts them more than death. We will ridicule their manhood. They think their 'Deze' are big, they think it is great fun to make them swell and wave them in my face. If it is alright with your women, we will make fun of how small their 'Deze' are?"

The women, including Lulu thought that would be fun. Lad and I opted out. We went to find their horses. We knew how cruel women could be, they would have those young men in tears. They had about ten extra head, they had stolen somewhere. We would keep those. Leave them one mount each, to get home on. We stayed gone for the next hour. Till the Crows came running by us, they didn't even see us.

We went back to the campfire. The women were sitting there laughing. Happy Otter was setting by the fire with her legs crossed, showing her San-Wisan, she still hadn't got redressed. I noticed a little blood running down her thigh. I got Lizzy's attention and nodded toward Happy Otter. Lizzy said, "Happy Otter, I think your time of the month has started, do you need some dried moss, or do you have some?"

She looked down, "Oh, I think I have some, where did you throw my clothes?"

Lad stood there, transfixed. Turning redder by the second. If my memory served me, Happy Otter would only be three years older than Lad. As she got up, she glanced at Lad and winked. He turned and ran into the dark. It was after everyone was asleep before he came back and went to bed.

The next morning everyone was properly dressed. Every time Lad looked at Otter, he blushed. But that didn't keep him from looking. In fact it wasn't too long after we were on the trail before they were riding side by side, bringing up the rear so they could herd the extra horses.

Lizzy and Lulu were riding together, talking. Probably mother daughter stuff. I briefed the twins, before I rode ahead to scout the trail. There were more ranch's now than there were when I came through here before. I made sure our trail led around them. I didn't need any confrontations. I didn't know where they had stolen these horses from, I didn't need anybody accusing us of stealing them. All though none of them were branded.

We made camp beside another small stream that night. The Indian Ponies were used to us and were sticking close to our horses. The next night we stopped beside the Wind River. A spot with a thermal spring running into it. We had stopped with a couple of hours of daylight left. We put up our tents. Then the women decided to go swimming. Of course it was skinny dipping. I went on a short look see, to make sure the camp was secure.

When I got back the women were swimming. Lad was standing there with just his pants on. He had started to get undressed then stopped. "What's the matter, how come you're not in there?"

"I can't, my Deze will not behave. If I go in there like this, the women and Happy Otter will laugh."

"Oh yes, I remember. Let me tell you a story. When I was younger, and Happy Otter was a little girl. The whole bunch of us children used to go swimming. We had no clothes on. Yes, at first when one of us young boys was in that condition, the girls would laugh and titter. But as time went on, their laughter turned to smiles. Smiles of appreciation by the way."

I called out to Lizzy, "Have you been listening?"

"Yes, I will tell the girls not to laugh, but perhaps it would be better if you were in the same condition, it would make him feel better."

"What, no, I can control it now. How is it supposed to get that way?"

"I will talk to it, you know how it has a mind of its own. All I have to do is speak to it, it will do what I say."

"Ok, Lad, I will go swimming too. We will go in together, in the same condition. They will not laugh."

I took my clothes off, "Lizzy, make sure they do not laugh, at either one of us." We walked toward the water, it was all I could do to keep from laughing at myself. I felt like the whole world was looking at me. I glanced at Lad. He was looking straight ahead. His wasn't that bad, for his age.

If it was up to me, it would go soft, but Lizzy was talking to it. I was not listening at what she was saying. Talking about being led around by your dick, I was. I was very thankful when the water closed in around us. They didn't laugh. But they were smiling, all of them. We ended up playing toss the rock, then diving for it.

After that, the ice was broke. Otter and Lad were at ease with each other. In fact we had trouble getting their clothes back on them. By the time breakfast was over the next morning, I knew we had lost Lad. You couldn't pry them apart with a crowbar.

We made the Shoshone main camp on the Wind River the next day. The extra horses went to Happy Otter's father for her hand. It was like old home week. Not only did they get Otter back, but they were glad to see me also.

It was unusual for a woman to marry one so much younger and inexperienced. But being that Otter was a warrior, she could train him. And Lad had a lot of knowledge to share with her. He was a good student and learned a lot the last year in school. Which would come in handy as the invasion

J.D. Oliver

increased.

Lizzy came up and said, "Have you heard what they are saying about us, they call us, 'Mahpia Wicasta', what does that mean?"

"That means 'cloud people'. I wonder what they mean by that?"

"I don't know, I will ask Otter, she will tell us." Said Lizzy.

"He who speaks like thunder from the clouds, you come from him. Our Medicine Man told us this." Said Otter, when asked.

"Oh? We do? What makes him think so?" Said I.

"I don't know, I think he had a vision. But it only stands to reason, all the good things you do, like helping me."

"I don't think we come from the Great Spirit, oh maybe we accidentally do what he wants us to, but believe me, we are not Angels."

"So you say, so you say," she said as she and Lad walked away hand-in-hand. I looked around at the rest of our party, they were smiling, even Dog, as he sat there with his tongue lolling out.

"Come on now, you all don't believe that do you?"

"No, of course not," Said Lizzy. "We're not Angels. But that's no sign he doesn't use us at times. Even a blunt tool, is better than no tool at all."

"Well at least you got that right, we are pretty blunt." Said Yin-Li.

"Yes, forget all this heavy stuff, do you want to go swimming? That's where Otter and Lad are going." Yang-Su said.

"Heavy stuff? What do you mean by that?"

"You aren't the only one who has dreams about the

future, you know. We all do. We all are 'Mahpiya Wicata". 'Heavy' is a slang word from way in the future, I rather liked it."

"Well be careful about using what you see in your dreams. Let the future remain in the future." Lizzy said.

"Yeah," I added. "We have enough trouble with the present. As to swimming, I think we all could use a good cooling off."

Cooling off? How could you do that when everyone was naked? It was a good thing they couldn't see under the water. Except my wife of course, she could see. It wasn't long till we stole away to a secluded spot.

We stayed with the Shoshone for another week. Then we headed off for the south fork of the Shoshone River.

The sun had darkened all of our skin, being we hadn't worn much clothes for the last week. Even Lulu, with her fair skin. Of course she had to keep applying bear grease, or she would of burned. She had matured a lot, not just physically, but her personality also. She was becoming a lot like the twins. Of course they were also teaching her self-defense. And maybe a little offense also. She was a tall as Lizzy now, and muscling up fine. Even though all of the Shoshone boys had been trying to bed her, she kept them at a distance. We had been offered twenty ponies for her.

We arrived at the bluff overlooking the Castle Rock Ranch, four days later. We made camp. I wanted to scout things out, before we made our appearance. I had a pair of Army field glasses, so I put them to good use.

There seemed to be a lot of going and coming. It just wasn't the boys down there. I counted ten different men. There were also more shacks built. If I didn't know better I would say it was some kind of outlaw headquarters. And I didn't know better.

I mentioned that we made camp. Our camp was on the back side of the bluff. There was a cave that I had discovered years ago. It went back in for quite a ways, then opened up into a small valley or cove, you could call it. I could tell there had been no one in here, since the last time I was.

There was a spring that provided water to drink and sub-irrigated the grass. And it was just a short walk to where I could see down into the valley that held the Castle Rock Ranch. I knew those four would come to no good, and it looks like they had drug Pa into this mess.

I wondered about Caleb, Harriet and Penny. If they were Ok? Since their place was on the north fork, I hoped they were far enough away, so they had not been dragged in.

I seen Pa come out of the main house a couple of times. Anyway he was still upright. Both times a slattern looking woman dragged him back in. I went back to camp. Told them what I had seen.

"What are you going to do about it?" Lizzy asked.

"I don't know, what do the rest of you think we should do?"

Yang-Su said, "There is only one thing to do, go down there and clear the mess out. Course it would probably mean you would have to kill your so called brothers. But it is up to you, how far do you want to take it?"

"Well, we are U.S. Marshal's, we have the authority, we can deputize the three of you also." Lizzy said. "So whatever we decide to do, it would be legal."

"Alright," I said, "But lets watch them for a day or two more, just to make sure what is going on down there."

"Yes," Lulu said, "We would want to err on the side of caution."

The four of us turned to look at her, My, my, someone has grown up. I said, "Yes, Lulu, my thought exactly." She would, or maybe not, make someone a good wife someday. Who's to say she has to get married?

I hadn't decided, when I did go down there, whether to go as Buck or Phillip. My wife said that my eye color changes with my clothes. My eyes are green normally, but when I am Indian, they turn brown. Wouldn't it be strange if one was green and one was brown?

We waited for the dark to come. When I could go down there, unseen. "No, Lizzy, I am going to go alone. Don't worry, I won't kill anyone."

"It's not that, you clown. I don't want anyone killing you. Even though you're a big pain in the ass, you're my pain in the ass." She kissed me and ran her fingers through my hair, looking into my eyes as they turned brown.

The shadows of the moon were dark and friendly. As I flitted from one to another. A lot of people don't like the dark, but not me. I felt right at home. Well in fact I was home. I knew every rock, tree and bush. And they knew me and bade me well.

I came up to the main house, I slipped in through the open screen door and stood with the coats in the entrance way. Looking into the kitchen. Pa was sitting at the kitchen table drinking a cup of coffee. The woman was sitting opposite him, doing the same. She was speaking, "How many times have I told you not to go outside during the day. That bunch is just waiting for a chance go kill you."

"I know Tillie, but I'd just as soon be dead as a prisoner in my own home. Its not safe for you to go out there either."

"Why do you think I dress this way, I try to make myself as unappealing as I can."

The woman looked to be in her mid-fifties. Looking

J.D. Oliver

closer, she was decent looking, under her disguise. The woman continued on, "Ever since Charles and Wilbur left last year for California Carl and Robert have had things their way, they're the ones that brought their rustler buddies here."

"Do you think there is a way we can get word to Caleb to send for the law?" Pa said.

"I don't see how, I tried to sneak out, but they caught me. They would of raped me, but they thought I was too ugly."

I went, Psst, Psst, they lifted their heads up and looked around. I said, "Just sit natural like, its me, Buck. I'm in amongst the coats." They looked straight at me.

"Where, we can't see you?"

I moved the sheep skin coat a little so they could see my face. Tillie gasped. "It's an Indian."

"No, it's my boy Buck, thank goodness he's come back, we'll be alright now, he's hell on wheels."

"How many are out there?" I asked.

"Twelve, counting Carl and Robert, I'm afraid they went all the way bad." Pa said.

Tillie spoke up, "Can you get word to the law?"

"Yes, of course, I talk to myself all the time, I am the law, my posse is up on the bluff. Pa, I heard you say that Carl and Robert had gone all the way bad, is that right?"

"Yes, son, it is. They have been raping and murdering right along with the rest of that scum."

"Are there any women out there with them?"

"No, thank goodness, but that is why we have been trying to make Tillie so unattractive to them, so they would leave her alone."

"Not to be rude, but how did Tillie get here and just who is she?"

"She's an old friend of Ma's. About six month's after

Ma died, I wrote to her. She came out and we were married."

"Alright, enough said about that. But it wouldn't bother you if both Carl and Robert got killed in the coming melee?"

"Well of course it would bother me, no one wants to see their children killed. But I know they deserve to die, for what they've been a'doin."

"Are they all here now, or are some out on a raid?"

"They are all here, they don't get up till almost noon, bunch of lazy bastard's. I overheard some of them talking, they are planning on going out in a couple of days." Pa said.

"So they sleep late, good, it's always best to beard the lion in his den. You two sleep well tonight, it will all be over by breakfast." Then I just faded away, left them gawking with their mouths open.

I checked each shack and the main bunkhouse. So I would know who slept where. Then I tripped through the friendly shadows on my way back to camp. They were grouped around the campfire, playing poker. They didn't have any chips. So they had broken twigs, different sizes for different values. I stood there in the shadows watching them.

"You might just as well come and join us, we know you're there." Lizzy said.

"You could of played strip poker you know, it would of been more fun." I said.

Lulu spoke up and said, "Not without you here, it wouldn't of been. Because you would lose of course."

"Why do you think I would lose?"

"Because you want to. You know you like to tease us" Lizzy said, as she threw in her hand.

"Come on lets go to bed. All of sudden I'm horny." I made her wait though, as I explained what we were going to do on the morrow. Lizzy said that she had enough of her special weave clothes for all of us. That was good, because I sure didn't want any of the women to get hurt.

The weather was warm for it being so early in May. We didn't bother to set tents up. The girls were sleeping in the cave. Lizzy and I had laid our bedroll at the mouth of the cave that led to the little valley. Of course we were sleeping in our regular night clothes, bare skin.

Lizzy fell asleep right after we made love. For some reason I wasn't that sleepy. The moon was just peeking over the hills surrounding the valley. The pale beams were making a pattern on Lizzy's naked legs, then upward over her perfect belly. I watched with interest. A slight breeze started, just as the beams reached her nipples. They hardened with its touch. Funny, she was sound asleep and they still responded to stimuli.

I lay on my back watching the moon argue with the stars. The moon won I guess, because the stars closest to the moon, bowed and retreated. I got to thinking about our task in the morning. Wondering about those outlaws. Who they were? I mean, not just their names, but their background?

Did they have mothers and fathers, brothers and sisters? Of course they must have. But if given the chance, would they repent or die? Did I want to give them that chance? Yeah, I guess I did. I believed in an eye for any eye, but was it my place to be their judge, jury and executioner? No, by rights, I guess I was supposed to arrest them and bring them to justice. But shit, Cheyenne was a long ways off. With many a pitfall between here and there. And I didn't want to fall into any pit.

"What are you doing? Why aren't you asleep? Didn't you get enough, must not of, by the way that is pointing at the moon." Lizzy said, as she rolled on her side, watching me. I glanced down. I hadn't even noticed it.

"No, I'm fine, I guess. Sex wise, that is. But I was just

thinking." Then I told her about my thoughts. Then added. "What about you, does it bother you?"

"If I had any doubt, I wouldn't do it. We have never killed anybody that wasn't trying to kill us. Same goes for that bunch down there tomorrow, if they don't try to kill us we won't kill them. Go to sleep. Wait, I have always lived by the adage, 'waste not, want not', I'm not going to waste that." And she didn't.

We were up at dawn, having washed in the spring, we were dressed, all five of us. I gave detailed instructions on what I wanted them to do. I had no worries about Lizzy and the twins, they had been seasoned under plenty of fire. The twins had been teaching Lulu how to shoot and throw a knife. I looked into her face and could not detect one hint of nervousness. Well, we would see.

We left the horses in the valley. The distance was short enough to walk, we all had new moccasins that we got from the Shoshone's. I had my two .44's and the Henry .44 rifle, plus of course my knives. Lizzy and the twins were armed the same. Lulu had knives and a double barrel 12 gauge, plus a twelve shot .36 stuck in her waistband. We had enough firepower to kill fifty men, much less twelve.

We thought we would catch them in bed, we were wrong. They were up and roping their horses. I guess Pa had it wrong, as to when they were going on their next raid. Timber and brush ran close to the corral. We were not discovered till we stepped out. We were spaced about twenty feet apart.

All twelve were milling about on different tasks. Carl and Robert were smoking and leaning against the corral, looked as if they were too important to saddle their own horses. They were the last ones to see us. The rest of them stopped in their tracks as we came into view. Most of them were not looking at me. Why should they, when they had four beautiful women to look at.

Carl looked up and seen the others standing there with their jaws on their boots and said, "What the hell, you guys get to work." Then he seen me. His jaw dropped, "What are you doing here, you red bastard?"

Robert turned to look, his hand came to rest on his gun butt. I said, "Take it easy boys, I'm here to arrest you, you've been very bad boys. Now what do you think Ma would think of you?"

"Who cares what that old lady would think, she's dead, just like you're going to be."

"Boy's that's being very disrespectful to Ma's memory, and you know how much I loved her. Now be careful or you will make me mad. And you wouldn't like me when I'm mad."

The others still hadn't come out of their shock of seeing the women. Now, most men on the frontier had a deep respect for women. Especially white women, and I guess Lizzy and the twins fit that bill, but most of them were looking at Lulu. That blond hair was sure a magnet. But to get back to that respect. About six of them, when Lizzy told them to drop their weapons, did just that. That left six that needed a little prodding. Of course, really only four, cause Carl and Robert were mine.

Carl looked at those four and said, "Robert and I will take this stinking Indian, you four shoot them pussies. Or aren't you men enough?"

I braced myself, I let them draw and shoot first, the impact of the bullets on my vest hurt like hell. Then I drew both guns at the same time and put a bullet, each, threw their eyes, Carl the left eye, Robert, his right eye. I heard shots from the women, they didn't let them shoot first.

Lulu didn't use the shotgun, she had pulled her .36 from

her waistband faster than the guy could get his gun clear. Of course Lizzy and the twins, were faster then greased lighting. I was rubbing my chest when Lizzy came over.

"I thought we agreed that you weren't going to let them shoot first anymore?"

"I'm sorry Honey, but I was thinking about Pa. I wanted to make sure he knew I had to kill them. Besides I had a dream last night, I knew they would shoot at my badge, they hated anyone who was an authority figure. Knowing that, I stuffed dry moss under my vest, it cushioned the blow somewhat."

We went back over to where the other three were holding the remaining six outlaws at gunpoint. Four of them were youngsters. The other two were on the downhill part of the slide.

"Well, well, what are we going to do with the bunch of you. Now being U. S. Marshal's we're supposed to get you back to Cheyenne for trial. But hell, I'm lazy. I might just decide to shoot the whole bunch of you. But again, me being lazy, you all are going to dig the graves for those other idiots. Like I said, I'm lazy, I don't feel like digging your graves. So I guess I won't shoot you, that is if you don't give me any more of a reason to do so."

One young fellow spoke up, "Uh, Sir, excuse me, but what did we do? The six of us was just hired on the day before yesterday. They, those two you shot, said we was needed for a roundup."

"Have you ever heard of cattle being rounded up for market this time of the year?"

"No, I reckon I haven't, but they were paying a hundred a month and found. So we didn't argue with them."

"Now weren't't you just a little suspicious they would pay regular hands that much?"

"Yes, I guess. But hell, you don't look a gift horse in the mouth, do you?" The young puncher said.

I looked at the whole bunch of them, "Is he telling the truth, or did he just open the outhouse door and fart?"

The oldest of the punchers smiled and said, "Well I did notice that he was a little windy, but what he says is the gospel truth. We weren't hired as gun hands, the fact is we ain't. You noticed how quick we shucked our fire arms, when them ladies asked us to?"

"Yeah, I reckon the six of you aren't as stupid as you look, that was the smartest thing you did since you learned not to poop in your pants. For sure, because they sure enough would of planted you." I said.

Lizzy said, "I believe them, look at them, their scared shitless."

"Yeah, I believe them too. Ok, boys, and you two also, your first task is, pick up your guns and then bury those vermin. And then if you still want a job, I'll talk to Pa. But I'm sure it won't be for a hundred a month."

I turned back to Lizzy, "Come on, I want to show you my room." The twins and Lulu came along also. On the way there, we met Pa and Tillie. They were just coming out of the house. Pa said, "The boys, did you kill them?"

"Yes, Pa I did. But only after they shot at me first. I had no choice."

"I know that son, I knew it was coming. When Ma was alive she kept them in line. But after she died, they just went crazy. It was Ma that ran the show, but you knew that of course."

"Yes Pa, I did." I looked at Tillie, "You have some pretty big bloomers to fill, do you think you're up to it?"

She said, "Well I guess, I'll have to be, won't I?"

Lizzy said, "We'll have a talk later."

The five of us went into the barn. My room was just as I left it. Someone had even been dusting it. Pa had followed us in. "It was me, son. I knew you would come back, I thought you would be upset if I didn't."

"No Pa, I wouldn't of been upset. But thank you, I do appreciate it." Come on everybody lets go see if Tillie can cook." I said, as I looked at Pa, he nodded.

All six of those hands signed on for thirty a month and found. The old timer that spoke up was hired as foreman. His name was Jake Long, he was paid fifty.

I don't know what Lizzy told Tillie, but she was sure all smiles. I thought Pa had even perked up a little bit. The second day there, Lizzy and I had decided to go over to Caleb's place. We thought we would leave the next morning.

Dog had decided to adopt Lulu, anyway they were always together. The twins and Lulu were never without their weapons. The hired hands gave them a wide berth. Which was fine with me, I didn't need the women to kill anymore of them. Which they would do if they stepped out of line.

Lizzy and I, left after breakfast. Lizzy seemed quite content, as she always was when we rode alone. "Liz, just what did you tell Tillie, she and Pa both seem happier."

"Funny thing, I didn't have to tell her too much. We got to talking about everything. The conversation got around to her past, seems her ex-husband was a religious nut. He didn't believe in sex, that is except to procreate. And after he died, her minister told her that widows shouldn't have sex. You know how some of these self-righteous Bible thumpers are, no one should have any fun, that is except them. All I told her was, that was a bunch of hogwash. It didn't take much convincing. Anyway the next morning both Pa and her had big smiles on their faces."

"Good for you sweetheart, good for you. It's not good for man or woman to be alone."

"Now that don't hold true for all people, some do alright by their lonesome."

"Come to think of it, I guess you're right, but I sure wouldn't want to go on without you." I said. As I leaned over and gave her kiss, along with a feel. She slapped my hand. Now why do women do that? You know darned well they like it. For some reason they just have to put on an act, that they don't.

We timed it just right, they were just setting down to lunch, when we rode up to their ranch on the North Fork of the Shoshone. Caleb came out, holding a rifle. He squinted at us, "What the hell, is that you Buck?" He said, lowering the rifle.

The screen door slammed back and out came Penny, I had just stepped down, when she attached herself to my neck. "Buck, Oh Buck, I thought you were dead." She said, kissing my cheek.

Lizzy stepped out of the saddle and said, "Whoa up there young lady, that is my husband you are kissing." Lizzy said with a smile.

Penny stepped back and said, "Oh, I'm sorry, but I'm just so glad to see him, he's my big brother, you know?"

"Yes Penny, I know, Phillip has told me all about you. You can kiss him if you want to."

"Phillip? When did you change your name Buck?"

"That's a long story Penny. So much has happened since I left, it'll take me days to tell it all. I suppose it would be easier to write a book, than tell it."

"Oh, I'm not going to wait for a book, come on, you can start telling us over lunch."

****

So now you know how I come to write this story. We sketched it all in for Penny. But of course we left out a lot of the details that I have told you. Figured she was a might young for some of it. But when it comes to women, are they ever too young for the truth? No one is really, but sometimes it should be sugar coated.

Of course that's not the end of our story, nor should it be. You see, we are still alive and its winter time. We are back in Denver, Caleb allowed Penny to come with us. She is going to school with Lulu. Next spring we are going to take her home.

There is some unfinished business that I need to take care of, before June of '76. We will drop Penny off and then head for the Little Big Horn. I don't know what good I can do, but maybe someone will listen to me. All I can do is try.

J.D. Oliver

Wail not! Wail not!
My children, Wail not!
For it's but dust we are
'Till life be Regained
For Hope Lives
Within our beating hearts
Wail Not, my Children!